A NATION INTERRUPTED

A NATION INTERRUPTED

A Novel
by Kevin McDonald

BOOKS

Aura Libertatis Spirat

A Nation Interrupted

Copyright © 2019 by L&J Publications

12th Edition

This is a work of fiction. Names, characters, businesses, places, events, and incidents are either the products of the author's imagination or are used in a fictitious manner.

Braveship Books

www.braveshipbooks.com

Edited by Linda Morrow

Cover Design by Rossitsa Atanassova
99designs

ISBN-13: 978-1-64062-111-4
Library of Congress Control Number: 2020904788
Printed in the United States of America

For Chris Storer—an outstanding coach and an even better history teacher

Contents

Acknowledgments

In addition to thanking my editor, Linda Morrow, I wish to express my appreciation to the following individuals for their selfless contributions to this book:

Garry Crain
Tyler Damron
Terry Dill
Iris Farber
Marilyn Galloway
Harold Graebe
John Litchfield
Mark Lorance
George Martin
Darcy McDonald
Charlie Morrow
David Murray
Mark Parcell
Howard Polden
Kelly Polden
Chuck Reynolds
Elza Rosinger
Patrick Shaub
Mark Siena
John Spence

I am especially grateful for the inspiration and encouragement I received from my former commanding officer, George Galdorisi. A retired Navy Captain and *New York Times* bestselling author, George is much more than an accomplished naval aviator and writer. He is a loyal friend and a great literary mentor.

Author's Note

This is a work of fiction. Even though the plot presents an alternate history, there are many historical figures, as well as actual historical events, intertwined within the story. Some of the dialogue and writings attributed to the historical figures are public record. Much of their dialogue, however, is fictional, as are many of their actions. This book is not intended to be a true and accurate historical reference.

History, often the result of planning and painstaking effort by people of great stature, occasionally pivots on happenstance. Beginning with the Civil War, this is a story of two separate American nations, both struggling to survive in a world that not only could have been—but a world that very nearly was.

<u>*Chapter One*</u>

13 September 1862 *(4 days before the Battle of Antietam)*

On this hazy morning in late summer, Barton Mitchell and his fellow Union soldiers temporarily halted to rest in a meadow. Mitchell, a corporal in the 27th Indiana Infantry Regiment, was about to begin a chain of events that would ultimately determine the fate of a nation—a nation that, up until this crucial moment in history, had been destined to become the most powerful on earth.

Recently the site of a Confederate encampment, the meadow in which the war-weary corporal lay sprawled was a day's march south of Frederick, Maryland. The grass, littered with refuse left behind by a retreating regiment of South Carolinians, was still wet from the morning dew. As he tried to rest with his Springfield musket lying across his chest, Corporal Mitchell felt something pressing against the small of his back. Using his left hand to balance his musket above the ground, he rolled onto his left hip and elbow. Mitchell reached behind his back with his right hand and removed the source of his discomfort—three Carolina-tobacco cigars, bundled and wrapped in a soggy envelope.

Energized by his good fortune, the corporal immediately sat up, placed his weapon on his lap, and unwrapped his prize. Discarding the envelope, Mitchell was pleased to find that all three of the stogies were still dry and intact. Offering one to his sergeant, who was reclining several feet away, Mitchell sprang to one knee. He rested the musket on his other knee and began rummaging through his pack, searching for his tin of matches.

Sergeant John Bloss was happy to accept his junior benefactor's offer as he tucked the cigar into his woolen uniform jacket, faded and tattered from eighteen months of continuous wear. Bloss, however, was not so quick as Mitchell to dismiss the tobacco-stained envelope that had come to rest in the grass next to where he was leaning back on his elbows. Sitting up, Bloss surveyed the object of his curiosity. There was writing on it, but the morning dew had blotted out the ink, making it unreadable.

The veteran sergeant was vexed by his corporal's apparent lack of interest in the sealed envelope. Casting a look of mild disdain toward Mitchell, still preoccupied with finding his matches, Bloss retrieved it himself. Removing the bayonet from his musket, he used it to slit the lengthwise edge of the envelope. As he removed several folded sheets of paper, Bloss was surprised to discover they were relatively dry. The ink had partially bled through to the opposing sides of the pages, but the text was still legible.

As he began to study the freshly penned script in Special Order 191, Sergeant Bloss could barely believe his eyes. It was a dispatch from Confederate General Robert E. Lee, commander of the Army of Northern Virginia. The dispatch was one of a half dozen Lee had sent to his field generals in advance of three planned attacks against Union targets along and on either side of the Potomac River.

The order prescribed in detail how the Confederate Army was to divide into four separate forces along the Potomac. Three of the divided armies would launch simultaneous major assaults at Lovettsville and Harpers Ferry on the Virginia side of the river, as well as Sharpsburg on the Maryland side. The dispatch was addressed to General D.H. Hill, whose army was to serve as the rear guard for the other three. Generals James Longstreet, John George

Walker and Stonewall Jackson were to spearhead the coordinated morning attacks beginning on the 17th of September—a mere four days away.

Corporal Mitchell watched in bewilderment as Sergeant Bloss jumped to his feet, reaffixed his bayonet to his musket, and nearly tripped over Mitchell's pack as he began sprinting toward his company commander. Within hours, the critical news contained in the lost dispatch was on its way, via mounted courier, toward a farmhouse east of Sharpsburg—the farmhouse where Major General George B. McClellan, commander of the Army of the Potomac, had established his temporary headquarters to coordinate the search for General Lee and the Confederates.

It was a seventeen-mile ride.

Confederate Captain Emmett Baldwin was a military man ahead of his time. In an age when armies still formed up against one another in open fields of battle, Baldwin regarded such tactics as folly. He had managed to convince his superiors to let him pick a dozen men from the ranks of traditional units and train them in the art of guerilla warfare.

For months, Captain Baldwin and his men had been operating behind Union lines, mapping out troop positions and disrupting supply lines ahead of the now-imminent Confederate incursion into Maryland. Even though Maryland had not seceded from the Union, there were still some in the state who were loyal to the Confederacy. Many others, though not overtly supportive, were at least sympathetic to the Confederate cause.

General Lee hoped to capitalize on those divided loyalties, and Baldwin's mission was part of that effort. With only four days left until the beginning of Lee's planned offensive, Baldwin's men were en route from Sharpsburg (where they had charted Union troop concentrations around General McClellan's headquarters) to the township of Frederick, twenty miles east. Their task in Frederick was to covertly approach local merchants and discern whether they would be willing to sell food and other supplies to the approaching Confederate Army.

Baldwin's commandos had little in common with other military units of the day. They wore no uniforms, did not march in formation, and carried an assortment of weapons ranging from Bowie knives to Henry repeating rifles. They were also exceptionally resourceful. They would occasionally appropriate provisions from known partisans in the area, but they largely lived off the land. They also survived on the spoils of their insurgency, having scavenged coffee and flour from a derailed Union supply train only days earlier. Even their repeating rifles, along with most of their ammunition, had been stolen from a Union armory.

As they walked along a secluded dirt road, Baldwin and his men were several miles east of General McClellan's headquarters. The surrounding woods were thick with brush. As he led his men toward a sharp crook in the road, Baldwin heard the muffled sound of hoofbeats coming from around the bend.

He dispersed his men into the woods, six on either side of the road.

Private Stanislaw Tobias Pozniak was an exceptional equestrian. The eldest son of Polish Jewish immigrants, Pozniak had spent his childhood working on his family's horse farm in western New York State.

At the beginning of the war, in 1861, Stanislaw had been only sixteen years of age when two U.S. Army procurement officers showed up looking to purchase mounts from his father. Like many

Polish Americans, Stanislaw was fiercely patriotic. He pleaded with his father for permission to go with the men and join the Union Army.

At first disinclined to allow it, Stanislaw's father eventually yielded to his son's request, but only after striking a deal with the two procurement officers. He agreed to sell them the horses they had selected at a cut-rate price, and they agreed to enlist Stanislaw into the Union Army as a mounted courier instead of an infantry soldier. The procurement officers departed the farm with fourteen of the Pozniaks' finest steeds and the eldest of their two sons. Stanislaw Pozniak had gone on to become one of the most accomplished mounted couriers in the Union Army.

Now, as Private Pozniak was nearly a half hour into the most important ride of his life, he was hell-bent on reaching McClellan's headquarters. Though he didn't know the contents of the dispatch in his leather satchel, the Union colonel who had tasked him with delivering it had impressed upon him, in no uncertain terms, that he was carrying a document critical to preserving the Union.

As he approached the next bend in the road, Pozniak was only minutes from his destination. For most of the ride, the young private had cantered his mount, letting him run at a three-beat pace. Now, as he rounded the bend, he kicked the animal into a full gallop, pressing him hard toward his objective.

Suddenly, Pozniak felt a burning sensation in his right shoulder. The reins began to slip from his hand. For an instant, he had no idea what had caused his arm to go numb. Then, he heard the report of a rifle shot, followed immediately by more shots. The salvos echoed through the trees behind him, prompting the wounded courier to spin his head as he transferred the reins to his left hand. Standing in his stirrups, he rose from the saddle and looked to the rear—nothing.

He returned his gaze to the woods directly ahead. Swirling rings of smoke, clearly visible as they jetted from behind the trees on either side of the road, revealed the shooters' positions. As the shots continued to ring out, Pozniak's survival instinct told him to pull back on the reins and reverse course. He knew that stopping his horse and turning would be a slow, cumbersome maneuver, making him a near-stationary target for several critical seconds.

Instead, the young trooper pushed ahead, leaning forward and down as he rode straight into the teeth of the ambush. He leaned so low that rider and horse became one—a desperate, two-thousand-pound beast galloping at more than thirty miles per hour.

When Pozniak reached the epicenter of the melee, Baldwin's men ceased firing. They waited. As soon as Pozniak was no longer directly between them, Baldwin's men opened up again, firing at the fleeing Union soldier until he was no longer in range.

Miraculously, Pozniak had managed to race through the fusillade of bullets unscathed. But as the courier continued riding away at a breakneck pace, one of Baldwin's men, armed with a Whitworth sniper rifle, stepped out into the middle of the road. He steadied himself, taking dead aim. The sniper fought hard to calm his rapid breathing. He choked momentarily from the smell of gunpowder that filled the surrounding air. Finally, he held his breath for several seconds and lightly squeezed the trigger.

As his horse continued toward Sharpsburg at a full gallop, Private Pozniak lay dying—his aorta pierced by the sniper's .45 caliber bullet. By the time Baldwin and his men covered the nearly seven hundred yards to reach the fallen courier, Stanislaw Tobias Pozniak had taken his final breath.

Quickly scanning the road in both directions, Captain Baldwin knelt beside the lifeless body of a boy young enough to be his son. He removed the leather satchel from around the dead private's neck and shoulder. Still scanning the road, he quickly opened it and examined the contents.

As he read the intercepted dispatch from his own general, it didn't take Baldwin long to discern the extent to which the information that had fallen into the enemy's hands could undermine the Confederate war effort. He slung the satchel over his shoulder and dragged the slain courier's body from the road into the woods. Without saying a word, he pointed east, signaling his men to continue toward their objective in Frederick.

One of the men stayed behind. He picked up a fallen branch and swept the road until the blood-soaked soil was no longer visible. He continued sweeping toward the woods, masking the drag marks from their victim's boots. Tossing the branch into the woods, he raced to catch up with the others.

Baldwin's band of marauders knew it wouldn't be long before a Union patrol came along to investigate the circumstances behind the riderless horse. They moved at a brisk pace, trying to distance themselves from the site of the ambush. But as he contemplated the significance of the dispatch he and his men had intercepted, Baldwin suddenly shortened his gait, slowing their progress. He began to question what his next move should be. How was this all going to play out?

Obviously, he needed to get word to General Lee that the Confederate plan had fallen into Union hands. And he needed to do it quickly, while there was still time for Lee to countermand his order.

It stood to reason that the Confederate general would have to abort his plan in favor of a new strategy. General McClellan, even though Baldwin's men had prevented the Union courier from delivering Special Order 191 to his headquarters, was still sure to learn of the planned three-pronged assault. The Union field commander who had sent the dispatch would almost certainly follow up to confirm that it had been successfully delivered. The fact that Baldwin's men had temporarily delayed the message from reaching McClellan was of no consequence.

But, then again, it *could* be of consequence. As Baldwin suddenly realized—it could be of tremendous consequence. He held up his hand, stopping the small detachment of Rebels in its tracks. He turned and stared at the road behind him. His men stood silent, studying the deliberate expression on their captain's face as he weighed his options. They had seen this expression before. Emmet Baldwin was not an everyday, run-of-the-mill junior officer. He was a tactician, one who possessed a shrewd military intellect. Without saying a word, Baldwin began retracing his steps toward the site of the ambush.

Without asking any questions, his men turned and followed him.

The following day, when General Robert E. Lee learned of Captain Baldwin's decision to leave the critical dispatch on the fallen courier's body, the usually calm Confederate commander was seething with rage. Those in his inner circle, including his chief of staff, Brigadier General Robert H. Chilton, had never seen the general this animated.

Chilton tried to calm his boss, carefully interjecting his speech between Lee's repeated rants against Baldwin and his men. "But, General…*sir*, Captain Baldwin's actions were quite sound in retrospect. His strategy is not without—"

"Strategy!" Lee shouted, interrupting Chilton. "*What* strategy? Allowing an intercepted order intended for my field generals to remain in Union hands is a strategy? Pray tell, Robert—exactly *how* does this damned reckless action constitute a strategy on the part of our renegade captain?"

Chilton tried again. "Sir…as Baldwin explained in his message, he replaced the dispatch and purposely moved the courier's body back onto the road. He *wanted* the Union patrol to discover it there, along with the contents inside the satchel. Even if he'd not done so, McClellan would have still, in due course, become aware of the order the courier was carrying. Baldwin couldn't have prevented that by removing the dispatch from the courier's body."

Lee's chief of staff could see the general was still skeptical. "Had Baldwin retained the satchel," Chilton continued, "McClellan and his staff would have surmised that we are aware Special Order 191 has been compromised. They also would have correctly reasoned that we must now abandon our planned three-pronged assault in favor of a new strategy."

Lee was still angry, but he was at least listening with interest. Chilton seized upon the opportunity to drive home his point. "Thanks to Captain Baldwin's deception, the enemy will continue to believe we have no knowledge that your order has fallen into their hands. Therefore, they have no reason to believe we will deviate from the plan they have in their possession. They are, no doubt, still expecting us to execute the details of Special Order 191 exactly as you drafted them. Don't you *see*, General? Captain Baldwin has cleverly maneuvered your enemy into a false position. His ruse has placed you one move ahead of McClellan on the chessboard."

Chilton watched as a calm slowly descended over his boss. He waited patiently for a response from the now-ruminative general.

After several minutes, Lee spoke. "General Chilton, we must move swiftly."

Chapter Two

17 September 1862 (the day of the battle)

At Harpers Ferry, Virginia, near the confluence of the Potomac and Shenandoah Rivers, the sun was just beginning to rise above the surrounding hills. Down below, inside the large federal garrison, fourteen thousand Union soldiers waited. Commanded by Colonel Dixon S. Miles, the soldiers girded themselves for the Confederate assault that was to be led by General Stonewall Jackson.

The assault never came.

The same was true at Lovettsville, where General John George Walker was to have attacked a large encampment of Union soldiers.

Jackson and Walker were nowhere near Harpers Ferry and Lovettsville. They weren't even in the state of Virginia. They were with Generals Hill and Longstreet—in Maryland. The four divisions assigned to Hill, Longstreet, Jackson and Walker had rejoined the main body of General Lee's army. A massive Confederate juggernaut was moving north, along Antietam Creek—straight toward Sharpsburg and General McClellan's headquarters.

McClellan was completely exposed. The Union commander had spread his forces to defend against the multi-pronged attack detailed in Special Order 191. He was ill-prepared to fight a decisive battle at

Sharpsburg—not against an approaching Confederate army four times larger than the one he had expected. His fate was now sealed.

The ensuing battle was nothing short of a Union massacre. By noon, the badly outnumbered defenders at Sharpsburg had been overrun, suffering casualties in the tens of thousands. Shortly thereafter, George B. McClellan, the commanding general of the Union Army, was taken prisoner. McClellan's surrender meant that the only Union commander who still possessed an army large enough to prevent Lee's forces from marching into Washington, D.C., was Major General Ulysses S. Grant.

Grant's army was seven hundred miles to the west. The American Civil War was effectively ended.

When President Abraham Lincoln received word of his army's defeat at Antietam, he realized his quest to preserve the Union had failed. "The war is lost—our Union put asunder," Lincoln muttered to General Henry Halleck, his chief of staff. "This changes everything we know—everything we've tried to safeguard for posterity."

In the weeks that followed, Lincoln sent his emissaries to Richmond. There, they received the surrender terms that had been dictated by Jefferson Davis—the president of the Confederate States of America.

Soon thereafter, the United Kingdom issued a proclamation recognizing the Confederacy as an independent nation. France, Germany and Spain quickly followed suit. At the time of its inception, the CSA constituted the fourth-largest economy in the world.

But it was an agrarian economy—one built upon the institution of slavery.

<u>Chapter Three</u>

1863–1913 (the aftermath)

In 1862, President Lincoln had hoped for a strategic opportunity to issue an emancipation proclamation. Had McClellan successfully deflected Lee's Maryland campaign, the momentum gained from such an important victory could have provided that opportunity. But because of the Union Army's defeat at Antietam, Lincoln never issued his proclamation.

Even if the Union Army had prevailed at Antietam, Lincoln's proclamation would only have freed persons being held as slaves in the states that had seceded. It would not have emancipated the half million souls who were enslaved in states that had remained part of the Union. Lincoln had planned to bring about a total end to slavery, not through his proclamation—but through a post-war amendment to the U.S. constitution. The proposed fourteenth amendment would have easily passed in the afterglow of a Union victory.

Now, it would be decades before such an amendment would pass.

In February of 1863, the status of five Union states still hung in the balance. Under the terms of the U.S. capitulation, Maryland, Kentucky, Missouri and Delaware—because they were slave states that had not seceded—had been granted referendums to determine their allegiance. Citizens in each state would go to the polls to decide whether to remain part of the Union or join the Confederacy.

Additionally, in what turned out to be one of the most controversial provisions of the surrender, Kansas voters were permitted to determine their fate as well. The state had long been at the center of pre-war turmoil over the question of slavery in America. After years of contentious negotiations, Kansas had eventually been admitted to the Union as a free state in 1861, a move which had greatly exacerbated an already-volatile situation during the leadup to the war. Now, even though it had been a free state during the conflict, Kansas was once again the nucleus of controversy over the issue of slavery.

When the referendums were held, Maryland and Delaware voted to remain part of the United States. Kentucky, Missouri and Kansas elected to join the Confederacy, although there was a great deal of suspicion surrounding the Kansas vote. Few in the U.S. government doubted that the vote had been surreptitiously skewed by pro-slavery factions in neighboring Missouri; but having already suffered a humiliating defeat at the hands of the Confederates, the United States lacked the political fortitude to press the issue.

The die was now cast. The boundaries of a new, self-governing nation had been drawn: Missouri, Kentucky, and Virginia to the north—Kansas, the Oklahoma Territory, and Texas to the west. Together with Arkansas, Louisiana, Tennessee, Mississippi, Alabama, Georgia, Florida and the Carolinas, these states now constituted the Confederate States of America.

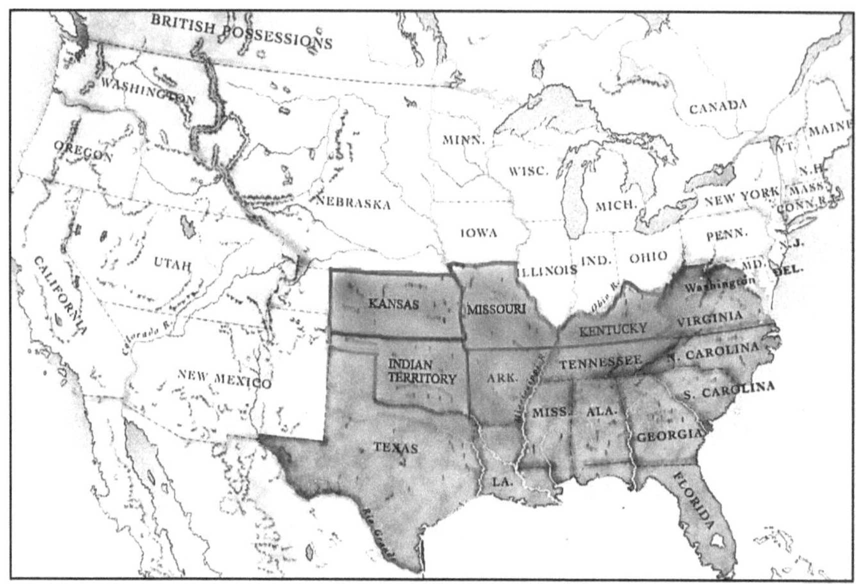

The Confederate States of America (February 1863)

The liberation of millions of African Americans had been indefinitely delayed. In addition to those states holding slaves in the newly independent Confederacy, two Union states (Maryland and Delaware) continued to hold slaves as well.

There was still a viable abolitionist movement, of course—even within the Confederacy. It wasn't long before many began to openly question the institution of slavery on moral grounds. In the end, it would take a seismic convergence of the industrial revolution and this Southern abolitionist movement to, once and for all, bring an end to slavery in the Confederate States.

In 1886, barely a quarter century after waging a bloody war to defend their "right" to hold slaves, the Confederate Congress voted overwhelmingly to pass an emancipation amendment. The amendment freed every remaining Southern slave and granted them full citizenship in the Confederate States of America. It was ratified that same year. Ironically, it wasn't until 1888 that a similar amendment was added to the United States Constitution.

Slavery in America was finally ended. It had died, as most corrupt institutions do, from natural causes.

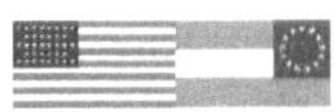

The decades that followed emancipation were a time of peaceful coexistence between the two American nations.

The United States, continuing President James K. Polk's earlier vision of a "manifest destiny," expanded to the Pacific coast—but not beyond. Once destined to become a formidable world power, the defeated nation never extended its sovereignty beyond its own shores.

The newly independent Confederate States were even less interested in expansion. Perhaps their isolationism was an effort to exorcise the twin demons of slavery and secession from their national conscience. Whatever the reasons, the Confederates stubbornly adopted a myopic foreign policy designed to avoid potential overseas entanglements even in situations where it might jeopardize their own national security interests.

All of this led to a world in which European nations continued to hold a firm grip on their respective Pacific and Caribbean protectorates. Many of those protectorates had once been on a path that would have eventually brought them inside the U.S. sphere of influence. Now, with America in a weakened state, the Monroe Doctrine, which had compelled the European powers to refrain from interfering in affairs within the Western Hemisphere, simply fell by the wayside.

The Philippines and Guam in the Pacific, as well as Cuba and Puerto Rico in the Caribbean, remained under Spanish control. Alaska remained a part of Russia, and Hawaii remained independent. Even though the United States negotiated a lease on a Pearl Harbor naval base with Hawaii's provincial government, very few U.S. Navy assets were ever deployed there.

When the French abandoned construction of a canal across the Isthmus of Panama late in the nineteenth century, President Theodore Roosevelt saw an opportunity for the U.S. to step in and acquire a strategic asset. Congress, still suffering from the malaise of the Civil War defeat, was reluctant to expend resources on foreign ventures. Roosevelt was unable to convince the shortsighted Congress to take on the project.

As a result, the canal, which would have been a tremendous military and economic resource to both American nations, was never completed.

At the beginning of the twentieth century, shadowed by a rapidly changing geopolitical environment, both the United States and Confederate militaries were third rate—each barely serviceable as a homeland defense force. That would slowly change when, as the Great War erupted in Europe, nations all around the globe began plummeting into the most extensive armed conflict in recorded history.

By then, however, the world was a vastly different place than it would have been if Corporal Barton Mitchell—while resting in a meadow near Frederick, Maryland, in 1862—had not happened upon that seemingly innocuous bundle of cigars, thus beginning a chain of events that changed the course of history.

Chapter Four
1914–1918

On Sunday, the 28th of June in the year 1914, Franz Ferdinand, the Archduke of Austria, was assassinated in Sarajevo. His assassin, a militant Bosnian Serb named Gavrilo Princip, had just toppled the first in a series of dominoes that would eventually lead to a global conflict known as the Great War—"the war to end all wars."

An ocean and half a continent away from Sarajevo, in the small town of Kerrville, Texas, a young boy lay sleeping in his bed. He was blissfully unaware of how the death of this person about whom he knew nothing, in a place he didn't know existed, was going to change his life.

Roderick Hurley was eight years old when the world decided to go to war. The second of four children, Rod was the oldest son. Even at eight years of age, he was a natural leader. Several hours after Franz Ferdinand had died in the streets of Sarajevo, the windup alarm clock next to his bed began clanging. He quickly set about rousting his brother and two sisters out of bed, ordering them to get ready for church. It was this propensity to shepherd his siblings that prompted his father to rely heavily upon Rod when, three years later, Clarence Hurley went north to volunteer with the United States Army.

When the Great War began in 1914, both American nations declared their neutrality. But while the Confederate States would continue to stand on the sidelines for the entirety of the conflict, their neighbors to the north would eventually commit themselves to the Allied cause in 1917. Three years after the war had started, the United States began sending American "doughboys" to France to fight against Germany and the other Central Powers.

When the U.S. finally entered the war, Clarence Hurley was not the only Southerner who opposed the CSA's continued neutrality stance. There were a significant number of Confederate men who went north to join the U.S. war effort. More than eight hundred thousand of them left home wearing the uniform of their nation's former enemy.

At about the same time that Rod Hurley's father was leaving Texas to fight in Europe, Toby Pozniak's father was celebrating his son's bar mitzvah (the Jewish coming of age ritual) at the Kane Street Synagogue, in Brooklyn, New York. Lawrence Pozniak had named his son after his own father's older brother. Toby's full name was the same as that of his great-uncle—Stanislaw Tobias Pozniak.

Toby didn't know much about his great-uncle, only that he had been a member of the Union Army during the Confederate War of Secession. He also knew that Stanislaw Pozniak had been killed in the line of duty. Toby's father had never shared much more than that—and for good reason. He hadn't wanted to explain to his son that the circumstances of his great-uncle's death had always been enveloped in controversy. Fairly or unfairly, some historians had placed blame for the Union defeat on Stanislaw Pozniak, faulting the young courier for the events leading up to the decisive battle at

Antietam. The Pozniak family had always vehemently rejected that judgment.

Now that Toby was moving into adulthood, Lawrence Pozniak decided it was time to level with his son about his namesake's notoriety. After all, he was the one who had saddled Toby with his great-uncle's name, even though Lawrence had done it out of compassion toward his own father, who often lamented the loss of his older brother. As they were leaving the synagogue that evening, Lawrence asked his son if he would like to take a ride down to Luna Park, on Coney Island.

"Sure, Pops—I'd love that. Is Mom coming too?"

"She's gonna ride home with the Krbecs. We'll make this a men-only outing. Whatta ya say?"

Toby was thrilled to hear his father refer to him as a man. Riding to Coney Island in their Model T Ford, he listened intently as his father engaged him in *adult* conversation. "How are things going at school these days?" his dad asked him. "How'd you and I fare on that Tesla coil we made for the science fair?"

"Scored an 'A'-*plus*, Pops."

Toby Pozniak loved school. He especially loved science. Even during recess, when his classmates were pouring onto the playground, Toby would sit in the lab with his science teacher. The two of them would talk about the universe and how it works. They talked about the planets, the stars and the speed of light. They even discussed things that weren't visible to the human eye—things like atomic particles.

As much as Toby enjoyed talking about science with his teacher, he enjoyed talking about spiritual things with his father even more. And he never had any difficulty reconciling the two. "Pops, why do you think God made electricity?" he asked.

"That's an easy one," his father answered. "He did it so you and I can take a ride on *A Trip to the Moon* after dark."

Toby grinned at his father. He loved that ride. It was his favorite attraction in the entire amusement park.

A Trip to the Moon was an animated experience within the confines of a huge domed building. The surrounding light show made riders feel as if they were soaring over New York City in a grand airship, up into the clouds and onward to the moon. There was even a papier-mâché lunar surface where riders disembarked and interacted with costume-wearing "moon dwellers."

This was a fantastic adventure in 1917.

Staying late into the night, Toby and his father rode every ride at Luna Park, right up until closing time. He had already enjoyed such a wonderful experience earlier in the day, celebrating his bar mitzvah with his parents and all his friends. The trip to Coney Island with just his dad had topped off a perfect day for Toby.

But now, on the drive home, his father took on a more serious tone. "Tell me something, Toby—how much do you know about your Great-Uncle Stanislaw?"

"Not much. Only what you and Mom told me—that he died when Grandpapa was young. Grandpapa never talks about him."

"That's because your grandfather still mourns the death of his brother, even after all these years."

"Why is that, Pops?"

"It's because of what some people, some *ill-informed* people, say about him. Your great-uncle fought in the Confederate War of Secession in the last century. Well…he didn't actually *fight*. He was a messenger. Just before the decisive battle, he was on his way to deliver some especially important papers to the Union headquarters. Unfortunately, he rode into a Confederate ambush. He could've turned and ridden away, but he tried his best to get past the ambush and deliver the papers. Only, he didn't make it. That's why some people blame him for losing the battle that cost the United States the war."

"But if he died bravely like you say he did, why do they think it was *his* fault? It wasn't his fault, *was it?*"

"*Absolutely not!* Your Great-Uncle Stanislaw was only a few years older than you are when he died. He died doing his duty…for his country. He was a *hero*. And don't you ever let anyone tell you differently."

Toby swore he wouldn't.

During the year and a half that his father was fighting in Europe, Rod Hurley matured rapidly. When the Central Powers surrendered to the Allies in 1918, Clarence Hurley returned home to discover his little boy, now twelve years old, had grown into manhood, both in appearance and mental toughness.

Rod was taller than normal for his age. He was a little on the slender side, but his muscular frame gave him the appearance of someone who could handle himself in a scrap. That masculine physique, along with his friendly face and pleasant demeanor, also made him popular with the girls at his school in Kerrville. One, in particular, had taken notice of Rod and often sat with him at lunch. Margaret Swanson was a striking, blue-eyed blonde.

Rod, although he was initially a little embarrassed by Margaret's attention, was not altogether unhappy to be in her frequent company. He and she would typically engage in small talk over their sack lunches. It wasn't long before they became more than just friends. Soon, they began sharing their private thoughts with one another.

One day, Rod took Margaret's hand—not really holding it, just touching it—and asked her, "What are you gonna do after school, Margie?"

Margaret looked at him and smiled. "I'm supposed to help my little sister with her social studies homework, but if you're asking to pay me a social call, then I suppose I could—"

"*No,*" Rod interrupted. "That's not what I'm talking about. I mean after we graduate. What I mean is…*well*…what are you gonna do with your life? What is it you long for?"

She was taken aback. She had never seen her beau this passionate. "I'm not sure, Rod. What is it *you* long for?" Margaret was secretly hoping that *she* was the object of Rod's passion.

"Remember when that barnstormer flew his airplane into town not long ago?"

Margaret tried not to let her disappointment show.

"That's what I wanna do, Margie. I wanna be a flyer."

Rod Hurley was dressed in his brown wool suit and tie, wearing boots and a cowboy hat. Margaret Swanson wore a modest linen dress and Victorian lace-up shoes. Sitting beside Rod, with her blond curls dangling beneath a flimsy bonnet, she dreamed of one day marrying him.

The two of them together were a classic Norman Rockwell painting. They epitomized small-town America in 1918. They represented ideals common to both American nations—ideals that recognized no border between Confederate and Union states.

The years that followed the end of the Great War were a time of gradual reconciliation between the two American nations—not a political reconciliation, but a cultural one. Contrary to what the maps depicted—and contrary to what most Europeans and their leaders believed—there was, in a practical sense, only one America.

Chapter Five
1919–1924

On the 6th of January in 1919, Theodore Roosevelt passed away at his home overlooking Long Island Sound in New York. One of the former president's final acts was to pen a lengthy letter to his son. In the letter, he lamented that one of his greatest regrets had been his inability to convince Congress to complete the canal across the Isthmus of Panama.

Two days later, at his state funeral, the flag-draped coffin of the deceased president was carried into Christ Episcopal Church, near his home in Oyster Bay. The flag that adorned his casket that day bore thirty-two stars. Standing among the dignitaries attending the ceremony was Confederate President William P. Hobby, the man who represented the sixteen stars missing from that flag.

The Great War had ended in 1918. In 1923, a defeated Germany, burdened by reparation payments imposed by the Allies in the Treaty of Versailles, began to suffer hyperinflation. At one point, a single American or Confederate dollar was worth seven thousand German marks.

The resulting civil unrest gave rise to several extremist political factions, one of which was the National Socialist German Workers' Party. It was led by a former lance corporal who had served as a regimental messenger in the German Army.

His name was Adolf Hitler.

In the fall of 1924, Toby Pozniak left Brooklyn, New York, to study physics at the University of California at Berkeley.

The following year, Rod Hurley left Kerrville, Texas, and entered the Citadel (the Confederate military academy) in Charleston, South Carolina.

<u>*Chapter Six*</u>
1925–1929

In the spring of 1925, F. Scott Fitzgerald published his acclaimed novel, <u>The Great Gatsby</u>.

Set in the fictional Long Island town of West Egg, it's the story of an opulent New York lifestyle during America's Jazz Age. The story's main character is James (Jimmie) Gatz. After coming to New York, Gatz legally changes his name to Jay Gatsby to conceal his Jewish heritage and help himself assimilate into an Anglo-Saxon Protestant society.

Many literary critics believe the fictional town of West Egg in <u>The Great Gatsby</u> is fashioned after the village of Great Neck—a wealthy Long Island community that, ironically, was home to a sizeable Jewish population at the time Fitzgerald wrote his novel.

Saul Rosenbaum and his wife Esther were both second-generation German Americans. A New York real estate mogul, Saul had accumulated most of his wealth buying and selling property in and around New York City. As highly respected members of the Temple Beth-El Synagogue, Saul and Esther had many friends throughout the community. In short, they were contented with their lives in Great Neck.

Saul, however, had come to detest the daily commute to his office in Lower Manhattan. Forty-five minutes to Penn Station on the Long Island Railroad and another twenty minutes by cab to his Wall Street office was beginning to make him regret moving away from the city.

One reason he and Esther had moved to Great Neck was for the sake of their only child. A fifth-grader at the Kensington-Johnson Elementary School, Natalie Rosenbaum was happy at "KJ"—the moniker she and her friends had affectionately given to their school.

But, then again, Natalie was the sort of person who could find happiness anywhere she happened to be. It was a trait that, in Natalie's case, was not entirely attributable to a child's natural naiveté. Like most "only children," she possessed a high sense of self-esteem, but she was not arrogant by any stretch of the imagination. Unlike some children raised with no siblings, Natalie was kind, gracious and selfless toward others.

So, when Natalie's father asked her if she would like to move back into the city, it was no surprise that she was enthusiastically in favor of the idea. To Natalie, this meant an opportunity for a great adventure. It was a chance to make new friends in a new neighborhood.

That's who Natalie Rosenbaum was. Her inclination was to see the good in every new circumstance she encountered, as well as every new person she met. Whenever Natalie was introduced to someone new in her life, she always assumed he or she was a decent person.

Even at twelve years of age, Natalie Rosenbaum was easy to like.

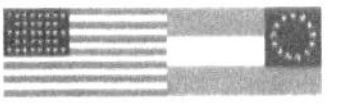

In the summer of 1925, Adolf Hitler published his autobiography, <u>Mein Kampf</u>. He wrote it while he was incarcerated for a failed coup attempt against the Weimar Republic—Germany's post-war democratic government.

Hitler asserted that Judaism and communism were to blame for Germany's tribulations. He alleged that a cabal of Jewish bankers and Marxists had conspired to undermine Germany's war effort in 1918. <u>Mein Kampf</u> was an early glimpse into the void that was Adolf Hitler's soul. His hatred for Jews percolated throughout his writing:

> *The nationalization of our masses will succeed only when, aside from all the positive struggle for the soul of our people, their international poisoners (the Jews) are exterminated. If, at the beginning of the war and during the war, twelve or fifteen thousand of these Hebrew corrupters of the nation had been subjected to poison gas...then the sacrifice of millions at the front would not have been in vain.*

In May of 1928, the Nazi party gained twelve seats in the Reichstag, Germany's house of parliament.

In the spring of 1929, Mr. and Mrs. Clarence Hurley, along with Margaret Swanson, loaded several pieces of luggage onto a Greyhound bus in Kerrville, Texas. Following a two-hour ride with several stops south and east, they arrived in San Antonio, where they boarded a train to Charleston, South Carolina.

On the 22nd of May, the Hurleys and Margaret proudly watched as Roderick Hurley graduated third in the Citadel's 1929 class of cadets. Following the ceremony, most of the new graduates were sworn in as second lieutenants in the Confederate Army. Rod Hurley was one of the few who were sworn into the CAAF (Confederate Army Air Force).

Margaret Swanson stood next to Rod Hurley as he raised his hand and repeated the commissioning oath. Margie was an extremely attractive young woman. Her hourglass figure made it difficult for the other cadets not to notice her as she pinned the shiny gold "butter bars" onto Rod's dress uniform.

Four days later, Mr. and Mrs. Hurley were joined in Charleston by Arthur and Elizabeth Swanson—Margie's parents. That afternoon, they assembled inside the Citadel's large chapel, along with two hundred other people, many of them recently commissioned second lieutenants and their fiancés awaiting their turn at the altar. Together, they watched Rod and Margie exchange their wedding vows.

In August of 1929, Toby Pozniak, having earned his bachelor's degree from UC Berkeley in only three years, completed work on his master's degree at that same institution.

The following month, the young physicist began earning his doctorate, concentrating heavily on the rapidly growing field of quantum mechanics. Pozniak's grasp of the subject was not only superior to that of his fellow doctoral candidates—it was also superior to that of the Berkeley professors.

Toby Pozniak was well on his way to becoming a star in the world of atomic theory.

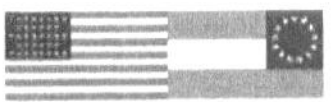

In October of 1929, the U.S. stock market crashed, plunging both Americas and most of Europe into an economic depression. In desperate need of funds, the United States government recalled the post-war recovery loans it had made to Germany. The recall further worsened an already crippled economy within the Weimar Republic.

In German elections held the following year, the Nazis would gain one hundred and seven more seats.

Chapter Seven
1930

The midsummer sun cast its rays across several rows of bright-yellow PT-3 biplanes as it peeked just above the horizon. The planes were parked in front of a dozen hangars at San Antonio's Brooks Field, the primary flight training base for the Confederate Army Air Force.

It had been more than a year since Rod Hurley had graduated from the Citadel. Unfortunately, the budget constraints of a depressed economy had delayed his entry into primary flight training for what seemed to Hurley to be an eternity. The logjam of prospective military aviators waiting to begin flight school in both the Confederate and United States of America had resulted from a shortage of airplanes and instructors within the respective training commands of both nations. It was symptomatic of the sorry state of both militaries in July of 1930.

All of that was not important to Second Lieutenant Rod Hurley. Finally, after a rigorous course of ground instruction and training sorties, he was about to make his first solo flight. For most of his twenty-four years leading up to this moment, Hurley had dreamed of taking to the sky in command of his own plane.

Wearing a brown leather flight suit and fur-lined boots, he approached his air machine with long-awaited anticipation. With his broad-shouldered build and black wavy hair, Hurley's likeness could have easily graced a recruiting poster for his nation's air force. As he finished his preflight inspection and climbed onto the lower wing of his airplane, the young aviator projected a dashing, almost celebrity-like image. After strapping on his bulky parachute and donning his tight-fitting leather helmet, he hopped into the PT-3's open cockpit with childlike excitement.

As the sun rose into the clear Texas sky, Rod Hurley fastened his seatbelt for the thrilling adventure that lay ahead.

On the other side of the Atlantic, two of the world's brightest theoretical physicists were having lunch at a beer garden in Göttingen, Germany.

Werner Heisenberg was a Nobel Prize recipient, renowned for his work in the field of quantum mechanics. Toby Pozniak, having earned his doctorate in that same field, had traveled to Germany to study under Heisenberg at Göttingen University. The campus was a repository for advanced atomic research, making it a magnet for the world's most talented and ambitious physicists.

Heisenberg and Pozniak enjoyed each other's company. They often came to this place, not far from campus, to discuss their work over a plate of schnitzel. At twenty-eight years of age, Heisenberg, who was born in Bavaria, was only two years older than his American protégé. The two men shared common interests and even possessed common physical traits. Each man was slight in stature, with a receding hairline that added years to his appearance. Despite the oppressive summer heat that pervaded the open-air beer garden, each was dressed in a suit and tie.

As much as Pozniak enjoyed these outings, today's after-lunch topic of conversation was about to make him uncomfortable. Perhaps fueled by the hot temperatures and one too many steins of warm lager, the discourse took a turn that began to make the normally self-assured physicist feel uneasy.

Reaching into his double-breasted jacket, Heisenberg took out a tin case and removed a cigarette. He leaned sideways and pulled a box of matches from his pants pocket. Casually striking the match under the table, he lit the cigarette and pushed aside his empty plate. Waving the match to extinguish it, he smiled. It was the sardonic smile of a person who knows he will relish an argument he is about to incite. Passing a cigarette to his associate, he struck another match and held it at arm's length across the table. "So, tell me, Tobias—what do you think of Herr Hitler?"

Pozniak accepted the cigarette and leaned forward, allowing his friend to light it. He exhaled a billowing white plume. "Hitler? Why should I care at all about him?"

"Come now—surely you have an opinion about the man." Heisenberg tapped his finger on the table. "He spoke at this very hall just last week."

"Did you come to hear him?" Pozniak asked.

"Certainly, I did. The fact that I'm a man of science doesn't preclude me from taking an interest in politics. These are hard times in my country."

"These are hard times in *my* country as well, Werner."

"*Yes, yes*—sure they are; but you and I both know the Allies took advantage of an opportunity to humiliate the German people at Versailles. And now we're paying a heavy price because of it. Hitler is merely calling on our citizens to stand up and make something of themselves. He wants to see the Fatherland prosper again."

Pozniak fidgeted with his tie. Reaching for an ashtray, he flicked the ashes from his cigarette. "I *also* would like to see the German people prosper. It's just that I'm concerned for those Herr Hitler has chosen to blame for the current state of Germany's affairs."

Sensing his associate's anxiety, Heisenberg now attempted to diffuse the tension he had intentionally created. "You mean the disparaging remarks he's made about Jewish merchants? You mustn't take that literally, my friend. That's just part of his rhetoric, designed to offer up an accounting for a failed economy. I'm quite sure he doesn't actually—"

"Designed to offer up *scapegoats* is more like it," Pozniak retorted, cutting Heisenberg off mid-sentence.

"Oh, be reasonable, Tobias."

"Reasonable? You think Hitler and his cronies are *reasonable?*" For the first time in their association, animus now hung in the air. "I think we should be getting back to the university now." Pozniak stood and reached into his pocket. He pulled out a wad of Weimar Republic currency and peeled off two dozen bills. Unaware of the irony, he tossed twenty thousand German marks down on the table. Twenty *thousand* marks—it was barely enough to cover his meal and a small tip for the waitress. Pounding his cigarette into the ashtray, Pozniak turned and left.

Heisenberg glanced at the pile of cash and looked back up at Pozniak. He watched as his perturbed colleague walked away. When the waitress came to collect the money from the table, Werner Heisenberg smiled at her and ordered another stein of beer.

That evening in Albany, New York, Franklin Roosevelt, the forty-fourth governor of that state, sat in his office and contemplated his political future. Nine years earlier, Roosevelt had been afflicted with polio. His legs were now paralyzed. Despite being confined to a wheelchair, he had managed to salvage his career, rising to the governorship of the most populous state in the Union.

Now, Roosevelt was intent on taking his political comeback one step further. The next presidential election was two years away. If anyone possessed the political cunning to overcome a physical disability and become president of the United States, it was Franklin Delano Roosevelt.

In Missouri, the presiding judge of Jackson County had spent most of that spring and summer constructing inroads that would lead to future political opportunities. Many of the state's most knowledgeable pundits believed he was positioning himself to run for a seat in the Confederate Senate.

Unbeknownst to even his closest political associates, however, the former haberdasher from the small town of Independence had loftier aspirations. Specifically, he was positioning himself for a run at his nation's highest office.

His name was Harry S. Truman.

In Berlin, Heinrich Brüning, Chancellor of Germany, worried that his proposal for a deflationary economic policy would be defeated by moderates in the Reichstag.

On the 16th of July, Brüning decided to invoke Article 48 of the Weimar Constitution, which allowed him to institute laws without parliamentary consent. The move proved to be a slippery slope for an already-unstable German democracy.

Waiting in the wings, Adolf Hitler took special note of Brüning's implementation of the Article 48 provision. With political ambitions of his own, Hitler had a keen interest in how the German chancellor's powerplay would be received by a disgruntled German electorate.

Chapter Eight
1931

Stuyvesant High School, a stately ten-story building situated on a scenic parcel of land north of Battery Park, was one of the best public schools in New York City. Overlooking the Hudson River, it was the school of choice for the sons and daughters of wealthy socialites living in Lower Manhattan. There were grand columns of marble guarding the main entry. Together with the ornate Art Deco doors, they gave the secondary school a university-like appearance that comported well with the high standards to which its students were held.

On a beautiful spring day in late May, eight hundred and thirty-nine graduating seniors lined up outside the entrance to Stuyvesant High School's large auditorium. The room was filled with excited family members and friends of the graduates. A formally dressed, middle-aged woman was seated behind an open grand piano, below and to one side of the stage.

As the pianist began playing "Pomp and Circumstance," the guests stood in unison. They turned and watched as the long procession of graduates began marching from the back of the auditorium toward rows of empty seats in front of the stage. Following the graduates' march, the local Episcopal bishop strode to the microphone and delivered a lengthy invocation. There were several announcements by the school's principal, as well as speeches by dignitaries from Stuyvesant High School's administration and the New York City Department of Education.

Finally, it was time for the valedictorian's address. As an attractive and smiling young woman made her way from the front row of seats toward the stage, the auditorium fell silent. Sudden shouts of encouragement from the embarrassed girl's friends and family made her blush and drew a smattering of laughter from the crowd. Preparing to climb the stairway to the podium, the young woman used the hand in which she held her speech to lift the hem of her graduation robe. As she gracefully ascended the half dozen steps, she raised the other hand to steady the ill-fitting mortarboard on her head. Even though she wore a not-so-flattering pair of wire-rimmed eyeglasses, those seated closest to the front of the auditorium could tell she was a radiant beauty.

After adjusting the microphone on the rostrum, Stuyvesant High School's valedictorian confidently and eloquently delivered her brief remarks:

> Friends, family and teachers—I cannot begin to thank you enough.
>
> Thank you all for your support in helping my classmates and me to reach this most-exciting benchmark in our lives. Without you, none of this would have been possible. Thanks to you, we, the Stuyvesant High School graduates of 1931, stand ready to take our places in society.
>
> Four years ago, when this class of graduating seniors first entered these halls, our great nation was

experiencing a time of growth and prosperity. It was a time of optimism and hope for future generations.

Today, my fellow graduates and I will depart this institution against the backdrop of a devastating economic depression. Many of the families inside this auditorium have been affected in some way by the challenging times that have fallen upon our country. Most of us here today, however, are doing very well compared to many of our fellow Americans.

My classmates and I pledge to work as hard as we can to make a difference during these challenging times. I call upon everyone here, not just the graduates, to do his or her part to help a fellow citizen.

My friends, God is incredibly good to us. Deep down inside my heart, I believe that individuals are good as well. If people of all faiths unite to help one another, we can rise above any unfortunate circumstance that might beset our great nation.

I ask God to bless us all. I pray He will lift our souls and fill each of us with great compassion. I pray He will bestow upon us a desire to share our blessings with our brothers and sisters who are less fortunate than we.

I pray He will help us to be good Americans.

Thank you very much.

Almost immediately, there was a spirited response from the audience. The entire graduating class rose from their seats and applauded wildly. It wasn't long until the guests were standing and cheering as well. The young woman had, in just a few short sentences, struck a chord in the hearts of everyone in attendance that afternoon.

At eighteen years of age, Natalie Rosenbaum was still easy to like.

In San Antonio, Margie Hurley was busy unpacking boxes at her husband's new duty station. Randolph Field had been scheduled to open the preceding year, but just like most government projects, it had been delayed because of bureaucratic inefficiencies.

Those same bureaucratic inefficiencies, however, had likely saved the project from being scrapped altogether. The funds budgeted for construction of the new base had been allocated just prior to the 1929 stock market crash. Once the money had been earmarked, it was easier for the Confederate government to complete the project than to exercise the unwieldy political processes necessary to cancel it.

Randolph Field was the final training stop on Rod Hurley's quest to become a pilot in the CAAF. The new two-bedroom house that Margie and Rod now occupied was simple, yet nice. So too were the other houses and buildings that surrounded it. The red Spanish tile atop the white stucco walls made this place much more pleasing to the eye than the government housing on most military bases. Margie Hurley didn't know how long she and Rod would be living here, but she was doing her best to make it feel like home.

While his wife was settling into the young couple's new residence, Rod Hurley, now a first lieutenant, was checking in with the personnel sergeant at the 232nd Advanced Training Squadron. The 232nd had just received brand-new airplanes. The Boeing B-9 was the first all-metal monoplane bomber produced in America. Even though Boeing was a U.S. company, a mutually beneficial trade agreement between the two governments allowed U.S. and Confederate defense contractors to sell their wares to both nations' militaries.

After stamping Rod Hurley's orders, the personnel sergeant escorted him to meet the man who commanded the 232nd, Lieutenant Colonel Charles Morrow. Holding his training folder under his arm,

Hurley stood at attention and rapped on the colonel's open door. "First Lieutenant Hurley reporting for duty, sir."

"Come on in, Hurley." Morrow pointed to a chair across from his desk. "Take a seat," he said, smiling. He reached into his desk drawer and took out a pack of Lucky Strikes. He placed them on the desk in front of the young lieutenant. "Cigarette?"

"No…thank you, sir."

"Let's have a look at your training records." Colonel Morrow's pleasant demeanor helped to put Hurley at ease as he handed the folder across the colonel's desk.

The young lieutenant waited patiently, glancing around the office as the colonel looked through his records. Hurley noted there were photographs from every stage of Morrow's career. He divided his attention equally between the many photos until he became fixated on one in particular. Displayed atop the colonel's metal file cabinet was a picture of a much younger Colonel Morrow dressed in the uniform of a British Royal Air Force pilot. Morrow was posing in front of a Sopwith Camel, the RAF's frontline pursuit [fighter] plane during the Great War.

Morrow looked up and noticed Hurley's preoccupation with the photo. "That was a fine airplane, Lieutenant."

"Sir?"

"The Sopwith Camel—isn't that what you're staring at?"

"Oh…*yes sir*, Colonel—that and the RAF uniform. My father served in the United States Army Infantry during the war."

"Yes, I know."

"You *know*, sir?"

"My brother was an infantry officer in the U.S. Army. He commanded a company of Texas volunteers in France. He speaks very highly of your father—said he was one of his best men."

"I had no idea we shared that connection, Colonel. I guess it's a pretty small world."

"Well, it's no great coincidence that my brother and your father know one another. The fraternity of Texas volunteers who fought in that war is pretty tight."

"Yes sir. I imagine it would be." Hurley hesitated before continuing. "May I ask you a question, Colonel?"

Morrow nodded.

"Why the RAF instead of the U.S. Army Air Corps?"

"Simple," Morrow replied. "I joined up in 1915, two years before the U.S. entered the war. Guess you could say I cut out the middleman and got right down to business. Besides, it's a better-lookin' uniform, don't you think?"

Both men chuckled. The U.S. and Confederate armed forces not only shared much of the same military hardware, they also shared similar-looking uniforms. While the two nations' navies wore uniforms that closely resembled those of their British counterparts, the olive-drab uniforms of both the U.S. Army Air Corps and the Confederate Army Air Force were dreary and dull compared to the flashy blue uniforms worn by RAF officers.

"Now—let's cut to the chase. We need to talk about *you*, Lieutenant." The senior officer looked back down at the folder he was holding. "It says here that you graduated at the top of your class over at Brooks. Says you were selected for a slot as a pursuit pilot. Even says your instructors all believed you're a natural pilot. *Are* you a natural pilot, Lieutenant?"

"Well, I'm not sure I'd go that far, sir. I don't have enough experience to know what that means."

Morrow unexpectedly slammed the folder onto the desktop in front of a startled Rod Hurley. "That's a load of *horseshit*, Hurley! And you can stow that duplicitous self-deprecation crap. There's not an aviator worth his salt who doesn't believe he's the best stick-and-rudder guy ever to strap into a cockpit."

Hurley tried to gather his composure but found himself stammering. "I suppose you could say I'm very *comfortable* in the air." He was certainly more comfortable in a cockpit than he was sitting across from Colonel Morrow at that moment.

Morrow looked at the young officer sideways and smirked. "If that's so, what's the story with this pursuit slot? Why didn't you take it?"

"That class isn't slated to start for another eight months, Colonel. I took this slot because I can earn my wings as a bomber pilot before that class even starts. I already waited a year just to start my primary training. The last thing I want now is to be placed in another holding pattern." Hurley knew his explanation sounded trivial.

"And you think earning your wings a few months earlier is worth giving up an opportunity to become a pursuit pilot?"

Hurley paused momentarily before answering. He weighed the fact that Morrow had flown as a pursuit pilot with the RAF against the fact that he now commanded a training squadron for bomber pilots. He wasn't sure what his new commanding officer wanted to hear.

After a few seconds of silent deliberation, the anxious young lieutenant opted in favor of candor. "To be honest, sir, I think flying bombers will be just as rewarding as flying pursuit planes—maybe even more so. Being part of a crew is an idea that appeals to me." Hurley was hopeful he had successfully extricated himself from his unpleasant situation. The stoic expression on the colonel's face did little to reassure him.

Morrow sat silently for a moment, his expression unchanged. He leaned back in his chair and placed his clasped hands over his polished brass belt buckle.

Hurley waited.

Finally, Morrow leaned forward, calmly pushing Hurley's training folder to one side of the desktop. Resting his forearms on the spot where the folder had been, he brandished a wry smile and spoke. "Very well, Lieutenant—let's see what we can do about making you into a bomber pilot."

In Munich, twenty-three-year-old Angela Raubal was living in an apartment with Adolf Hitler, her forty-two-year-old half-uncle. There were widespread rumors that Hitler was physically and mentally abusing his niece. At the very least, the two maintained a volatile relationship.

On the 18th of September, following a heated argument with Hitler, Raubal shot herself with his pistol, committing suicide.

Adolf Hitler fell into a state of deep depression. His depression, however, would be short-lived.

Chapter Nine
1932

It was a pleasant February afternoon in San Antonio. Margie Hurley could barely contain her excitement. Not only was she proud to be attending her husband's graduation from flight school, she was happy for other reasons as well—reasons known only to Margie. Sitting in a grandstand with the families and friends of the other sixteen members of Class No. 3103, she watched the impressive ceremony unfold.

By virtue of his top-grad status, Rod Hurley led his classmates, marching beside him in dual eight-man columns, onto the Randolph Field parade deck. The band that marched ahead of the graduating aviators was playing John Philip Sousa's "The Invincible Eagle" as they passed the reviewing stand. The flag-draped platform, prominently situated in front of the large grandstand, was filled with high-ranking military officers and several local luminaries. The two columns of graduates stopped directly in front of the stand, where they continued marching in place until, just as the band played their final note, Hurley brought the formation to a complete halt.

"Right...face!" Hurley barked. The young lieutenant and his classmates executed the command in unison, turning smartly toward the dignitaries. Still at attention, Hurley saluted the reviewing stand. Holding his salute, he announced to Colonel Jim Jackson, commanding officer of the 43rd Training Air Wing, that Class 3103 was "reporting for graduation."

Colonel Jackson returned Hurley's salute and ordered him and his classmates to stand at ease. Colonel Jackson then delivered a lengthy address, replete with patriotic platitudes and dutiful acknowledgments of every VIP in attendance. After speaking for longer than anyone wanted to listen, the colonel stepped down from the platform, along with the wing admin officer, and walked toward Hurley and his classmates.

Returning his formation to attention, First Lieutenant Rod Hurley became the first member of Class 3103 to receive his wings.

After congratulating Hurley with a handshake, Colonel Jackson made his way through the ranks, where each of Hurley's classmates anxiously awaited his hard-earned prize. As Jackson paused in front of each man, the admin officer handed the colonel a set of wings. Greeting each new aviator with a handshake, Colonel Jackson presented the wings, one by one, to the sixteen men standing in the formation. By tradition, the actual "pinning-on" of the wings would be left to each graduate's wife, girlfriend or mother following the conclusion of the ceremony.

As he stood alone in front of the ranks, Hurley held his wings in the palm of his hand. He rubbed his thumb back and forth across the textured metal feathers. The sensation filled him with a feeling of accomplishment the likes of which he had never experienced. From his perspective, even his graduation and commissioning at the Citadel was not as gratifying as this occasion. Rod Hurley had finally achieved his lifelong dream. He was a pilot in the CAAF.

After every man had received his wings, Colonel Jackson returned to the reviewing stand. The clear blue sky provided a perfect backdrop for the seven B-9 bombers as they approached the parade deck from several miles away. The flyby of twin-engine monoplanes, the same planes in which Class 3103 had trained, would officially close the ceremony. The fourteen radial engines produced an exhilarating airborne symphony as they neared the grandstand. The climax was a combined 8000-horsepower crescendo that reverberated for several seconds as the low-flying formation passed just above the crowd. The awe-inspiring display added a thrilling exclamation point to the day's proceedings.

As Rod Hurley dismissed his class, the parade deck was inundated in a sea of excited well-wishers. Proud family members and friends poured from the stands to congratulate the newly designated aviators.

Emerging from the crowd, Margie Hurley flew into Rod's arms. Not allowing her feet to touch down, Rod wrapped his arms around Margie's waist and swung her through two complete revolutions before placing her back on the ground. He kissed her and held her in his arms for several seconds.

As the embrace continued, Margie stood on her toes and whispered something into Rod's ear.

"You're kidding!" he said, holding Margie out in front of him where he could see the smile radiating from her face.

Margie batted her eyes and hugged him again, giving him another kiss.

Rod Hurley was on cloud nine. Not only was he now an aviator—he would soon be a father as well.

Six months later, in Germany, Toby Pozniak watched with great concern as the Nazi party gained two hundred and thirty more seats in the July federal elections. The Nazis, though they had failed to gain a clear majority, were now the largest political party in the Reichstag.

Four months after the German elections, Franklin Delano Roosevelt was successful in his bid to unseat Herbert Hoover, the incumbent U.S. president.

Hoover had presided over the worst financial collapse in American history. It was a resounding defeat for the outgoing president and a colossal victory for his successor. In garnering 89% of the electoral college, FDR had been presented with a great mandate.

The nation had turned to him for guidance during a time of great turmoil.

Chapter Ten

_1933_

On the 30th of January, the man destined to plunge the world into a second world war culminated his rise to power in Germany. Adolf Hitler became chancellor of the German government.

Three weeks later, a communist extremist, protesting the decision to put Hitler in charge, set fire to the Reichstag, burning it to the ground. Hitler pointed to the incident as evidence of a communist plot against the German people. On the 28th of February, citing his Article 48 powers under the Weimar Constitution, he unilaterally passed a law that ended civil liberties in Germany.

Three weeks later, he succeeded in passing the "Enabling Act"—a contrived law that, for all intents and purposes, granted him dictatorial powers. He would eventually assume the title "der Führer" [the leader].

Adolf Hitler could now rule as he pleased.

On the 4th of March, Franklin Roosevelt was sworn in as the thirty-second president of the United States. In his inaugural address to the nation, Roosevelt attempted to calm Americans' anxieties over the

economy and the growing unrest across the Atlantic. "The only thing we have to fear," the new president said emphatically, "is fear itself."

For Toby Pozniak and the millions of Jews living in Europe, there was much more to fear than fear itself.

At her father's suite of offices in Lower Manhattan, Natalie Rosenbaum sat behind the receptionist's desk, sorting letters and filing miscellaneous real estate documents. As she leaned over to open the file drawer on one end of the desk, she heard static on the desktop intercom. A familiar voice came over the hollow-sounding two-way speaker box. "Natalie, can you come in here please?"

"Be right there, Papa." Natalie continued retrieving the folder in which she intended to file a property tax receipt. To mark her place in the long drawer full of files, she partially lifted the folder immediately behind the just-removed folder. That way, the tab would be noticeably higher than the others when she returned to complete her task. She gracefully spun her chair and stood in one motion. She made her way past several offices belonging to various members of her father's firm, toward the end of the hall where Saul Rosenbaum's private office occupied the lion's share of the suite.

Behind his closed door, Saul could hear the heels of his daughter's oxford pumps clacking against the marble-tiled floor. He toggled another switch on his mahogany intercom board, buzzing his accountant.

"Yes, Mr. Rosenbaum?"

"Miss Witherspoon, Natalie's going to be in my office for a while. Would you cover the front desk please?"

"Of course. I'll head up front right away. Will you and Natalie be needing any coffee?"

"No, thank you. I'll send Natalie back up front as soon as we've finished with our business."

Though it wasn't necessary, Natalie paused to knock before opening the door that led into her father's corner office. Perched forty stories above Wall Street, the office provided a breathtaking panorama to the east, south and west of Manhattan's southern tip. The Brooklyn Bridge, Governors Island and the Statue of Liberty were just a few of the landmarks visible from the lavishly appointed workspace. As many times as Natalie had been in this office, the view always mesmerized her when she entered the room. Stopping just inside the doorway, she paused several seconds to take it in. "You wanted to see me, Papa?"

"Come on in, Ketzel." Saul often called Natalie by this name in private. It was the Yiddish word for *kitten*.

Natalie closed the door. She walked across the Persian rug in the center of the office, toward the three leather-upholstered chairs that sat in front of her father's desk. "What did you want to see me about?" she asked, settling into the middle chair.

Smiling, Saul picked up a letter from his desktop and showed it to Natalie. "I heard from Isidor Gordimer again."

Natalie lowered her head and glared at her father over the top of her glasses. "We've talked about this, Papa. I don't want to go to college. I'm perfectly happy doing what I'm doing. I appreciate what you're trying to do for me, but I wish you'd let this go."

Abandoning his smile, Saul returned his daughter's disdainful look. "*So*—you intend to spend the rest of your life working as my receptionist and volunteering at soup kitchens? You have so much more to offer, Natalie. Besides, Miss Witherspoon will be retiring in the next few years, and I'm going to need a good accountant."

"I know…and I'm flattered you think I'd be a good accountant; but I still don't want to go to college. Besides, I haven't taken my entrance exams. I can't be—"

Saul held up his hand. "Listen to me, Ketzel. Izzy still owes me a favor. I was the one who helped him acquire that property up on the West Side several years ago when Columbia expanded its business school. Izzy knows you haven't taken the entrance exams. He says not to worry. He still sits on the board of regents, and he can authorize the director of admissions to accept you based on your status as a Stuyvesant valedictorian."

"That's all well and good, Papa, and I don't want you to think I don't appreciate your help. It's just that I've been saving my money to travel to Europe with my friends next fall. You *know* that."

Saul became animated. "Don't you read the papers, Natalie? This is no time for you and your friends to go gallivanting around Europe!"

Natalie wasn't accustomed to receiving such a terse rebuttal from her father. She grew flustered. In a rare display of insolence, she raised her voice. "But if I don't go now, I'll probably never have another opportunity! My *friends* don't seem to be worried about going to Europe!"

Her father's expression became deadly serious. "Your friends aren't *Jewish*, Natalie."

On the 14th *of July, Hitler decreed the Nazi party to be the only legitimate political party in Germany. Many German citizens, fearing they would be ostracized if they resisted, reluctantly registered as party members. Even those who continued to oppose Hitler and the Nazis dared not voice their dissent in public. In Germany, it was a time of subjugation.*

Conformity was the order of the day.

It was late evening in Göttingen. On his way to visit Werner Heisenberg at his campus apartment, Toby Pozniak was filled with a sense of uncertainty that bordered on fear. He was trying to decide if he should leave Germany. He was hesitant to relinquish his prestigious position as one of Werner Heisenberg's top associates, but he was becoming concerned for his personal safety. He was hopeful that a frank discussion with his friend would help to reassure him and put his fears to rest.

As Pozniak rounded the corner of Heisenberg's ivy-covered apartment building, he stopped in his tracks. Straight ahead, under a streetlight, he spotted two brown-shirted men with Nazi armbands walking toward him.

Startled, Pozniak quickly retreated. Peering from around the corner of the building, he watched the two men as they stopped in front of Heisenberg's apartment and knocked on his door. A few seconds later, Werner Heisenberg opened the door and cordially greeted the men. They exchanged smiles and handshakes before Heisenberg invited them into the apartment and closed the door.

Pozniak was stunned. He stood motionless for almost a minute. Not knowing what else to do, he started walking back to his apartment on the other side of the Göttingen campus. As he made his way across the shadowy grounds, he began to survey his surroundings. It was as if he had been transported to a place he had never been before. He felt alone.

Halfway home, he stopped. It was eerily quiet. Standing beneath a campus streetlight, he slowly turned a complete revolution, casting his gaze in every direction. He took notice of the buildings he had passed every day for the past three years as if he were seeing them for the first time. He realized something had changed profoundly, almost overnight.

Seemingly surrounded by a sea of banners bearing the Nazi swastika, Toby Pozniak knew the time had come to get out of Germany.

Chapter Eleven
_1934_

Captain Rod Hurley was usually comfortable sitting at the controls of his B-9 bomber. He had logged more than 2,000 hours in it. But on this cold and rainy night in February, he was anything but comfortable. Flying in an open cockpit, though it might have been glamorous and exciting, left him at the mercy of the elements. In the clouds at 5,000 feet, Hurley and his crew were somewhere over Northeast Kansas—in pitch darkness.

Unable to communicate with his copilot, who was flying the aircraft from the forward cockpit, Hurley correctly surmised that the rain had shorted out his interphone (the B-9's internal communication system). He also correctly surmised that he and his crew were lost. To make matters worse, he could see ice beginning to form on the edges of his windscreen.

With the interphone not working, Hurley shook the stick to signal his copilot that he was taking control. Blind to anything on the ground, his only tools for keeping the 14,000-pound bomber upright were his altimeter, his airspeed indicator, and a rudimentary attitude gyro. Unable to hear anything on his radio, he climbed, hoping to pick up the low-frequency radio range signal out of Sherman Army

Airfield. He predicated those hopes on the assumption that his radio was not also shorted out.

Hurley was in luck. Reaching 7,500 feet, he heard the Morse code signal from the four antennas arrayed 3.2 miles northwest of the Sherman Field runway. The pulsating tones in his headset let him know he needed to turn right to intercept the radio beam that would guide him to the antennas.

He banked right and held the turn through forty-five degrees on his compass. Leveling his wings, he maintained his heading and waited for the steady tone that would let him know when he had intercepted the beam. Several minutes later, Hurley heard the reassuring steady tone. He turned forty-five degrees back to the left. The B-9 bomber was on the beam, headed toward the antennas.

After several more minutes, the steady tone began to pulsate again. The distinctive pattern of the tones let Hurley know he had drifted right of his course. He turned slightly left. Within seconds, he had reacquired the beam. Hurley continued in this manner for nearly forty-five minutes, relying on nothing but the tones in his headset to keep his bomber on course toward the antennas. The closer he got to Sherman Field, the quicker the tones shifted and the more tedious the corrections became.

Finally, the tones stopped altogether. His headset went silent. Far from being a malfunction, this was a good thing. The aircraft was in the cone of airspace directly above the antennas—a place where no radio waves were propagated. This was Hurley's indication that he was on top of the transmitting station.

The veteran pilot turned his aircraft to intercept the course depicted on his navigational chart. It was a maneuver designed to carry him away from the airfield, giving him time to lower his altitude in airspace free of obstructions. Reacquiring the radio signal, he began descending to the prescribed altitude of 2,900 feet. After tracking the outbound beam from the station for the specified amount of time, he reversed his course, back toward the station.

In accordance with his chart, Hurley descended to 1,800 feet; but he was still unable to see the ground. After several minutes tracking the beam inbound, Hurley crossed the station for the second time. He continued on his course, straight toward the runway at Sherman Army Airfield. This was the final segment of the approach. Hurley started his stopwatch and descended to the minimum prescribed altitude of 600 feet above the ground. He gazed into the darkness below, desperately searching for the runway—nothing.

In 1934, there were only a handful of pilots in the world who possessed the necessary skills to fly this kind of approach. Fortunately for the other three crew members aboard the low-on-fuel B-9 bomber, Rod Hurley was one of them.

Hurley's stopwatch told him he was only seconds from the airfield. He was still flying blind. He contorted his neck from side to side, straining for any sign of the airfield. At last, he began to make out the two rows of flare pots that illuminated the Sherman Field runway. He guided the lumbering, ice-laden B-9 onto the wet sod and chopped the throttles.

As Hurley taxied toward the row of hangars at the edge of the field, he and his crew were miserably wet and cold. All four men were physically and mentally exhausted from the grueling five-hour flight that had originated at their home base in Montgomery, Alabama. They were not the slightest bit saddened knowing this would be their final flight in the obsolete B-9.

As they neared their parking spot, their prize for surviving this trip was clearly visible inside one of the brightly lit hangars. Through several rows of paned glass windows in the hangar's huge sliding doors, they saw the shimmering, bare-metal airframe of a new Martin B-10 bomber. The freshly polished B-10 was a sight for sore eyes. In the coming days, following several orientation flights, Hurley's crew would be flying their new bomber back home to Maxwell Field.

Rod Hurley took special note of the new bomber's modern, fully enclosed cockpit. Even though his face was numb from the freezing weather, he still managed to produce enough of a smile to be seen by his copilot, who was looking back at him from the front cockpit.

His copilot returned the smile, flashing an enthusiastic thumbs-up.

In March, a thirty-two-year-old Italian physicist published an article in which he described a series of experiments conducted in his laboratory at the University of Rome. Based on the results of the experiments, he concluded that the atoms of certain elements could be split by bombarding them with neutrons.

The physicist's name was Enrico Fermi. He would eventually be heralded as "the architect of the nuclear age."

The 30th of June would come to be known as the "Night of the Long Knives." It was the beginning of a brutal three-day purge in Nazi Germany. It was also the German people's introduction to a paramilitary organization known as the Schutzstaffel—the "SS."

The SS, made up entirely of Aryans loyal to the Nazi party, was tasked with Adolf Hitler's personal protection. During the bloody seventy-two-hour rampage, hundreds of SS troops carried out a series of targeted assassinations against political figures deemed by Hitler and the Nazis to be enemies of the state.

Also complicit in the murderous campaign was the Gestapo, the Führer's secret police.

If any in Germany still questioned Adolf Hitler's resolve to rule the Reich with an iron fist, the Night of the Long Knives completely removed those doubts.

In late July, Toby Pozniak returned to New York City. Not long after his return, he interviewed for a research professorship at Columbia University.

Relieved to be back in New York, Pozniak rented an apartment in his childhood neighborhood of Prospect Heights, in Brooklyn. Though his father and mother had both passed away, he took up residence near his parents' old home, where he renewed a significant friendship from his youth.

Toby Pozniak had not seen Marc Krbec since leaving for college a decade earlier. While growing up on the same block, the two had once been very close. Krbec was now a supervisor at one of the Brooklyn Navy Yard dry docks. He was also a community outreach volunteer at their old synagogue on Kane Street, the same synagogue where Pozniak had celebrated his bar mitzvah seventeen years earlier.

Although Pozniak had never been exceptionally devout in his Judaism, his experiences in Germany had caused him to reevaluate his commitment to his faith. When Marc Krbec invited him to "come back to the old *shul* (Yiddish for *school*)," Pozniak decided to take him up on it and began attending the Saturday afternoon services at Kane Street.

Still, he often found himself questioning whether he really knew who God was. He even questioned if he really knew who Toby Pozniak was. It wasn't exactly a midlife crisis, not in the classic sense of someone trying to recapture his youth. Pozniak was looking for something to replace the aspirations he had left behind in Germany. He was filled with anxiety as he waited to hear back from Columbia University; but his emptiness stemmed from more than just that. He was searching for his purpose in life.

Sitting alone in his apartment one day, Pozniak thought he might try finding his purpose at the bottom of a gin glass. As he sat there in his kitchen, staring at the half-empty bottle on the table, he thought of his great-uncle—Stanislaw Pozniak. He thought about how, during the Confederate rebellion, his great-uncle had "failed" in his mission to deliver the all-important dispatch to General McClellan in the days leading up to the decisive battle.

The despondent physicist had no idea why these morose thoughts of his great-uncle had crept into his consciousness; but now that he was reflecting on his namesake's place in history, he wondered to himself, *When my own defining moment comes, will I also fail?*

Then, as if God were tapping him on the shoulder, he remembered the promise he had made to his father years earlier—his promise never to let anyone convince him that his great-uncle had been anything less than a hero. Toby Pozniak had loved his father deeply. Choking back tears of remorse, he poured the contents of his glass back into the bottle.

With an apologetic smile on his face, he raised the glass skyward, as if to show his father it was empty. "Sorry, Pops," he said out loud.

The following morning, Toby Pozniak learned he had been accepted to fill the professorship at Columbia University.

Chapter Twelve
1935

Young Sam Hurley, sweating in the oppressive Alabama heat and humidity, couldn't understand why he was being forced to sit quietly. It made no sense. His mother had tried explaining that he and she were there to watch his dad participate in an important ceremony, but that didn't much matter to Sam. All he knew was that the huge building surrounding him was filled with airplanes, all of them practically begging to be explored.

Still four months shy of his third birthday, Sam was primarily interested in the two shiny planes parked only feet away from where he was sitting. They were positioned on either side of a platform full of men wearing fancy uniforms. He grinned and waved at one of the men on the platform. Sam's father, trying not to be noticed by anyone else in the crowd, winked and waved back at him.

Barely six years after receiving his commission, Captain Rod Hurley was about to assume a title not normally conferred upon junior officers. This was a change-of-command ceremony. A new commanding officer was assuming the reins of the 405th Bombardment Squadron, and Hurley was being instated as the new CO's executive officer (XO), a billet usually reserved for officers two grades above his rank.

Hurley had mixed emotions as he sat there during the ceremony. His rapid ascension to this position was unprecedented. He was gratified that his superiors in the CAAF were exhibiting such confidence in his ability to lead, but unfortunately, his new responsibilities were going to mean less time in the cockpit. It was a prospect that left Hurley feeling melancholy about his early advancement up the chain of command.

Following the ceremony, Hurley's new commanding officer, Colonel Glen Hatch, asked his new XO to join him in his office. "Bring Margaret and Sam with you," Hatch said to Hurley.

Hurley, still a bit uneasy in the presence of a full bird colonel, wasn't sure why his new skipper was asking him to bring his family to their first command-level meeting. The request seemed a bit unorthodox to the young captain, but he set about trying to round up his wife and son. Not surprisingly, he found Sam climbing up onto the landing gear strut of a B-10. After successfully plucking his adventurous son from the bomber's undercarriage, he looked around for Margie. He spotted her in the corner of the hangar, talking with several of the other squadron wives. Carrying Sam in his arms, he walked up behind her and waited for an opportunity to interrupt the conversation. Then he waited some more…followed by more waiting.

Finally, one of the other wives noticed the anxious look on Hurley's face. She tapped Margie on the shoulder. "I think the new executive officer needs to talk to you," she said, smiling.

Hurley saw his chance. "Actually, the new executive officer's *boss* is asking to see her," he interjected.

Margie turned and glanced at Rod and Sam for just a moment. "All right, dear—I'll be right there." Wrapping up her conversation, Margie turned to walk with Rod and Sam toward the stairwell. "Okay, dear—what does your new colonel want to see me about?"

Hurley shifted Sam into his other arm. "He didn't say, but it must be bad news if he wants you there with me."

When they reached the foyer at the top of the stairs, Colonel Hatch's door was open. Hatch got up from behind his desk and waived them in. He stepped outside the doorway and summoned the squadron admin officer. "Captain Beale, will you find that message from the Bureau of Personnel and bring it in here please?"

"Right away, Colonel." Beale grabbed the message from his desktop and joined the Hurleys in Colonel Hatch's office.

As Beale handed him the message, Colonel Hatch asked everyone to sit in the chairs that lined the walls of the office. Returning to his desk, Hatch studied the message Beale had handed him. After a minute or so, he looked up with a stern expression on his face. "Captain Hurley, we haven't had a chance to discuss this yet, but when I learned my new exec was only a captain, it gave me pause."

Hurley was immediately uncomfortable as Hatch continued. "I informed the wing commander, General Pitt, that, as a full colonel, I felt I rated someone more senior as my next-in-command. I told the general that if he expected me to accept command of this outfit, we were going to have to remedy this situation."

Hurley's heart sank. He feared Colonel Hatch was letting him know that he was bringing in someone from outside the squadron to replace him as XO.

"Well," Hatch continued, "I guess General Pitt must have agreed with my position on this delicate matter, so he flexed his muscle up the chain and expedited a solution to the problem. Will everyone please stand." Still impassive, the colonel opened his desk drawer and took out a set of gold oak-leaf collar devices. As he stood and walked from behind the desk, Colonel Hatch flashed a smile and presented the oak leaves to Margie Hurley. Then he marched to the front of his desk and executed an about-face. "Captain Hurley, front and center!"

Surprised and relieved, Rod Hurley awkwardly lowered Sam to the floor. He knelt and asked his son to wait there quietly. Captain

Beale, helping to ensure Hurley's orders would be followed, reached down and took Sam by the hand.

As Hurley stood at attention, Colonel Hatch recited the contents of the promotion letter. Moving up next to her husband, Margie stood ready to pin the new collar devices onto his uniform. Upon completing the short letter authorizing the promotion, Hatch shook Hurley's hand and turned to Margie.

"Congratulations, Mrs. Hurley. Your husband is now the youngest major in the Confederate Army Air Force. Will you please do the honors."

On the first Monday in September, the fall semester was convened at Columbia University. Among the returning sophomores that year was an attractive and ambitious young accounting student. Natalie Rosenbaum, complying with her father's wishes, had cancelled her trip to Europe and had enrolled at Columbia the previous year. Now, at the start of her second year on campus, Natalie was glad she'd listened to her father. She had made a stable of new friends, one of whom was her dormitory roommate.

Karen Berkovich was the granddaughter of Ukrainian immigrants. Her father worked as an architect for a Manhattan design firm and lived in Yonkers, where Karen had grown up. Her mother had died during the 1918 influenza pandemic when Karen was just a baby. Her grandparents had helped to raise her while her father, using the benefits from her mother's life insurance policy, was earning his architecture degree at The City College of New York.

Unlike Natalie, Karen had struggled just to graduate in the top quarter of her high school class. Given her modest background and unremarkable grades, she didn't exactly project an Ivy League persona. Karen had only gained admission to Columbia by the thinnest of margins. Unlike Natalie, Karen was easily overlooked in a crowd. And even though Karen's father had provided well for her during her childhood in Yonkers, she hadn't been exposed to the kind of wealth that Natalie, as the daughter of a New York City real estate mogul, had enjoyed while growing up in Lower Manhattan.

These details didn't seem to matter much to either of the girls. Their different stations in life were never discussed. Like most people, Karen was fond of Natalie. The feeling was mutual. As far as Natalie was concerned, Karen was the perfect roommate. The fact that both girls were Jewish only served to strengthen their friendship.

On the 15th of September, at the Nazi Party's annual rally in Nuremberg, Adolf Hitler introduced legislation that further escalated Germany's state-sponsored animus toward its Jewish population. A complex matrix was adopted to define who was and who was not a citizen of the Reich.

According to the "Nuremberg Laws," A Jew was defined as anyone descended from at least three Jewish grandparents. The definition also included anyone descended from at least two Jewish grandparents if that person actively practiced the Jewish faith. Anyone who was descended from Jewish grandparents but did not practice Judaism was labeled a "Mischling," the German word for mongrel.

Under the new laws, Jews and Mischlings were no longer considered German citizens. They were stripped of their rights and banned from participating in civic life. For most of these unfortunate souls, the window of opportunity for escaping the brutal Nazi regime had already passed.

Chapter Thirteen
_1936_

It was late January, two weeks into Columbia's spring semester. Just as he did every morning when classes were in session, Toby Pozniak boarded the train at Brooklyn's 7th Avenue Subway Station. He was looking forward to that afternoon's meeting with the university provost. During the hour-long commute to his campus office, he sat re-reading the many letters he had exchanged with Enrico Fermi while the two were in Europe.

Pozniak and Fermi not only shared a passion for nuclear physics—they also shared a concern over the cancerous fascism that was spreading throughout Europe. Fermi's wife was Jewish. Because of the anti-Semitic policies of the Benito Mussolini government, the Italian physicist was becoming increasingly concerned for his wife's safety in their home country. Though the two had never met, Pozniak and Fermi had become friends through their frequent correspondence. Pozniak hoped to help his fellow physicist get out of Italy by bringing him to Columbia University as a member of the school's faculty.

He knew it wouldn't be easy. Ironically, even though many of the university's stately buildings were modeled after those of the

Italian Renaissance, Columbia's administration was not in the habit of hiring Italian professors.

Two years earlier, Pozniak had experienced the institutional prejudices at Columbia during his own hiring process. Reflecting back on his interview in front of the faculty search committee, Pozniak recalled the condescension from several of the committee members toward his Eastern European and Jewish lineages. He had also been subjected to an even more sinister form of bigotry—elitism. Instead of earning his credentials from a "proper" Ivy League university, his degrees were from Berkeley. Had it not been for George Pegram, who chaired the physics department, he most likely would not have been hired.

Pegram had held his position at the top of Columbia's physics department for nearly a quarter century. As far as the rest of the faculty was concerned, when Professor George Braxton Pegram spoke, it was as if his words were coming from the burning bush of the Old Testament.

Fortunately for Toby Pozniak, Pegram had recognized that the young Berkeley product was one of the world's preeminent experts in the field of nuclear physics. In the end, the venerable professor had used his considerable academic weight to quash any attempts to blackball Pozniak.

Today, George Pegram would be accompanying Toby Pozniak to his meeting. The two men hoped to convince the provost to invite Enrico Fermi to Columbia as a summer lecturer.

A couple of hours later, when the meeting was over, they had succeeded in doing so.

In November, President Franklin Roosevelt was easily reelected. Even though the world was still in the midst of a depression, the U.S.

gross national product had bottomed out and was making modest gains.

The U.S. economy was on the slow road to recovery.

In the South, the Confederate economy was lagging far behind that of the younger nation's northern neighbor.

Running on an economic platform that mirrored Roosevelt's "New Deal" policies, Huey Pierce Long, a flamboyant and controversial senator from the state of Louisiana, was elected president. Long's vice-presidential running mate was also a Confederate senator—from the state of Missouri.

Seventeen days after his narrow victory, President-elect Huey P. Long was assassinated in Baton Rouge by the son of a political rival. Under the provisions of the Confederate Constitution, Vice President-elect Harry S. Truman would now succeed him as the thirteenth president of the Confederate States of America.

In Germany, the Nazis established a concentration camp in Sachsenhausen. It was the first of many to come.

Located twenty-two miles north of Berlin, the camp was used to incarcerate political prisoners. By the end of 1936, approximately sixteen hundred people had been interned at Sachsenhausen.

That small number was only the beginning.

Chapter Fourteen
1937

On the 7th of July, troops from the Japanese Empire invaded the Republic of China. It was the beginning of a Japanese expansion that would spread unchecked throughout the Western Pacific.

On Easter morning, at the Messerschmitt aircraft works in Augsburg, Germany, seven crew members climbed aboard an experimental aircraft. With a wingspan of more than one hundred feet, the Me 261 *Adolfine* was the largest airplane ever constructed. The Messerschmitt engineers had designed it to be a long-range reconnaissance plane; but the German Air Ministry had other plans for the top-secret airframe.

The massive Me 261 left Augsburg shortly before dawn. Nine hours later, it landed at Ponta Delgada, in the Azores—a flight of nearly 2,000 miles. After taking on fuel, the plane departed on a record-setting roundtrip flight that was expressly not publicized. Nearly twenty hours after becoming airborne, the *Adolfine* returned and touched down again at Ponta Delgada.

While the aircraft was being refueled, one of the Me 261's crew members chatted with several of the local ground handlers who were servicing the mysterious German plane. He showed the curious men a sketch he had drawn during the return leg of the flight.

It was a sketch of the New York City skyline.

Confederate President Harry Truman had a vision—a plan for resurrecting his nation's failing economy. Thanks to the nonrestrictive trade agreements between the CSA and the USA, Confederate and U.S. corporations could conduct business across the border in either country. Truman hoped to lure successful U.S. companies to the Confederacy by offering them generous tax incentives.

One of the companies on which Truman had set his sights was the Boeing Aircraft Company. Boeing had recently introduced the B-17 *Flying Fortress*, a heavy bomber that represented a dramatic leap in aviation technology. Apart from naval vessels, the B-17's $200,000 price tag made it the most expensive piece of military hardware in the world. According to most military experts, it was well worth the price.

When the United States Army Air Corps held a competition to replace its aging fleet of Martin B-10 bombers, Boeing's *Flying Fortress* was the odds-on favorite. That was before the Boeing crew inexplicably failed to remove the B-17's exterior control locks prior to the demonstration flight. Only after takeoff did the pilot discover he was unable to move the control surfaces. Boeing's prototype crashed, prompting an impatient U.S. government to award the contract to the Douglas Aircraft Company instead. Two hundred Douglas B-18 *Bolos* were purchased at a much lower cost of $58,500 each. It saved the U.S. government 28.3 million dollars and left the Boeing Company in serious financial trouble.

General Harold F. Ramsey, commanding general of the Confederate Army Air Force, hoped to capitalize on Boeing's misfortune. Ramsey still believed in the B-17. What's more, he was looking to replace his own B-10 bombers. President Truman was an easy sell, especially after Boeing agreed to sell their bombers at a reduced price and move their B-17 production facility to Fort Worth, Texas. At a time when the Confederate government was strapped for cash, Truman was able to convince the Confederate Congress to appropriate nine million dollars for the purchase of sixty B-17 *Flying Fortresses*.

The U.S. government would eventually recognize it had erred in awarding its contract to Douglas instead of Boeing. Just two years later, the U.S. Army Air Corps would begin replacing all its *Bolo* bombers with *Flying Fortresses*. Regaining its financial footing, the Boeing Company would ultimately renege on its promise to relocate to Texas.

For the time being, however, General Ramsey had pulled off an enormous achievement. Unlikely as it might have seemed, his diminutive CAAF suddenly possessed one of the finest bomber fleets in the world.

Rod Hurley had never seen the Pacific Ocean. He had never been west of El Paso. Hurley went forward to the C-47's cockpit. He knelt between the pilot and copilot. "You fellas think we could take a quick tour of the coastline before we set it down?"

"*Sure thing*, Colonel." The young pilot's response was the first time Hurley had been addressed as "Colonel" since being promoted only hours earlier.

Hurley patted the pilot on the shoulder. "Thanks, Lieutenant. I'll let the boys in the back know what we're doing."

"Yes, sir. I'll get on the horn and let 'em know we're gonna be a little late."

Hurley got up and shuffled back toward the rear of the plane. He stopped halfway down the aisle and made his announcement. "*Good news*, boys. We're gonna take a little sight-seein' tour before we land."

"Can we please stop at the next gas station, Colonel. I've gotta piss like a racehorse!" The voice had come from behind him. As the other men were laughing, Hurley turned to see who the comedian was.

At eighteen years of age, Corporal Garry Crain was the youngest of the three radio operators on the trip. Hurley had only met him the previous day. For that matter, most of the twenty-nine men aboard the C-47 transport were new to Hurley. Beginning with his last-minute flight from Montgomery to Shreveport two days earlier, things had happened so quickly over the past forty-eight hours that it was all still a blur. From the moment Colonel Hatch had informed him he'd been selected to command his own squadron, the events leading up to this mission had been a reassignment whirlwind.

His old CO in Montgomery had even neglected to inform him he'd been promoted to Lieutenant Colonel. He had only learned about that after arriving at Barksdale Field, in Shreveport. Three hours before he and his men were to board this flight, the Barksdale wing commander had tossed him a set of silver oak leaves while briefing him on his assignment. Hurley had not even had a chance to tell Margie about his promotion. She and Sam, along with all the family's personal effects, were still back at Maxwell Field in Alabama. He would have to rely on Margie to make the move to Louisiana on her own.

The seat next to Corporal Crain was empty. Hurley settled in next to him. "Where you from, Crain?"

"*Gabby*, sir."

"I beg your pardon?"

"*Gabby*. My buddies all call me 'Gabby.' I'm from Enid, Oklahoma, sir. Well, I was *born* in Enid. I actually grew up in Edmond. Edmond's just north of Oklahoma City. *Well*...Enid's north of Oklahoma City too—they both are. Edmonds's closer, though. It's only about eight miles north of the city. Enid's almost sixty. I guess they call me 'Gabby' because I'm a radio operator. That—and I talk a lot."

Hurley chuckled at the young airman. He liked this kid. "Well, I guess that's a good trait for a radio operator to have, Corporal. Tell me, do you really have to piss?"

"Oh, *yes sir*. I'd never joke about somethin' like that. Well...I *might* joke about it; but I'm not jokin' now, sir. I really do need to piss. If we don't land soon, I'm gonna...I don't know *what* I'm gonna do. I've gotta piss *really bad*."

"Well, hang in there, son. It won't be too much longer."

"Yes sir."

Hurley patted the young corporal on the shoulder and moved several rows back to an empty window seat. He stared out at the radial engine on the front of the wing. He had barely slept over the past two days. The steady drone from the power plant made him want to close his eyes and surrender to his fatigue. Instead, he refocused his attention away from the plane's engine toward the terrain below.

As it reached the Columbia River, the C-47 descended to 700 feet. The pilot followed the river on a westward heading past Portland, Oregon, all the way to the Pacific Ocean. As he banked northward, all eyes were focused on the panorama out the right-hand side of the plane. The green forests and rocky coastline were awe-inspiring. The snowcapped peaks in the distance were spectacular. None of the men aboard the plane had ever seen anything like it.

After forty minutes along the coast, they rounded the Olympic Peninsula and flew east until they reached Puget Sound. Turning to the south, they flew just west of downtown Seattle and set up for their final approach.

As they gazed out through the C-47's windows, Lieutenant Colonel Rod Hurley and his men could see them lined up on the ramp. Parked in front of the huge Boeing assembly plant were three magnificent B-17s, each freshly painted in CAAF markings.

In November, Germany, Italy and Japan entered into a military alliance. The three nations would eventually sign the Tripartite Pact and come to be known as the Axis Powers.

The world edged closer to war.

Chapter Fifteen
1938

On the 12th of March, German troops marched unchallenged into Austria and claimed it for the Third Reich. It was the first step in Adolf Hitler's plan to provide "living space" for the German-speaking people of Europe.

Marc Krbec was a shipbuilder. At thirty-one years of age, the Brooklyn native looked the part. His stocky frame and muscular build reflected his rugged, blue-collar background. Abandoned as an infant, he had spent his toddler years at Brooklyn's Hebrew Orphan Asylum. At age three, Marc had been adopted by Sid and Edna Krbec, who took him into their Prospect Heights residence, three doors from the home where Toby Pozniak's family lived.

As boys, Marc Krbec and Toby Pozniak had been inseparable. Neither had siblings, which probably accounted for their close, fraternal relationship. The fact that one of them had grown up to become a shipbuilder while the other was now a nuclear physicist belied the strong bond the two men shared.

Still living alone in the home his parents had left him when they passed away, Krbec was elated when Pozniak returned from Germany and took up residence in the old neighborhood. They socialized often, attending the same Saturday services at the Kane Street Synagogue. When the Dodgers were in town, the two of them often spent their leisure time in the center field bleachers at Ebbets Field.

That night's game between the Dodgers and the New York Giants had gone into extra innings. When the Dodgers failed to score in the bottom of the twelfth inning, Krbec let his friend know it was time to leave.

"*No*—not *yet*. One more inning," Pozniak pleaded.

"Can't do it, pal. Got a big day tomorrow. Wouldn't do for the section supervisor to come draggin' in late. Let's go. We can listen on the radio in the car." With that, Krbec downed his beer. He got up and slid along the crowded row of upper deck seats, toward the aisle. Pozniak followed close behind, trying not to trip over the feet of those fans intent on sticking around however late into the night it took for the Dodgers to beat their crosstown rivals from Upper Manhattan.

In a rush to get to the car so they could hear the end of the game, Krbec and Pozniak hurried down the ramp and out of the stadium. Once outside the gate, they crossed the street to the overcrowded parking lot behind the left-field bleachers. Zigzagging between the parked cars that belonged to fans who had arrived early enough to find a spot, they exited the lot onto the next block.

They made their way toward the pizzeria where they had eaten prior to the game. Krbec's car was parked out front on the street. As they neared the car, they were still close enough to Ebbets Field to hear a loud chorus of cheers erupt from inside the ballpark. They both quickened their pace, anxious to find out what was happening. By the time they reached the 1936 Chevrolet Coupe, they were in a full-on sprint, laughing at themselves like little boys.

As soon as Krbec started the motor, Pozniak turned on the AM radio and tuned the dial to 1010 kHz. The cheers they'd heard had been for a Tony Malinosky triple leading off the Dodger half of the thirteenth inning. Out of breath and perspiring, they both rolled their windows down as Pozniak turned up the volume.

They sat and listened, knowing all it would take for the Dodgers to win the game was a sacrifice fly or a well-placed ground ball. Both men voiced their displeasure when the next two batters each struck out on 3-2 pitches. Their disappointment was compounded when, as soon as the next batter had stepped to the plate, Malinosky ended the Dodgers' scoring threat by wandering away from third and getting picked off.

"That's about right," Krbec murmured. Disgusted, he stood on the clutch and forced the shifter into first gear, grinding it in a fit of exasperation. He popped the clutch, chirping one of the rear tires on the pavement as he sped away from the curb.

Even though he was laughing at Krbec's outburst, Pozniak shared his friend's frustration. As boys, the two had spent more time at Ebbets Field than at the Kane Street Synagogue. To Toby Pozniak and Marc Krbec, both places were holy. Just as most Brooklynites did, they felt a tremendous sense of personal ownership in their team. In the 1930s, the Brooklyn Dodgers represented more than just the local professional baseball team. They were woven into the fabric of the community.

As the two men drove past block upon block of multi-family brownstones, they listened to Red Barber's play-by-play description of the game on WHN. They waited until the commercial breaks between innings to talk. Pozniak lit a cigarette and offered one to his friend. Krbec waved off the cigarette and lifted his hat, wiping the summer sweat from his brow with the back of his forearm.

In the top of the fifteenth, the Giants loaded the bases with two outs. Brooklyn Manager Burleigh Grimes came out of the dugout for a pitching change. During the lull, Pozniak turned to his friend and asked him what was so important about tomorrow's shift at the Navy Yard.

"We're gonna start laying a keel," Krbec replied. "This one's special—the USS *Washington*. It's gonna be the biggest battlewagon we've ever built."

"The largest you've built at the Yard, or the largest in the fleet?"

"Biggest in the *world*, pal. Unfortunately, I hear those Nazi bastards are buildin' one even bigger. Still, this bad boy's gonna be sportin' three huge turrets, each with three sixteen-inch guns. Those ain't exactly peashooters, you know. The shells those things fire are heavy as your papa's old Buick. Trust me, you wouldn't wanna be on the receivin' end of one of those babies."

Red Barber began reciting Ralph Birkofer's stats while the Dodgers' relief pitcher was throwing his warmup tosses. Pozniak reached over and turned the volume down on the radio. "Tell me something, Marc. You think we're headed for another war?"

Krbec mused for several seconds before answering. "I don't know from nothin', Toby boy…I sure hope not." He shook his head and repeated himself. "I sure as hell hope not."

Just then, they heard Red Barber preparing to call Birkofer's first pitch. Pozniak turned up the volume just in time to hear Barber's call. "There she *goes*. A long drive to right—*grand slam!*"

Krbec and Pozniak turned to one another and winced. "Dem *bums*," they muttered in unison.

On the 1ˢᵗ of October, Germany annexed the Sudetenland, a region of Czechoslovakia mostly inhabited by ethnic Germans. Most Western leaders hoped this would be the extent of Adolf Hitler's territorial ambitions.

In England, one man, the First Lord of the Admiralty, recognized that it was a false hope. He warned that if Hitler's encroachments went unchecked, it would lead to further German expansionism.

His name was Winston Churchill.

Chapter Sixteen
1939

On the 15th of March, German troops invaded the remaining independent regions within Czechoslovakia.

They met little resistance.

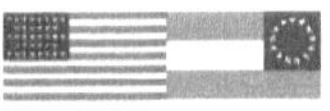

In April, following a three-year civil war in Spain, Generalissimo Francisco Franco succeeded in overthrowing Spanish President Manuel Azaña. Franco established a fascist dictatorship in the same fashion as the man who had supported him in his war—Adolf Hitler.

Natalie Rosenbaum had graduated in May and was working in the Columbia University Bursar's Office. Although she enjoyed the work, she knew it was only temporary. Miss Witherspoon, Saul Rosenbaum's longtime accountant, would be retiring from his firm in a few months, and Natalie would return to work for her father as planned. In the meantime, working on campus gave Natalie a chance to remain in touch with many of her college friends, including Karen Berkovich, her former roommate.

Karen had failed several required courses during her junior and senior years but was finally set to graduate at the end of the current summer session. Although Natalie was no longer living in the dormitory with Karen, the two spent many of their evenings together. That night, they were dining at Barbetta, one of the most popular Italian restaurants on Manhattan's Upper West Side.

Two men, both older than Natalie and Karen, were seated at the table next to theirs. One looked to be in his early thirties. The other was somewhat older. Though she wasn't eavesdropping, Natalie noted that the eldest of the two spoke with an obvious Italian accent. It was the younger man, though, who piqued Natalie's interest. She found herself staring at him. The man glanced at her several times as well.

As the evening wore on, they glanced at one another more frequently. For the first time in her life, Natalie became self-conscious of her eyeglasses. Taking them off, she folded the wire rims and placed them in her purse. When it came time to pay, she discreetly took them out again. She held them to her eyes just long enough to read the total at the bottom of the check and then quickly tucked them back inside her purse, hoping the man at the next table hadn't noticed.

Karen thought her friend's behavior odd until she also noticed the man who had garnered Natalie's attention. She winked at Natalie and smiled. "Don't you think he's a little old for you?"

"I'm sure I haven't the slightest idea what you're talking about," Natalie retorted. She reached into her purse and fumbled for the proper amount of cash to cover the check and tip.

Just then, the two men pushed their chairs back and began to leave. The younger man stopped to toss several folded bills onto the table. He hurried to catch up with his friend as they headed out of the restaurant. Nearing the exit, the man turned his head and glanced at Natalie one last time.

Lieutenant Colonel Rod Hurley stood alone by his father's grave. Clarence Hurley had been in a state of decline for several years, ever since Rod's mother had passed away unexpectedly from pneumonia. Now his parents were reunited, lying side by side in a small cemetery next to the First Baptist Church in Kerrville, Texas.

The graveside funeral service had ended more than an hour ago. It seemed as though everyone in town had attended. Most of them had stuck around to offer their sympathies to the Hurley family before heading home. Rod had sent Margie and Sam on their way with Margie's parents so he could spend some time alone with his father. He stood there, quietly studying the polished granite marker at the head of his father's grave. Under the etched outline of a Texas flag was the following epitaph:

Clarence Robert Hurley
August 4, 1885–July 17, 1939
Husband, Father, Soldier
Served with the Allied Forces in the Great War

Rod Hurley was deep in thought, his head down, when he realized someone was standing next to him.

"The flag's a nice touch," the man said.

Hurley looked up. He was surprised to see a face from his past wearing an out-of-date CAAF uniform. It was Colonel Charles Morrow, Hurley's old CO from his Randolph Field training squadron. "Colonel *Morrow!* How are you, sir?"

"I'm doin' well, Hurley. I'm sorry for your loss."

"Thank you, sir. I never expected to see *you* here."

"Well, your father went out of his way to attend my late brother's funeral in Houston several years back. I figured I needed to pay my respects. I don't remember if I ever told you my brother was your father's company commander in France."

"Yes sir, you did."

"You know, it's kinda funny. My brother wanted a Texas Flag on his headstone just like the one on your father's. I think all those fellas who volunteered for that outfit thought of themselves as Texans first and Confederates second. That's probably why they didn't have any disinclination toward fighting with the U.S. Army."

"I'm pretty sure you're right, Colonel. I think my dad was always privately ashamed that our nation stood by while the U.S. military did all the fighting in that war. He never said so, but I think it saddened him."

"It saddened me too, Hurley. A man shouldn't have to fight under another flag to be on the right side of things. I truly hope we never allow that to happen again." Morrow paused a few seconds, looking down at Clarence Hurley's grave. He contemplated the gravity of his own words as if someone else had spoken them. When he raised his head again, Morrow wore a mournful expression that revealed the true depth of his conviction. Then, as if not wanting to linger on the subject, he turned to Hurley and quickly changed his tone. "On a happier note," he said, smiling, "how are you liking your command at Barksdale? I'd give my left nut for a chance to fly one of your B-17s."

Hurley chuckled. "Well, you don't have to give up a nut, Colonel. Next time you're in Shreveport, I'll make it happen. Just let me know when you're gonna be there, and I'll set it up. We'll take one out on a post-maintenance check flight."

Morrow's smile grew wider. "Don't make a promise you don't intend to keep. I'm liable to take you up on that offer."

"I'm serious, sir. You give me a little notice, and I'll make sure we have a bird available. Do you have a place to stay tonight? You're welcome to stay with Margie and me at my dad's old place. There's more food there than we could possibly eat in a week. I think every mother and grandmother in Kerrville cooked a meal for us."

"I appreciate the offer, Hurley. I sincerely do. Unfortunately, I need to be gettin' back home to San Antonio. My wife's not doin' so well these days. I just wanted to drive over and pay my respects to one of the old Texas volunteers."

"Well, I'm sorry to hear about your wife, but I appreciate your stoppin' by. It means a lot to me, Colonel." Hurley came to attention and saluted his old CO, wishing they had more time to visit.

Colonel Morrow returned Hurley's salute. Then he smiled and shook his hand. "I'm gonna hold you to that B-17 ride," he said as he turned to leave.

"I'm countin' on it," Hurley replied.

Morrow began walking toward his dusty pickup truck.

"*Oh!* And, Colonel…"

Morrow stopped and turned.

"I hope so *too*," Hurley said earnestly.

"You hope *what?*" Morrow asked.

"I hope we never again stand by while someone else fights our war for us."

The summer months were quiet at Columbia University. Aside from the small number of students attending summer sessions, the campus resembled a ghost town.

Toby Pozniak and Enrico Fermi walked together. They were excited that their upcoming trip to Chicago had been approved by the Columbia administration. George Pegram had initially disappointed the two men. Their boss had denied a request to pursue their ambitious nuclear project on Columbia's New York City campus. Instead, he had put them in touch with one of his close colleagues.

As a result of Pegram's referral, the dean of physics at the University of Chicago was now anxious to discuss their proposal.

Pozniak and Fermi were set to board a flight to Chicago the following week. They were on their way to the bursar's office to pick up their airline tickets and travel funds. After climbing several steps to the building entrance, Pozniak opened one of the double doors and held it open for Fermi. Once inside, Pozniak pointed to a large stairwell in the foyer. "Second floor," he told his friend.

The two climbed the stairs to another foyer outside another set of double doors. A bronze sign hanging above the doors let them know they were in the right place. They entered a waiting area lined with empty chairs. Along one of the walls, there were a dozen windows resembling bank teller stations. All but one had shades pulled down. Pozniak went to the window and explained the purpose of their visit to an uninterested young female, who was studying a textbook on the other side of the glass.

"You'll need to come to the back through that door," she said, pointing to an entrance near the last window. "I'll open it for you."

The young lady unlocked the door and escorted Pozniak and Fermi into a back office. It was filled with twenty or so desks. Because it was summer, only two of the desks were occupied. The entire room was surrounded by rows of large filing cabinets. A middle-aged woman at one of the desks looked up at them from behind a stack of papers. "Professor Pozniak and Professor Fermi?"

"Yes," Pozniak replied as their escort left them with the woman. "We're here for our travel packets."

"I have them right here," the woman said, pointing to two large manila envelopes on her desk. She picked up a couple of clipboards and pointed toward a pair of metal chairs beside her desk. "I'll need you to fill out these forms before I can release your airline tickets and per diem."

"Thank you," Pozniak said, taking the clipboards and handing one to Fermi. The two nuclear physicists meekly sat and began filling out the tedious accounting forms.

Pozniak finished first and handed his clipboard back to the woman behind the desk. He stood to stretch his legs. Casually looking around the room, he noticed a young woman working at a desk on the other side of the office. Even though her back was toward him, Pozniak felt there was something vaguely familiar about the woman. He could see that Fermi was only halfway through the stack of forms on his clipboard. He thought about asking his colleague if he needed any help. Instead, he casually strolled toward the desk where the young woman was working.

Not knowing why, he walked around in front of her. It was as if he were being drawn to the anonymous woman. As Pozniak stood in front of her desk, the young woman instinctively looked up at him. He could tell she was startled, just as he was. Neither knew what to say.

After several awkward seconds, Pozniak broke the silence. "I like the glasses," he said, smiling.

"I beg your pardon?" the young woman responded.

"The eyeglasses. They look nice on you."

The young woman blushed, nervously straightening the glasses.

"I'm sorry," he said, his own face reddening a bit. He extended his hand. "The name is Toby…Toby Pozniak."

"I'm Natalie," she replied, placing her hand in his, "Natalie Rosenbaum."

On the 1ˢᵗ of September, Adolf Hitler invaded Poland. Two days later, Britain and France declared war on Germany. Italy would eventually declare war on Britain and France.

Within weeks, the Soviet Union invaded Poland from the east. In Asia, the Japanese advanced into the interior of China. For the second time in a quarter century, the world was at war.

Once again, just as they had done at the beginning of what would henceforth be known as World War I, both American governments declared their neutrality.

Chapter Seventeen
1940

On the 10th of May, the Germans turned their imperialist aggression westward. They invaded France, as well as Belgium, Luxembourg, and The Netherlands. Within three weeks, the German "blitzkrieg" [lightning war] had pushed the Allies to the brink of defeat, pinning them against the English Channel at Dunkirk.

As many in his own government urged him to sue for peace, Winston Churchill, now the British Prime Minister, ordered every available seafaring vessel in England—military and civilian—into service. Over a ten-day period, 861 ships and boats rescued more than 338,000 British, French and other Allied troops off the beaches at Dunkirk.

Having failed to secure an Allied surrender, Hitler began planning for a cross-channel invasion of England. The Battle of France was over. As the Battle of Britain loomed, Winston Churchill looked for assistance from the other side of the Atlantic. The British Prime Minister appealed to both American presidents for help in defending the free world.

No help was forthcoming...not officially.

Toby Pozniak and Natalie Rosenbaum sat atop the *Wonder Wheel*, the giant Ferris wheel on Coney Island. Eight months earlier, they had come here on their first date. Now, it was one of their favorite spots.

It was late spring and unseasonably cold in New York City. Even though it was midafternoon, the sun was barely a bright spot behind the thick cloud layer. The amusement park below was doing a fair business, but the beach next to it was practically deserted, save for a few well-bundled people strolling the blustery shoreline. As Toby and Natalie looked out across the sand from their elevated vantage point, the white-capped ocean presented a dreary, gray backdrop.

Toby reflected on his years in Göttingen. He remembered feeling insecure after fleeing Germany and returning home to Brooklyn. He was thankful Marc Krbec had been there to help him resettle in his old neighborhood. He thought about the hollowness he had felt, even with Marc's support, as he had searched for a sense of purpose in his life. As he held Natalie Rosenbaum in his arms, Toby Pozniak was certain he had found that sense of purpose. Natalie had filled the void in his life.

Natalie snuggled as close as she could, trying to stay warm. "When do you and Henry have to go back to Chicago?" she asked, laying her head on his shoulder. Natalie always referred to Enrico Fermi by his Americanized name. She did it mostly to needle Toby, who refused to take the same liberty with his colleague's Italian given name.

"Next month," he answered. "It looks like the government might step in and provide some funding for our reactor. The War Department seems to be concerned the Germans are working on one of their own. They believe Werner Heisenberg is running the project."

"Isn't he your friend from Göttingen?"

"I collaborated with him at Göttingen. Let's just leave it at that."

"But what does all this have to do with the project you and Henry are working on? Why does the War Department care if the Germans build a reactor?"

"I guess they're worried they might try to develop atomic energy and use it as a weapon."

"I still don't see why our government should be concerned. We're not at war with Germany."

Toby shook his head. "No…not *yet*."

"But I guess I don't understand. How could they use energy as a weapon?"

Toby thought for a moment, searching for a way to answer Natalie's question. "Think of it this way," he said. "Every time an atom splits, it releases energy. The process is called nuclear fission. When Enrico and I build our reactor, we'll be able to regulate the speed of the fission. That way, we can control the amount of energy produced by the reactor."

"So, what are you going to do with this energy?"

"We're not going to do anything with it. Enrico and I merely intend to prove it's possible to produce it. Eventually, it could be used to heat water and produce steam. The steam can be used to propel a turbine, and the turbine can be used to produce electricity. Our work could lead to an endless source of energy—enough to power the entire world into infinity."

Natalie began laughing.

"What are you laughing at?" he asked with a confused smile on his face.

"You! I'm laughing at *you!* You sound like a professor."

"I *am* a professor!"

"Well, Professor Pozniak. You still haven't explained why the War Department is interested in your reactor."

"I'm getting to that. You didn't let me finish."

"Go ahead, sweetheart. I'm listening." Natalie grinned, pleased with herself for getting a rise out of her normally reserved suitor.

"So, you're gonna *listen* now?" Toby nudged her in the ribs, causing her to laugh again.

"I *said* I was listening. Go ahead."

"Like I said, Enrico and I plan to build a reactor we can control; but, theoretically at least, it might be possible to set off a nuclear reaction in which the fission is allowed to progress unimpeded. The rate at which energy is released would increase with every atom that splits, like a chain reaction. It would produce an unimaginable explosion—a blast powerful enough to destroy everything for as far as you can see from up here."

Natalie suddenly pushed herself away from his side and looked into his eyes. "You mean a *bomb?*"

"*Yes*, Natalie—an *atomic* bomb."

Throughout the summer that followed the Allied retreat from Dunkirk, Adolf Hitler's Luftwaffe (the German Air Force) waged a relentless bombing campaign over the whole of England. Badly outnumbered, Royal Air Force fighter pilots continually rose to intercept the German attackers in the skies above their homeland.

Hitler was desperate to establish air superiority over England in advance of his planned invasion. Churchill was even more desperate to deny it to him.

At the end of August, it became obvious the RAF had succeeded in fending off the German onslaught from the air. Hitler was forced to call off his invasion, resulting in a temporary stalemate along the shores of the English Channel. Thanks to a handful of brave aviators, England had—for the time being at least—halted the Nazi war machine. Winston Churchill delivered an epic speech before the

British House of Commons in which he declared, "Never in the field of human conflict was so much owed by so many to so few."

At Barksdale Field, in Louisiana, Churchill's words were not lost on Lieutenant Colonel Rod Hurley.

Rod Hurley leaned back in his chair and propped his flight boots on the corner of his desk. Chomping a cigar, Hurley spread open that morning's edition of the *Shreveport Times*. He began reading the newspaper's account of Winston Churchill's speech from the previous day.

Halfway through the article, Sergeant Garry Crain appeared in the hallway outside his door. The cigar still in his mouth, Hurley mumbled, "What's up, Gabby?"

"I'm not exactly sure, Colonel. There's an old codger out on the flight line says you told him he could take one of our birds up for a spin."

"What the *hell?*" Hurley tossed the newspaper aside, sprung to his feet, and grabbed his sunglasses. Plunging his cigar into a wall-mounted ashtray, he followed Sergeant Crain down the hallway, down the stairs, through the hangar and out onto the flight line. Standing there between the two long rows of shiny B-17s was a man he instantly recognized. "That's not an 'old codger,' Gabby. That's Colonel Morrow, my old CO."

"He looked like an old codger to me, sir. *Look* at him. He's wearin' a cowboy hat and boots. How am I supposed to know he's a colonel?"

"He's *retired*, Gabby." Visibly annoyed with the sergeant, Hurley pointed toward the hangar. "Go back inside and find some flight gear for him. And while you're at it, tell the operations officer to round up a crew for me…everybody except a copilot. And tell him to find us a bird that needs a few in-flight maintenance checks."

"I still don't know how I was supposed to know he's a colonel," Crain groused.

"*Dammit*, Gabby—just *go!*"

"I'm *goin'*, sir." Sergeant Crain dutifully turned and walked toward the hangar. "The guy's wearin' boots and a cowboy hat," he muttered to himself.

An hour and a half later, a *Flying Fortress* was rumbling west at 220 miles per hour, flying at 5,000 feet above a forest of East Texas pines. For those on the ground who had never seen one, the B-17 was an awesome sight. For Charles Morrow, a man who had racked up seven air-to-air kills flying a Sopwith Camel in World War I, flying it from the copilot's seat was surprisingly close to the thrill of a lifetime. "This gal's one *hell* of a beast!" he exclaimed over the interphone.

Hurley smiled at him from across the cockpit. "We need to throttle 'em up for a power check, Colonel. She's gonna try to climb on you, but we need to stay at five thousand."

"Roger that."

Hurley put his palm against all four throttles and slowly began working them forward. Morrow pushed against the yoke to keep the bomber from climbing. He instinctively reached down and rolled the elevator trim wheel forward, relieving the pressure on the yoke. The retired colonel giggled like a kid with a new toy as the B-17, absent a bomb load and less than half full of fuel, began to accelerate, eventually reaching more than 280 miles per hour.

"I'm sold," Morrow said, smiling at Hurley. "That's almost three times faster than my old Sopwith Camel."

"Pretty impressive, isn't it?" Hurley pointed at the altimeter. "If we were up at altitude, she'd top out around three twenty-five on true airspeed."

By this time, the Dallas skyline was coming into view on the horizon.

"You hungry for lunch?" Hurley asked.

"I'm gettin' that way," Morrow answered.

"I know a really good place—Bailey's Barbecue over in Fort Worth. Whatta ya say we grab some chow?"

"I'm in," Morrow said. "*And…*I'll buy for the crew."

Another voice abruptly chimed in on the interphone. "*See,* I told you this guy's not really a colonel."

Morrow flashed a quizzical look at Hurley.

Hurley looked down and shook his head. "Sorry, Colonel. That was Sergeant Crain. My radio operator *talks* too much."

"That's okay," Morrow laughed. "I'm still gonna buy the sergeant's lunch."

"I don't think you know how much these boys can eat, Colonel."

"Well, seein' as how y'all are payin' my pension, it's the least I can do."

"Have it your way," Hurley replied. "Gabby, get on the horn to Tarrant Base Ops and let 'em know we're comin' in for fuel. Tell 'em we're gonna need a couple of sedans from the motor pool."

"You got it, sir. That dead-cow place sounds great."

Hurley looked over at Morrow. "When we get over Fort Worth, we'll take a little spin around town before we land."

Crain spoke up. "Let's not do that, Colonel. I gotta piss."

"I guess you're gonna have to tie a knot in it, Sergeant."

"Awh, Colonel! I gotta piss *real bad!*"

The B-17 was not a common sight over Fort Worth. When Hurley and his crew began circling the city, the loud drone from the four 1200-horsepower radial engines caused people to stop what they were doing and stare skyward.

It wouldn't be long, however, until the sight of large bombers over the city would become commonplace. Confederate President Harry Truman, unable to lure Boeing to Texas several years earlier, had convinced the Consolidated Aircraft Company to come in their place. The CAAF was building a production facility for Consolidated on the west side of Fort Worth, right next to Tarrant Army Airfield. The Consolidated Company would soon be using the government-owned plant to assemble their new B-24 *Liberators.*

As they approached the airfield, Colonel Morrow passed the controls back to Rod Hurley. "I'd better let you take her in, Skipper."

Hurley was humbled at the deference shown to him by his former mentor. "Check out the size of those hangars," he said to Morrow as he maneuvered his B-17 onto short final. "That's where they're gonna build the B-24s."

"You'll be flying one of *those* behemoths soon," Morrow said. "They just keep makin' 'em bigger and bigger."

"We'll see," Hurley responded unenthusiastically.

Morrow sensed something unusual in the young squadron commander's tenor. He was unaware that earlier that morning, just prior to their flight, Hurley had placed a call to the Bureau of Personnel in Richmond. Lieutenant Colonel Rod Hurley was already in the process of resigning his commission in the CAAF. He was just waiting for the right moment to announce his intentions.

For the time being, Margie Hurley was the only person who knew that her husband would soon be crossing the Atlantic to fly with the Royal Air Force in England.

Chapter Eighteen
Spring, 1941

On the 11th of March, President Franklin Roosevelt signed the Lend-Lease Act, authorizing the shipment of arms, including warplanes, to Great Britain. Just as in World War I, the official U.S. stance was one of neutrality; but Roosevelt anticipated his nation would eventually be dragged into the conflict by circumstances beyond his control. Roosevelt hoped that by arming the British early on, he could shorten the conflict.

Though many in the U.S. accepted the prospect that America might eventually be forced to go to war—few, if any, believed there was any danger the war might someday come to America.

In late spring, it had been almost a year since Western Europe had fallen to the Nazis. Despite being forced to postpone his invasion of England, Adolf Hitler was beginning to believe the Third Reich was invincible. If he was unable to continue his blitzkrieg across the English Channel, he would redirect it to the east while he waited for the British to capitulate. He spent months amassing three huge army groups comprising one hundred and fifty divisions (more than three million soldiers) for *Operation Barbarossa*—the planned invasion of the Soviet Union.

Hitler's staff gathered at the Reich Chancellery, the Führer's official residence, to finalize their preparations for *Barbarossa*. But as he and his inner circle congregated around the map on the planning table, some of Hitler's generals were less than enthusiastic about a war with the Soviet Union, especially while England still represented a threat. Two of those not on board with the operation were Generals Erich von Manstein and Alfred Jodl.

Von Manstein was a battle-tested field commander and a master of blitzkrieg warfare. Jodl was the strategist most responsible for Germany's early successes in Poland and France. Both generals believed the ill-conceived Russian invasion was ripe for failure.

With arms and supplies now flooding into England from America, the two generals seized on the meeting as a last opportunity to convince Hitler not to invade the Soviet Union. Much to the astonishment of the other war planners, especially those who routinely parroted every word their Führer uttered, von Manstein and Jodl offered up an alternative proposal.

They argued that the Soviets posed no immediate military threat. It was the British stalemate, they contended, that constituted the more pressing danger. If not defeated soon, England would continue growing stronger with every shipment of Lend-Lease arms that arrived from the United States. German U-boats were picking off many of the convoy ships, but most of the supplies were still getting through. Why not isolate the British by cutting their supply line at the source? Although the United States was a formidable industrial power, their military was weak. The Confederate States also possessed a military, but it was even weaker. And it was doubtful the Confederates would risk their own security to defend their former enemy.

Instead of taking on the Soviet Union, the two generals suggested the Nazi war effort would be better served if the Germans mounted an invasion against the United States. If successful, they could shut off the North American spigot and starve the British into submission.

Most in attendance expected the Führer to explode. They waited nervously for him to berate von Manstein and Jodl for daring to question his strategy, especially at this late stage.

But Adolf Hitler hated the Americans as much as he hated the Russians. He despised the Russians for their soviet system of government. The contempt he felt toward the Americans, however, was personal. He considered the United States to be racially impure—a ragtag nation of mongrels. The American ideal of a "melting pot" society was anathema to Hitler. He was also furious over Roosevelt's Lend-Lease program. To Hitler, it represented an act of cowardice, a way for the U.S. to fight against Germany without getting bloodied in the process.

Adolf Hitler stood silent for several seconds. Finally, he spoke—calmly. "What would the logistics be for such an invasion?"

Chapter Nineteen

04 June 1941

The three DH.98 *Mosquitos* took off from RAF Wick, on the northern tip of Scotland, shortly after 1300 GMT (Greenwich Mean Time). Powered by two Rolls-Royce *Merlin* engines, the de Havilland *Mosquito* was a swift and agile light bomber. But these specially outfitted *Mosquitos* were "pathfinders." Instead of bombs, they carried reconnaissance cameras by day and flares by night.

Climbing out on a southeasterly heading, they leveled off at 300 feet over the North Sea and set a course for the Nazi-occupied province of South Holland in the Netherlands. Flying at 270 miles per hour, the undetected formation reached the target in less than two hours.

Crossing the coastline, the formation scattered. Each *Mosquito* descended to 100 feet and began making multiple high-speed passes over the target, each from different directions, each with cameras rolling. On the first set of passes, flown at nearly 400 miles per hour, the pathfinders encountered no resistance. The Germans manning the surrounding anti-aircraft batteries had been caught completely off guard.

As each aircraft made subsequent runs, it was met with a barrage of anti-aircraft artillery and small arms fire. The planes were flying too fast and low for the defenders to take aim at them. They simply tried to put enough ordnance into the air to score random hits. On the fourth and final pass, the bombardier/navigator in the second *Mosquito* was killed when multiple machine gun rounds haphazardly found their mark and ripped through the cockpit on his side of the aircraft.

Their mission complete, the three *Mosquitos* turned northwest and headed back out to sea.

Chapter Twenty
05 June 1941

Across occupied Europe, Jews were being loaded onto trains and transported to concentration camps, the largest of which was Auschwitz, in Poland. Heinrich Himmler, head of the SS, met with Rudolf Höss, commandant of the Auschwitz camp, to deliver the following message: "The Führer has ordered the 'Final Solution' to the Jewish question. We (the SS) must carry out this order…I have therefore chosen Auschwitz for this purpose."

In accordance with Adolf Hitler's wishes, the following statement was published in an editorial from <u>Der Stürmer</u>, a Nazi newspaper: "Now judgment has begun, and it will reach its conclusion only when knowledge of the Jews has been erased from the earth."

"So, what are your intentions toward my daughter?"

Seated across the table, next to Natalie, Toby Pozniak was flustered by Saul Rosenbaum's question. "I'm not sure I know what you mean, sir?"

"I simply want to know your plans for my daughter. She tells me you're headed off to Chicago this fall for some kind of science fair."

Pozniak took a sip of wine and raised his napkin to his lips. He was stalling, trying to think of a diplomatic way to respond to this unexpected line of questioning.

Natalie interceded. "That's *not* what I said, Papa. I told you Toby was going to Chicago to conduct important research for the government. And we certainly didn't invite him into our home so you could give him the third degree—*did* we, Mama?"

"No—we *didn't*," Esther Rosenbaum replied, casting a contemptuous look at her husband. "Show some manners, Saul!"

Having regained his composure, Pozniak spoke up on his own behalf. "It's okay, Mrs. Rosenbaum. It's a fair question." As he began speaking to her father, he turned to look at Natalie. "I can assure you my intentions toward your daughter are honorable," he said, smiling at her. He turned his attention back to Natalie's father. "My colleague and I have been given a grant by the War Department to conduct research at the University of Chicago. He's there with his wife now, lining up the people and equipment we'll need for our project. I'm supposed to join him there in September. I asked Natalie to accompany me, but then we both decided it wouldn't be proper."

Pozniak reached over and took Natalie's hand. "We plan to stay in touch. Natalie will, hopefully, come to visit once or twice—but only if that's acceptable to you and Mrs. Rosenbaum. When I return to Columbia in January, we'll resume seeing one another."

"Of course, Natalie may go to visit you in Chicago," Mrs. Rosenbaum declared. "Saul and I think that would be wonderful." She glared at her husband. *"Don't we, Saul?"*

Chapter Twenty-One
07 June 1941

Like his father before him, Rod Hurley had been unable to stand by while the fight between freedom and tyranny raged in Europe. He was not the only one. From across the Atlantic, men had journeyed from both the United and Confederate States of America to fight alongside the British.

Most were airmen.

As a result of England's victory in the Battle of Britain, Hitler's blitzkrieg had stalled at the western reaches of mainland Europe. With the advancing and retreating armies now separated by the English Channel, the conflict had evolved into a struggle between the Luftwaffe and the Royal Air Force. Day after day, bombers flew from either side of the channel. Day after day, fighters rose from the opposite side to meet them. It was an air war, a deadly duel in the skies over England and the occupied nations of Western Europe.

Eventually, in an effort to lessen their losses from German fighters, the British began sending their bombers across the channel in darkness. At the Lindholme bomber base in South Yorkshire, England, the RAF's No. 121 Squadron was preparing for another night of aerial combat. Under the command of Group Captain Rod

Hurley, the squadron had just completed their early-evening mission brief.

The target for that night was a Dutch Coast oil refinery. The refinery, near the port of Rotterdam, was supplying much-needed fuel for the Nazi war machine. It was heavily defended by a triad of anti-aircraft artillery batteries, each armed with five 88-millimeter cannons. There were also two fighter squadrons based forty miles away, near Eindhoven. Even though the fighters would be reluctant to come up at night, the exploding shells (known as flak) from the anti-aircraft guns surrounding the port would pose a serious threat to the RAF bombers as they approached the refinery.

The aircrews of 121 Squadron were composed entirely of volunteers from North America and Eastern Europe. Rod Hurley had logged more B-17 flight hours than any pilot on either side of the Atlantic, which was why the RAF had chosen him to lead the makeshift squadron of twenty-four Lend-Lease *Flying Fortresses.* The other men in Hurley's crew were experienced as well, having already flown eight nighttime missions together. One at a time, the ten crew members took their positions inside the dark interior of the *"Yellow Rose,"* the nickname given to Hurley's B-17.

First to board through a door on the right side of the fuselage was the tail gunner, Aleksander Nowak. Having fled Poland after the Nazi invasion a year earlier, Nowak was the only member of the crew not from North America. His English, though not perfect, was good enough to communicate with the other crew members, even in the heat of battle. Nowak was one of several Poles in Hurley's squadron, all of whom were stalwart fighters and all of whom reviled the Nazis for having ravaged their homeland.

Next to enter were the two waist gunners, Jack Reardon and Bill Pruett. Reardon was the youngest of the *Yellow Rose* crew members, still six days shy of his nineteenth birthday. Both gunners were two years out of high school—Reardon from Cincinnati, Ohio, and Pruett from a small town in Indiana. Both had enlisted in the U.S. Army Air

Corps (later the U.S. Army Air Force) after graduation. Both had flown as waist gunners aboard B-17s back in the States.

After Reardon and Pruett came the ball turret gunner, Stan Kempema. A native of Erie, Pennsylvania, Kempema had won his state's amateur welterweight boxing title in 1938. At just five feet, four inches tall and a hundred and forty-five pounds, he was easily the smallest member of the crew. His diminutive physique was well suited to the tight confines of the B-17's lower turret.

Following Kempema was the last of the five crew members stationed aft of the B-17's bomb bay—Garry "Gabby" Crain. When Crain had learned that Rod Hurley was leaving the Confederate Army Air Force to fly with the RAF, he had insisted on coming along to fly as Hurley's radio operator. After making a half-hearted attempt to dissuade his young sergeant, Hurley had pulled the necessary strings to get him discharged from the CAAF and assigned to his squadron at Lindholme.

The remaining five crew members entered the *Yellow Rose* through the forward hatch, a four-foot square entrance on the left underside of the nose section. First to reach up and grab the top edge of the open hatch was the copilot, Thomas Damron. The West Point graduate and veteran flyer was a native of the Bronx. Damron had been a high-time B-17 commander in the U.S. Army Air Force before volunteering for the RAF. Hurley had chosen him to be his copilot as an insurance policy. If Hurley became incapacitated during a mission, he wanted someone with Damron's experience leading the formation. Damron grasped the spar at the top of the hatch and swung his feet up through the opening, into the fuselage. He climbed and contorted his way up into the cockpit and began strapping into the copilot seat.

Dave Murray, the *Yellow Rose's* flight engineer, was the next to hoist himself into her nose section. His station was just behind the cockpit, where he could stand and man the top-turret machine guns when not performing his flight engineer duties. The slight-framed

Murray, like Garry Crain, was from Oklahoma. He was an avid reader and had a knack for analyzing mechanical problems and repairing them on the fly. Fascinated with airplanes, he had grown up maintaining machinery on his father's farm. When he enlisted at age twenty, he was destined to become a flight engineer. Over the past six years, he had been one of the best in the CAAF.

The next two crew members were both Texans, which is one reason they had requested to fly with Rod Hurley aboard the *Yellow Rose*. Mark Lorance, the bombardier, was from the Piney Woods region of East Texas. John Spence, the navigator, had grown up in a small town north of Fort Worth. Both were good at the jobs for which they had volunteered, although Spence was a bit of an enigma. Outwardly recalcitrant, he was at the same time fiercely devoted to duty. John Spence was the kind of guy who seemed to emerge unscathed from just about any crisis—but only after convincing everyone else around him that the situation was hopeless. Those who understood him, including Mark Lorance, overlooked Spence's cynicism because they knew that, even in the most desperate situations, they could count on him to do whatever needed to be done.

Last to climb aboard was Rod Hurley. After hoisting himself up into the fuselage, he reached down through the hatch and grabbed the handle on the door. He pulled it closed, latching it securely, before making his way into the cockpit.

Using flashlights, the crew went through their final preflight checks, ensuring every piece of their equipment was in working order. Once they had completed their checklists, they sat at their stations in silence, waiting for the prebriefed startup time. Each man girded himself for the mission that lay ahead. As the crew waited in darkness, the minutes seemed to drag on forever. For some, it was an opportunity for introspection. For others, it was a time of prayer.

Finally, at 2205 GMT, those on the flight deck—Hurley, Damron and Murray—got down to the business of starting the engines. The nighttime silence was broken as the electric starter whined from inside the cowling on the first of four 1200-horsepower Wright *Cyclone* engines. The starter strained to turn the weight of the massive propeller and all the moving parts attached to the engine's crankshaft. Slowly, the blades began to turn. After several revolutions, the engine began to cough. The initial explosions inside each of the nine cylinders produced fire and smoke from the exhaust stacks. The mighty engine shook on its mounts, sputtered momentarily, then roared to life. Illuminated in the beam from the lineman's flashlight, the spinning propeller became translucent. Only the arc created by the bright yellow tips of the blades remained visible.

One by one, the other three engines were started in the same manner. Following more checks by the cockpit crew, the *Yellow Rose* was ready to taxi. Gabby Crain patched Hurley's throat-mounted microphone through to the external radio. Hurley pressed the mic and called for the rest of the squadron to check in.

"*Borrowed Time* is up," came the first call.

"*Duchess of FUBAR*'s up."

"*Deuces Wild* is down—mechanical."

"*West Coast Lady*'s up."

The roll call continued until every crew, using their plane's nickname, had reported in. Two of the twenty-one B-17s dropped out with mechanical problems, leaving nineteen for the mission. Thirteen of those were carrying conventional high-explosive bombloads. Six, including the *Yellow Rose*, carried incendiaries.

Rod Hurley checked his watch. At 22:17 GMT, he gave the order. The *Flying Fortresses* of No. 121 squadron began streaming from their individual hardstands onto the taxiway, each in its preassigned sequence, each falling in behind the *Yellow Rose*. Five thousand miles from his home in Kerrville, Texas, Group Captain Rod Hurley led his squadron toward the longest of three concrete runways at RAF Lindholme.

The *Yellow Rose* paused for a quick runup check, then taxied into position on the runway. The crew members completed their final takeoff checks before Hurley grasped the yoke and called for takeoff power. Thomas Damron grabbed all four throttle levers and pushed them forward. As soon as the engines were at takeoff power, Hurley released the brakes. The sluggish B-17, carrying a maximum payload of bombs and fuel, begrudgingly rocked forward, gradually gaining momentum.

From his flight engineer station, just behind the cockpit, Dave Murray leaned forward and kept one hand on the four propeller levers to ensure they remained at the correct RPM. Not far into the takeoff roll, the tailwheel rose from the ground and the bomber assumed a level attitude. At just more than halfway down the 5000-foot runway, Hurley pulled back slightly on the yoke and coaxed the giant bird into the air.

Hurley called "gear up" and began climbing into the darkness. His bomber rose at 700 feet per minute toward a cruising altitude of 9,000 feet. Over the next fifteen minutes, eighteen more B-17s took off into the night. Each fell into a loose-trail formation behind the *Yellow Rose*.

They were one hour from Rotterdam.

The three pathfinder *Mosquitos* were flying barely above the waves. At 2233 GMT, the lead bombardier/navigator estimated their position. They were 30 miles northwest of the target. The *Mosquitos* slowed their airspeed from 270 to 120 miles per hour and entered a wide holding pattern in the darkness over the North Sea.

Twenty-two minutes later, they received a radio transmission from Sergeant Garry Crain aboard the *Yellow Rose*. The pathfinders departed their holding pattern and accelerated toward the Dutch coastline. The mission commander rocked his wings, passing the formation lead to the second *Mosquito*. Leaving his two wingmen, he added power and began a slow climb to 3,000 feet while keeping pace with the other two aircraft. Flying well above the other two planes in the formation, the mission commander had exposed himself to the German coastal air defenses.

A short time later, at the Luftwaffe fighter base near Eindhoven, ground crews began running up the BMW engines on a row of prepositioned Focke-Wulf Fw 190s. Eight specially trained "night-fighter" pilots scrambled toward their planes. As the flight leader, a decorated ace from the Battle of Britain, was strapping into his cockpit, he looked up into the pitch-black, moonless sky. He shook his head. *"Verdammt in die Hölle,"* he muttered to himself. [Dammit to hell.]

The pilots quickly strapped themselves in and returned the salutes from their ground crews. Spread line abreast, the eight Fw 190s simultaneously launched from the sod airfield and raced toward the coast. Four minutes later, the German pilots, flying in a loose formation consisting of four two-plane sections, began to see the half dozen searchlight beams swirling above Rotterdam.

The RAF pathfinders were already marking the target for the approaching B-17s of 121 Squadron. While the pathfinder mission commander circled overhead, his bombardier/navigator vectored the other two *Mosquitos* to the target, telling their bombardiers when to drop their flares.

Ironically, it was the Germans themselves who were supplying the necessary reference points the pathfinders needed to complete their mission. RAF analysts, using the film from the pathfinders' daylight reconnaissance mission, had charted the position of each searchlight relative to the target. As the searchlight operators haphazardly chased the low-flying *Mosquitos*, they were unwittingly providing the RAF pilots with the navigational fixes they needed to pinpoint the refinery.

All it took was a series of high-speed, low-level passes to properly disperse the flares around the target. When the mission commander dove and dropped 2,000 pounds of incendiaries into the middle of the flares, the fire from the incendiaries provided the approaching B-17s with an aiming point at the center of the previously darkened refinery.

Arriving overhead at 7,000 feet, the German night fighters surveyed the scene below. The second section leader asked for permission to dive on the low-level pathfinders.

"*Forget* the pathfinders!" the flight leader snapped. "Look for the bombers!"

"Twenty miles from the target," came the call from John Spence. "Come right to one seven six." Using the stars above the North Sea and radio beams out of England, Spence had navigated the formation to the IP (the *initial point* from which the bomb run would begin). They were almost due north of the refinery. The German anti-aircraft gunners would most likely be expecting the bombers to approach the target from the west, the shortest route across the North Sea.

Rod Hurley ordered his six-mile-long line of B-17s to begin climbing and descending to their previously assigned bombing altitudes. Staggering their altitudes would make it more difficult for the gunners to target the bombers as they streamed single file over the refinery. The gun crews had to manually set a timer on the fuse of each individual shell before loading it. When the shell was fired, the fuse was activated. The timer would detonate the explosive flak at the desired altitude, sending shrapnel over a wide area. With each bomber flying at a different altitude, the gun crews' task of finding the correct range and making the necessary adjustments was made more difficult.

"Pathfinders are clear. Target illuminated." The radio call over Garry Crain's headset let him know the low-flying *Mosquitos* were vacating the airspace above the refinery. "Happy hunting, Yanks."

The *Yellow Rose's* radio operator acknowledged the transmission from the pathfinder flight leader. "We're not all Yankees up here, partner; but we sincerely appreciate you fellas lightin' up the target for us. Happy trails." Sergeant Crain quickly passed the word to the cockpit. "We're cleared for the bomb run, Colonel."

Crain, along with the rest of the *Yellow Rose* crew members, refused to address Hurley as "Group Captain" whenever the RAF brass wasn't around. This was understandable coming from the North American volunteers. However, Aleksander Nowak, the tail gunner, had also adopted the practice. In doing so, the fiery Polish refugee had earned an added measure of acceptance from his American crewmates.

Rod Hurley pressed the microphone strapped against his throat. "Clear your guns," came the order through the interphone. "Let's be sharp. Keep an eye out for exhaust stacks and tracers." Each of the gunners fired a short burst from his .50 caliber machine guns to ensure they weren't jammed. Every fifth round in each ammunition belt was packed with a pyrotechnic charge to illuminate the round as it flew toward the target. This made it easier for the gunners aboard the bombers to direct their ordnance onto the attacking fighters.

Similarly, the attacking fighters routinely utilized tracers to target the bombers. However, tracers worked both ways. The pyrotechnic rounds also gave away the position of the attacker. The RAF crews were unaware that the specially trained night-fighter pilots out of Eindhoven had removed their pyrotechnic rounds. Instead of using tracers to zero in on their targets, the Germans hoped to approach the RAF bombers undetected, holding their fire until they were at point-blank range.

To pull this off, the aerial assassins would have to pinpoint the RAF bombers by tracking the glow from their exhaust stacks. After locating the unsuspecting bombers, the German night fighters would carefully creep in until they were flying in formation with their prey. It was a deadly game of cat and mouse.

The *Yellow Rose* was twelve miles from the target. The searchlights over Rotterdam were clearly visible to everyone but the tail gunner. It wouldn't be long until the searchlights would illuminate the lead B-17, giving its position away to the German gunners on the ground.

Just then— "*Dixie Jane* is hit!" The frantic radio call came from the B-17 directly behind the *Yellow Rose*. "*We're taking fire! Where the hell—*"

The radio screeched and went silent.

"*Skurwysyn!*" [Son of a whore!] Aleksander Nowak shouted from his tail gunner station. "Is massive fireball, six o'clock low!"

The pilot of the lead Fw 190 had successfully positioned himself immediately behind and just below the bomber without being seen. From a range of only 100 yards, he had opened up with his two 20-millimeter cannons, raking it mercilessly.

The ten crew members inside the B-17 never had a chance. The armor-piercing shells shredded the underside of the fuselage and penetrated the bomb bay, igniting the four tons of incendiaries inside. The resulting explosion broke the bomber apart in midair, splitting the fuselage just forward of the waist gunners' stations. Most of the men were killed in the explosion. Several rode the fluttering, burning wreckage all the way down into the North Sea—8,000 feet below.

The cloud of debris that resulted from the exploding incendiaries inside the *Dixie Jane's* bomb bay was more than the attacking German pilot had bargained for. His heart skipped as he flew through the conflagration and emerged on the other side with only minor damage to his Fw 190.

Several minutes later, when his pupils once again had dilated, he began to make out the faint glow from another set of B-17 exhaust stacks. They belonged to the *Yellow Rose*. Rod Hurley's bomber was 2,000 yards in front of and 1,000 feet above the Fw 190. The German ace began moving in for another kill. Slowly…steadily, he began closing the gap.

Aboard the *Yellow Rose*, Mark Lorance leaned forward into the plexiglass portion of the nose bay and peered through the donut-sized lens on his Norden bombsight. After several minutes, he pressed his throat mic. "Target in sight," he announced. "I'm ready to take it, Skipper."

"It's your aircraft," Hurley answered, toggling the switch to transfer directional control of the airplane to the bombardier.

Now controlling the B-17's heading from his station in the nose of the aircraft, Lorance manipulated a series of knurled knobs on the bombsight. As Hurly maintained altitude from the cockpit, every adjustment Lorance made produced a corresponding correction to the bomber's flightpath, taking it on a course toward the release point.

Meanwhile, the unseen Fw 190 was creeping closer and closer from behind.

His navigation skills no longer required, John Spence abandoned his chart table and manned the ported machine gun several feet behind Lorance. This was the part of the run Spence, along with everyone else in the crew, feared the most. Unable to maneuver until the bombs were released, they were forced to fly straight and level toward the target. The steady flight profile made them even more vulnerable to the German cannons on the ground.

Suddenly, the entire nose bay filled with a bright light. No longer flying in darkness, the *Yellow Rose* had been spotted by the searchlight operators below.

The Germans knew the RAF bombed in trail formation. Once they had acquired the lead bomber, they would concentrate all their fire on that one aircraft until they destroyed it or until it completed the bomb run. Only then would they direct their fire onto the next bomber. For now, the *Yellow Rose* became the only target that mattered to the gunners manning the deadly 88-millimeter cannons.

"It's our turn in the spotlight," Spence grumbled sarcastically. "I *hate* this horseshitty job."

The gun crews hurriedly estimated the bomber's altitude, set the fuse timers on their first round of shells, and opened fire.

Seeing the B-17 illuminated by searchlights, the Fw 190 pilot knew it was now or never. He didn't want to stick around for the inevitable flak that was now only seconds away. He rammed his throttle forward, committing himself to the attack. The hardened fighter pilot raced in for the kill. He centered the *Yellow Rose* in his gunsight. Climbing and accelerating at the same time, he opened fire just as the first burst of flak sent a piece of shrapnel through his canopy and into his right shoulder.

The orange flash from the flak was just enough to make the Fw 190 visible for a fleeting instant. Startled, Stan Kempema caught a glimpse of the attacking German and opened fire from the ball turret. "*Bandit! Six o'clock low!*" he shouted. Tracers began streaming from the twin machine guns that protruded from the plexiglass dome on the bottom of his turret. The rounds deflected wildly as he trained the turret toward the position where he had momentarily seen the fighter climbing toward him. Kempema was firing blindly into the abyss.

The Fw 190 was close—dangerously close. Had the wounded German pilot not been busy dodging tracers and flak, he would have been able to see the fear on Kempema's face as he sat exposed inside the brightly illuminated ball turret.

"*Verdammt!*" [Dammit!] Aborting the attack, the German pilot grimaced from pain as he used his bloody right arm to roll the Fw 190 hard over to the left. Inverted, he chopped his throttle and pulled back on the stick until his fighter was 60 degrees nose down. Using the artificial horizon on his cockpit instrument panel, he rolled the plane upright again and continued diving at 400 miles per hour into the darkness, away from the deadly shroud of flak that now surrounded the bomber.

The *Yellow Rose* shook and rattled as she droned straight ahead toward the target. The closer the flak bursts came to her airframe, the harder she bucked. Twice, pieces of hot shrapnel penetrated the fuselage and burned inside the aircraft. Each time, the crew quickly doused the flames with carbon dioxide from portable fire extinguishers.

"Can't this crate move any faster?" John Spence muttered to himself. He turned and looked at his partner in the nose bay. Mark Lorance was glued to his bombsight, staring through the lens. *"Come on, Mark! Just drop the damn bombs!"*

Spence hadn't keyed his mic, but Lorance was able to hear the impatient navigator shouting in the background. The steady bombardier calmly reached back and toggled a switch while still staring at the crosshairs in his lens. "Bomb bay doors open," he announced.

The next several seconds seemed an eternity. The constant "krumppp" of exploding shells was becoming increasingly intense as the German gunners zeroed in on the vulnerable B-17.

Finally, the bombs were released. *"Bombs away!"* Lorance shouted. "She's all yours, Skipper!"

"It's about damn time," Spence murmured under his breath as Lorance closed the bomb bay.

Hurly disengaged the autopilot. "We're outta here!" he declared as he turned away from the target and called for max power. The searchlight operators began spinning their beams away from Hurley and his crew, probing the skies for the next bomber in the formation.

As the *Yellow Rose* descended and accelerated toward the coastline, her entire complement of incendiaries found their mark inside the perimeter of the massive oil refinery. Soon thereafter, more incendiaries fell from the next bomber—then more from the one after that. A number of them missed, but with each incendiary that hit the target, the flames inside the refinery became more and more intense. Before long, the target was fully engulfed—a raging, petroleum-fueled inferno.

Then came the B-17s carrying 500-pound general-purpose bombs. They pounded the burning refinery, sending even more flames, along with heavy debris, high into the night sky. Soon, there were vortexes swirling within the blaze. It became a self-perpetuating firestorm.

The view from the bombers was apocalyptic. One after another, the crews of 121 Squadron ran the gauntlet above Rotterdam. Two of the squadron's B-17s were destroyed by the deadly flak. Beginning with the ten men killed when the *Dixie Jane* was taken down by the German night fighter, thirty-four Allied airmen died in the shooting gallery over the target. A half dozen more were critically wounded. Eight went missing in action when they bailed out of their crippled B-17 over the North Sea.

Each man that night was there of his own accord. Some of them were outwardly calm and deliberate during their bomb runs. Most were scared out of their wits. They all, by virtue of their willingness to voluntarily fly into harm's way, exhibited exceptional valor.

When the reconnaissance *Mosquitos* returned to Rotterdam the following morning, their photos revealed the strategic oil refinery had been obliterated. Rod Hurley's squadron had pounded the fiercely defended target with twenty tons of incendiaries and forty-eight tons of general-purpose bombs.

As the sun climbed high into the sky over RAF Lindholme, most of the exhausted crew members of 121 Squadron slept soundly. One man, however, sat alone in his office. Group Captain Rod Hurley, an ocean away from his own family, was busy writing letters to the families of those who hadn't returned.

Chapter Twenty-Two
04 July 1941

As the air war raged over Europe, life in the United States was business as usual. In Brooklyn, the Nathan's Hot Dog Eating Contest had been an annual Independence Day tradition since 1916. Every 4th of July, people came from across New York City to see who could consume the most hot dogs at the popular Coney Island eatery.

Each year, there were qualifying competitions to determine the final twenty contestants. In the summer of 1941, however, one of the contestants was there by special invitation from Nathan Handwerker, the hot dog company's founder. Handwerker was a Jewish immigrant from Eastern Europe. The Brooklyn Hebrew Orphan Asylum had fallen on hard times and was in danger of closing from a lack of funds. Handwerker had organized a charity drive and had publicly pledged to award an at-large contest invitation to the individual who raised the most money for the struggling orphanage.

Marc Krbec, having spent his early years at the orphanage, had enthusiastically accepted the challenge. He had taken advantage of his position as a supervisor at the Brooklyn Navy Yard to strong-arm his co-workers into donating generously. Then, after having squeezed all he could from his fellow shipbuilders, Krbec had successfully solicited—with a little help from his best friend's gal—

a sizeable check from Saul Rosenbaum's real estate firm. Rosenbaum's contribution had put him over the top.

As Krbec took to the stage with the other contestants, Toby Pozniak and Natalie Rosenbaum cheered him on. Natalie had also invited her former college roommate to attend the event. Karen Berkovich was not nearly so enthusiastic about the prospect of watching twenty grown men stuff themselves with hot dogs. "Are those things even kosher?" she asked Natalie.

Natalie pretended not to hear the question as she continued cheering for Krbec.

"Look at him," Pozniak said, laughing. "I haven't seen him this excited since the Dodgers won the pennant when we were kids. I think this is the proudest day of his life."

But when the contestants had finished lining up behind the long table, there was an empty spot. Nathan Handwerker began quizzing several of the more-tenured contestants to determine who was missing and why. After several minutes, he huddled with everyone on the stage to discuss the situation.

When the conference ended, all but one of the contestants who were present returned to their stations behind the table. Marc Krbec joined Nathan Handwerker as he stepped to the microphone at the front of the stage. "Ladies and gentlemen, we have a situation," Handwerker announced. "One of our qualifying contestants has fallen ill."

"*He's just getting a head start!*" someone yelled from the crowd, drawing laughter and applause.

Handwerker waited for the laughter to die down. "All right, then. Here's what we've decided to do. This is Mr. Marc Krbec. He's here at my invitation because he raised nearly three thousand dollars for the Jewish orphanage here in Brooklyn." There was a smattering of applause. "I'm going to allow Mr. Krbec to pick another contestant from the crowd." There was more applause, this time loud and enthusiastic. Handwerker motioned for Krbec to move in closer to the microphone. "Okay, Mr. Krbec. Who's it going to be?"

People began to cheer excitedly as, throughout the crowd, hands went up from people wanting Krbec to pick them. The smiling shipyard worker played along, teasing the anxious crowd as he poised himself to point at the lucky winner. He raised his finger and rotated it in circles. After several revolutions, he lowered his finger and pointed it straight at his lifelong friend. "I choose…Professor Toby Pozniak!" he shouted.

As several good-natured boos came from the crowd, Toby Pozniak declined, waving his arms and shaking his head. The crowd voiced its displeasure, both with Krbec's choice and Pozniak's refusal to accept the invitation. Someone standing behind Pozniak pushed him toward the stage. The embarrassed physicist immediately turned around and retreated as the crowd grew more impatient and booed louder.

Handwerker placed his hand on Krbec's back. "Looks like your friend doesn't want—"

"*I'll do it!*" a loud female voice interrupted.

A hush came over the crowd.

"Natalie! What are you doing?" Karen Berkovich asked her friend incredulously.

"I'll do it!" Natalie shouted again, making her way toward the stage.

The crowd began to cheer loudly.

Unsure what to do, Krbec looked quizzically at Handwerker for an answer. The hot dog mogul just smiled and shrugged his shoulders. As Krbec turned to wave Natalie onto the stage, she was already at the top step of the stairs.

Natalie walked matter-of-factly across the stage and removed her eyeglasses. She handed them to Nathan Handwerker. "Here—hold these," she said as the audience applauded her chutzpah. With the crowd enthusiastically supporting her, Natalie Rosenbaum took her position behind the table.

As the giant platters stacked with hot dogs were paraded onto the stage, the crowd cheered and whistled. Nathan Handwerker held up his hand to quiet the crowd. "All right, ladies and gentlemen—before we begin, let me go over the rules again. Once the bell rings, each contestant will have ten minutes to consume as many hot dogs as he—"

Handwerker cut himself off mid-sentence and started again. "Each contestant will have ten minutes to consume as many hot dogs as he—or *she*—can." He paused while the crowd chuckled and clapped. "The contestant who consumes the most hot dogs before the final bell will be the winner. ...There *is* one caveat," he added.

Knowing what was coming, the crowd began to cheer and laugh. Handwerker raised his voice over the crowd. "The hot dogs *must* stay down for at least three minutes after the bell. If the contestant suffers a 'reversal of fortune,' that contestant will be disqualified." The crowd laughed louder. Handwerker turned to face the anxious contestants. "Gentlemen...and lady, *arrrre you ready?*"

Some gave a thumbs up. Others simply nodded.

Handwerker pointed at the large clock atop the platform's backdrop. "Very well, then. Here we go! *Ten...nine...eight—*" As he got closer to the end of the countdown, more and more spectators joined in. "*—three...two...one!*"

As the starting bell rang, the sweep-second hand on the clock began to move. The crowd roared raucously as the contestants flew into action. They began grabbing hot dogs from the platters and frantically shoving them into their mouths. Some were attempting to swallow the hot dogs whole. A few, including Natalie Rosenbaum, grabbed one in each hand so as to have the next dog ready as soon as the previous one had been devoured. The judges watched to ensure that only a modicum of crumbs fell from the contestants' pained faces.

As the crowd continued to cheer, Karen Berkovich turned to Toby Pozniak and rolled her eyes in disgust.

Pozniak looked back at her with a peculiar expression on his face. As the crowd roared louder and louder, something came over him. The normally reserved physicist suddenly became caught up in the moment. He flashed a big grin as he put both his little fingers inside his lips and stretched them taught. He whistled as loudly as he could, loud enough to draw the attention of everyone in the crowd. *"Come on, Natalie!"* he shouted at the top of his lungs. *"Show 'em how to eat some hot dogs!"*

Pozniak's childlike antics took Karen Berkovich by surprise. She began to laugh. She decided she might as well embrace the spectacle for what it was…*whatever* it was. She started clapping her hands together. *"Get goin', Natalie! Suck 'em down!"*

By nine minutes into the competition, the once-frenetic pace set by the competitors had slowed considerably. Several had all but given up.

With forty-five seconds to go, Marc Krbec decided he'd had enough. The burly shipbuilder slowly placed a half-eaten hot dog back onto his platter. He leaned forward, resting his hands on the red, white and blue tablecloth. He had a look of capitulation on his face.

Meanwhile, Natalie Rosenbaum continued eating at the same workmanlike pace she had maintained since the opening bell. At five feet, five inches tall and a hundred and eighteen pounds, Natalie was the smallest of all the competitors. And yet, a survey of the platters revealed she had consumed as many hot dogs as the two-hundred-and-eighty-pound construction worker standing next to her.

As the clock ran down, the crowd began counting down toward the final bell. With seven seconds to go, Marc Krbec could no longer hold it. He sheepishly turned his back to the crowd and deposited most of his day's work into the bucket he had been issued prior to the contest. The crowd whooped and cheered at his hard-luck exit from the competition.

When the final bell rang, the competitors were allowed to finish chewing and swallowing any hot dog they had begun eating prior to the expiration of time. This led to the disqualification of one more competitor, who was flagged by the judges for shoving a still-pristine hot dog into his mouth after the bell.

The clock continued to run for another three minutes as the remaining competitors did their best to digest the massive quantities of bread and frankfurters they had crammed into their gastrointestinal tracts. This additional three minutes of soul-searching led to the disqualifications of two more contestants, one of whom was the thickset construction worker who had been eating next to Natalie.

When the three minutes were up, Natalie Rosenbaum was declared the winner. The crowd erupted, cheering louder than they had all day.

Natalie, as if nothing at all unusual had taken place, walked calmly across the stage and retrieved her eyeglasses from Nathan Handwerker. She put them on as she turned to the cheering crowd and waved. Then, she looked straight at Toby Pozniak and began laughing.

In that small moment, Toby Pozniak experienced an epiphany. That was the moment he realized he loved Natalie more than he loved life itself.

Chapter Twenty-Three
09 July 1941

As a result of the American Civil War, the United States, once destined to become a world power, was split into two nations. Neither of these smaller, weaker nations was capable of rising to the top of a restructured global hierarchy.

Though the U.S. was still an economic and industrial force, its limited sphere of influence in foreign affairs had resulted in a world map that looked different than it otherwise might have. This was especially true in the Western Hemisphere, where European nations still held real estate that, under the Monroe Doctrine, would have surely slipped from their political grasp.

Two of the largest Caribbean islands, Cuba and Puerto Rico, were strategically located near the North American mainland. Had the Union prevailed in 1862, there is little doubt the U.S. would have helped both Spanish colonies attain their independence. The same was true for the Philippines in the Western Pacific. Because of history's altered course, however, all three were still Spanish protectorates.

Ironically, Japan now had designs on the Philippines as part of their expansionist war in the Pacific. Adolf Hitler saw this as an opportunity. In exchange for military access to Cuba and Puerto Rico, the German Führer promised to intercede with the Japanese on Spain's behalf.

Generalissimo Francisco Franco, the Spanish dictator, was already indebted to Hitler for his support during the Spanish Civil War. Even though he had hoped Spain could remain neutral in the current global conflict, Hitler's offer to dissuade the Japanese from seizing the Philippines was a proposition he was unable to refuse.

Over the past two months, the military assets originally amassed for the now-postponed invasion of Russia had been covertly sealifted into Cuba and Puerto Rico. More than a million soldiers, along with tons of military hardware, were hidden throughout the remote interiors of both islands.

More men and equipment, including dozens of disassembled and crated Junkers Ju 52 trimotor transport planes, were arriving each day at ports all across the two islands.

The airport terminal southwest of downtown Havana was not exactly a hive of activity. The few incoming airliners, when they did arrive, were typically DC-3s sparsely loaded with American tourists. Most of the incoming flights were cargo planes ferrying freight from both North and South America. Most of the freight from North America comprised innocuous mercantile goods headed to Cuban markets. Much of the South American freight, however, was hurriedly transported away to unidentified destinations—for unknown purposes.

At the port facility in Old Havana, east of the main city, there was still the occasional cruise ship arriving from America; but on most days, the outmoded passenger terminal there received even fewer visitors than the one at the airport. Gone were the days when large cruise ships filled with vacationers from Europe arrived several times a week. The war had made transatlantic travel a thing of the past.

In stark contrast to the nearly empty cruise-ship terminal, the several cargo piers on the opposite side of the port were bustling. Every day, unmarked crates were being offloaded from various European-flagged freighters at a swift pace. Largely unnoticed by most observers, this had gone on for months.

From a tree-covered hill overlooking the port, one man took special note of the increased activity. Alejandro Cruz focused his binoculars on the large crates. He also studied the man who was supervising the process. The man was dressed in traditional Cuban attire, wearing a beige button-up guayabera shirt over white cotton slacks. He even wore a Cuban fedora, made of white straw—but the man was not Cuban.

It was late afternoon. Cruz took the binoculars from around his neck and placed them in his satchel, alongside his camera. He knew the man would be leaving the port soon, just as he had done each of the three days Cruz had been observing him. On this day, Cruz decided to follow the man. He made his way from the hill down to the street, tossed the satchel into the back of his car, and drove the short distance to the port. Parking near the pier where the man had been supervising the longshoremen as they offloaded the crates, he waited there for more than an hour, watching the gate next to the pier.

Finally, the man emerged and got into a taxi. Cruz followed the taxi to the Hotel Saratoga in Old Havana, not far from the port facility. Parking a block away, Cruz watched as the man got out of the taxi and disappeared through the large open-air entrance into the hotel.

Cruz turned and reached over the seat, retrieving his satchel from the back of the car. He got out and crossed the street, casually walking into the hotel, where he took a seat inside the Saratoga's luxurious lobby. He was determined to wait there to see if the mysterious man would come down from his room. Cruz lit a cigarette and picked up a discarded newspaper from the empty chair next to his. He casually skimmed the paper while casting frequent, furtive glances toward the white marble stairway that led up to the guest rooms.

After ten minutes or so, Cruz set the paper aside and extinguished his cigarette in the freestanding ashtray next to his chair. He removed a pen and a pad of paper from his satchel and began writing detailed notes to himself, documenting his observations from earlier that afternoon.

After another forty-five minutes, he stood and carried his notepad to a phone booth in the corner of the hotel lobby. He tucked the notepad under his arm and took a handful of coins from his pocket. After looking toward the stairway to make sure the man hadn't reappeared, Cruz sidestepped into the booth and closed the folding doors. Dropping the coins into the payphone, he asked the operator to put him through to the U.S. Embassy.

Just as the phone began to ring on the other end of the line, the man he had been observing came down the stairs and walked toward the exit. Cruz quickly hung up the phone and exited the booth. Following the man outside the hotel and onto the sidewalk, he watched as the man removed his fedora and used it to hail another taxi. It was the first time Cruz had gotten a closeup look at the man. He quickly reached into his satchel for his camera, but the man turned and glanced in his direction. Cruz froze until the man had turned his attention back toward the street. By the time he pulled the camera from his satchel, it was too late. The man was getting into the taxi.

Cruz sprinted toward his parked car, but in his haste to grab his keys from his pocket, he dropped them onto the sidewalk. Picking them up, he jumped behind the wheel, tossed his satchel into the passenger seat, and started the car. Screeching away from the curb, he began trying to catch up to the taxi, now two blocks in front of him. Running through a red light, he drew the ire of a cross-traffic driver, who laid on the horn and stuck his head outside his car to shout obscenities at Cruz. When he was within a block of the taxi, he slowed down, maintaining a safe distance so as not to be noticed.

It was now early evening. Alejandro Cruz tailed the taxi along the palm-lined boulevard next to the seawall, to a waterfront restaurant on the city's northwest side. The man got out at the curb, paid the driver through the passenger window, and went inside.

With no place to park his car, Cruz drove past the restaurant and made a U-turn. He found an empty spot on the opposite side of the street, directly across from the restaurant. He waited several minutes before darting, satchel in hand, across the busy four-lane boulevard. Cruz stopped to wipe the sweat from his brow before entering the restaurant. Once inside, he slipped the maître d' twenty pesetas to seat him several tables away from the man he'd been following.

The man was seated alone, but it wasn't long before another man joined him—a man whom Cruz recognized. Francisco Gómez-Jordana was the foreign minister of Spain. He had fought against the Cubans during their failed war for independence in 1898 and was hailed as a Spanish military hero. The man Cruz had been tailing rose and greeted Gómez-Jordana with a handshake. It was obvious from their demeanors the two had met before.

Hoping to remain inconspicuous, Cruz summoned the waiter and ordered a drink. He perused the menu, occasionally glancing toward the table where the Spanish foreign minister and the still-unidentified man were engaged in conversation. He watched them throughout dinner, hoping for an opportunity to photograph the pair without being noticed. Cruz finished his meal as the two men continued to converse through several rounds of drinks and cigarettes.

At one point, Cruz made a trip to the men's room, carrying his satchel with him. After making sure no one else was present, he removed his camera and attached the telephoto lens. He held the door slightly ajar with his foot and quickly focused the lens on the two men still seated at their table. He snapped several photos in rapid succession before he was startled by another patron, who opened the door from the other side.

The patron was wary when he saw Cruz with the camera, but he said nothing and slipped past him without incident. Cruz tucked the camera back into his satchel and returned to his table as the waiter was clearing it. "*¿Habrá algo más, señor?*" [Will there be anything else, sir?]

"*No, gracias,*" Cruz answered. "*Solo la cuenta, por favor.*" [Just the check, please.]

Cruz settled his bill and headed out to his car. He waited for ten minutes or so until the man he had been following emerged from the restaurant, accompanied by the Spanish foreign minister. The two got into Gómez-Jordana's car and drove away.

Cruz followed them as they turned off the boulevard onto a narrow side street. After several blocks, they stopped briefly at another local hotel and picked up two more riders. As he continued to tail the four men into the night, Alejandro Cruz tried his best to remain inconspicuous.

The Tropicana nightclub was an iconic landmark in Havana. The clientele at the swanky club was an eclectic mix of Cuban aristocrats, Spanish government officials and American tourists. With luxury seating for nearly a thousand people, each of the large tables was adorned with an elaborate floral centerpiece that included a complimentary box of Cohiba cigars and a bottle of Bacardi rum.

Visitors to the Tropicana were greeted curbside by beautiful dancers wearing extravagant gowns and exotic headdresses. The dancers posed for photographs with each arriving patron; but on this night, the first of four men emerging from one of the cars abruptly informed the photographer that under no circumstances was he to aim his camera in their direction. Francisco Gómez-Jordana tossed his keys to the valet as he and his three companions walked past the hospitality station. They made their way through the swinging glass doors into the ornate vestibule. There, they were welcomed by a maître d', who introduced them to their waiter for the evening.

The waiter escorted the men down the sculpture-filled hallway, out into the large amphitheater filled with tables. Aside from the entrance hall, kitchen and backstage dressing rooms, the Tropicana was an outdoor venue, surrounded by six acres of tropical jungle. The seating area was completely covered by a lush, natural canopy of trees filled with hundreds of multicolored lights.

The main stage was enormous. A half dozen tall palm trees, each wrapped with strands of flashing lights, stood on either side. There was a network of rigid metal beams spanning the tops of the palms, each beam serving as an anchor point for the massive array of spotlights suspended above the stage. To the left of the main stage, elevated twenty feet above it, was another stage. It was recessed into the jungle and comprised three levels, each backdropped with vines, lavish flowers and still more lighting. To the right of the main stage, also recessed into the thick vegetation that surrounded the seating area, was a raised orchestra stand. A red velvet curtain was draped from the edge of the stand to conceal the steel latticework that supported it.

With the orchestra playing softly in the background, the waiter led Francisco Gómez-Jordana and the other three men to the front-row table that had been reserved for the Spanish foreign minister and his guests. The tables immediately adjacent to theirs had been reserved as well, providing the men with a buffer of empty tables for privacy.

Seated next to Gómez-Jordana was the man Alejandro Cruz had followed from the pier that afternoon. Colonel Wilhelm Schmidt was a personal assistant to the second-most powerful man in Germany— Hermann Göring. As head of the Luftwaffe, Göring had sent Schmidt to Cuba to oversee the offloading and reassembly of airplanes that had been dismantled and shipped across the Atlantic in crates.

Lighting a cigar, Gómez-Jordana mumbled something inaudible to Schmidt.

"I beg your pardon?" Schmidt responded.

Gómez-Jordana finished lighting the Cohiba. He puffed it several times before speaking again. "My apologies, Colonel. I asked what you think of the Tropicana."

"It's wonderful," Schmidt offered. "I had no idea we would be sitting outdoors…and in such a beautiful setting."

Gómez-Jordana turned his attention to the man seated directly across from Schmidt. "How about you, Field Marshal? Are you enjoying your stay in Cuba?"

Field Marshal Friedrich von Essen was a no-nonsense military officer. "I'm not here on vacation, Herr Gomez. I'm here to prepare my troops. That said, I sincerely appreciate your invitation tonight. The show will be a welcome respite."

"You are most welcome," the Spanish foreign minister said, smiling. "Is there anything my government can do to assist you with your preparations? I trust the Ju 52s are being delivered to your airfields in satisfactory condition?"

"They are."

"Do you need help with the reassembly process? I understand they are to be fitted with auxiliary fuel tanks to extend their range."

Von Essen found the question patronizing at best, insulting at worst. "We don't require any assistance from the Spanish government. We only require confidentiality."

"*But of course*, señor. Do you have any idea when you'll be prepared to move ahead with your plan…what are you calling it…Operation *Atlantis?* You *do* know the longer you delay, the greater the likelihood your operation will be compromised. Just look around you. There are many Americans in Havana."

"Speaking of which," Colonel Schmidt interrupted. "You see that man who just sat down alone over there…next to the curtain below the orchestra stand?"

Gómez-Jordana pointed at the man to confirm he was the one in question. *"Him?* He's not American. He's not even a tourist. I've actually seen him before. I think he's a member of the Cuban governor's staff here in Havana."

"Be that as it may, I saw him outside my hotel this afternoon…and again at the restaurant. I think he's following me."

This was the point at which the fourth man, until now uninterested in the small talk and pleasantries, became keenly interested in the conversation. Smaller in stature than the rest, Ernst Kruger was the only man at the table dressed in black. "You say he's been following you?" Kruger asked.

"Yes, I believe so," Schmidt replied. "I think he even tried to take my photograph outside the hotel."

Just then, the house lights went down. The orchestra struck a loud chord and broke into a lively, rhythmic mambo melody. The stage lights simultaneously cast a kaleidoscope of swirling colors down onto the dance floor.

Two dozen scantily clad female dancers burst onto the stage and began gyrating to the music. They swayed, pirouetted and dipped, all while delicately balancing large exotic headdresses. As they danced beneath the lights, the skin on their bodies glistened with perspiration and glitter. Several bars into the song, they were joined by two dozen male dancers, each of whom sensuously ran his hands up and down the bare midriff of his female partner, tracing every seductive curve as the couple moved in unison to the beat of the music.

At the same time, a dozen more female dancers streamed onto all three levels of the elevated stage. The surrounding jungle came to life in a dazzling display of pulsating emerald lights. The Tropicana's cabaret was a mesmerizing spectacle, especially to those seeing it for the first time. No one seated at the foreign minister's table seemed to notice when, a half hour into the show, Ernst Kruger stood and made his way to the back of the amphitheater. Nor did anyone seated at the tables farthest from the stage take notice when Kruger slipped into the darkened jungle behind them. Only when their colleague later returned did Colonel Schmidt and Field Marshal von Essen realize that Kruger had been absent from the table.

The orchestra played late into the evening. The singers sang—the dancers danced. Shortly after midnight, the show ended to thunderous applause. Even Field Marshal Friedrich von Essen stood and cheered, along with Colonel Wilhelm Schmidt and Francisco Gómez-Jordana.

Throughout the entire club, only two men remained seated during the ovation. One was SS General Ernst Kruger, who—unimpressed with the pomp and pageantry—sat stoically at the front-row table. The other was Alejandro Cruz, who sat next to the curtain beneath the orchestra stand.

Long after the other Tropicana guests had left, the head waiter looked across the empty amphitheater and noticed a man still sitting at his table. He yelled at the man, trying to get his attention. When the man appeared to ignore him, the waiter weaved his way through the labyrinth of tables toward the orchestra stand. "Señor!" he shouted at the man.

Though he was looking straight back at the waiter, the man said nothing.

Only when the waiter was within a few yards of him did he notice the blood oozing from the corner of the man's mouth. "Señor! ¿Estás enfermo?" [Are you sick?]

Glassy-eyed, the man continued staring straight ahead.

The waiter reached out and tapped him on the shoulder. The man slumped forward.

As Alejandro Cruz fell face-first onto the table, the red curtain beneath the orchestra stand slowly ripped. A large, blood-soaked swath of the curtain clung to the back of Cruz's once-white suit jacket as he lay prone in the floral centerpiece. His fedora bounced to the edge of the table and fell to the floor, landing at the waiter's feet.

The waiter stepped back, startled, as he saw the dagger that had been plunged deep into Cruz's back from behind the curtain.

Chapter Twenty-Four
18 July 1941

The crates containing disassembled Ju 52s and heavy equipment continued to arrive in Havana daily. There were also a number of crated fuselages and wings belonging to fighters, most of them Messerschmitt Bf 109s. While the Ju 52 transports were trucked into the interior for reassembly, the fighters remained in their crates, stacked along the piers.

Meanwhile, Cuba's southern ports were also busy. Though these ports lacked the infrastructure for the offloading of substantial freight, their relative seclusion made the smaller ports ideal locations for German troops to continue flooding onto the island far from the eyes of any Americans.

One of the paradoxes of a peacetime military is that militaries are not in the business of peace. In the absence of war, armies and navies often devolve into political bureaucracies.

At the U.S. embassy in Havana, Lieutenant Commander Mike Crofford was becoming increasingly frustrated. It had been more than a week since his operative inside the Cuban governor's office had turned up dead. His gut told him something ominous was occurring on the island where he ostensibly served as the U.S. naval attaché.

Unfortunately, the decision makers back in D.C. were not interested in Crofford's gut. His superiors at Naval Intelligence were more concerned with cracking the code used by the Nazis to communicate with the U-boats that were wreaking havoc on the Lend-Lease convoys to England. He had repeatedly asked for permission to venture into the interior of Cuba to confirm the presence of a German military buildup. Each time he had asked, he had been instructed to remain at his post in Havana. Had he been just another naval attaché, Crofford most likely would have understood his superiors' reluctance to turn him loose undercover. Mike Crofford, however, was not just another naval attaché. He was a trained intelligence officer—and a good one.

Following his graduation from Annapolis, Crofford had spent nearly a year at the Navy's intelligence school, where he had graduated at the top of his class. After spending three years in the fleet, he had been assigned to an exchange tour with the Confederate military. During that time, he had spent two years teaching intelligence courses at the Citadel.

While at the Citadel, Crofford had become close with one of his fellow instructors—an unassuming Confederate major from Kansas. The major, who was teaching courses in tank warfare and military leadership, had taken it upon himself to make sure the young Navy lieutenant, who had grown up in Nebraska, felt welcome at the Confederate academy.

That unassuming major was now the highest-ranking officer in the Confederate military. General Dwight David Eisenhower was more commonly known as "Ike." He was anything but flamboyant. His meteoric rise to the top of the Confederate Army had been enigmatic. While many of his peers had exhibited superior warrior skills, Eisenhower's most valuable attributes were leadership and judgment. His organizational talents were second to none.

Perhaps more than anything else, Dwight Eisenhower possessed the ability to learn, not just from his superiors—but from his subordinates as well. He was one of those rare leaders who professed to have an open-door policy and actually did. He encouraged his junior officers to use him as a sounding board for their ideas. No detail was too insignificant to garner Ike's attention.

In decided contrast, not one of Mike Crofford's superiors shared his concern over a possible German buildup in Cuba. Could it be he *was* paranoid?

Perhaps.

But, if his suspicions were correct, all of North America could be at risk. He knew his old friend would listen to him and offer wise counsel. As Lieutenant Commander Crofford picked up the phone to call General Eisenhower, he knew he was risking his career.

<u>*Chapter Twenty-Five*</u>
Monday, 28 July 1941

It was an impulse.

Toby Pozniak, changing trains at the Penn Station subway terminal, had just missed the 4:50 p.m. "A" train to Brooklyn. As he stood waiting for the next train to carry him home on his evening commute from Columbia University, he made a spontaneous decision.

Pozniak began shuffling and weaving his way through the other commuters on the crowded platform. He bolted up the exit to 8th Avenue and hailed a northbound taxicab in the midst of a driving rainstorm. Twenty blocks later, when the cab got stuck in the middle lane of rush-hour traffic, Pozniak paid the driver and continued on foot. He jumped from the cab and weaved his way through the maze of sitting cars to the sidewalk.

After running the final six blocks through the storm, he was welcomed by a doorman beneath an Art Deco awning. The doorman helped him remove his rain-soaked suit jacket and handed it back to him. He held the door as Pozniak shook the rain from his hat and entered the building.

"Welcome to Tiffany's," the saleswoman said from behind a showcase filled with diamonds. "How may I help you?"

"I'm not sure," Pozniak responded, out of breath and dripping on the marble floor. "I've never shopped for an engagement ring before."

Chapter Twenty-Six

Wednesday, 30 July 1941

Confederate President Harry Truman sat in his office, eating lunch at his desk.

"Mr. Truman, I have General Eisenhower on the line. You wanted me to let you know as soon as he returned your call."

"Thank you, Miss Conway. Put him through." Truman swallowed the remainder of his sandwich, washing it down with several gulps of iced tea. He intentionally let the phone ring several times before picking it up. "You too busy to take my calls these days, General?"

"I'm sorry, Mr. President. I was tied up on a pressing matter."

"Would that pressing matter have anything to do with all the military maneuvers around Richmond the past week and a half? If I didn't know better, I'd think you were getting ready to stage a coup."

"Nothing as drastic as that, sir. Just routine exercises."

"You can cut the crap, Ike. Something's going on, and I need to know what it is."

"I'm not sure _anything_ is going on, Mr. President; but you're right—you _do_ need to know what's in the wind. If you can see me this afternoon, we need to talk in person."

Chapter Twenty-Seven
Thursday, 31 July 1941

For months, ships had been coming into Cuba's southern ports and surreptitiously offloading men and cargo. Then the ships would leave the ports empty, only to return weeks later with their cargo holds full once again.

Today, as the ships left the ports, they were not empty.

Meanwhile, high overhead, a nondescript DC-3 flew along Cuba's southern coastline. No one thought much about it. Commercial DC-3s were coming and going over Cuba all the time.

What those on the ground didn't know, however, was that this unmarked DC-3 was not just another airliner or cargo plane. This one belonged to the First Reconnaissance Wing of the Confederate Army Air Force.

Chapter Twenty-Eight
Friday, 01 August 1941

As he walked the halls of the Navy Department in Washington, D.C., Lieutenant Commander Mike Crofford was sure his career was finished. Twenty-four hours earlier, he had been recalled from his naval attaché post in Havana. His stomach was in knots as he entered the office of Naval Intelligence.

The receptionist looked up from her desk. "May I help you, Commander?"

"Yes, ma'am. I'm Lieutenant Commander Crofford—here to see Captain Fuller."

"Oh yes. He's expecting you," she said in an ominous tone. "Follow me."

As the receptionist led him down one of several passageways leading from the outer office, Mike Crofford, dressed in his summer white uniform, felt conspicuous among the other naval officers, all wearing service dress blues.

"_Here_ we are," the receptionist said, stopping outside Captain Fuller's office. She knocked lightly on the open door. "I have Lieutenant Commander Crofford here, Captain."

"Send him in," came a brusque voice from inside the office.

The receptionist stepped aside, clearing the doorway. As Crofford turned sideways and slid past her into the office, she looked at him somberly, as if she were sending him to his execution. With his hat tucked under his left arm, Crofford marched to the front of Captain Fuller's desk and stood at attention. "Lieutenant Commander Crofford reporting as ordered, sir."

Fuller sat quietly, reading an open file folder on his desktop.

Crofford continued to stand at attention.

After several uncomfortable minutes, Fuller looked up at him with a stern expression on his face. "You're out of uniform, mister. The uniform here in Washington is service dress blues."

Crofford was taken aback. The term "mister" was customarily used when addressing officers below the rank of lieutenant commander. "My apologies, Captain. I only arrived from Havana several hours ago. It won't happen again."

"Do you know why you're here, Commander?"

"I'm not exactly sure, sir."

Fuller rose and walked around to the front of his desk. He placed his face directly in front of Crofford's. "You're not *sure*, Commander?"

"Well, I'm not positive, sir. You see..." Crofford relaxed his posture before continuing. "You see, sir, I'm—"

"I didn't tell you to stand at ease, Commander!"

Crofford snapped back to attention. He wasn't accustomed to being treated like a junior officer. "Sorry, sir. You see...I have an idea why I'm here...but I'm not certain."

"Were you certain the Germans had overrun Cuba, Commander? Fuller took a step back and paused. He turned and walked back to the chair behind his desk. He motioned toward the chair next to Crofford. "Awh *hell*, son—sit down."

Crofford sat.

"Do you realize what you've done, Commander? You didn't just go outside your chain of command and embarrass those of us in this office. You embarrassed the United States Navy. You dishonored the entire United States military! *Hell*, son—*what you did was tantamount to treason!* Did you think we wouldn't find out you called the head of the Confederate military? And what in God's name were you trying to accomplish?"

"I'm sorry, Captain. I didn't know what else to do. I had a good relationship with General Eisenhower back when I taught at the Citadel. I guess I thought he might be able to advise me on how to proceed."

"Proceed with *what*, Commander?"

"I know you don't believe me, sir, but something's going on in Cuba…something big. But I can't confirm it if I'm stuck inside the embassy. I need to get out into the interior of the island and do some digging."

"Well, you can forget about that. You won't be returning to Cuba. You've been relieved as naval attaché."

Crofford sat silently. After several seconds, he stood. He once again placed his hat under his arm and snapped to attention. "Is that all, sir?"

"*No*, Commander Crofford! That is *not* all! Captain Fuller took no pleasure in what he was about to say. He had read Crofford's heretofore exemplary service record. His demeanor suddenly shifted from anger to solemnity. "Crofford, you've been reassigned to my staff pending your court-martial. Report back to my office Monday morning. We'll set you up with a temporary admin assignment."

As Lieutenant Commander Crofford walked dejectedly from Captain Fuller's office, a lieutenant on Fuller's staff passed him in the passageway. "Afternoon, Commander."

Crofford didn't even look at him.

Lieutenant Hank Wilson shrugged off Crofford's breach of etiquette. He stopped outside Fuller's office and rapped on the door.

"Come on in, Hank."

"Sir, we just received an unusual communication from our CSA counterparts in Richmond. I thought you should see it right away."

"What is it?"

"They transmitted a series of facsimiles to us." Lieutenant Wilson handed a red file folder to Captain Fuller. "They're aerial reconnaissance photos from the southern ports in Cuba. I think you'd better take a look at them."

As darkness fell across Southern France, the final chess pieces were being moved into place for the start of Operation *Atlantis*. At a dozen Luftwaffe airfields, wave after wave of German bombers launched into the western sky. Normally, the medium-range Heinkel bombers from these airfields would have turned north and headed across the English Channel for nighttime raids over England.

But these were not Heinkels. These bombers were long-range Messerschmitt Me 264s. They would not turn north for England. They would continue west across the Atlantic—all the way to their staging fields in Puerto Rico.

With a staggering maximum range of 9,320 miles, Adolf Hitler had fondly dubbed the Messerschmitt Me 264 his *"Amerika Bomber."* In less than forty-eight hours, the Me 264s headed for America's doorstep would have an opportunity to live up to their billing.

<u>*Chapter Twenty-Nine*</u>

Sunday, 03 August 1941

"... few, if any, believed there was any danger the war might someday come to America."

1236 EDT—It was a glorious afternoon for baseball. The blue skies over Ebbets Field were bright and clear behind a line of thunderstorms that had blown through New York City the previous evening. The smell of popcorn and freshly cut grass permeated the unseasonably cool late-summer air.

The Dodgers were still taking batting practice as Toby Pozniak and Marc Krbec descended the steps toward the third row, just behind the visitors' dugout. The crack of the bat striking the ball echoed throughout the half-empty stadium as groups of early-arriving fans made their way from the concourse to their seats.

All along the third-base foul line, directly in front of Pozniak and Krbec, mitts popped in rapid succession as the visiting Boston Braves warmed up almost within reach of the stands. One aisle over from where the two men now took their seats, the familiar cry of "beer here!" rang out from a roving vendor.

"Yoh—over here!" Krbec shouted at the vendor, raising his hand. "We should sit here more often," he said to Pozniak. "Any particular reason you decided to pony up for these high-dollar seats today?"

"I'm celebrating," Pozniak replied, grinning like the cat who ate the canary.

Clumsily hauling a metal ice chest, the beer vendor began sidestepping his way across an empty row of seats, toward Pozniak and Krbec.

Meanwhile, Krbec was trying to size up the expression on his friend's face. "Those eggheads up at Columbia give you a raise or somethin'? If *that's* what's up, you're not just payin' for the tickets, you're buyin' the beers too."

Reaching the aisle next to Krbec's seat, the vendor plopped his heavy ice chest down onto the concrete step and opened it. He pulled a cold bottle from deep down in the ice and popped the top with an opener tied to his apron. Reaching back into the chest, he retrieved a waxed-paper cup that bore the familiar *Dodgers* logo in royal blue script. He poured the beer and handed it to Krbec, who passed it to Pozniak. The vendor repeated the routine and handed the second beer to Krbec, who gave him two bucks. "Keep the change," Krbec said as he turned to resume his conversation with Pozniak. "Okay, pal. You gonna tell me what's goin' on, or *not?*"

"You're not gonna believe it."

"Believe *what?* Just tell me already."

"I asked Natalie to marry me last night." Pozniak waited for the animated response he was certain would be forthcoming from his longtime friend—nothing.

"*And?*" Krbec asked.

"What do you mean, '*and?*'"

"What did she say?"

"She said '*yes*,' you knucklehead. What do you *think* she said?"

"That's great, Toby boy! That's great! Krbec paused for several seconds, not knowing what to say next. Then he punched his friend hard on the shoulder. "Why don't you *tell* somebody before you go off and get engaged?"

Pozniak rubbed his shoulder. "I didn't think I needed your permission," he said, laughing.

"So—when are you two lovebirds gonna tie the knot?"

"In January, when I get back from Chicago."

"Why not before you leave? You could take Natalie with you."

"We considered that, but I leave in four weeks. Natalie said she and her mother need more time to plan a wedding."

"Plan *schman*," Krbec said sarcastically. "You pick a day the synagogue and the rabbi are available, and *bam*—you got yourself a wedding plan."

Yeah, *well*…dream on, pal. Trust me when I say it doesn't quite work that way with women. Her mom's gonna turn this thing into a big-time production."

Just then, a loud voice reverberated over the public address system. "Ladies and gentlemen—welcome to Ebbets Field for today's game between the Boston Braves and the Brooklyn Dodgers."

Just north of the National Mall, at the Office of Naval Intelligence, Captain Chauncey "Chace" Fuller was in his Washington, D.C., office. He and his exhausted staff had been working almost nonstop since Friday afternoon, poring over a series of aerial reconnaissance photos taken four days earlier. The CAAF photos showed a large number of ships leaving several of the ports along Cuba's southern coast. Though none were Kriegsmarine (German Navy) warships, many of them did appear to be transporting military hardware.

The ships on which no topside cargo was visible presented even more cause for concern. Most of them were large bulk-cargo ships. Ships of this type had steel doors above their cargo holds. The doors were normally closed when the vessels were under way, but the ships in the reconnaissance photos were steaming with the cargo holds open. The doors might have been propped open to provide fresh air for personnel being transported belowdecks. Fuller and his staff couldn't be sure because the resolution of the photos wasn't sufficient to see inside the dark interiors of the holds. If those bulk-cargo ships *were* filled with German troops, it meant that, based on the number of ships in the photos, they could be transporting well over 100,000 troops.

To where? And for what purpose?

Captain Fuller was hoping against hope that the obvious answers to those questions were not the reality. He had already alerted Admiral Harold Stark, chief of naval operations, about the reconnaissance photos. Admiral Stark had been dismissive of the report; but just to be safe, he had ordered every ship capable of putting out to sea to blockade the waters off the Mid Atlantic Coast. If there *was* to be an amphibious invasion, Stark speculated it would take place in proximity to Washington, D.C.

That view was shared by the Army's chief of staff, General George C. Marshall, though he also doubted the threat was real. Marshall had passed the intelligence along to General Douglas MacArthur, who was in command of the U.S. Army's two East Coast divisions. MacArthur had put his units on alert but had seen no reason to reposition them along the coastline.

Maybe this actually is a false alarm, Captain Fuller thought to himself. The more Fuller thought about it, the more he was able to convince himself there was nothing to the shadowy reconnaissance photos. If all those ships were getting under way to launch an amphibious invasion, they would have seen landing craft in the photos. They didn't really know what was in those cargo holds…and they had yet to see a single German warship.

A hundred miles east of Washington, D.C., a Kriegsmarine task force was steaming west at 17 knots. At 39 degrees north latitude, the task force was several hundred miles south of the U.S. convoy routes, hoping to avoid detection. The armada included three of Germany's six heavy cruisers, as well as two K-class light cruisers and dozens of destroyers and smaller combatants. At the center of the formation was KMS *Tirpitz*—the Battleship *Bismarck's* massive sister ship. If they maintained their steady course of 267 degrees, the task force would arrive off Cape May, at the entrance to Delaware Bay, in just under five hours. But Washington, D.C., was not their objective. The ships would soon alter course.

Seventy miles farther east, a massive formation of bombers was slowly passing above an even larger formation of trimotor transport planes. Flying at 1,000 feet over the Atlantic, the nearly three hundred planes in the lower formation were carrying three battalions of lightly armed paratroopers and five battalions of fully equipped airborne assault troops—almost five thousand German soldiers.

1428 EDT—At Ebbets Field, the Boston Braves had just put up three runs in the top of the fifth inning to take a 4-2 lead over the hometown Dodgers. Boston pitcher Jim Tobin had just started throwing his warmup tosses in the bottom half of the inning. At the top of the right field scoreboard, the clock on the Schaefer Beer sign read 2:28 p.m.

Tobin zipped a fastball to Al Montgomery, crouched behind the plate. The Braves' catcher stood and cocked his arm, preparing to toss the ball back to his pitcher. Standing on the mound, Tobin watched in bewilderment as the catcher suddenly halted his throwing motion. Staring out toward right field, Montgomery slowly lowered his arm and dropped the baseball in the dirt. From where he was standing at home plate, the massive swarm of approaching airplanes appeared to black out the entire sky. The breathtaking stream of Me 264s seemed to trail into infinity as the leading edge of the formation overflew the steel light standards atop the southern rim of the ballpark.

Soon, everyone in the stadium was fixated on the hundreds of bombers passing overhead. The roar from the planes' engines was earsplitting. No one knew what to do. Even as the trail planes in the formation were still visible from Ebbets Field, the distant sound of bombs exploding at the Brooklyn Navy Yard sent the crowd into a panic.

As Marc Krbec made a move toward the aisle, Toby Pozniak grabbed him by the arm. *"You need to drive me to the city!"* Pozniak shouted. *"I've gotta get to Natalie!"*

At the Office of Naval Intelligence, Captain Chace Fuller was just about to head home. He had finally managed to convince himself that the mysterious cargo in the reconnaissance photos had been nothing more than large commercial shipments back to Spain.

As Fuller buttoned his uniform jacket and reached to take his hat from the coatrack next to the door, Lieutenant Hank Wilson burst into his office. "It's *New York*, sir!"

"What?"

"New York City, Captain. Hundreds of German bombers—*as we speak!*"

"But that can't be," Fuller declared. "Bombers from *where?*"

"We're not sure. We think they might be out of Puerto Rico…maybe Cuba."

Captain Fuller's mind began to race. "Get me a map of New York and the surrounding beaches," he barked as he headed down the passageway to a large conference room. "Do Admiral Stark and General Marshall know? And get all our people in here—*now!*"

A thousand feet above Floyd Bennett Field, four miles southeast of the Dodgers' now-empty baseball stadium, nineteen Ju 52s were streaming German paratroopers from their cargo doors. Three hundred and forty-two parachutes descended onto the grass infield bounded by the New York Naval Air Station's three concrete runways. Once on the ground, the paratroopers quickly shed their parachutes and formed themselves into six-man squads. They fanned out from the center of the airfield, making their way toward the surrounding buildings.

It was over in less than twenty minutes. The few Navy sailors and U.S. Marines who did manage to lay their hands on weapons were quickly killed or captured by the marauding German paratroopers.

To the west, at the entrance to New York Harbor, the same scenario was unfolding at Brooklyn's Fort Hamilton and Staten Island's Fort Wadsworth. Although some of the paratroopers missed their drop zones and drowned in the Verrazano Narrows, the majority of them landed without warning in the middle of both installations. The U.S. Army soldiers at both bases were quickly defeated by the German attackers. Many of the defenders, unable to retrieve rifles from locked armories, surrendered without a fight.

All of the huge 16-inch gun batteries that guarded the entrance to America's busiest harbor quickly fell into German hands.

As Toby Pozniak and Marc Krbec raced toward Krbec's car, the bombs decimating the Brooklyn Navy Yard were still booming in the distance.

Now, a second wave of planes began flying over their heads. They flew lower and slower than the bombers that had passed overhead minutes earlier. They flew so low that the black and white swastikas on their tails were clearly visible from the ground. Pozniak and Krbec stopped momentarily to watch them pass. They looked on in disbelief as, first one—then a dozen—and finally, hundreds of white streamers inflated over the northern end of Prospect Park, two miles from the entrances to the Brooklyn and Manhattan Bridges.

As the parachutes filled the sky above the entrances to the bridges, Marc Krbec looked at Toby Pozniak. "I don't think we're gonna make it into the city today, pal. We gotta get off the streets."

As the several hundred paratroopers who had landed in Prospect Park moved to secure the two bridges that linked Brooklyn to Lower Manhattan, farther north, several squadrons of Me 264s were pummeling the Williamsburg and Queensboro bridges.

Unchallenged, the heavy bombers were able to accurately deliver their bombs from low altitude. Both bridges fell into the East River. The only alternate passage from the Atlantic Ocean into New York Harbor had been rendered unnavigable. The entrance through the Verrazano Narrows was now the only waterway in or out of the most strategic port in America—and the Germans already controlled it.

At the same time, long lines of Ju 52s were landing on the German-held runways at Floyd Bennett Field. Each plane that touched down carried eighteen heavily equipped airborne assault troops. As soon as the planes rolled to a stop on the large grass infield, the combat-ready troops disembarked. Half of them marched north, toward the two bridges already secured by the initial wave of paratroopers. The other half marched south, across the Marine Parkway Bridge, toward Rockaway Beach and the heavy gun batteries located at Fort Tilden. With the Fort Hamilton and Fort Wadsworth batteries already in German hands, the Fort Tilden guns were the only remaining coastal defenses capable of preventing German vessels from entering the harbor unmolested.

By this time, the soldiers at Fort Tilden were ready for the invading Germans. A fierce battle ensued at the southern end of the bridge, near the entrance to the base. The Fort Tilden defenders extracted a heavy toll from the Germans; but after a half hour of intense fighting, they were overwhelmed by the sheer number of attackers pouring across the bridge.

With all the New York City military installations now in German hands, there remained only one objective for the Nazi invaders—the huge complex of piers along Manhattan's west side.

The only rapid response assets the U.S. military could muster were two fighter squadrons out of McGuire Army Airfield, in New Jersey. Because it was a Sunday afternoon, most of the pilots were scattered throughout the town. By the time the first P-40 *Warhawks* arrived over New York City, the German columns had already advanced into Lower Manhattan.

Several of the P-40s made strafing runs, taking out a number of German paratroopers unlucky enough to be caught crossing the Brooklyn and Manhattan Bridges. But because of the cover provided by the urban environment, the American pilots' efforts to dissuade the invaders from moving westward through the city were ineffective.

The advancing German troops continued unabated toward the strategic piers along the Hudson River.

In Washington, D.C., details of the attack were, at best, sporadic. Most of the information available to the higher-ups was coming in the form of news bulletins over the public airwaves.

In the large conference room at the Office of Naval Intelligence, Captain Fuller and his staff were trying to piece together the puzzle. Why were the Germans attacking New York instead of Washington? Where were the cargo ships from the reconnaissance photos? More importantly, were there any German warships off the coast?

The answer to the last question came when the U.S. Coast Guard reported receiving a frantic radio message from a commercial fishing vessel near Long Island. The ship's captain had sent out a distress call after his vessel began taking fire from two destroyers in the KMS *Tirpitz* task force. The incident had occurred forty miles south of Jones Beach. Before going silent in the middle of his transmission, the captain had reported the task force was headed north.

"This makes no sense," Lieutenant Wilson said to Captain Fuller. "It looks like their target for the landing is Jones Beach—but where are the landing craft? We know they're not on the cargo ships. Are they being transported with the task force?"

Captain Fuller was silent for several seconds. Finally, he turned to Lieutenant Wilson with a look of stunned realization. "There *are* no landing craft," he said grimly. "There isn't going to be an amphibious assault. Jones Beach isn't the target. They're headed straight for New York Harbor. And here we sit with our entire Navy parked two hundred miles south. There's not a *damn* thing we can do to stop them."

"My *God*," Wilson exclaimed. "If they get those cargo ships into the harbor, they can offload a hundred thousand troops in a matter of hours."

In Berlin, Adolf Hitler and Hermann Göring were ecstatic. The reports they were receiving from Field Marshal Friedrich von Essen communicated a perfectly executed blitzkrieg. In one afternoon, the Nazi war machine had seized the most important harbor in the United States of America. All but three of the long-range Me 264 bombers had made it back to Puerto Rico, and every single Ju 52 had landed safely at Floyd Bennett Field.

Field Marshal von Essen's plan had been audacious. He had recognized that relying on a few hundred lightly armed paratroopers to take the New York Naval Air Station would be a roll of the dice. The JU 52s, despite being fitted with auxiliary fuel tanks, only carried a ferry range of 1,440 miles. They had flown 1,330 miles from Cuba. Without those runways, the low-on-fuel Ju 52s, carrying more than four thousand airborne assault troops, would have had to make forced landings twenty miles to the north, at the New York Municipal Airport in Queens. With no mechanized assets available during the airborne phase of the invasion, that would have necessitated a march through city streets. At best, it would have taken the better part of a day for the heavily equipped troops to reach their objectives, giving the U.S. military time to intervene.

But Von Essen's men had executed his plan flawlessly. It could not have been more perfect.

Back in D.C., as Captain Fuller's fatigued staff continued to work well into the evening, Lieutenant Commander Mike Crofford appeared at the entrance to the large conference area. The room gradually fell silent as, one by one, those gathered around the long table stopped what they were doing and looked toward Crofford.

Captain Chace Fuller was an austere, no-nonsense naval officer. He was not about to tolerate a theatrical display of disrespect from someone under his command—not even from someone who had been unjustly accused of impropriety. Fuller looked Crofford squarely in the eyes. "Evening, Commander Crofford. You come to revel in your vindication?"

"Not at all, Captain. I came ready to work. I'm at your disposal."

Disarmed by the younger officer's deference, Fuller's forbidding expression slowly changed to one of countenance. He motioned Crofford into the room as he spoke. "Very well, Commander. Work you shall."

Chapter Thirty

Monday, 04 August 1941

As dawn broke over the Brooklyn Navy Yard, yesterday's blue skies were a distant memory. Smog from the still-smoldering fires filled the harbor, partially obscuring the extent of the devastation.

The once-bustling shipyard was in ruins.

It could have been even worse. The attack had come on a Sunday afternoon, which meant that most of the shipbuilders and other civilian employees had been spared. Also, many of the military personnel stationed there had been away on weekend liberty. Even so, more than two thousand lives had been lost. Many of those killed were senior naval officers living in a section of base housing known as Admiral's Row.

All along the piers and dry docks inside the main basin, giant gantries had collapsed into grotesque heaps of twisted steel. Just north of the main basin, along one of several piers that jutted into the East River, shreds of decorative red, white and blue bunting lay scorched and tattered, strewn throughout the debris from a flattened wooden grandstand. Alongside the pier, directly in front of the fallen grandstand, the USS _Washington_ had settled to the bottom.

Preordained to become the pride of the U.S. Navy's fleet, the mighty battleship's badly damaged superstructure was now all that was visible. Just four days before celebrating the completion of their ship in what was to have been a grand commissioning ceremony, eight hundred and twelve of her crew members had been violently entombed inside the bowels of her hull.

Not long after daybreak, those New York City residents with a view of the outer harbor were witnesses to a surreal scene—the foreboding image of the KMS *Tirpitz* task force steaming past the Statue of Liberty. In the task force's wake, a convoy of bulk cargo ships was making its way north, toward the Hudson River and the huge complex of piers along Manhattan's west side. Each was heavily laden with German troops and military hardware. Perhaps even more unsettling was the long line of German cargo ships headed *out* of the harbor—those that had already offloaded their deadly consignments during the previous night.

In Prospect Heights, Toby Pozniak and Marc Krbec hunkered down inside Krbec's row house. Like most New York City residents, they were afraid to venture out onto the streets. During the initial hours of the invasion, Pozniak had repeatedly telephoned Saul Rosenbaum's residence in Lower Manhattan, trying desperately to reach Natalie. All during the night, the switchboards had been inundated. None of the calls had gotten through. Then, as morning approached, the lines had gone dead.

Pozniak and Krbec, along with most of their fellow residents, were now riveted to the radio. With the New York City stations off the air, they were listening to WBYN, out of Newark, New Jersey. With each passing hour, the continuous news bulletins painted a more desperate picture.

The U.S. Army had reportedly begun mobilizing out of Fort Dix, in New Jersey, but they were still nowhere to be seen in or around New York City. Around midmorning, more P-40s from McGuire

Army Airfield began strafing the Manhattan piers, but it was too little too late. Many of the U.S. fighters were lost to anti-aircraft fire from the *Tirpitz* and the other German warships supporting the invasion from inside the harbor.

Through it all, the Germans kept flooding more troops and hardware, including tanks and planes, onto the New York City piers. As quickly as the crates containing fuselages and wings from Luftwaffe fighters were offloaded, they were transported to Floyd Bennett Field and quickly reassembled. By late afternoon, less than eighteen hours after they had been delivered in the initial wave of late-night cargo ships, the first Messerschmitt Bf 109s were providing critical air cover above the piers.

By early evening, a full panzer division—a hundred and ninety tanks, along with twenty thousand soldiers—was rolling through the Holland and Lincoln Tunnels. The sight of German tanks emerging on the New Jersey side of the river caused many residents there to angrily question why their own military was still nowhere in sight.

In Washington, President Roosevelt was rapidly losing patience with General MacArthur. He wanted MacArthur to advance his two East Coast divisions toward the invading Germans without delay.

MacArthur was slow to react. He was reluctant to use his limited resources offensively. Instead, he chose to fall back and form a defensive line around the nation's capital. The Americans under siege in and around New York City had no way to know that the assets from Fort Dix were not advancing toward the Nazi invaders. As those trapped behind the German lines waited to be rescued, the U.S. Army was retreating southward.

As night fell, Douglas MacArthur scrambled to organize his defenses around the D.C. perimeter. Inside the Oval Office, Franklin Delano Roosevelt sat despondent. Rolling his wheelchair back, he slowly spun it away from his desk. As he stared through the window onto the darkened White House grounds, he wondered how this could have happened.

The more he thought about it, the more Adolf Hitler's decision to invade America began to make sense. Roosevelt's Lend-Lease agreement with Winston Churchill had transformed the U.S. into what Roosevelt himself had described as "the great arsenal of democracy." Instead of trying to sink the convoys after they were en route to England, Hitler had elected to shut off the massive flow of badly needed military supplies at the source. In doing so, the Nazis had also extended the Third Reich into the Western Hemisphere. By co-opting America's vast resources, Hitler hoped to achieve world domination.

The president now wondered if he had made a terrible mistake. While turning out weapons to prop up Churchill and the British, he had allowed his own military to linger in a state of unreadiness. As he thought about it in retrospect, he realized his actions had made it much too easy for Hitler to believe he could successfully invade America.

While FDR despaired inside the White House, the mood inside the Reichstag was one of elation. Adolf Hitler and his staff were becoming more confident with every report they received. Field Marshal von Essen's invasion was succeeding well beyond their greatest expectations.

When they received word that the 24th Panzer Division had secured the piers on the New Jersey side of the Hudson, it seemed as though Operation *Atlantis* was going to be over in a matter of weeks. With more than a hundred thousand German soldiers already ashore and two million more en route, the ground invasion that had begun with a few hundred paratroopers was now in full stride.

During the leadup to the invasion, the German high command had seemingly planned for every contingency. But despite their attention to even the smallest detail, they had overlooked an important intangible.

Hitler and his staff had known that America's military was weak. They had assumed that America's resolve would be weak as well. It was a serious misjudgment. New Yorkers were already beginning to defy the Nazi invaders. At City Hall in Lower Manhattan, Fiorello H. La Guardia, New York's pugnacious mayor, refused to cooperate with SS General Ernst Kruger's staff. In several Brooklyn neighborhoods, residents hurled bricks and bottles at German soldiers as they marched in the streets. Although their efforts were disorganized and ineffective, they represented the genesis of an American resistance movement.

In Richmond, Virginia, an even greater German miscalculation was about to manifest itself. While Operation *Atlantis* had caught President Roosevelt and General MacArthur flat-footed, President Truman and General Eisenhower had anticipated the German invasion. All along the northern border of Virginia, the Confederate military was cocked and ready.

Prior to the invasion, Adolf Hitler had dismissed the possibility that the Confederate States of America might come to the aid of their former enemy. Had he possessed even a modicum of insight into the Southern psyche, the German Führer would have recognized the danger in making such an assumption. Even the staunchest Confederate isolationists were loath to stand by and watch the Nazis overrun their northern neighbors.

At seven minutes before midnight, Eisenhower sat across from Truman at his desk. The general watched as the Confederate president picked up the telephone. "Miss Conway," he said calmly, "you may place the call to President Roosevelt now."

More than three thousand miles away, initial reports of the invasion were still coming across the BBC airwaves.

At RAF Lindholme, Rod Hurley and the other North American volunteers of No. 121 squadron gathered around the console radio in the corner of their briefing room. As they listened to the news reports, the men knew their days flying for England were numbered.

In the coming weeks, they would be returning to fight in the skies above their own homeland.

Chapter Thirty-One
Tuesday, 05 August 1941

Less than forty-eight hours after the first bombs had dropped on New York City, President Harry S. Truman stood before a combined session of the Confederate Congress and called for a declaration of war against Germany. The lawmakers were unaware that four divisions of Confederate troops had already moved north across the border. Eighty years had passed since Confederate soldiers last set foot inside the state of Maryland. This time, however, they were there, not as adversaries—but as allies. This time, they were there at the behest of the U.S. president.

Truman was not a particularly talented orator, but he delivered an impassioned, compelling speech that lasted twenty-two minutes. When he closed, the chamber erupted into thunderous applause. Even those who were hard-line isolationists stood and joined in the ovation.

It took only three hours for the declaration to formally pass both houses of the Confederate Congress.

Chapter Thirty-Two
Wednesday, 06 August 1941

The U.S. Military was in disarray. Both of MacArthur's East Coast divisions, one armored and one infantry, were retreating toward their own capital. Field Marshal Friedrich von Essen's forces were advancing faster than MacArthur's forces could retreat. More importantly, the Germans were bringing thousands of troops and tons of equipment ashore by the hour.

General George S. Patton was incensed. He understood that the retreat was playing into von Essen's hands. He recognized that the best chance to thwart the invasion was to advance on New York City and attack the port facilities before the Germans had a chance to strengthen their foothold. Watching his tanks roll southward instead of northward was agonizing to Patton.

General Dwight Eisenhower understood the situation as well. All four of his Confederate divisions were headed up the coast at a breakneck pace. His goal was to put as much real estate as he could behind his army before they made contact with the invading Germans. Despite their status as allies, Eisenhower and MacArthur were executing opposing strategies.

Back in Washington, D.C., it didn't take long for Franklin Roosevelt to make his first critical wartime decision. He placed an emergency phone call to Richmond, Virginia. Roosevelt and Truman quickly decided to appoint General Eisenhower as Supreme Commander of the North American Allied Forces.

Eisenhower's first action as commander of the combined North American military was to countermand MacArthur's retreat order. He ordered Patton to halt his retreat at the Susquehanna River, just south of the Pennsylvania-Maryland border. His tanks were to take up defensive positions on the south side of the river and make a stand against von Essen's advancing panzer divisions. It was a risky decision. Eisenhower was hoping the Confederates' two armored divisions would reach Patton before the Germans did.

The Susquehanna represented the last best line of defense north of Washington and Richmond. If the Confederate divisions failed to reinforce Patton's defenders in time, the Germans would likely break through his tenuous barricade. If they did, there would be nothing to stop the panzers from rolling into both American capitals.

Patton was just south of Wilmington, Delaware, when he received Eisenhower's order. The Supreme Commander's directive to stand and fight was the first palatable order the hawkish general had received. With von Essen's panzers in close pursuit, Patton raced his tanks down U.S. Highway 40.

He was thirty miles from the mile-long bridge that spanned the Susquehanna.

Chapter Thirty-Three
Thursday, 07 August 1941

Eddie Ramirez was the youngest of four sons in his family. He and his three brothers had grown up in the Barrio Logan section of San Diego, just blocks from the large naval base that served as home port to the U.S. Pacific Fleet.

If someone had asked Maria Ramirez whether there was anything special about her fourth son, she would have been hard-pressed to say that there was. He was not nearly as outgoing or self-assured as his older siblings. Frankly, Eddie's mother, along with his brothers, had always considered Eddie to be a bit of a mollycoddle.

Hector Ramirez, Eddie's late father, had served in the First World War and had retired from the Navy as a chief petty officer. Maria was understandably proud when each of Eddie's older brothers joined the Navy as well.

But Eddie was miserably prone to seasickness. As a child, even on the protected waters of San Diego Bay, he often became violently ill in his father's small fishing boat. So, after graduating from high school, instead of upholding his family's proud tradition, Eddie had opted to join the U.S. Army.

Now, on the fifth day of Adolf Hitler's Operation *Atlantis*, nineteen-year-old Eddie Ramirez was driving one of two hundred and twelve Sherman tanks rumbling toward the Susquehanna River Toll Bridge. An entire U.S. armored division rolling down a four-lane public highway was, in and of itself, a bizarre circumstance. The fact that they were being pursued by three hundred German panzers exponentially compounded the surreal nature of the situation in which Private Ramirez now found himself.

By the time Patton's forces reached the northern bridgehead, the lighter U.S. tanks had managed to separate themselves from their heavier, slower pursuers by almost fifteen miles. Even as the last M4 Shermans were clearing the southern end of the bridge, a team of combat engineers began hastily rigging the bridge for demolition.

On General Patton's order, the Shermans fanned out to both sides of the bridge, taking up positions in the trees on the southern side of the river. There they sat, waiting to engage the Germans, who would likely fan out along the northern shore once the bridge was destroyed.

Working high in the bridge's metal superstructure was proving difficult for the half dozen combat engineers. Forty minutes later, as they were still struggling to rig the charges in the arched framework above the bridge's center span, the head of the German column arrived at the northern end of the bridge. The lead panzer, a *Panzer III*, thundered onto the bridge and opened up on the defenseless engineers with its ported machine guns. The engineers were easy targets. One by one, they fell from the arched trusses onto the deck of the bridge. Their lifeless bodies were crushed beneath the treads of the advancing panzers. The Americans' "last best line of defense" was in danger of being breached.

The German column began rolling across the mile-long bridge that spanned the river. Patton's forces quickly tried to reposition themselves to engage the panzers that were exiting the southern end of the bridge. A chaotic tank battle erupted as the German and American crews began firing shells at one another on the move. The Americans initially had a sizeable numbers advantage, but as the

German column continued pouring across the bridge, more and more *Panzer IIIs* joined the fight.

Following commands from his sergeant, who was looking through a periscope in the top of the turret, Eddie Ramirez drove his tank to within two hundred yards of the point where the Germans were exiting the bridge. He could hardly hear himself think as the gunner inside his tank began firing the 75-millimeter main gun above his head. Ramirez cringed with each blast from the gun. Then he cringed again as each empty shell casing clanked against the Sherman's steel deck. The pungent smell of sweat and spent gunpowder filled the stifling interior of the tank's hull. It was the first taste of battle for every man in the crew.

It would be short lived.

Ramirez's tank had fired only four rounds before it was struck. The armor-piercing shell from the *Panzer III's* gun hit the Sherman at more than twice the speed of sound. It penetrated the hull just below the turret, instantly killing the gunner and loader. The lightly armored American tank should have been destroyed, but the shot had come from close range. The shell's momentum had carried it through the far side of the hull, limiting the damage.

Still, the force of the impact and the resulting shower of shrapnel inside the tank had killed all but one of the Sherman's five crew members. Miraculously, Eddie Ramirez had survived. His leather helmet had been ripped from his head, along with his left ear and a portion of his left cheek. His back and shoulders were full of shrapnel, and his right ear was ringing from the concussion of the impact.

Ramirez was covered in blood, most of it from his dead comrades. The young private was in a state of shock. His senses were totally overwhelmed by the horrific carnage that surrounded him. He climbed through the hatch and stumbled from the tank onto the grass. He dropped to his knees, coughing and vomiting. The deadly blow from the *Panzer III's* gun had abruptly claimed whatever propensity to fight the fledgling warrior might have possessed. In tears, he sprawled himself onto the ground and lay there, facedown—motionless.

Through the ringing in his remaining ear, Ramirez could hear the battle raging around him. He felt the earth shake beneath him with every round that was fired. He smelled the acrid smoke from the exploding shells and burning tanks. Not knowing why, he slowly raised his head and looked toward the Susquehanna Bridge in the distance. Something inexplicably caught his eye. His blurred vision gradually sharpened as he focused his attention on the objects of his curiosity. He could see the network of satchel charges the engineers had strapped to the latticed framework of the bridge's superstructure.

The German column continued to advance, bludgeoning its way across the bridge.

Ramirez rolled onto his back. Propping himself up onto his elbows, he looked at the jagged hole where the shell had ripped through the half-inch armor plate on the side of his tank. The Sherman was damaged but still functional. He quickly regained his situational awareness as his mind began to process the deaths of the four men still inside the idling tank. He had known those men. They had been brothers to him, maybe even more so than the three older siblings in whose shadows he had spent his childhood.

Suddenly, the usually meek private swelled with anger. Numb to his wounds, he rose to his feet and climbed back into the tank. Closing the hatch, he ignored the gruesome scene that surrounded him inside the hull. He shifted the tank into gear and drove it away from the southern bridgehead. The front end of the Sherman dipped and rocked as Ramirez headed it straight down the steep bank that led to the edge of the river. After plowing through a row of trees near the bottom of the slope, he braked hard, sending the tank into a sideslip. The spinning Sherman skidded to a stop several yards short of the southern shore, beneath and to one side of the bridge.

Forcefully shoving the remains of the gunner to one side, Ramirez swung the turret toward the arch above the bridge. He raised the main gun and opened the breech. After loading a high-explosive shell, he closed the breech and fired.

The shell struck the superstructure and took out several girders. Ramirez reloaded and fired again, taking out several more girders. The steel debris bounced off the pavement at the bridge's midspan—directly in front of an approaching *Panzer IV*. The panzer commander recognized what was happening and ordered his driver to stop. He opened the top hatch and stood, extending his upper body out of the turret so he could see to either side of the bridge. He waited for the next shot. When it came, he spotted the lone Sherman tank to his left, on the bank of the river.

The German commander shouted the Sherman's relative bearing to his gunner and ordered him to engage it. The gunner trained the turret left and lowered the gun. The first shot from the much heavier *Panzer IV* missed.

Ramirez fired a fourth time, hitting the superstructure again.

The second shell fired from the *Panzer IV* glanced off the side of the Sherman's turret, causing it to rock on its treads. If he was going to survive a third shot, Ramirez desperately needed to cease firing and reposition his tank. Less from courage and more out of a desire for vengeance, Ramirez ignored the incoming fire from the *Panzer IV* and continued to target the trusses directly above it.

The German gunner adjusted his aim. Ramirez adjusted his.

Just then, it was as if the seconds turned to minutes. Time became irrelevant to Eddie. His senses heightened to a level he had never experienced. Even with only one ear, he could hear himself breathing over the reverberation from the battle, which was raging even louder and more intensely than before. He could feel his heart pounding in his chest. He shoved another round into the breech and slammed it shut. As he kissed the crucifix that hung from the same chain as his dog tags, he calmly stepped on the foot pedal that actuated the trigger mechanism. Eddie knew he was drawing his final breath.

The two shells exited their respective muzzles at the same instant. Both found their targets. As Eddie Ramirez died in the explosion that sent the turret of his tank a hundred feet into the air, the shell from his own gun struck one of the satchel charges. The satchel detonated, setting off the remaining charges in rapid succession. The panzer commander heard the creaking and groaning from the metal arches as they gave way overhead. He ducked inside his turret and slammed the hatch. *"Vorwärts!"* he implored the driver. [Forward!]

It was too late. The *Panzer IV* had barely begun to move when it was buried under tons of twisted steel. The tank commander held his breath and waited for the end. He was ecstatic when he realized his sturdy panzer hadn't been crushed. He and his crew had been spared.

A heartbeat later, he and the other four men inside the German tank plummeted to their deaths as the 50,000-pound panzer plunged into the Susquehanna River—along with the midspan section of the bridge.

The panzers on the south side of the fallen bridge, most of them *Panzer IIIs*, continued to fight; but they were now cut off from the bulk of the German column, which was still on the north side of the river. The larger *Panzer IVs* had no way to advance and join the battle.

Not long after the bridge had collapsed, the first of two Confederate armored divisions arrived to reinforce Patton's forces. The tide of the battle quickly turned in favor of the North American Allies. A few of the stranded panzer crews bailed out of their tanks and ran for the banks of the Susquehanna. The remaining German commanders begrudgingly surrendered their vastly outnumbered panzers, ending the bloody fight. The deadly Nazi juggernaut had been halted.

From a bluff overlooking the river, General George Patton had observed the battle from start to finish. From his vantage point above the bridge, the general had been an eyewitness to Private Eddie Ramirez's selfless act of courage.

Several days later, in San Diego, a Western Union delivery man arrived at the home of Maria Ramirez.

After reading that her youngest son had been killed in action, Eddie's mother slumped to her knees and dropped the telegram. Tapping her forehead, she made the sign of the cross. She cried Eddie's name aloud as she fell prostrate onto the ground and pounded it with her fists. The Western Union man tried to console Maria, but she continued crying Eddie's name until all she could do was sob. As the telegram fluttered away in the breeze, the delivery man continued doing his best to comfort Eddie's anguished mother. Maria refused to acknowledge him. Nothing he could say was going to bring Eddie back to her.

Months later, Maria received a certified personal letter from U.S. Secretary of War Henry Stimson. As Eddie's mother sat at her kitchen table reading the narration in her son's citation, she once again began to weep. This time, however, instead of slumping to her knees, Maria got up from her chair. After learning exactly how Eddie had died, she stood, clutching the letter against her heart. Maria Ramirez knew now that her youngest boy had indeed been something special.

Eddie Ramirez had been awarded the Medal of Honor.

Chapter Thirty-Four
15 August 1941

Twelve days had passed since the Nazi invasion. In the days that followed the battle on the Susquehanna, the Germans continued pouring men, supplies and equipment onto the piers in New York Harbor. Now that they had broken out and advanced south, the Nazi invaders were bringing assets ashore at Philadelphia as well. More than two and a half million German troops had moved onto U.S. soil.

With his southern advance halted eighty miles short of the U.S. capital, Field Marshal von Essen began expanding the stalled front to the west, probing for another way to move his forces across the Susquehanna River basin.

Eleven miles upriver, General Eisenhower's Allied forces successfully secured the road across the Conowingo Dam before the Germans could use it as a crossing point. Eisenhower then made a gut-wrenching decision. After sending trucks equipped with loudspeakers to warn residents living downriver, he ordered General Patton to destroy the dam. Most of those on the southern shoreline were evacuated in time; but many residents on the German-held side of the river never heard the broadcasts. Several hundred drowned in the resulting torrent.

As a stalemate developed along the river, armored and infantry forces dug in on both sides. Above them, German and Allied planes battled for air superiority while they strafed and bombed opposing forces on the opposite side of the river.

For the first time since the Civil War, American civilians were caught in the crossfire as their towns became battlegrounds. Ironically, the ground war was concentrated along the old Mason-Dixon Line, which had once separated slave states from free states in pre-Civil War America.

Now, however, it was Americans on the northern side of the line who were subjugated—primarily in Pennsylvania, New Jersey and New York.

Even though Massachusetts and the other New England states were cut off from the rest of America, citizens there were not yet under the boots of the Nazis. Residents in Boston and other major cities were able to move about freely. They also had access to radio newscasts and other sources of information.

The same was not true for Americans trapped behind the German lines in Philadelphia and New York City. Many of them, especially Jewish Americans, were facing an existential crisis.

Toby Pozniak had given up hope of reaching Natalie by telephone. Even though the Rosenbaum's Lower Manhattan residence was less than five miles from his Brooklyn apartment, it might as well have been on the other side of the world.

The Germans had co-opted the switchboards for their own use. The only means of communication available to New York City residents was word of mouth. Because of Nazi-imposed curfews and prohibitions on movement, it was impossible for New Yorkers to contact anyone outside their immediate neighborhoods. No passage was permitted between the five boroughs. The few Brooklynites who had defied the restrictions and attempted to cross into Manhattan or Queens had paid with their lives.

Every local radio station had gone silent. Pozniak barely knew what was going on ten blocks away. He knew nothing of what was transpiring on the other side of the two remaining bridges into Manhattan. With each passing day, he grew more concerned for Natalie's welfare.

To make matters worse, rumors were beginning to circulate about German SS squads sweeping through neighborhoods and rounding up Jews. The Kane Street Synagogue had been ransacked. Every window had been broken. Even more concerning, the synagogue's files, including the membership rolls, had been taken by the raiding SS troops.

Toby Pozniak was desperate to know Natalie's fate.

Meanwhile, Marc Krbec was working behind the scenes to organize a local resistance effort. Krbec had no family, and unlike Toby Pozniak, he had no love interest. Krbec was a man unto himself. The fiery shipbuilder had no intention of allowing himself to be tyrannized by the invading Nazis. As he plotted to create a network of like-minded insurgents, Krbec was careful to exclude Pozniak from his plans. As much as he liked and respected his lifelong friend, he knew he was not a warrior.

In addition to that, Krbec worried Pozniak's obsession with Natalie might cloud his judgment. He thought it better not to entangle his pal in such a dangerous undertaking.

<u>*Chapter Thirty-Five*</u>
16 August 1941

Group Captain Rod Hurley was incredulous when the order came down that night. He recognized right away what it meant. His squadron—his men—had become expendable.

Rod Hurley's aircrews were among the most decorated in the RAF. The planners at British Bomber Command understood that No. 121 Squadron would soon be standing down permanently. Nearly all the squadron's North American volunteers had submitted letters of resignation. As volunteers, they were not obligated to wait for their official releases, but they had agreed to do so as a matter of courtesy to the British government.

Now, within days of their discharges, they were being asked to do something no other RAF bomber squadron was being asked to do—fly a daytime, low-level raid against one of the most heavily defended targets in occupied France.

The U-boat pens at Saint-Nazaire were fortified beyond anything else the Nazis had constructed. The fourteen pens along the entrance to the Loire River were collectively covered by twenty-six feet of reinforced concrete. Atop the mammoth concrete slab was the most extensive array of anti-aircraft defenses west of Berlin. In addition, the Luftwaffe had stationed four Fw 190 and three Bf 109 squadrons at two airfields close to the pens. The RAF's previous raids on the pens, all flown at night, had been both ineffective and costly. Rod Hurley knew he was being ordered to send his men on a suicide mission.

The following morning, as his aircrews noisily assembled for the mission brief, every man knew something was not right. An early-morning brief could mean only one thing—a daylight raid. There was much conjecture, none of it positive, among the anxious crews. At precisely 0700, the squadron adjutant entered at the back of the large hall, stepped to one side of the door, and shouted above the noise from the talking aircrews. "Atten...*hut!*"

The men stood and snapped to attention as Group Captain Rod Hurley entered the hall. He marched down the aisle with his adjutant following behind. As the pair climbed the several steps that led to the briefing platform, Hurley, without looking back, told his men to take their seats.

When he turned to address them, his men could see the troubled look on Hurley's face. Gazing down from the elevated platform, he stood motionless and silent for several seconds. Each man felt as if his CO was looking straight at him. Hurley turned and motioned for his adjutant to pull back the curtain on the giant briefing map. A wave of murmurs swept across the disbelieving aircrews. John Spence, Hurley's petulant navigator, sprang to his feet. "This is total *bullshit*, Colonel!" The hall fell silent as the astonished airmen waited to see how their CO would respond to Spence's outburst.

His expression unchanged, Hurley looked down at his navigator and said nothing. He turned around and faced the map as Spence sat back down. With his hands behind his back, Hurley appeared to study the map intensely. Finally, he turned and faced his men again. "Flight Lieutenant Spence is absolutely correct," he announced to the surprise of everyone in the room. "This absolutely *is* bullshit. Each of you is here as a volunteer. Each of you has performed your duties with honor. Now, with our homeland under attack, you and I are doing what anyone in our position would do. We're asking to return home so we can fight the enemy *there*, where our countrymen—and our families—are under attack. No one can fault us for that decision"

Hurley paused for several seconds, choosing his words carefully. "It's obvious what the RAF brass is doing by sending us on this mission. They're attempting to squeeze every drop of blood from 121 Squadron before standing us down. We don't have to do this. We can simply refuse to fly today. And we might do just that."

Every man listening was dumbstruck. They had never heard this kind of talk from their CO.

Hurley continued. "Before we make that decision, however, let's look at this thing logically. If we fly today, there's a chance—a very *good* chance—that we don't come back. There's also a chance, even if we refuse to fly this mission, that we won't get home to America. Ships are going down every day. It's not a given that our transport makes it back across the Atlantic. We might even be blown out of the water by one of the U-boats out of Saint-Nazaire."

A few in the room nodded in agreement.

"So…here's the deal, gentlemen. I'm not going to stand up here and try to con you into signing up for what is likely to be a one-way mission. If any man in a crew wishes to opt out, that entire crew will stand down today. God knows you've already given more than you owe to the Brits. I promise you—no one will think less of you if you sit this one out. I certainly won't. I wanna get home to my family as badly as you do."

Hurley paused again. He looked squarely at Flight Lieutenant Spence. "John, you and the rest of the *Yellow Rose* crew talk it over among yourselves. If you choose to stay back, I'll lead the mission from another aircraft. For those of you who decide to fly with me, we'll resume this briefing in one hour."

Group Captain Rod Hurley stepped down from the platform. Every member of 121 Squadron rose to stand at attention as their commanding officer marched to the back of the hall and out through the door.

As the men in 121 Squadron took stock of their situation in Lindholme, it was still pitch dark over Long Island Sound. Just inside the entrance to Port Jefferson Harbor, the moonless night bore no witness to the wake from the periscope. The water in the main channel of the harbor was dead calm. Slowly, placidly…quietly, the USS *Billfish*, a *Balao*-class submarine of the United States Navy, breached the surface a mile from the port.

As soon as the submarine's upper hull was above the waterline, three men emerged from the hatch on her forward deck. One of the men, clad in civilian clothes, looked out across the harbor as the other two knelt and hauled up a heavy, cigar-shaped object that was passed to them through the hatch. As the two deckhands unfurled the black rubber raft onto the deck, the third man reached back into the hatch and accepted his duffel bag.

One of the deckhands returned to the hatch and hauled up two oars. The other jerked hard on a lanyard, discharging the CO_2 canister that inflated the raft. The two deckhands saluted the third man and scurried back belowdecks, securing the hatch behind them.

Alone in the darkness, the third man took his place in the raft and waited. As the submarine slipped beneath the surface, water cascaded across both sides of her curved steel hull and converged beneath the wooden slats that formed the flat portion of her deck. The resulting confluence percolated up between the slats and gently floated the raft away from the submerging sub. Facing aft, the man watched the superstructure disappear back into the water. He placed the oars into the rowing fulcrums on either side of the raft and began sculling his way toward Port Jefferson, two thousand yards away.

By the time he reached land, the eastern sky was glowing faintly on the horizon. Still under cover of darkness, he steered away from the port facility and beached his raft on a strip of secluded shoreline. He dragged the raft into some nearby woods and deflated it. After burying it there, he made his way through the dormant town to the local train station.

The station was dark and empty. The Long Island Railroad hadn't run for three weeks—not since the first day of the invasion.

He sat alone on the platform. Reaching into his duffel bag, he removed a Navy-issue Colt .45 pistol and tucked it into his outer coat pocket. Then he reached back into the bag and pulled out a box of C-rations. He opened the cardboard carton and retrieved one of the tin cans and a P-38 can opener. After unfolding the P-38's sharp edge, he used it to puncture the lid. He worked the tiny opener around the edge of the can, carefully peeling it open. Sitting and thinking, he ate all three hardtack biscuits before tossing the can into the nearby woods, where it wouldn't be found.

Reaching back into the carton, he removed a pack of Chesterfields. He opened the pack and turned it upside down, tapping it against the palm of his hand until a single cigarette protruded from the rest. Taking the cigarette with his lips, he reached inside his coat and slipped the pack into his shirt pocket. From the same pocket, he took out a Zippo lighter and flicked the lid open. After lighting the cigarette, he flicked the lighter shut with a distinctive click and returned it to his pocket. He took a long, deep draw and held it for several seconds. Exhaling, he leaned forward and looked westward, down the dark and lonely tracks.

Finally, he stood and walked to the edge of the platform. He tossed the duffel down onto the ground beside the tracks. He squatted, placing his hand on the platform, and leapt down beside his bag.

He picked it up and began walking.

As the lone figure began his silent trek toward New York City, eighteen bombers climbed into a clear, midday sky over RAF

Lindholme. Every available B-17 under Rod Hurley's command was flying.

In the nose of the lead aircraft, navigator John Spence plotted a southward course, toward the submarine pens at Saint-Nazaire. All eighteen of the aircrews—a hundred and eighty members of 121 Squadron—were knowingly flying into the teeth of a Nazi buzz saw on what was to be their final mission in the RAF.

Reaching the English Channel, the formation altered its course to the southwest, around the western tip of the French coastline. No longer flying in trail formation as they had done during their nighttime raids, the bombers were tightly grouped into three flights. Rod Hurley and the other *Yellow Rose* crew members were at the front of the lead flight, which consisted of six *Flying Fortresses* in a box formation. Below and to their left was another box of six, trailing slightly behind. Also trailing slightly behind, above and to their right, were six more.

It was a formation designed to concentrate their defensive firepower. Any German fighter attacking a B-17 within the formation would be vulnerable to machine gun fire from at least five other bombers. Unfortunately, the tightly packed formation—flying low, at just 4,000 feet—would also make it that much easier for the anti-aircraft gunners on the ground to target the bombers with their deadly flak.

The mission began going badly as soon as the formation rounded the western reaches of the French coast. As they turned southeastward, toward the submarine pens, the bombers were jumped by all seven fighter squadrons out of Saint-Nazaire. The gunners inside the B-17s were quickly overwhelmed. Beginning at the rear of both the low and high boxes, the Fw 190s and Bf 109s began chewing up the formation, one B-17 at a time. By the time Rod Hurley's bombers reached their IP and started the bomb run, he had already lost half his squadron.

As what was left of the formation continued toward the target, the swarm of fighters suddenly peeled away. Then came the flak from the 88-millimeter guns. Halfway through the bomb run, copilot Thomas Damron was struck in the thigh by shrapnel that had penetrated the right side of the fuselage. He took the scarf from his neck and tied it around his leg to stop the bleeding.

From his bombardier station, Mark Lorance took control of the *Yellow Rose*. He struggled to make the necessary bombsight adjustments as the B-17 was tossed about violently in the storm of exploding shells from the German 88s.

More of the attacking bombers fell from the formation as it neared the target.

Finally, Lorance released his bombs. On his cue, the other bombardiers released theirs at the same time. Most of the bombs fell harmlessly into the Loire River. The few that did hit their mark did only minor damage to the reinforced concrete pens.

As the remaining B-17s turned toward home, the Germans granted them no clemency. After having survived the flak, Rod Hurley and his crew were once again attacked by fighters near the entrance to the English Channel. Stan Kempema, the ball turret gunner, was killed during the first of more than two dozen passes by the unforgiving Luftwaffe pilots. The German fighters were methodically conducting a merciless execution, strafing the wounded formation from above and below.

Inside the nose bay, John Spence had exhausted his entire belt of ammunition. In a futile act of defiance, he pulled the .50 caliber machine gun from its port and tossed it aside. He ripped his sidearm from the shoulder holster on his flight suit and began firing it through the empty port.

After sustaining multiple hits, the *Yellow Rose* lost both her inboard engines and fell out of formation. One of the Fw 190 pilots followed her down, continuing to pound the badly damaged bomber with his two wing-mounted 20-millimeter cannons. When one of the two still-operating engines caught fire less than 500 feet above the water, he broke off the attack, assuming the B-17 was finished.

Inside the *Yellow Rose's* cockpit, Thomas Damron had already feathered the props on the two inboard engines to stop them from spinning. When the number four engine caught fire, Damron reached down to secure the number four fuel valve on the center console. Rod Hurley reached out and stopped him. *"Let it burn!"* Hurley shouted. "At least it's makin' power! We're gonna put her down in the channel!"

The crew frantically prepared to ditch. John Spence quickly calculated their position and carried it back to Garry Crain in the radio compartment. Crain transmitted it over the British Air/Sea Rescue frequency. Seconds later, Crain and Spence were thrown against the bulkhead immediately forward of the radio operator's station.

Water began to rush into the fuselage through the shattered ball turret and the seams in the bomb bay doors. Crain had dislocated his shoulder. In excruciating pain, he stood and reached with his one good arm to pull the life raft deployment handles at the top of the bulkhead. On the uppermost sides of the fuselage, two external doors fell open. Two five-man life rafts, one on either side, inflated and unfurled onto the wings of the sinking bomber.

Spence was momentarily dazed. His face was covered in blood from a large gash on his forehead. Lying flat on his back inside the radio compartment, he felt himself losing consciousness. A surge of cold water rushed over his body, reviving his senses. His first instinct was to scramble out through the radio compartment hatch behind Garry Crain. As he grabbed a steel frame and pulled himself to his feet, he realized Mark Lorance was still in the nose of the sinking aircraft. While the other crew members were scrambling out through their nearest emergency exits, Spence scrambled forward, through the rapidly flooding bomb bay.

When he reached the nose section, he could see Lorance, with his head barely above the rising water, struggling to free himself from his parachute harness. The harness had become entangled around the bombsight pedestal and wouldn't budge. Within seconds, the water had rushed over the panicked bombardier's face.

Spence took a deep breath and dove down to help Lorance. Both men groped desperately at the harness release, but it was jammed. Spence came back up for another gulp of air. There were only a couple of feet between the rapidly rising water and the top of the compartment. When Spence dove back down, his were the only hands working to unlock the harness. He broke his middle finger trying to dislodge the release lever.

In an act of rage, Spence put his feet against the top of the pedestal and pulled on Lorance's harness with all his might. He relaxed momentarily to improve his grip and pulled again, one last time. The bombsight mounts separated, freeing the limp bombardier's harness from the pedestal. Spence pushed Lorance to the top of the compartment and followed him up. There were only a few inches of air left. Lorance was unconscious.

Spence knew he couldn't make it back to the radio compartment with Lorance in tow. He took one more breath before shoving the immobile bombardier beneath the water. He pulled him aft, out of the nose bay and up into the cockpit, where the pair emerged from the water. Gasping for air, Spence contorted his way through the pilot's sliding window while holding onto Lorance's harness. Once he was outside the aircraft, he braced his feet against the side of the fuselage. He struggled to pull Lorance, still wearing his bulky parachute pack, through the small window.

As Lorance cleared the window, the pair fell several feet into the water. Spence pulled the toggle to inflate Lorance's Mae West before inflating his own. The still-unconscious bombardier's flotation bladder, because it was ripped during the egress from the cockpit, failed to inflate. Spence reached out and grabbed Lorance just as he was slipping beneath the surface of the frigid water.

Spence was cold and exhausted. Just as he was about to lose his grip on Lorance, he felt someone tugging on the neck of his Mae West from behind. Rod Hurley pulled him up and over the side of the life raft. John Spence watched as Dave Murray and Garry Crain, groaning from the pain in his injured shoulder, pulled Mark Lorance into the same raft. As Lorance lay flat on his back, he expelled a fountain of water from his mouth and began choking. Murray rolled Lorance onto his stomach and pumped the seawater from his lungs.

Spence looked back toward the *Yellow Rose* and watched it disappear beneath the murky waves. The once-majestic B-17 settled to the bottom of the English Channel with Stan Kempema's bullet-riddled body still strapped inside the ball turret. Shivering uncontrollably, John Spence sat up and ran his aching hand across the gash on his forehead. He looked around at the other broken, disheveled men in the bobbing life raft. He shook his head in disgust. "I told you this mission was bullshit," he said somberly.

Chapter Thirty-Six
17 August 1941

Toby Pozniak walked several blocks from his apartment to the market. The invasion had interrupted the city's mercantile system, leaving food and common household goods in short supply. The Germans had implemented a rudimentary system of rationing, restricting each local resident to one bag of groceries per week.

This was Pozniak's second trip. When he entered the store that morning, he was stunned to see the shelves were nearly bare. A pair of German soldiers met him just inside the door and motioned for him to stop. Without speaking, one of them handed him a leaflet and then let him pass. Pozniak took the leaflet, trying hard not to make eye contact with the menacing soldier. He stepped farther inside the store, away from the door and the guards, and began to read the one-page document.

A swastika was emblazoned at the top of the leaflet. The first sentence proclaimed that the citizens of New York were now under the jurisdiction of the Third Reich and were subject to the orders of Adolf Hitler and his local administrators. Residents were admonished to comply with all directives from the occupation forces for their own safety. Lastly, there was a proclamation ordering all citizens to listen to a radio broadcast on Wednesday, the 20th of August, at 8 p.m.

Four nights later, Toby Pozniak, Marc Krbec and several of their Prospect Heights neighbors gathered around the radio inside Krbec's home. After two and a half weeks of silence, radios all across New York City once again crackled to life. As they listened to the broadcast coming from the WOR studios in Manhattan, Toby Pozniak and his neighbors heard an ominous voice—the voice of Ernst Kruger.

Chapter Thirty-Seven
27 August 1941

The men were scheduled to board a westbound Liberty ship the next morning. As they waited to catch their bus to the Port of Southampton, seven of the nine surviving *Yellow Rose* crew members were gathered inside London's Old Bell Tavern, just north of the River Thames.

It was still early afternoon, but it was already turning into a raucous affair. There was a sizeable collection of empty pint glasses stacking up on the table, evidence the men were succeeding in their mission to blow off steam before beginning the long journey across the U-boat-infested North Atlantic.

"The next round's on me!" Rod Hurley announced.

"*All* the rounds are on you!" John Spence yelled, drawing boisterous cheers from the other men.

Hurley laughed and waved the waitress over to the table. He asked her to bring three bottles of Johnnie Walker Black Label whisky and eight shot glasses. When the bottles arrived, he filled all but one of the glasses. After passing the charged glasses all around, he slid the empty glass to the center of the table and stood. The still-chattering men instinctively quieted down and stood to join their CO in a toast. Hurley asked the men to raise their drinks. "To Stan Kempema and all our fallen brothers from One Twenty-One Squadron," he said solemnly.

"To Stanley." Garry Crain seconded.

The men drank to their dead squadron mates. As they collectively slammed their empty glasses onto the wooden table, a loud thwack rang throughout the smoke-filled pub. "*Waitress—we're done here!*" Hurley shouted.

The waitress shouted back at him in a thick Cockney accent. "Keep your shirt on, Yank! I've still got to tally your bloody tab."

Garry Crain looked at Hurley and laughed. "*Dammit*, Skipper. We've been over here for nearly a year, and these Limeys still think we're all Yankees."

Hurley smiled back at him. "Well, Gabby—as of three weeks ago, I guess maybe we all *are*. Grab those bottles and follow me, men! Bring your glasses too!" Hurley picked up the unused shot glass from the center of the table and headed for the door.

The flustered waitress stepped in front of the exit. "*Hold on*, Yanks. You can't take those glasses with you. And your tab is thirty-seven quid."

Hurley reached into his pocket and pulled out a £100 banknote—a little more than $400 at that time—and handed it to her. "Will that cover the tab and the glasses?" he asked.

Wide-eyed, the waitress smiled. She took the money and slipped it down her low-cut blouse, into her brassiere. She stepped aside. "*Clear off*, sport. For that much money, you could've had *me*."

As the men filed past her, John Spence reached out and gave her a gentle tap on the backside. "*Hell*, darlin'—we *all* could've had you for *that* much." He quickly ducked as she drew back her hand and threatened to slap him across the face.

As the unruly men poured onto Fleet Street, Rod Hurley motioned for them to follow. The men complied, still carrying the whisky bottles and shot glasses. Garry Crain turned to Dave Murray. "Where do you think the skipper's taking us?" he asked.

"Beats me," Murray said, shrugging. "I would've thought he'd be takin' us to receive personal farewells from the king and queen, but Buckingham Palace is in the other direction."

Several blocks later, the drunken gaggle arrived in front of St. Bartholomew's Hospital. "*Did we come here to check Spence into the syphilis ward?*" Mark Lorance bellowed—much to the amusement of everyone except John Spence, who showed his buddy the splint on his broken middle finger.

Hurley continued through the entrance with his rowdy troops trailing behind. He walked to the front desk, where he spoke to a wary, middle-aged nurse. "Howdy, ma'am. Can you tell me what room Squadron Leader Thomas Damron is in?"

The nurse looked down at the desk, flipping through cards in a Rolodex. "He's in room four twenty-two"—the men started moving—"but, *see here!* The whole *lot* of you can't go up there!"

The frustrated nurse might as well have been trying to stop a marauding band of pirates. Before she could get the words out of her mouth, the inebriated men headed up the stairs. Climbing one step behind Rod Hurley, Garry Crain reached up and tugged his former CO's sleeve. "Hey, Colonel, how'd you know Major Damron was here?"

"Listen, Gabby. For the *last* time—until we get back home and get reinstated, we're civilians. If and when that happens, you'll be a sergeant, and I'll be a colonel. Until then, we're just Gabby and Rod."

"Yes sir, Colonel."

Hurley shook his head and continued up the next three flights of stairs. The fourth-floor medical staff could hear them coming. The head nurse intercepted the unruly cadre just outside the stairwell and stepped in front of them. "Two visitors per patient, gentlemen."

"*Gentlemen?*" John Spence howled. "Lady, you obviously have us confused with somebody else." The other men began laughing.

Rod Hurley turned and held up his hand, signaling for quiet. He looked back at the nurse. "Look, ma'am. We're all shippin' out tomorrow. We just wanna have a drink with our squadron mate before we go."

"Oh…*Yanks*. I might've guessed. Look here, Mr. …"

"Hurley…Rod Hurley."

"*Well*, Mr. Hurley. I don't care what you and your rabble want, you can't—"

A voice from down the hall cut her off mid-sentence. "It's okay, nurse. I'll handle it."

"They're all yours, doctor." The nurse turned and walked away as Hurley and his crew continued down the hallway. The doctor who had intervened on their behalf was standing just outside Thomas Damron's room.

"Are you Group Captain Rod Hurley?" the doctor asked, extending his hand. "I was very sorry to hear about your squadron."

"Thanks, Doc; but I'm no longer a group captain. One Twenty-One Squadron was disbanded—what was left of it anyway. We've all been discharged from the RAF, and we're headed home tomorrow. Squadron Leader Damron can't be discharged until you fellas are done with him. We just wanted to have a little farewell drink before we go."

The doctor looked toward the door to Damron's room. "I happen to know you Yanks have done a bang-up job since coming over here to lend our lads a hand." The doctor looked back at Hurley and smiled, though the smile seemed uneasy. "My son piloted one of the pathfinder *Mosquitos* when your boys took out the refinery at Rotterdam. He said your squadron was the best heavy bomber outfit in the RAF." The doctor paused and looked once again toward Damron's room. "Go ahead in, Group Captain. You and your men take all the time you want with your mate. The whisky will do him good. Just try to keep the noise down, could you?"

"Sure thing, Doc—and thanks."

As they entered the room, Thomas Damron was sitting up in the hospital bed with a big grin on his face. His right leg was elevated and wrapped with bandages. "What the hell is this?" he asked, laughing. "I could hear you guys all the way down in the lobby. Looks like you're short one. How come Nowak's not with you?"

"Alek is headed back to Poland," Hurley answered. "Says he's gonna fight with the Resistance there."

For the next hour and a half, the men swapped stories and jokes as if they were a bunch of teenagers hanging out in a high school parking lot. Despite Hurley's promise to the contrary, the party grew louder and louder. On three separate occasions, the head nurse popped her head into the room and admonished the men to lower their voices. Each time she did, they promised to comply and offered her a drink.

Finally, after the bottles were empty, they said their goodbyes and filed out into the hallway. As they made their way toward the stairwell, the doctor who had rescued them from the head nurse stepped out from an adjoining room. "You chaps have a safe passage home," he said, once again reaching out to shake Hurley's hand.

"Thanks again, Doc. By the way—be sure to tell your son how much we appreciate the top-shelf work he did for us over Rotterdam."

The doctor hesitated slightly. "I wish I could, Group Captain. He was shot down over France four days ago. I'm still hoping he's in a Jerry POW camp."

Hurley didn't know what to say.

The doctor could see that the veteran aviator was unsettled. He quickly spoke again, attempting to alleviate Hurley's embarrassment. "I'm sure I'll see him again. When I do, I'll be sure to give him your regards."

"Thanks, Doc. Good luck to you and your son."

"Good luck to you and your men, Group Captain. You're going to need it."

The next morning, seven hungover men lugged their gear aboard an empty Liberty ship. They settled in for a fifteen-day transit back to one of the still-viable North American ports.

A day later, in Edinburgh, Scotland, Aleksander Nowak boarded a Russian freighter bound for the Baltic.

Two days after that, Thomas Damron's doctor received word from the RAF that his son had been killed in action.

Chapter Thirty-Eight
09 September 1941

Four weeks after the German spearhead had been blunted at the Susquehanna River, Field Marshal Friedrich von Essen's forward units had extended their westward expansion all the way to the Appalachian Highlands.

Determined not to allow the Germans a southern advance, General Eisenhower had continued to stack U.S. and Confederate divisions all along the Allied side of the front. The German invasion was no longer a blitzkrieg. It had become a brutal, toe-to-toe slugfest. The front was now spread across most of southern Pennsylvania.

Adolf Hitler was livid that the German advance had bogged down short of the two American capitals. The German Führer implored von Essen to create a second front by attacking the North American Allies along their southern coast.

Von Essen knew he didn't possess the resources for such an assault. The operation to seize New York Harbor had succeeded largely because it had taken the Americans by surprise. Another such attack would likely be disastrous. He managed to convince the Führer that the best strategy was to continue pouring assets into Pennsylvania.

Meanwhile, in Lower Manhattan, SS General Ernst Kruger had spent a month setting up the Third Reich's provisional government. As Hitler's direct representative, Kruger was responsible for administrating all the occupied regions in North America. His first order of business had been to get New York City up and running under German rule. He had reopened the subways and ordered all city residents to return to work at their former places of employment—provided their former places of employment were located inside the borough in which they resided. Travel from one borough to another was still forbidden.

The city had slowly begun to function amid a climate of fear and uncertainty. No one had seen nor heard from Mayor LaGuardia since the first day of the invasion. His whereabouts and fate were unknown. The roving SS squads had arrested many of the city's most prominent residents—a number of whom were Jewish. This had added fuel to the rumors of a concentration camp.

They were more than just rumors. The SS had cleared out the municipal jail facility on Rikers Island and had established the first Nazi concentration camp on U.S. soil.

The building at 2nd Avenue and 12th Street had been completed a year before the start of the American Civil War. Located in Manhattan's Jewish Theater District, it housed the Yiddish Art Theater.

On this Thursday evening, several of the theater's wealthiest benefactors were meeting inside the dimly lit, smoke-filled business office. One of the three men in the office was Saul Rosenbaum. "We need to do this," he said glumly. "If we surrender our will to the Nazis, I promise you—our wealth and status won't save us. You've seen the SS making arrests on the street. You've heard the same rumors I've heard. If there is to be a viable resistance movement in

New York City, we've got to help. I, for *one*, do not intend to let them persecute me and my family without a fight."

"I don't either," the second man said. "But why should we throw our weight behind the group being organized by this Navy intelligence officer. We should be forming our own *Jewish* resistance. *We're* the ones being arrested in our homes."

"I agree," said the third man. "If the U.S. government wants to organize a resistance, let *them* fund it."

"The government's not asking us for money, gentlemen. They'll supply the weapons and the training. They're only asking us to use our influence in the business community to get their resistance fighters hired into jobs where they can do the most good—places where they can gather intelligence and disrupt the Germans' day-to-day operations. As for a separate Jewish resistance movement, I'll just say this—the only way Jewish Americans will survive this war is if *America* survives this war. Right now, anyone who fights against the Nazis is our brother, whether he's Jewish or not."

"That's a valid point," the second man said. "But aren't we sticking our necks out by helping these resistance fighters? If they're discovered, won't it come back on *us?*"

"We're *already* targets," Rosenbaum answered. "Why do you think we're holding this meeting in secret? We're being tyrannized because of our Jewish lineage. The only pertinent question is whether we're going to surrender—or fight."

"He's right," the third man said. He looked at Rosenbaum. "Tell us what you need us to do, Saul."

For the next hour, Rosenbaum outlined the plan that had been given to him by the naval intelligence officer who had discretely approached him outside his office. The other two men listened, making detailed notes to themselves. When it came time to leave, the three men left the darkened theater several minutes apart so as not to draw attention to themselves.

The sun had already set as Saul Rosenbaum walked south, toward his apartment. Eight blocks into the twelve-block walk, he stopped beneath a streetlight to look at his watch. He had ten minutes left until the 8 p.m. curfew. He caught a glimpse of two dark figures walking behind him. As they passed under the streetlight a block away, he could see them clearly. He knew from the way they were dressed—black suits and fedoras—they were Gestapo agents.

Rosenbaum grew nervous. He froze in his tracks for several seconds before continuing toward his apartment. *I can't go home*, he thought to himself. *If they're going to arrest me, I don't want to lead them to Esther and Natalie.*

Three blocks from his apartment, Rosenbaum stole a quick glance to confirm the men were still behind him. He turned the next corner and began heading west, away from his apartment. It was almost 8 o'clock. He didn't know what to do. He kept walking, looking back to the intersection every few seconds to see if the men were going to turn the corner and continue shadowing him. When they emerged from behind the building, they continued walking south—straight through the intersection.

Rosenbaum continued to the next corner. He stopped in front of a locked-up bodega, a place where he routinely bought short-list grocery items on his way home from his office. Though he was relieved the agents had not tailed him around the corner, his heart was still racing. He leaned back against the darkened glass door to gather his thoughts. Removing his hat, he was wiping his brow when he was startled by something rapping on the glass behind him. As he jumped away from the storefront and turned to see what it was, the door slowly opened. A familiar face emerged. It belonged to Mateo Vargas, the middle-aged man who ran the bodega.

Vargas held up his pocket watch and pointed at it. "Señor Rosy," he called out in a Puerto Rican accent. "*Quickly*—come inside."

Rosenbaum ducked into the store. Vargas closed the door behind him, locking it quietly. Rosenbaum turned to thank him, but he saw

Vargas, silhouetted by the streetlight just outside the door, holding his finger to his lips. The two men stood in silence.

Several seconds later, two German soldiers passed in front of the store, turning the corner onto the sidewalk where Rosenbaum had just been standing. Vargas held his hand up for several more seconds before speaking. "It is okay, señor. They are gone now. You can set your watch by those two. They pass my store every night at eight o'clock sharp. Come—let us go upstairs to my apartment."

As the two men climbed the stairs in the corner of the store, Rosenbaum spoke. "I can't thank you enough, Mateo. I can't believe I let myself run up against the curfew like that."

"It is nothing," Vargas replied, opening the door at the top of the stairs. "You and Mrs. Rosenbaum are two of my best customers. I have an extra bed up here." He switched on the light and led Rosenbaum into a spartan, one-room apartment. Two neatly made twin beds occupied the corners on either side of the entry. A refrigerator and gas stove were centered along the opposite wall, next to a small pantry. There was a curtain-covered, plywood closet in one of the far corners. An open door in the other corner revealed a dreary but sanitary bathroom. A square kitchen table filled the center of the room, surrounded by four mismatched chairs.

Rosenbaum took off his hat and handed it to Vargas. "That's very generous, Mateo, but I can't stay here all night. Esther and Natalie will be worried sick if I don't come home. I'll just lay low for a little while before heading out."

"No—you must not, señor." Vargas placed the hat on top of the refrigerator. "The Germans are everywhere after the curfew. If they spot you out on the street, your wife and daughter will have plenty of reason to worry about you. *No*—you should stay here." He offered Rosenbaum a cigarette as the two men sat down at the table.

Rosenbaum reached out and took the cigarette. "I suppose you're right...*dammit*." He leaned over while Vargas lit the cigarette for him. "I just wish there was some way to let my family know I'm okay. I wish those bastards hadn't shut down the switchboards."

"Perhaps it is better they did. If we were able to use the telephones, they would be listening to everything we say. We would just end up getting arrested anyway."

"I suppose you're right again, Mateo. *God,* I wish we had some way to fight back."

"I expect we will find a way to fight back soon," Vargas said. "Until then, we must do our best to survive. We must not do anything to draw attention to ourselves. Would you like a beer while I make us some supper?"

"That sounds good, actually."

Vargas opened the refrigerator and took out a bottle of Schlitz. He closed the door and reached up to retrieve an opener from atop the fridge. He opened the bottle and handed it to Rosenbaum. "Here you go," Vargas said with a smile. "I hope you like corned beef hash." He turned and walked back to the refrigerator. "It came from Katz's Deli, so I am fairly certain it is kosher."

"You're too kind, Mateo. I'm sure it'll be great."

As Vargas lit the stove and began heating their supper, Rosenbaum took a draw from the cigarette and looked around the windowless apartment. He studied a wall-mounted shelf that held a free-standing crucifix, along with paintings of Christ and the Virgin Mary. He glanced at a nightstand next to one of the beds. He noticed a wedding photograph.

Curious, Rosenbaum got up from the table and walked over to take a closer look. The photo was of a much-younger Mateo Vargas and a woman he had never seen. "You were *married*, Mateo?"

"Her name was Clarita," Vargas replied proudly while stirring the hash in a pan.

"She's beautiful," Rosenbaum commented.

"She died from influenza several years after we came here from San Juan. Clarita loved America. She especially loved New York. She was so proud when our baby was born here."

"You have a child?"

"A daughter…Amanda. She is married and lives in New Jersey. I also have three grandchildren—two boys and a girl. I have not heard from any of them since the invasion." Vargas turned away from the stove and looked at Rosenbaum. "I have heard the rumors about Rikers Island, Señor Rosy. Perhaps you and your family should think about moving into my apartment until this is over. I can sleep downstairs in the store."

Rosenbaum was taken aback. "We couldn't ask you to do that, Mateo. You'd be putting yourself at risk by hiding us."

"You are a child of Israel, señor. The Bible says God will bless those who bless *you*."

"You're Catholic, aren't you?"

"Yes."

"Yet, you would sacrifice yourself for me and my family?"

"*Yes*, señor."

"Why would you do that?"

"Because we worship the same God, Señor Rosy. The only difference is, you are still looking for the Messiah—I believe he has already come. He is the one who tells me to care for those less fortunate than I am."

Rosenbaum was visibly moved. He marveled at how this modest storekeeper, a man whom he barely knew, would be willing to risk his life for a wealthy, "less-fortunate" real estate mogul. "Mateo, I have no idea what it takes to achieve sainthood in the Catholic Church, but I know a saint when I see one. I'm deeply grateful to you."

"It is nothing, señor." Vargas turned back toward the stove and shut it off. "Our supper is ready," he announced. "Now we eat."

After their supper, the two men drank and talked late into the evening, retiring just before midnight. Even though Mateo Vargas's extra bed was plenty comfortable, Saul Rosenbaum tossed and turned. He couldn't stop thinking about Esther and Natalie—worrying they would assume the worst.

Finally, he drifted off to sleep.

"I can't believe Papa didn't tell you where he was going," Natalie said. She and her mother were growing more concerned with each passing hour.

"He was going to a business meeting," Natalie's mother said. "That's all he would tell me. When I pressed him, he told me not to worry. He said he'd be home for dinner well before the curfew." Tears began flowing down Natalie's cheeks as she sat next to her mother on the sofa. Esther Rosenbaum took her daughter into her arms and stroked her hair. "These tears aren't just about Papa, are they?"

Natalie began to weep more intensely.

Her mother held her tighter. "I'm sure Toby is fine, sweetheart. I know you'll hear from him soon."

"You can't know that," Natalie sobbed.

"I know he loves you very, very much. I've seen the way he looks at you. I think he would move heaven and earth if that's what it takes to get to you."

"I know he would, Mama. That's what scares me." Natalie regained her composure enough to sit up and look her mother in the eye. "That's also what scares me about Papa. I'm afraid he's going to challenge the Germans and end up getting arrested. I'm already separated from Toby. Now I'm afraid we're going to lose Papa as well. It's all too much, Mama. I'm afraid…afraid of what's going to happen to us." Natalie began crying tears again.

Her mother held her and tried reassuring her once more, but it was no use. Esther decided to let her weep. Natalie, exhausted from worry, cried herself to sleep in her mother's arms. Standing up, Esther gently placed her daughter's head on a cushion and raised her legs onto the sofa. She covered her with a blanket and kissed her goodnight.

At 5:30 a.m., the clattering alarm bell pierced the silence in Mateo Vargas's apartment. Vargas switched on the lamp as both men sat up on the edges of their beds. Saul Rosenbaum, in his boxer shorts and undershirt, looked especially ragged and disoriented in the dim light from the yellowed lamp shade.

Vargas spoke first. "Buenos días, señor. How did you sleep?"

Rosenbaum leaned forward and put his elbows on his knees. He sighed and ran his fingers through his uncombed hair. "Not very well, I'm afraid. I need to get home, Mateo."

"*Not yet*, señor. The sun will not be up for another half hour. The curfew is still in effect." Vargas got up and put on a threadbare flannel robe. "I will go down to the store and start the coffee while you dress. When you come down, we will find you something to eat."

"Thanks, Mateo." Rosenbaum remained seated on the edge of the bed, thinking. How was he going to apologize to Esther and Natalie for putting them through this anguish? Did he really want to jeopardize his family by getting involved in a resistance movement?

Rosenbaum stood slowly, stretching and yawning. He shuffled across the wooden floor as he made his way to the bathroom. He looked down and squinted as he pulled the chain on the dangling light fixture. Leaning forward, he washed his face in the rust-stained porcelain sink. He raised his head and looked into the mirror. He rubbed his hand across the stubble on his tired, wrinkled face.

…She and her parents are stranded on an island with no food or water. Her parents look horribly emaciated. Natalie doesn't know where the island is, how they got there, or how long they've been stranded.

She suddenly finds herself standing alone on the shore as her parents sail away on a boat. She runs up and down the shoreline, pleading with them not to leave her.

Her mother blows a kiss to her. "I love you, Natalie!"

Her father looks at her and speaks softly. Even though he is a hundred yards offshore, she can hear him plainly. "It's going to be okay, Ketzel. He'll send for you soon—"

Natalie was awakened by the sound of her father's key turning the lock on the door. She sat up quickly on the sofa. "He's *home*, Mama!"

Esther Rosenbaum came running out of her bedroom just as Natalie was hugging her father's neck. "*Saul Rosenbaum*, you big *nudnik!*" she shouted as tears filled her eyes. She ran to Saul's open arms as Natalie stepped aside. "Where on God's earth have you been?" she asked, sobbing on his shoulder.

"With a friend, Esther…I've been with a friend."

Chapter Thirty-Nine
23 September 1941

A stagnant battlefront had emerged. It stretched some three hundred miles, from Pittsburgh in the west, eastward to the northern tip of the Chesapeake Bay. Even though the Germans controlled the northern half of the Delmarva Peninsula on the eastern side of the bay, the strategically vital naval base at Norfolk, Virginia, remained operational, as did the other Confederate Navy bases and ports along the Atlantic Coast and Gulf of Mexico.

Admiral Harold Stark, the Allied chief of naval operations, ordered the U.S. Pacific Fleet to begin moving from the West Coast into the Atlantic—a four-week passage around Cape Horn, at the tip of South America.

Confederate Fleet Admiral Chester Nimitz, serving as deputy CNO, was the next-senior naval officer in the Allied chain of command. He warned against leaving the West Coast undefended. Even though no one in Naval Intelligence anticipated a Japanese attack against America, Nimitz saw it as a possibility.

Not knowing that Field Marshal Friedrich von Essen had already rejected the idea of a German assault along the southern coastline, Admiral Stark was desperate to guard against it. He ignored Nimitz's admonition against leaving the West Coast undefended.

Meanwhile, as Thomas Damron recovered from his wounds in a London Hospital, the other surviving members of the Yellow Rose's flight crew reached their destinations.

Aleksander Nowak disembarked the Russian freighter in Gdańsk and joined the Polish Resistance. He was reunited with a large group of insurgents operating out of a remote airfield at Debki, near the Baltic.

Rod Hurley and the other North American crew members survived a harrowing journey across the North Atlantic. Their convoy was attacked twice by U-boat wolfpacks. By the time they reached the Confederate port in Charleston, South Carolina, seven of the twenty-nine Liberty ships had been lost.

After one last night on the town, the men went their separate ways, hoping to spend time with their families while they awaited reinstatement orders from their respective air forces.

It was the first day of autumn in Kerrville, Texas. The weather was sunny and hot.

At the Swanson ranch, just outside of town, it was already ninety-three degrees at one o'clock in the afternoon. Elizabeth Swanson stood at her kitchen sink, washing dishes in front of an open window. A warm breeze ruffled the red-and-white-checkered curtains. Just behind Elizabeth, Margie Hurley was still clearing the leftovers from her mother's table. As Elizabeth scrubbed a plate, she lifted her head to look out the window. Her grandson was playing in the yard.

In the distance, a half mile away, she noticed a Greyhound bus on the farm-to-market blacktop that ran past the entrance to the ranch. She didn't think much of it. The Swanson's ranch was located along the bus line's regular route from San Antonio to the station in Kerrville.

To her surprise, however, she heard the faint sound of the Greyhound's diesel engine winding down. She watched curiously as the bus gradually slowed and stopped at the end of the dirt driveway that led to the house. She heard the wisp of air expelled from the brakes as the Greyhound sat idling for several seconds. As the bus pulled away, the black exhaust partially obscured the lone figure left standing on the far side of the road. He lifted his heavy duffel bag and tossed it over his shoulder. As he began walking toward the house, Elizabeth realized what was happening. *"Margaret!"* she shouted. "Come *quick—it's Rod!"*

Margie Hurley rushed to the kitchen window. Standing on her toes next to her mother, she leaned forward and peered out past her son, down the long driveway. Seconds later, Sam Hurley watched curiously as his mother leapt from the porch and ran past him without saying a word. She tore off her apron and let it fly as she sprinted down the driveway with her long blond hair flowing behind her. It was then that Sam noticed the man walking toward the house. He watched as the man dropped his bag and began running toward his mother.

Reminiscent of the day Rod had earned his wings, Margie flew into his waiting arms. Just as Rod had done that day a decade earlier, he wrapped his arms around her waist and swung her through the air. Unlike that day at Randolph Field, however, he continued to hold her off the ground. He kissed her passionately, holding her in a tight embrace. As the embrace continued, Margie wrapped her legs around Rod and squeezed them together. Her white cotton dress rode up on her shapely thighs.

Watching from the kitchen window, Margie's mother blushed. Then, she chuckled. Nine-year-old Sam didn't know what to make of his mother's bizarre behavior. Finally, as the man lowered his mother to the ground, Sam recognized the father he hadn't seen in more than a year. He took several steps—then began running.

As his son drew near, Rod dropped to his knees and held out his arms.

"*Daddy!*" Sam shouted as he jumped into his father's arms and hugged his neck.

Still watching from the kitchen, Elizabeth Swanson laughed again. Then, she shed a tear. Margie's mother removed her apron and hung it on the hook next to the refrigerator. She made her way onto the porch and waited for her daughter's family to finish the long walk to the house.

The first day of autumn in Brooklyn had been unusually cold and dank. The afternoon temperature had barely reached fifty degrees beneath the misty, gray skies. It was just past 6:30 in the evening. Even though the sun wouldn't set for another twenty minutes, darkness was already settling across the city.

Toby Pozniak left his apartment. This was the night Pozniak had been anticipating for the past week, ever since Marc Krbec had come to him with the plan to get him across the East River and into Lower Manhattan. This was the night he would finally be with Natalie.

The Gowanus Canal, a two-mile-long industrial waterway on the west side of Brooklyn, was a complex network of docks and warehouses. One of Krbec's associates, a former contractor at the Brooklyn Navy Yard, owned a warehouse next to the Fourth Street Basin. Located on the backwaters of the canal, the dilapidated building afforded the perfect backdrop for a clandestine operation such as the one the two men had planned for tonight.

Inside the warehouse was a small boat, equipped with twin outboard motors. Krbec had arranged to meet Pozniak in front of the warehouse shortly after sunset. The two of them were plotting to lower the boat into the secluded basin under cover of darkness.

From the basin, Pozniak planned to make his way southwest, through the canal and into New York Harbor. Once in the harbor, he would turn north along the Brooklyn shoreline until he passed Governors Island. From there, Pozniak hoped to make a dash across the entrance to the East River and land the boat along the Battery Park seawall at the southern tip of Manhattan. It was a dangerous scheme—one that could easily get him killed.

Toby Pozniak didn't care. He was desperate to finally reach Natalie.

The Fourth Street Basin was more than twenty blocks from Pozniak's Prospect Heights apartment. It was a long walk, and he didn't want to push up against the 8 p.m. curfew. If he did, he would risk being stopped by the German authorities. He was so intent on reaching the warehouse ahead of the curfew that he failed to notice the shadowy figure pacing him from behind, less than a block away.

As he neared his destination, a light fog rolled off the canal and into the surrounding neighborhood. It wasn't until he rounded the corner onto Fourth Street, headed for the dock and adjacent warehouses, that he caught a glimpse of the man walking behind him. Pozniak slowed his pace, unsure what to do next. He continued ahead and cast a quick glance back just as his pursuer passed beneath the misty halo of a streetlight. The unfamiliar man was dressed in a trench coat and fedora.

Pozniak's heart sank. *Is he Gestapo?* he thought to himself. He considered aborting the rendezvous, but he had already tipped his destination by turning onto the dead-end street. He broke into a sprint. As he ran along the dimly lit dock, Pozniak desperately searched for his accomplice in the maze of fog-shrouded warehouses. His heart was racing, partially from exertion—mostly from fear.

Finally, near the end of the dock, he spotted Marc Krbec waving him into one of the darkened warehouse doors. Pozniak ducked inside. The two men stood just inside the open door. Frantic and almost out of breath, Pozniak warned Krbec of the approaching Gestapo agent. When he saw the look on Krbec's face, he knew something was not right. "What's wrong, Marc?"

"I'm sorry, Toby. I'm sorry I had to do it this way."

"You had to do *what?* What are you talking about?"

Krbec didn't answer. He focused his gaze over Pozniak's shoulder. Sensing a presence behind him, Pozniak slowly turned his head. He saw the ominous figure of the man who had been following him silhouetted in the doorway. Krbec finally spoke. "Toby, this is Lieutenant Commander Mike Crofford—US Naval Intelligence."

Crofford extended his hand. "Dr. Pozniak—I've come to take you out of here."

Pozniak was stunned and confused. "What the *hell* are you talking about?" he asked, refusing to shake Crofford's hand. "Take me *where?*"

"To Washington, D.C.," Crofford answered.

"I don't know you from Adam," Pozniak said. "I'm not going to D.C. with you. I'm not going *anywhere* with you." He turned back to Krbec. "What's going on here, Marc? I thought you were gonna help me get across the harbor. We had a plan. You were supposed to help me get to Natalie. Isn't that why we're here?"

Krbec hesitated. He looked at Lieutenant Commander Crofford for help. Crofford closed the door and switched on the light. He pointed to a table and chairs in the corner of the warehouse. "Have a seat," he said to Pozniak.

The three men sat. Crofford looked across the table at Pozniak. "There's no easy way to tell you this," he said. "Natalie and her family aren't at their home. They were arrested ten days ago—along with the bodega owner who was hiding them in his apartment. We're pretty sure they're being held at Rikers Island."

"*No—you're lying!*" Pozniak shouted.

Krbec intervened. "*Toby, look* at me," he said with a pained expression on his face.

"He's *lying*," Pozniak said to Krbec. "He's just trying to get me to go with him. For *what*, I don't know—but he's *lying!*"

Krbec tried once more. "*Look at me.* He's *not* lying. We've known about Natalie for the past week. We desperately wanted to tell you, but we couldn't."

"Who the hell is '*we*,' Marc?"

"The Resistance."

"*Resistance?* What the hell are you talking about? *What* resistance?"

"The one Commander Crofford helped us organize."

"And this all just slipped your mind? You never thought to mention to me you were putting together a resistance?"

"I thought it better you didn't know," Krbec said sheepishly.

"Thanks for the confidence, buddy. To hell with *you* too!"

"Look, Toby. I was trying to keep you—"

Crofford cut them off. "Gentlemen, we don't have much time here." He glanced at his watch and then looked straight at Pozniak. "Tell me, Doctor—do you know someone named Enrico Fermi?"

The question, though it caught him off guard, lessened Pozniak's anxiety. "I know him. What's *he* got to do with all this?"

"Well…apparently, he's a pretty important person to someone back at the War Department. It seems he's managed to convince that same someone that *you're* an important person as well. Whoever that someone is must have a lot of pull in D.C., or I wouldn't be sitting here telling you this."

Crofford leaned in closer, looking into Pozniak's eyes. "So, here's the skinny, Doc. I'm sorry as hell about your gal and her family. I know we threw you a nasty curveball here tonight, but time is running out. You're gonna have to trust me when I tell you that the Nazis have arrested Natalie and her family. I know that's shitty—but that's how it is. And as sorry as I am that it happened, I can't do a damn thing to change it."

As Crofford continued, his tone intensified. No longer sympathetic, he became indignant, raising his finger and pointing it at the startled physicist. "Furthermore, Professor Pozniak—*you* can't do anything to change it either—at least not *here*. You also need to trust me when I tell you that some good men are risking their lives to get you out of New York, so I'm guessing that whatever it is you do is somehow important to the war effort. So, what's it gonna be, Doc? You gonna hide here in this warehouse, pissing and moaning about something neither of us can change?"

Crofford leaned in even closer. "Or…are you gonna get off your ass and help us fight back against the bastards who've taken Natalie away?"

From the window in the darkened prisoner barracks, Saul Rosenbaum could see the headlights of the trucks as they crossed the only bridge onto Rikers Island. For the past eight nights, he had watched as the new inmates were hurriedly offloaded by the SS soldiers, pushing and shoving them into two groups. The men were always separated from the women and children. Then, the two groups were forced to stand in separate ranks under the harsh spotlights at the camp entrance.

The routine was always the same. A couple of guards would carry a small wooden platform from a nearby shed and place it on the ground, directly in front of the newly arrived prisoners. A few minutes later, SS Colonel Helmut Kraus, the camp commandant, would emerge from his office and march to the platform, where he would "welcome" the new arrivals to Rikers Island.

Rosenbaum couldn't hear the commandant's speech, but he knew what he was saying. He was telling the new prisoners that their services were required by the Third Reich and that they would be treated well if they worked hard.

The initial internment process always ended the same way. At the conclusion of his speech, Kraus would read a series of job skills from a list and order anyone who possessed those skills to step forward. Those who stepped forward were taken into the shack just inside the gate. The others were immediately marched off to the male or female barracks, where their personal effects were confiscated and they were issued crude canvas uniforms with blue and white vertical stripes. Unless the inmate was a non-Jewish political prisoner, the uniform would include a yellow Star of David on the left breast.

Saul Rosenbaum thought back to his family's arrival at the camp. He recalled his fear at having heard the word "accountant" announced as one of the skills on the list. He remembered feeling relieved when Natalie had quietly remained in the ranks.

It wasn't until the next day that Rosenbaum had learned what happened to the people taken inside the shack that first night. He had recognized one of them—a barber—that next morning as he stood in line to have his hair sheared. He had noticed the man was wearing an armband on his uniform that read, "WU." When it was his turn to be sheared, Rosenbaum had asked the barber what the letters meant.

"Workers' Unit," the man had responded quietly, so as not to draw attention from the guards. Then, the man had rolled up his sleeve to show Rosenbaum the fresh, painful-looking serial number tattooed on his left forearm.

Saul Rosenbaum was an intelligent man. As he watched the new prisoners being processed into the camp that night, he understood why the Nazis were only assigning numbers to the Workers' Unit inmates.

He had not seen his wife or daughter since the night they first arrived; but Rosenbaum knew he had to get word to Natalie that she must volunteer her accounting skills to the Workers' Unit.

Lieutenant Commander Crofford, standing at the helm of the small boat, carefully navigated his way through the foggy, dark canal. Despondent, Toby Pozniak sat quietly behind him.

Pozniak's head was spinning with emotions. He wondered how his close friend could have been helping to organize a resistance movement without his knowing about it. He hated that he and Marc had parted on bad terms. He wondered when, or even *if*, he would get a chance to set things straight with his friend; but more than that, *much* more than that, Pozniak feared for Natalie. He was aware of the rumors surrounding Rikers Island. He was overcome with grief and trepidation, so much so that he was barely conscious of the danger he and Crofford now faced as they attempted to reach their rendezvous point just outside New York Harbor.

As they exited the canal into Gowanus Bay, Crofford continued steering to the southwest, through the Bay Ridge Channel and around the westernmost tip of Brooklyn. Approaching the Verrazano Narrows, they entered the main channel of the harbor and left the fog behind. Their eighteen-foot boat carried only twenty inches of freeboard. The waves threatened to swamp their small craft as they ran in total darkness to avoid detection from the German harbor patrol and the gun batteries on either side of the channel.

Lieutenant Commander Crofford called upon the seamanship skills he had learned at Annapolis to safely carry his now-seasick passenger toward the rendezvous point off the western tip of Coney Island. High above, the crescent moon provided just enough light for Crofford to align his boat directly between Hoffman Island, on the west side of the channel, and the Coney Island Lighthouse, a thousand yards to the east.

After checking his watch, Crofford steadied himself on the helm with one hand as he used the other to point a large flashlight due south. He clicked the light on and off three times and waited. The small craft tossed the two men about violently. For the next fifteen minutes, Crofford alternately placed the twin throttles in *forward* and *reverse* to maintain his position in the choppy waters.

Toby Pozniak, even though he was miserably seasick, became mesmerized by a bizarre sight some two thousand yards away. There it was, towering above the starlit eastern horizon. The skeletal framework of the *Wonder Wheel* made him long for a happier time. He and Natalie had ridden the giant Ferris wheel on their first date to Coney Island. Over the next year and a half, it had become one of their favorite places. Seeing it now only intensified his anxiety over Natalie's fate.

Pozniak stared at it, hypnotically fixated on the ghostly image of the now-lifeless amusement park ride. He was suddenly startled back to reality as the glimmering superstructure of the USS *Billfish* breached the surface, rose from the water, and eclipsed his view of the gigantic Ferris wheel.

"This is where you get off," Crofford said to Pozniak.

"You're not coming, Commander?"

"Not *this* trip, Doc. I still have work to do here with the Resistance. Besides—you're the one they came for. I hope you're really as big a deal as they seem to think you are."

At their Ranch in Kerrville, Texas, Arthur and Elizabeth Swanson had been sleeping for hours. In the bedroom next to his grandparents, Sam Hurley was sound asleep as well.

In another bedroom, at the far end of the house, Rod and Margie Hurley were sharing a year's worth of passion in a single night.

Chapter Forty

20 October 1941

It had been almost a month since Rod Hurley had reunited with his family at the ranch that belonged to Margie's parents. He and Sam were tossing the baseball in the yard beside the house.

Sam was getting better at catching his dad's slow knuckleball. He had learned to relax his arms and legs so he could move his glove in front of the dancing knuckler at the last second. Hurley let a good one fly. Sam could see the faded red stitches in the seams. There was almost no rotation as the ball appeared to dart up and down—left and right. Sam watched it all the way into his glove.

"Nicely done!" his dad shouted.

Sam looked back at his dad with a satisfied grin on his face. Then, he saw the dust trail behind the truck coming up the long driveway. "Somebody's coming," he said, pointing behind his dad.

As Rod Hurley turned to see who it was, he knew his time with his family was nearly at an end. He recognized the truck. It belonged to Elmer Schott, who owned the Kerr County Western Union contract.

It could only be one thing—Hurley's reinstatement orders.

A frigid blast of northeast wind, the first of the season, swept across the entire hundred-plus miles of ocean in Long Island Sound.

The wind seemed to funnel down and intensify as the body of water that separated Connecticut from Eastern Long Island became smaller and smaller at the western end. The leading edge of the blast accelerated as it converged on a lonely, forsaken piece of New York real estate at the estuary of the East River.

Hart Island was a flat, barren, mile-long islet—a hundred acres of bleak, uninviting landscape. The gust whipped through the small stand of half-dead trees on the northeast shoreline, stripping them of their few remaining leaves. The leaves swirled through the ramshackle ruins of a dozen decaying buildings—eerie remnants of a Civil War prison, a tuberculosis sanatorium, and an insane asylum—all long since abandoned.

From Hart Island, the squall continued down into the East River, where it seemed to accelerate even more. By the time it reached Rikers Island, it was moving swiftly enough to strip the clipboard from Natalie Rosenbaum's hand and send it flying. The clipboard skidded to a stop near the edge of the concrete dock at the northernmost point of the concentration camp.

The SS guard who had handed it to her rammed the butt of his rifle into Natalie's abdomen, causing her to double over onto the ground as she groaned. "Pick it up!" he shouted.

Natalie struggled to her feet. She straightened her eyeglasses and hurried to reach the clipboard before the next gust carried it into the river. She reached it just in time. She covered the fluttering bills of lading with her hand to protect them from the wind.

Moored to the dock were several huge barges, each filled with various construction materials.

As Natalie made the long trek back to the shack near the camp entrance, the wind pierced her soul. She missed Toby so much. She wasn't sure what she feared most: never seeing him again—or seeing him in this hellhole. She turned the collar up on her prison uniform to cover her bare neck. Even in her tattered clothing, even with a crude tattoo on her forearm and nothing more than stubble on her scalp, Natalie Rosenbaum was still a striking woman. It was as if she possessed an inner beauty that radiated through her squalid outward appearance.

When Natalie reached the relative warmth of the shack, she took a seat on the crate that served as a chair at her workstation. She took the bills of lading from the clipboard and filed them away in the folder marked "HART ISLAND PROJECT."

On the opposite side of the camp, Saul Rosenbaum, grotesquely slouched over, was hobbling away from the foul-smelling latrine, thirty yards from his barracks.

He was becoming so weak that the trips to the latrine were his only exercise—and the trips were becoming less and less frequent. There had been no food in his barracks for the past week. There was barely enough water to keep the prisoners inside the overcrowded building alive.

As he approached the run-down barracks, he caught a glimpse of his reflection in one of the windows. He shuffled closer to the dirty glass pane to take a better look. It was as if his own ghost was staring back at him from inside the barracks.

In Washington, D.C., Toby Pozniak waited in the foyer at the Office of Naval Intelligence. As he sat reading news accounts of the war from the *Washington Post*, the receptionist's phone sounded one short ring. She picked up the receiver and listened for several seconds. "Yes sir," she said, hanging up the phone. She looked over at Pozniak. "You can go in now, Professor." She pointed off to one side of the desk. "Down this hallway. Captain Fuller is the fourth office on the right."

"Thank you, miss." Pozniak made his way down the hall and paused at Captain Fuller's open door. He started to knock, but a loud voice beckoned him to "*come on in.*"

Pozniak entered the office and was instantly greeted by the captain's outstretched hand as he walked from behind his desk. "It's a pleasure to finally meet you, Professor Pozniak. I'm Chauncey Fuller." The captain turned and pointed to another man, who was still seated, smoking a pipe. "I'd like you to meet someone."

Pozniak instantly recognized the man in the chair.

"This is Doctor Robert Oppenheimer," Fuller said.

Pozniak offered his hand. "It's an honor, Doctor Oppenheimer."

Oppenheimer reached out and shook hands but remained seated. "Pozniak, I've read your work. Enrico tells me you're the best quantum mechanics man he's ever worked with."

"Enrico's too kind," Pozniak replied.

"Let's hope not," Oppenheimer responded. "You're only here because we expect you to live up to your billing."

"Why exactly *am* I here?" Pozniak asked.

Captain Fuller pointed to the chair next to Oppenheimer's. "*Please*—take a seat." Fuller walked back to the other side of his desk and sat.

Pozniak took a seat beside Oppenheimer and waited for an answer to his question.

"First off, I heard about your fiancée and her family," Fuller began. "I want you to know how sorry I am."

Pozniak sat quietly.

"You're here because the reactor you and Doctor Fermi built was tested while you were trapped in New York—it worked."

"*And?*" Pozniak asked.

"We disassembled it and moved it out of Chicago. The Germans have already advanced into Ohio and are expanding their front lines farther to the west every day. We're racing the Germans on two fronts now—the one that stretches from the Atlantic to the Great Lakes…and the one too small for anyone to see. That's where *you* come in."

Pozniak leaned forward in his chair. "How so?"

Oppenheimer spoke up. "Enrico tells me you spent a great deal of time studying with Werner Heisenberg in Göttingen. We know he's working for the Nazis now. Tell us about the man."

Pozniak turned and looked at Oppenheimer. "What do you want to know about him?"

"Only one thing," Oppenheimer replied matter-of-factly. "Can he build an atomic bomb?"

Pozniak leaned back in his chair and looked at Oppenheimer. Then he looked straight at Captain Fuller. "*Yes*…I believe he can."

"Then we have to build one first," Fuller responded without hesitating. "Will you help us?"

Chapter Forty-One
January 1942

In New England, the bitterly cold winter of 1942 would come to be known as the "winter of frozen tears."

In a continuing effort to flank the North American Allies, Field Marshal Friedrich von Essen had extended his battle lines all the way to the Illinois River. In doing so, he had stretched his supply lines to their limits. His assets were spread so thinly across what was labeled the "Mason-Dixon Front," that it was virtually impossible to mount an effective southward offensive.

Making von Essen's task even more difficult, Adolf Hitler now insisted that he occupy the New England states. Even though those states had already been cut off from the rest of America, rendering them strategically insignificant, Hitler was adamant that the Jewish Americans living there should be included in his "Final Solution."

Venturing away from his headquarters in New York City, SS General Ernst Kruger traveled to Massachusetts that winter to visit the construction site of another major concentration camp, just outside of Boston. While traveling through New England, he would often personally participate in the murders of Jews who had been rounded up by local *Einsatzgruppen* units (SS death squads).

Ernst Kruger was the embodiment of evil—a depraved sadist who took pleasure in taunting those unfortunate souls whose lives were about to be violently snuffed out at the hands of the Einsatzgruppen.

One of the ways Kruger satisfied his sadistic compulsion was to use his personal sidearm to execute Jewish prisoners who had been selected for immediate termination. After forcing them to dig a long trench, the Einsatzgruppen would bind the prisoners' hands behind their backs and stand them next to one another, facing the trench, in groups of seven. Using his eight-round Luger, Kruger would systematically walk down the line, shooting each prisoner in the back of the head as he pushed them, making sure the victim fell forward into the trench. When he reached the seventh prisoner in the line, Kruger would purposely discharge the firearm beside the prisoner's head and push.

Some of the prisoners would lie motionless next to the other victims in the pit, pretending to be dead. Those who did were subsequently buried alive. Occasionally, the confused prisoners would roll over and look up at the smiling SS general. Studying the fear in their eyes, Kruger would let them languish for several agonizing seconds before shooting them in the forehead.

In the winter of 1942, these trench massacres became commonplace across New England. They were only a prelude to the mass exterminations that would begin once the new concentration camp was completed.

Satisfied that construction of the Boston camp was progressing on schedule, the brutal SS general returned to New York in late spring. Upon his return, Ernst Kruger was pleased to learn that his *Hart Island* project was nearing completion.

Even though the ground war had bogged down, for the Allied aircrews flying raids behind enemy lines, the war in the skies above America was anything but static that winter.

Flying with the CAAF's 257th Bomb Wing, Colonel Rod Hurley commanded one of five B-17 squadrons out of Eustis Army Airfield in Virginia. Hurley and his men flew mission after mission into German-held territory. Even when they weren't flying, the crews were subjected to Luftwaffe raids on their home base near Newport News on the James River.

Whereas the Allied bombers went to great lengths to minimize the amount of collateral damage they inflicted on their raids, the Luftwaffe often dropped their bombs indiscriminately.

By early summer, the German air raids were becoming so intense along the front that, on July 4th, it was decided to begin moving the two capitals out of Washington and Richmond. The U.S. and Confederate governments were both relocated to Atlanta, Georgia, six hundred miles behind the lines.

On August 2nd, the 257th Bomb Wing, combined with two wings of the USAAF, flew the first large-scale daylight raid over New York. The primary target was the Third Reich Expeditionary Headquarters, which was housed inside the Empire State Building. The port facilities in the harbor were also targeted.

The massive raid was a failure. It resulted in higher-than-expected collateral damage to the city, and the strategic port was operational again in a matter of days. As for the Empire State Building—it was virtually unscathed.

Even though the Allied bombers had fighter escorts all the way to the target, the losses on the New York City raid were unsustainable. In the year since the invasion, the Germans had transformed New York into the most heavily defended city outside of Berlin. Plans for future raids over New York were later scrapped.

<u>*Chapter Forty-Two*</u>

05 August 1942

The morning was warm and muggy.

Every day for the past nine months, a large group of Rikers Island inmates, most of them political prisoners, had been herded from a tightly segregated section of the camp onto construction barges bound for Hart Island. The group was known as the *Sonderkommando* (Special Unit).

Natalie Rosenbaum was the only other inmate with whom they were allowed to have any contact. Every morning, each of the Sonderkommando workers would show his left forearm to Natalie as he boarded one of the barges, and she would record the tattooed serial number in her ledger. When the barges returned in the evening, she would record the numbers in her ledger again.

But on this morning, as the last of the barges carrying the Sonderkommando was getting under way and Natalie began to leave, one of the guards shoved her with his rifle and ordered her to remain at the dock. She watched as two more empty, rust-covered barges approached from downriver.

In his overcrowded barracks, Saul Rosenbaum was lying on the wooden shelf he shared with a half dozen other inmates. Two SS guards suddenly kicked open the door at the other end of the barracks. "*Aufwachen!*" [Wake up!] they shouted, storming into the barracks. "*Aufwachen!*"

"*Stand!*" one of the guards shouted as the inmates slowly began to roust themselves out of the wooden racks. Those who couldn't stand on their own were helped by the others. They lined up on either side of the barracks—many of them hunched over, unable to stand upright.

The guards made their way down the two long lines of inmates, one guard inspecting each line. Every so often, one of them would stop and single out an inmate, motioning for him to join a line at the center of the barracks. Saul Rosenbaum was the last to be selected.

As he stood at the back of the line, ready to be marched from the barracks, Saul noticed that all the men in front of him had one thing in common. They were all elderly and sick. Several of those who had been chosen were unable to walk on their own, prompting the impatient guards to assign younger, healthier inmates to help them.

Out into the sultry morning they marched—a ragged, sorrowful procession of helpless old men whose only crime was being of Jewish descent. As they were herded across the camp, they were joined by other groups of old men. A comparable number of women, also elderly and sick, were marched in separate groups. By the time they reached the dock, where the two empty barges waited, their number had swollen to nearly five hundred.

The guards formed a barricade to keep the male and female prisoners separated. Saul desperately scanned the large huddle of female inmates at the other end of the dock. Even though they all presented the same shabby appearance, he was able to pick her out of the crowd. "*Esther!*" he shouted as he held his hand high above the throng and waved.

"*Saul!*" she shouted back, recognizing her husband's voice. She frantically scanned the crush of men but was unable to find him.

Saul began pushing his way through the mass of humanity. When he reached the dividing line between the male and female prisoners, one of the guards shoved him back.

Standing off to the side with her ledger, Natalie Rosenbaum noticed the scuffle on the dock. She caught a glimpse of her father. "*Papa!*" she screamed. As she started to run toward him, one of the guards reached out and grabbed her. He slung her hard to the ground, sending her glasses flying. They landed on the concrete, cracking one of the lenses. Slowly rising to her feet, she found the broken glasses and picked them up. By the time she put them back on, she could no longer see her father among the hundreds of other prisoners.

Natalie heard rumbling and booming in the distance. At first, she thought the Allied bombers had returned; but as she saw the dark black clouds churning over the Bronx, she realized a thunderstorm was moving in from across the river. The guard who had slung Natalie to the ground grabbed her by the collar and pulled her to the ramp next to the first barge. As the frightened women were forced into the cargo hold one at a time, Natalie began counting. Halfway into the count, there was a familiar face looking back at her, just out of arm's reach. "*Mama,*" Natalie said, in a frail whisper.

Esther Rosenbaum, her sunken eyes filled with tears, blew a kiss to her distraught daughter. "I love you, Natalie."

Several more prisoners passed down the ramp before Natalie could gather herself to resume counting. When all the women were loaded, she entered the total in her ledger. Several guards removed the ramp and carried it to the second barge.

As the first barge got under way, the loading process began again. Saul Rosenbaum managed to linger on the dock until all the other men had boarded.

When she saw her father at the end of the line, Natalie moved closer to the ramp. As the guards restrained her, she extended her hand. She managed to briefly touch her father's outstretched hand as he was pushed onto the barge. Natalie fell to her knees, weeping.

The barge moved slowly through the water. As Saul Rosenbaum stood with the other prisoners crammed into the steel cargo hold, the storm clouds opened up on them. Three hundred yards away, just north of the river, a flash of lightning showered sparks from the roof of a Bronx tenement building. A split second later, the clap of thunder left Saul's ears ringing.

The barge continued east as the heavy downpour drenched everyone on board. The rain became so intense that the shoreline was no longer visible from the middle of the river. Saul had no idea where the Nazis were taking him and his fellow inmates, but he was certain this would be his—and Esther's—final day on earth. He prayed that when Esther's time came, she wouldn't know until the very end. He also prayed that, for her sake, the end would be quick.

As the storm grew even more violent, the wind churned the waters around the barge. The overloaded vessel began to pitch and roll as it rounded Throgs Point and headed north, into Long Island Sound. Some of the men became ill. Because they had not eaten in weeks, dry heaves were all they could muster.

When they landed on Hart Island, the first barge had long since offloaded and departed. The women were nowhere in sight. The SS guards drove Saul and his fellow inmates from the barge and marched them toward one of two cinder block structures. Rectangular in shape, each building stretched more than a hundred yards. In the distance, just beyond the rear of the buildings, three red-brick incinerator stacks towered above the camp.

As they marched, Saul and the other prisoners passed an SS general and several aides. While the callous general watched the inmates slog past him in the driving rain, one of the aides held an umbrella over his head. Two more aides stood next to the general, behind cameras mounted on tripods. Several prisoners—members of the Sonderkommando, who had arrived ahead of the other inmates—held a canvas over the cameras as the aides snapped photographs.

When they arrived outside the entrance to the windowless structure, the rain suddenly stopped. The men stood silently outside the entrance to the building. As the storm clouds parted, the midmorning sun began beating down. Steam began to rise from the tops of the prisoners' shaved heads.

An SS officer, carrying a megaphone, stepped up onto a wooden platform next to the steel doors at the front of the building. He informed the men that they were fortunate to be the first Rikers Island inmates processing into a newer, cleaner camp. The SS officer's morose tone belied the cheerful message he was delivering. He told the men they would be issued fresh uniforms after they showered inside the building. He ordered them to remove their clothing.

As more prisoners assigned to the Sonderkommando began gathering the piles of discarded uniforms, a pair of guards opened the steel doors. The men were herded through the entrance—into a single, long chamber. Saul Rosenbaum was one of the last men shoved into the building. He heard the large metal doors groaning on their hinges as they clanked shut behind him.

A small glass skylight was the only thing that separated the men from total darkness. The lack of ventilation in the crowded space made it hard to breathe. Some of the men became claustrophobic. Others became uneasy as they looked up toward the large showerheads above them. Several nervous shrieks began to echo through the cavernous chamber. Then, as they heard boots reverberating on the metal catwalk above the ceiling, the men fell silent.

At the end of the chamber farthest from Saul Rosenbaum, the guard on the catwalk dropped the first open canister of Zyklon B pellets into one of the pipes. Everyone trapped in the building heard it ping against the inside of the metal showerhead. As the hydrogen cyanide gas began to vaporize, it flowed through the showerhead and into the chamber. Those directly under it were the first to inhale the deadly fumes. As they breathed the gas, they began to choke. Some tried in vain to hold their breath. Their lungs burned and their eyes watered profusely as they attempted to push their way toward the other end of the chamber.

Their efforts were futile. One by one, canisters fell into the remaining showerheads. Saul Rosenbaum could hear the pinging as it got closer and closer to him. He and several others began pushing against the metal doors. They were locked tight. The wave of panicked cries moved swiftly toward Saul and the other men at the door. By the time the last canister fell, the first victims were already foaming at the mouth and bleeding from their ears. Without enough room to fall onto the concrete floor, many began to convulse violently in a squatting position.

As he began to choke, Saul prayed for strength. He desperately wanted to die with dignity. Though he was suffocating, he found the strength to prop his back against the metal door.

His body began to seize. After spasming for several excruciating seconds, Saul felt a sudden sense of calm. As he closed his eyes, he heard Esther gently calling his name. Then, as his soul was slipping away, he saw Natalie. She was dressed in a beautiful white gown, standing alone beneath a chuppah—the traditional Jewish wedding canopy. Tears flowed down her cheeks.

Several heartbeats from everlastingness and unable to speak, Saul Rosenbaum reached out subliminally to communicate his dying message to the fading vision of his daughter—*It's going to be okay, Ketzel. He'll send for you soon.*

Chapter Forty-Three
07 August 1942

James Winston recoiled as he shuffled through the photographs stacked on the desk in Ernst Kruger's empty office. The demented general had organized them in chronological order to be sent to the head of the SS, Heinrich Himmler. Kruger was confident that his boss in Berlin would be impressed with how efficiently the first group of prisoners had been exterminated in his new death factory.

Winston, the janitor, was shocked by the first few photos that showed the physical condition of the prisoners packed shoulder-to-shoulder aboard the barge. He was repulsed when he saw the photos of the emaciated men standing naked in the sunlight. They were no more than skeletons. When Winston saw the grisly images from inside the gas chamber, he became physically ill. The grotesque mass of tangled bodies was incomprehensible. By the time he got to the photographs of the crematorium—where Sonderkommando prisoners had been forced to stack the corpses like so much cordwood—James Winston was enraged.

He took several of the photos from the huge stack and slipped them inside his shoe. As he continued cleaning the office, he tried to forget the ghastly images he had just seen. Winston swore to himself he wouldn't look at the photos again before doing what needed to be done.

Several hours later, after he had completed his shift, he waited to be searched by the German guards at the 34th Street exit from the Empire State Building. At six feet, four inches and a well-chiseled two hundred thirty pounds, the forty-year-old janitor was an imposing figure, even to the well-armed soldiers guarding the Third Reich Expeditionary Headquarters.

The grandson of a South Carolina slave, James Winston was one of three dozen African-Americans who had been part of the building's maintenance staff when the Nazis took possession of it. The guards patting him down at the checkpoint would never have imagined that, at the time of the invasion, Winston had been in the process of earning his master's degree in languages from New York University.

As the unsuspecting soldiers conversed with one another, they signaled for him to pass. They had no way to know his German was as good as theirs, probably better.

More importantly, the high-ranking Nazis whose offices he regularly cleaned would never have imagined that James Winston, a know-nothing cretin in their twisted minds, was arguably the most valuable member of the burgeoning American Resistance. At his next assigned drop, he would pass the photos to Lieutenant Commander Mike Crofford, along with the other intelligence he had gathered.

As daylight faded from the concrete canyons in Midtown Manhattan, Winston walked west on the sidewalk next to 34th Street. He made his way toward the subway station, where he routinely caught the No. 3 Train to Harlem. Along the way, he passed the bombed-out ruins of Macy's Department Store on the opposite side of the street. He looked to his left, around the corner, toward an all-too-familiar sight. It was the disquieting spectacle of armed German troops entering and leaving Penn Station en masse. High above the troops, stretched across the edifice of Madison Square Garden, was an enormous blood-red banner.

As James Winston gazed upon the illuminated black and white swastika at the center of the banner, he was determined not to let his children grow up slaves to a self-proclaimed "master race."

Chapter Forty-Four
13 September 1942

The young corporal set his coffee cup and food tray on one of the long tables in the center of the mess hall. After taking a seat next to the other men, he placed his palms flat on the table, examining his breakfast. Having already tasted the coffee on his way through the chow line, he knew it was barely lukewarm. The several strips of bacon were burnt to a crisp, and the heaping mound of eggs in front of him had been reconstituted from a box of powder. With a texture more like paste than scrambled eggs, they had retained the shape of the scoop used to slap them onto the tray.

His sergeant, sitting on the opposite side of the table, looked on as the corporal summoned up the courage to take his first bite. "You'd better eat 'em quick," the sergeant said sarcastically. "It's gettin' so we can't go more than three days without a goddamned air raid around here."

As if on cue, the sirens at Eustis Army Airfield began to wail. The large hall echoed as it erupted into a cacophony of sliding chairs and clattering utensils. Some of the chairs toppled over and crashed to the floor as the soldiers and airmen shoved them back from the tables. As everyone scrambled toward the exit, the young corporal, after jumping to his feet, paused to down his coffee. It was only a few seconds—not enough time to matter.

His sergeant, waiting next to the exit, snapped at him. "Let's *go! Now!*"

In his haste to get rid of the coffee, the corporal dropped the cup onto the floor. It shattered, exploding into jagged shards. The coffee splattered on his trousers as he hurried toward his waiting sergeant.

The two men bolted from the mess hall, racing toward their gun emplacement. As the door slammed behind them, they were both cut down by a single, low-flying Bf 109.

Colonel Rod Hurley emerged from his office. As he ran from the hangar, he slung his cigar away in disgust. He began heading toward one of two dozen bomb shelters scattered around the airfield. As he ran, he could hear the unmistakable sound of a Ju 87 Stuka—diving in a near-vertical descent—directly overhead. The Nazis had installed windmill-driven sirens on their deadly dive bomber, hoping to intimidate their enemies on the ground.

The sirens served their intended purpose.

Hurley sprinted as quickly as he could—for as long as he dared—before diving onto the tarmac. He skidded along the pavement just as the bomb from the Stuka struck the hangar behind him. As he lay facedown, the blast sent debris flying all around him. The shredded leather on the arms of his flight jacket revealed his bloodied elbows.

Hurley sprang to his feet and resumed running, along with dozens of other men, toward the relative safety of the nearby bunker. As he got closer, he wondered why no one was manning the .50 caliber machine gun above the entrance.

As the Stukas continued to rain bombs onto specific targets, Focke-Wulf and Messerschmitt fighters wreaked widespread havoc with a series of high-speed, low-level strafing runs.

Rod Hurley was tired. He was tired of losing men and airplanes on the ground. He was tired of cowering inside this bunker and waiting for the Allied fighters to repulse the Luftwaffe's incessant air raids. He was tired of Hitler and the Nazis. He was tired of the war.

His next action was borne not of heroism. It was a product of anger and frustration. Hurley, instead of scurrying down the steps to the underground shelter, ran straight toward the unmanned gun emplacement. He dove over the wall of sandbags that surrounded the gun. Scrambling to his feet, he swung the M2 Browning around on its mount and pulled the charging handle back. He began tracking a low-flying Fw 190 through the circular iron sights. He aligned the crosshairs on his target and began firing. The tracers passed so far behind the German fighter that they came closer to hitting the Allied P-47 that was pursuing it.

As Hurley looked around for another German attacker, he spotted a Stuka in a vertical dive. Once again, he failed to sufficiently lead his target. The rounds went nowhere near the dive bomber as it continued screaming down, zeroing in on another nearby hangar. Frustrated by his lack of success, Hurley decided it was time to abandon the gun and duck inside the bunker.

The Stuka pilot missed his mark, sending his bomb wide of the hangar. As Hurley attempted to vault over the sandbags that surrounded the gun emplacement, the errant bomb from the Stuka landed close enough to knock him back into the pit. He fell against the gun, striking the back of his head against the hot metal barrel. His scalp was split wide open as he continued falling.

As he lay there looking skyward, blood began to soak the ground next to his head. He felt a stinging sensation in his arms and legs. Unable to move, he watched the tracers from a P-47 catch up to the Stuka that had delivered the errant bomb.

Several hundred feet above him, the German dive bomber burst into flames and came apart. One of the main landing gear mounts from the Stuka's fixed undercarriage came cartwheeling out of the fireball. Rod Hurley watched helplessly as the heavy wheel and strut appeared to be tumbling on a path directly toward him. He closed his eyes and waited.

<u>Chapter Forty-Five</u>
04 November 1942

The barges were coming weekly now, always on Wednesday. On this particular Wednesday, for the first time since they had laid their plans, the weather and tide conditions were right. Watching from their two speedboats, Marc Krbec and the small band of Resistance fighters waited patiently in the small cove near Throgs Point.

A moderately thick fog had persisted into midmorning and showed no signs of lifting. The prevailing visibility was just good enough for the Resistance fighters in the cove—but not good enough for the SS guards on Hart Island—to see the barges rounding the point. The Sonderkommando barge had already passed. The barges carrying the inmates who were headed to the gas chambers would be rounding the point soon.

Located four miles south of Hart Island, Throgs point was situated at the southeastern tip of a mile-long peninsula. The peninsula extended from the Bronx into the East River estuary. The cove where the Resistance fighters waited was near the place where the river merged with Long Island Sound. The eastbound barges from Rikers Island routinely passed several hundred yards from the cove as they emerged from the river and turned northward into the sound.

Prior to the invasion, the nineteenth-century fort that sat on the point had been home to the New York State Merchant Marine Academy. Many of the men fighting with the Resistance were former cadets from the academy, including the men standing at the helms of the two speedboats inside the cove. A half dozen men sat in each boat, preparing to intercept the barges.

As he waited in the second boat, Krbec knew that even if their ambitious interdiction succeeded, it would only amount to a small victory. There would be two more barges next week—and two more the week after that. Still, if they managed to stop only these two from reaching Hart Island, they would deliver more than five hundred innocents from Ernst Kruger's incinerator.

Nearly a half hour after the Sonderkommando barge had passed, the ghostly silhouette of the barge ferrying female inmates to the gas chambers appeared through the fog. From his seat in the second boat, Krbec watched as the first boat slowly exited the cove. As soon as it was clear, he heard the rumbling motor rev to full power.

A minute later, Krbec heard shouts, followed by short bursts of automatic gunfire. Several minutes after that—another round of gunfire. He and the other men aboard the second boat strained to see through the fog. When they saw the barge turning away from Hart Island, they knew their fellow Resistance fighters had successfully pirated the vessel from the SS troops who were guarding it. They watched as the barge, resembling a fleeting apparition, faded back into the fog.

Krbec knew it would be his turn soon. His pulse began to quicken. He took the M1A1 machine gun from his shoulder and detached the magazine, examining it one last time. He shoved the magazine back into the receiver and pulled the charging handle aft. He released the spring-loaded handle, sending the first of thirty rounds into the chamber. Finally, he checked the four extra magazines he was carrying inside his jacket. He knew that if he had to use them all, it would mean their operation was failing. This was to be a lightning-quick assault. If they didn't succeed early on, they weren't likely to succeed at all.

The helmsman started the engine. Krbec sat listening to the powerful, uneven strokes of the camshaft inside the idling engine. He listened—and waited. He waited for nearly a half hour.

"There it is!" one of the men shouted. The six armed Resistance fighters stood and took their positions along the portside rail. With his head down, Krbec prayed the SS guards aboard the first barge had not had a chance to radio a warning to the second barge.

The helmsman engaged the propeller shaft. The idling boat began to make way, slowly moving out of the cove. The helmsman turned the boat toward the barge and rammed the throttle forward.

Standing near the stern, Krbec felt the aft end of the boat dip as the bow rose from the water. He and the other men held fast to the rail, leaning forward to maintain their balance. Each of the men used his free arm to aim his weapon toward the barge's pilothouse. Each held the gun's stock tightly against his shoulder. Marc Krbec had never experienced the sense of exhilaration he was feeling. The sudden rush of adrenaline throughout his body made him feel invincible. His heart was pounding.

Thirty yards from the barge, the men opened fire. The six machine guns sprayed the pilothouse, shattering the windows and killing all but one of the guards. As the lone surviving guard ducked beneath the windows, the barge's captain was also mortally wounded.

As the boat raced past the barge's stern, the remaining guard popped back up, firing several rounds from his rifle. Two hundred yards past the barge, the helmsman chopped the throttle and swung the boat around. Krbec and the other men shifted to the starboard rail. As the boat idled, they ejected the spent magazines from their guns and jammed reloads into the empty receivers. The helmsman again shoved the throttle forward.

This time, as they sped past the now-drifting barge and peppered the pilot house a second time, the helmsman suddenly reversed the throttle and threw the helm hard over to port. The agile boat turned sideways and decelerated before reversing course again, back toward the target vessel. Approaching the barge's port side on a parallel course, the helmsman brought the speedboat alongside.

One of the men swung a grappling hook on a rope up to the pilot-house deck. Krbec was the second man up the rope and over the rail. As the first attacker leapt aboard the barge, the last remaining SS guard stepped outside the pilothouse and fired once. The slain Resistance fighter fell just in front of Krbec, who sent a lethal burst of rounds into the guard, dropping him onto the deck.

From down in the cargo hold, forward of the pilothouse, two hundred and seventy-seven men began to shout with joy. Many of them fell to their knees, overcome with emotion. Others clasped their hands together and raised them toward the heavens.

As three more Resistance fighters jumped aboard, Krbec quickly took the helm and turned the hijacked barge away from Hart Island. The other armed fighter remained in the speedboat as the helmsman steered it in front of the barge. He began leading Krbec toward Kings Point, at the northern reach of the Long Island shoreline. A dozen minutes later, as the shore came into view through the fog, the speedboat's helmsman pointed his hand straight ahead in a tomahawking motion. He turned his boat and accelerated out of the barge's path as Krbec ran the captured vessel aground on a short stretch of beach in a municipal park.

A large cadre of men—some armed, some carrying ladders—emerged from several nearby trucks and ran to meet the barge. Moving quickly, they placed several of the ladders against the hull. As the first few men reached the tops of the ladders, they were handed more ladders to drop inside the barge's cargo hold. They climbed down into the hold, where they were greeted as saviors by the frail men who surrounded them. Many of the prisoners genuflected and kissed the hands of those who were helping them onto the ladders. Others simply shook their hands or embraced them. Some of the prisoners, too weak to climb on their own, had to be carried up the ladders by their rescuers. It would take almost half an hour to offload them all.

As the rescued prisoners were brought up out of the cargo hold, Marc Krbec and the other three men in the pilothouse carried the body of their fallen comrade forward, along the bulwark of the hull. Two of the men climbed down a side ladder and waited in the surf as Krbec and the other man got down on their knees and carefully lowered the body into their waiting arms.

As the first two men carried their fellow Resistance fighter ashore, the third man climbed down the ladder behind them. Krbec rose and stood alone atop the bulwark. He turned and gazed down into the half-emptied barge. Despite the loss of his comrade, Marc Krbec felt a tremendous sense of satisfaction as he watched scores of rescued prisoners being evacuated from the hijacked vessel.

Finally, Krbec climbed down the side of the barge and waded ashore to shake hands with his fellow Resistance fighters on the beach. The operation had come off just as planned. Counting the two hundred and ninety-one women from the first barge, they had saved five hundred and sixty-eight prisoners from the gas chambers. It was a good day—a *great* day.

As the rescued prisoners were escorted from the beach, they were introduced to several hundred local residents who had gathered to take them in and hide them. There was no shortage of New Yorkers willing to place their own lives at risk in order to protect those who had been liberated from the Nazi death camp. Because most of the Jewish population was either inside the concentration camp or in hiding, almost all the residents who showed up on the beach that day were not Jewish. Many of them even had German surnames. That was of no consequence. They were Americans—doing what they could to protect their fellow countrymen.

After the last of the prisoners had been taken from the barge, the empty hull was barely resting on the sand. As the tide rose, lifting the barge from the beach, a dozen men pushed it offshore, casting it adrift. In a few hours, the fog would lift and the Nazis would recover the empty barge from the middle of the sound. By that time, however, they would have no way to know where the prisoners had been put ashore.

In the midst of it all, Marc Krbec noticed one prisoner who refused to leave the beach. He kept shaking his head, declining to go with the family who was there to provide him refuge. Curious, Krbec walked toward the man and studied him. Unlike most of the others who had been rescued, he wasn't wearing the Star of David on his tattered prison uniform. Krbec spoke to the man. "You're not Jewish, are you?"

"I am not," the man answered.

Krbec recognized the accent. "You're Puerto Rican?"

"Yes, I am."

"Why won't you go with these people?" Krbec asked the man. "What is it you want?"

"I want to go with *you*." The man pointed to the machine gun slung across Krbec's shoulder. "I do not wish to hide from the Nazis. I wish to *fight* them."

"What's your name?" Krbec asked.

"My name is Mateo Vargas," the man answered.

"Why were you in the camp?"

"I was arrested for hiding my friends above my store."

Krbec was reluctant to let himself believe that the man standing in front of him could be the bodega owner who had hidden Toby Pozniak's fiancé and her parents from the SS. "Were your friends named Rosenbaum?" he asked.

"Yes, they were. How did you know that?"

Krbec was stunned. He wasn't sure he wanted to hear Vargas's answer to his next question. "Do you know what happened to them?" he asked.

"I fear that Señor Rosenbaum and his wife are dead," Vargas answered. "They were among the first to be sent away in the barges."

"What about their daughter—Natalie? Do you know what's happened to *her?*"

It was late, almost midnight. Robert Oppenheimer thought about waiting until morning to deliver the sealed message he had just received from the army courier. He sat inside his bungalow, yawning, as he studied the envelope from Admiral Fuller. Fuller had scribbled "URGENT FOR DR. POZNIAK" across it in his own handwriting.

Oppenheimer smugly thought to himself, *Just how urgent could this correspondence be? After all, if it was really that pressing, why hadn't the admiral delivered it himself?* He started to turn out the light and go back to sleep. Even though Fuller was technically his boss, Oppenheimer had never really thought of him as his superior. The arrogant physicist even believed he deserved the credit for the admiral's recent promotion. He figured the military brass had determined that a scientist of his stature rated someone higher in rank than a captain as his liaison.

As he reached toward the lamp to turn it off, Oppenheimer remembered how he had lectured Admiral Fuller about communicating directly with his scientists. He reluctantly concluded that Fuller was merely ceding to his demands by asking him to deliver this "urgent" message in the middle of the night.

Oppenheimer begrudgingly put on his robe and slippers and stepped into the crisp mountain air. He walked past several darkened bungalows, to Toby Pozniak's quarters. He knocked on the door and waited. After several seconds, he impatiently knocked again. He saw the window shade light up.

Pozniak opened the door, half awake. *"Robert?* What's going on?"

"This just came for you." Oppenheimer handed the envelope to Pozniak. Without saying another word, he turned and walked away. He really had no interest in what was in the message.

"Thanks," Pozniak said as Oppenheimer disappeared into the darkness.

He shut the door and walked across the sitting area, into the small kitchenette. He took a knife from a drawer and sat down at the table. He slit the envelope and removed a single piece of paper. Toby Pozniak unfolded the following short, handwritten message:

> Confirmation received from Lieutenant Commander
> Crofford—Natalie Rosenbaum alive.
>
> —Fuller

Chapter Forty-Six

30 November 1942

As an early snow began falling outside his window, Rod Hurley had no way to know. For the past eleven weeks, his entire world had been the ceiling directly above his head.

Since fracturing the second vertebra in his neck, the National Naval Medical Center in Bethesda, Maryland, had been Hurley's home. A "hangman's fracture" the surgeon had called his injury. Hurley remembered how the doctor, while showing him the x-rays, had remarked to him how lucky he was. "The paralysis is temporary," the doctor had told him. "It'll take a long time—six months maybe—but you'll likely make a full recovery."

As Hurley looked back on the past three months, he didn't feel all that lucky. The first few weeks following the injury had been filled with anguish. By the time the pain from the injury had finally subsided, his muscles had already begun to atrophy. The body cast that covered his entire torso and head had forced him to lie flat on his back and stare straight up at the ceiling twenty-four hours a day.

The irritation from the rash inside the cast had become excruciating. He had repeatedly begged the medical staff for a tool he could use to scratch it, but their answer had always been the same—the risk of infection was too great. Finally, one of the Navy corpsmen had taken pity on him and, on condition of anonymity, smuggled a wire coat hanger to him.

The boredom had slowly crushed Hurley's morale. The only excitement he had experienced was during air raids. Every time the sirens had sounded, the medical staff and ambulatory patients had taken cover in the bomb shelters. Hurley and the other bedridden patients had been left to ride it out. The nearby explosions had rattled the windows and shaken chunks of plaster from the ceiling, but—fortunately for Hurley and the other immobilized patients—the Luftwaffe had, so far at least, refrained from targeting the hospital.

Rod Hurley had done a lot of thinking over the past several months. Because he'd been laid up in his hospital bed, thinking had been about the only thing he could do. He had thought about how much he missed his family back in Texas. He had spoken to Margie by phone. He had also written her letters, although it had been difficult to hold the clipboard where he could see what he was writing.

That would all change today. Today was the day he was to be liberated from his personal-sized prison. As soon as the doctor removed the cast from his torso, he could begin his rehabilitation. The harder he worked, the quicker he would recover. The quicker he recovered, the sooner he could get back into the fight.

As he lay there in his hospital bed, thinking about everything that had happened over the past two years, Rod Hurley wasn't all that sure he actually *wanted* to get back into the fight.

Chapter Forty-Seven
03 December 1942

On the 1942 Jewish calendar, the Festival of Lights began on the first Thursday in December. It was day one of the eight-day Hanukkah celebration. Thirty days had passed since the American Resistance had rescued five hundred and sixty-eight prisoners destined for the Hart Island gas chambers. In the four weeks since, more than two thousand Rikers Island inmates had been gassed in mass exterminations.

For Ernst Kruger, that wasn't enough.

Kruger had been incensed upon learning of the raid. Now, the citizens of New York nervously waited to see if he would carry out his threat.

In the days following the attack, the enraged SS general had issued an ultimatum aimed at reclaiming his lost prisoners. Unless someone came forward to inform the SS of the prisoners' whereabouts before the beginning of Hanukkah, the Einsatzgruppen would begin carrying out random executions throughout the city.

Beginning on the first day of the Jewish celebration, seventy-one citizens were to be randomly pulled into the streets and summarily executed. If no one talked—seventy-one more would be executed on the second day. The executions would continue until someone came forward with the information Kruger sought. If necessary, they were to continue throughout the eight-day holiday.

Unless someone was willing to betray his fellow citizens, five hundred and sixty-eight New Yorkers would be randomly executed—one for each of the prisoners that had been taken from the SS in the raid.

Patrick Murphy was a twenty-two-year-old grandson of Irish immigrants. His grandfather, after processing through Ellis Island, had found a job washing dishes in Brooklyn. His father had been a New York City police officer. When Patrick was seven years old, his father had moved him, his mother and his five siblings from Brooklyn to Staten Island.

As a youngster, Patrick Murphy had attended Sacred Heart Catholic School. From there, he had enrolled at St. Peter's Boys' High School. Patrick had met Glennis, his future wife, during a Catholic high school mixer at St. Joseph Hill Academy, where Glennis was a student.

Following his high school graduation, Patrick had become a carpenter. He and Glennis had married and moved into a small house in the West Brighton section of Staten Island. One year later, Glennis had given birth to a baby girl—Katelynn. The Murphys had only recently celebrated Katelynn's third birthday.

Since the invasion, Patrick Murphy had been taking odd jobs anywhere he could find them. On this day, he was repairing a porch for a neighbor down the street. He was sawing a piece of lumber when he saw them coming from a block away. It was the Einsatzgruppen.

The twelve SS death-squad members, with rifles slung across their shoulders, were riding in the back of a Mercedes-Benz troop truck. There was no mistaking who they were. The white *SS* lightning bolts on the sides of their black helmets made them instantly recognizable.

Murphy, like everyone else in the city, had heard Ernst Kruger issue his ultimatum during the general's weekly radio address. He thought about darting inside the house but decided it might draw unwanted attention. He tried his best to look inconspicuous. *Surely the truck will just keep going,* he thought to himself as he continued sawing.

He held his breath as the truck continued rolling toward him, closer and closer. He began to shiver in the cold December air.

The young husband and father breathed a huge sigh of relief when the truck passed by without slowing down. A few seconds later, Patrick Murphy's heart sank as he heard the sound of the squealing brakes. When he heard the truck shift into reverse, he stopped sawing mid-stroke and froze. Unable to move, Murphy heard the low-pitched whine of the transmission as the truck quickly backed toward the house where he was working.

Glennis Murphy heard the frantic knocking on her front door. The young mother quickly got up from the living room floor, where she was helping Katelynn to dress her porcelain doll.

As soon as Glennis opened the door, she knew something was terribly wrong. It was Mrs. Shively, the widow whose porch Patrick had gone to repair. She was crying, unable to gather herself to speak.

"*What is it?*" Glennis shouted.

Try as she might, Mrs. Shively was unable to say the words. She just pointed toward the street in front of her house.

Glennis pushed Mrs. Shively aside and jumped from her porch. She sprinted toward the widow's house until she saw her dead husband lying in the middle of the street. The young wife and mother stopped in her tracks and fell to the ground. Several neighbors ran to her aid as a crowd gathered around Patrick's body.

Mrs. Shively, still shaken, looked through the Murphys' open door, into the living room. Katelynn was quietly playing with her doll. The crying woman composed herself as best she could and went inside.

She picked Katelynn up and held her in her arms.

By sundown, there were bodies in each of the five New York City boroughs—seventy-one of them in all. The SS simply left the bodies lying in the streets as an object lesson.

Still, no one came forward. Not one person in the entire city, at least no one who knew where the liberated prisoners were being sheltered, was willing to give up his fellow citizens.

Ernst Kruger was beside himself with rage. He wondered why these stubborn fools would sacrifice themselves for a bunch of worthless Jews. In the days that followed, more innocent New Yorkers were randomly executed.

Still—no one came forward.

Chapter Forty-Eight
11 December 1942

Nearly two thirds of New York's Jewish residents were being held on Rikers Island. The other third, including Marc Krbec and the other Jewish Resistance fighters, lived in the shadows.

When the New York City Department of Corrections had constructed the Rikers Island jail facility in 1932, they had intended it to house ten thousand short-term prisoners. By December of 1942, nearly one million inmates were crammed onto the four-hundred-acre site.

It was Friday, the last day of Hanukkah. Before the day was done, seventy-one more New Yorkers would die on the cold, damp streets of the city. Inside the Rikers Island concentration camp, Natalie Rosenbaum was making her morning rounds. Each day, she visited all the barracks in the camp. Her notebook contained a page for each building.

It had become routine. When Natalie was told someone inside the barracks had died during the previous night, she would enter the building and have the inmates take her to the corpse. She would record the number painted on the rack. At the completion of her rounds, the numbers would be passed to a "sanitation detail" within the Workers' Unit. They were tasked with gathering the corpses and stacking them on the dock. Later, the Sonderkommando would load the corpses onto a barge and take them to the incinerator on Hart Island.

On this particular morning, Natalie had already located a half dozen corpses. Most of them would barely be recognizable to anyone who had known the person before they were interned at Rikers Island. Still, there was something familiar about the face gaping back at her. It was something about the eyes. Even in death, Karen Berkovich possessed a look that was innocent and kind. Natalie wasn't even aware that her former college roommate had been imprisoned in the camp.

For the first time in a long time, the hardened defenses around Natalie's emotions were breached. Tears welled up in her eyes as she reached out and touched Karen's face. She sobbed and whispered her friend's name as she stroked what was left of her hair. Several of the other women stood beside Natalie and patted her shoulders, trying to comfort her.

That evening, sixteen hundred miles from Rikers Island, Margie and Sam Hurley decorated their Christmas tree. As Margie stood on a stepladder, draping garland onto the tree, Sam took considerable pride in hanging his miniature B-17 on one of the lower branches. Margie Hurley silently offered up a prayer for Sam's father, still recovering at the hospital in Bethesda, Maryland.

At the same time, Natalie Rosenbaum was lying on the hard plywood shelf that served as her bed. Because she was the longest-surviving inmate in her barracks, Natalie's rack was in a choice location. It was situated in the southeast corner, protected from the prevailing winter winds that drafted through the planks in the barrack walls.

Natalie shared the rack with five other female inmates, all of whom were asleep. She had been in the camp long enough that she was no longer cognizant of the foul stench that pervaded her bedding—a thin layer of dirty rags on top of the plywood. This secluded corner of the barracks afforded Natalie her only sanctuary from the hellish circumstances that surrounded her.

To commemorate the Jewish holiday, the women in the barracks had constructed a crude hanukkiah (a nine-branched candelabrum). It was prominently displayed atop a crate at the center of the room. Natalie watched the shamash (the "servant" candle) and the eight main candles flicker in the night. The candles provided a small bit of illumination in a place that would otherwise have been void of any light at all.

As she watched the candles flicker, Natalie's mind drifted. She thought about Karen Berkovich. She thought about her parents, knowing they had died a cruel and horrifying death. Lastly, she thought about Toby Pozniak—wondering what had become of him. Would she die not knowing?

As Margie Hurley was offering up her prayer far away from Rikers Island, a cold rush of wind suddenly penetrated the cracks on the north side of Natalie's barracks. The gust extinguished all nine candles of the hanukkiah, leaving nothing but darkness.

As she lay there in that wretched moment, Natalie Rosenbaum's faith in God was also extinguished.

<u>*Chapter Forty-Nine*</u>
January 1943

...Toby Pozniak slowly makes his way up the dark stairwell. It's a long, arduous climb.

Reaching the 86th floor, he pauses to catch his breath before cracking the door slightly ajar. He opens it just enough to spy into the hallway. Just as Lieutenant Commander Crofford had promised, the SS guard is nowhere in sight. He closes the door and removes the Navy-issue .45 from his coat pocket. He chambers a round. Holding the pistol in his right hand, he cautiously opens the door, checking the hallway one more time.

He steps into the empty hallway and moves silently toward the conference room where Adolf Hitler is scheduled to meet alone with Ernst Kruger. He hears muffled voices from a conversation within the room. He checks over his shoulder—still no guard.

Slowly opening the door, he peers inside the dimly lit room. He is surprised to see, not two—but three people sitting at the conference table. He recognizes Ernst Kruger, but the other two are sitting with their backs to the door. One is a woman.

Surmising the male with his back to him is Hitler, he commits. He steps into the room and points the .45 at the back of Hitler's head. Before he can get off a shot, Kruger has instantaneously risen and produced a Luger aimed straight at Pozniak. As Pozniak freezes, the SS general unexpectedly trains his pistol toward the woman and shouts, "If the Führer dies—she dies!"

The woman turns around to look at Hitler's would-be assassin. "Toby!" she shrieks, tears running down her cheeks.

Through her familiar wire-rimmed eyeglasses, Pozniak sees the terror in her eyes. "Natalie!" he screams, still pointing the gun at Hitler's head.

Just then, Pozniak feels the presence of another person in a pitch-black corner of the room. A wheelchair-bound man partially emerges from the darkness, his face still in the shadows. The faceless man points at Hitler and yells, "Do it, Pozniak! Pull the trigger!" Pozniak is still frozen. He doesn't know what to do. The two men continue shouting at him—one imploring him to shoot, the other warning him to lower his weapon.

This is it. This is his test—his moment of truth.

Natalie pleads for her life. Pozniak lowers the .45 to his side just as Kruger screams "you ignorant Jew!" and pulls the trigger—

Toby Pozniak sat straight up in bed, covered with sweat. It was the second time he had been haunted by the dream since learning Natalie was alive.

<u>*Chapter Fifty*</u>

22 February 1943

Rod Hurley held tightly to the rails of the mechanical treadmill. "That's enough," he barked to the Navy corpsman who was helping him to take steps with his atrophied legs. "I'm done for today."

The corpsman shook his head. "We're just gettin' started, Colonel. If you're gonna make any progress, you gotta keep goin' after it starts to hurt."

"I *said* that's enough," Hurley growled. "Take me back."

"Suit yourself, Colonel." The corpsman continued to shake his head disappointedly as he helped Hurley down from the treadmill and into his wheelchair. "You have a visitor waiting for you in your room."

"That's wonderful," Hurley said cynically. "Just what I need right now. Who is it?"

"Didn't get his name," the corpsman responded as he wheeled Hurley down the basement passageway toward the elevator. "But he did sound like he was from the same neck of the woods as you." The corpsman stopped and hit the button to summon the elevator.

The two men waited silently as they stared at the clock-like indicator above the elevator doors. The pointer slowly moved counter-clockwise until it reached the "B" on the left side of the dial.

The outer doors opened, exposing the steel cage. The corpsman slid the accordion-like gate to one side. After turning the wheelchair around, he pulled Hurly into the elevator. He closed the gate and pushed the button for the seventh floor.

Hurley sat brooding as the outer doors slowly closed. He heard the relay click, energizing the giant winch on top of the carriage. As the elevator began to rise, he could hear the noisy cables and pulleys echoing inside the tall shaft. Hurley watched as the painted floor numbers on the back sides of the outer doors scrolled past on the other side of the gate. "You got a cigarette, Smitty?"

The corpsman gave Hurley a cigarette and lit it for him.

When the elevator stopped at the seventh floor, the outer door opened. The corpsman slid the gate to one side and pushed Hurley's wheelchair out of the elevator. After closing the gate behind him, he wheeled Hurley down the hall. When they rounded the corner into his room, Hurley was greeted by a familiar face.

"Hello, Hurley—how you gettin' along?"

"Hello, Charlie. To tell you the truth, I've been better."

In all the years Charles Morrow had known Rod Hurley, he had never been addressed as anything other than "Colonel" by his former protégé.

"Chair or bed?" the corpsman asked Hurley.

"Bed," Hurley answered. "Charlie, you wanna sit? There's a chair there in the corner. Pull it up."

"No, thanks. I'm okay," Morrow replied.

The corpsman helped Hurley out of the wheelchair and into the steel-framed bed. He cranked the head of the mattress up until Hurley signaled for him to stop. "Anything else, Colonel?"

"No…thanks, Smitty."

"Sure thing, sir."

Hurley watched Morrow follow the corpsman to the door and close it behind him. His old CO turned and walked back to the side of the bed. Hurley wasn't sure why Morrow was there. "So, how've *you* been?" Hurley asked him. "You mind handing me that ashtray over there?" Hurley pointed to the table next to his bed.

Morrow picked up the metal ashtray and handed it to Hurley. "When did you start smokin' cigarettes?"

Hurley laid the ashtray on his lap. "Ever since a cigarette became the only thing I can get my hands on. There isn't a cigar to be had in this place." Not in the mood for small talk, Hurley pressed his old friend. "Hey—what brings you here, anyway?"

"When I get back to San Antonio, I'll be sure to send you a box of good cigars. It looks like you're gonna be here a while longer." Morrow got to the point of his visit. "I'm here because Margaret asked me to come."

Hurley tapped his cigarette on the edge of the ashtray.

"*Margie?* …She asked you to come see me? Why would she do that?"

"She's worried about you, Hurley."

"*Worried?*" Hurley became indignant. "Why would she be worried about me, Charlie? Just because I'm stuck in a hospital two thousand miles from home. Just because I'm laid up in one of the few buildings still standing in this bombed-out city? Just because I *can't walk?*"

Morrow stood silently for several seconds. He had never seen his former protégé this way. "She's worried about all those things, Hurley—but that's not why she sent me. She showed me some of the letters you've written since you've been here. She said she's never heard you say the kinds of things you wrote in those letters. You sounded like someone who's given up. She said the man who's saying those things is not the man she married. And…to be perfectly blunt…he's not the man I knew back at Randolph Field."

Hurley smashed his half-smoked cigarette into the ashtray and looked out the window. "I wish she hadn't shown you those letters, Charlie. She had no right to do that. And I wish you hadn't come here. I think I'm getting tired now. Please go."

"I'll go; but not until I tell you what I think. I think you're afraid."

Hurley looked back at Morrow. "That's bullshit, Charlie. You really think I'm scared of going back into combat? I don't give a *damn* what happens to me right now."

"I *know* you don't. That's your problem. I don't think you're worried about Rod Hurley. I think you're sick of watching *other* men die—the men under Rod Hurley's command. I think you're tired of writing letters to their families. I think—"

Hurley cut him off. "I don't give a damn *what* you think, Charlie. What would *you* know about what I've been through over the past three years?" Even before the words had left his mouth, Hurley regretted having uttered them. He knew Morrow had lost half his squadron over France during the last war. "I'm sorry, Charlie—I didn't mean that. I had no right to say it."

Morrow turned away and started to leave. As he opened the door, he stopped and turned back around. "You know, Hurley—I once stood with you next to your father's grave. You remember what you said to me that day? You said you hoped we would never again stand by and let someone else fight our wars for us." He looked Hurley straight in the eye. "This is *your* war, Rod. Who's going to fight it for you?"

Hurley's own words hit him like a ton of bricks.

Morrow turned and walked out the door, leaving it open behind him. He had taken several steps down the hallway when Hurley shouted at him from his bed. "*Colonel Morrow*—wait up!"

Morrow stopped. He turned and slowly walked back into the room.

"Were you serious about sending those cigars?" Hurley asked him.

"I'll send 'em," Morrow replied.

"Thanks. I appreciate that. Can you do me one more favor before you leave?"

"What is it?"

"Find Smitty for me. Tell him I'm ready to go back to the treadmill."

Chapter Fifty-One
29 March 1943

By early spring, Field Marshal Friedrich von Essen had begun launching offensives aimed at breaking the stalemate along the Mason-Dixon front.

Multiple times, his field generals managed to push the Allied defenders southward into Maryland and Virginia. Every time the German troops gained significant ground, bulging the front, General Eisenhower's forces managed to launch successful counterattacks on the invaders' flanks.

On one occasion, as the Germans were retreating, General Patton managed to drive his tanks fifty miles into German-held territory, all the way to Williamsport, Pennsylvania. He was eventually forced to retreat, but not before tens of thousands of refugees were able to escape southward to the Allied side of the front.

Meanwhile, across the Atlantic, England continued to fight the Germans in a massive air war. Although Hitler had managed to shut off the flow of war supplies from the United States, the resources he was allocating to the war in America were resources that couldn't be used to invade England. Ironically, the Americans were still indirectly helping the British to survive.

Through it all, the several hundred scientists under Rear Admiral Chauncey Fuller's top-secret command continued to work night and day on the weapon they hoped would end the war.

In Atlanta, Georgia, a small but powerful group of men were gathered inside the Allied War Department. Chauncey Fuller had a difficult job on his hands. To say that Robert Oppenheimer was a "loose cannon" in these situations would be a gross understatement. At any given moment, Fuller never knew what the eccentric physicist was likely to say—or to whom he was likely to say it.

"I have no way to be certain *when* we'll be ready to test a bomb," Oppenheimer answered, evoking a frown from President Truman, who had posed the question. "Possibly two months from now—possibly two *years* from now. In fact, it's entirely possible that the atomic bomb only exists in a theoretical universe. It might be unattainable."

Truman glared at Oppenheimer. "You're telling me that three hundred of our best scientists have been working on this bomb for more than three years now, and you don't even know if the damn thing is going to work?"

Oppenheimer was annoyed that anyone, let alone this boorish Southerner, would speak to him that way. "The device will work—theoretically. ...*Practically?* ...We won't know until we test it."

Admiral Fuller tried to right the ship. "If I *may*, Mr. President. We're confident the bomb will work. Unfortunately, based on the data we have, the bomb will weigh nearly thirteen thousand pounds. The outer casing will need to be eight feet long and more than six feet in diameter. There's not a bomber in our current inventory capable of carrying it."

President Roosevelt turned to General Henry H. "Hap" Arnold, commanding general of the Allied Army Air Forces. "How about it, Hap? Is that true?"

"As we speak…it is, Mr. President; but we're hoping the new B-29 will be in production before the end of the year. Even though they don't know what an atomic bomb is, Boeing's engineers—based on the specs Admiral Fuller's team has provided them—have designed the new bomber specifically to carry one."

Roosevelt was unable to hide his disappointment. "So, what I'm hearing is that, even if we had a bomb today, we won't be ready to deliver it to Berlin until sometime next year."

"I'm afraid that's true," General Arnold replied.

Roosevelt turned his attention to General Eisenhower. "Ike, how much longer can we hold out?"

Eisenhower answered candidly. "The Germans keep pouring men and equipment onto our shores every day, Mr. President. Add to that the fact that they've co-opted most of the northern production facilities for their own use, and…*well*…it's becoming harder and harder. Realistically, we can probably hold the line for another eighteen months; but unless something changes, it's just a matter of time until they overwhelm us. After that, I'm afraid the same will be true for England."

Roosevelt and Truman both sat silently, processing the gravity of Eisenhower's statement.

Finally, Truman spoke. He looked toward Admiral Fuller and Robert Oppenheimer. "Gentlemen," he said earnestly, "we need that bomb—and we need it *now*. We're giving you and your scientists every available resource. If you need resources that currently aren't available, let us know. We'll move heaven and earth to *make* them available. I don't care what it takes. If we don't get that bomb, it won't be long before the Germans are marching into Atlanta. I'm gettin' too old to pack up and move again. Eventually, there won't be any place left for us to go."

Having delivered his message to Fuller and Oppenheimer, a frustrated Truman turned to Hap Arnold. "General Arnold—we know the Nazis are gassing hundreds of people a week in that death camp off Long Island. I know we got our asses kicked the last time we tried to bomb New York, but isn't there some way in God's name we can take that damned thing out?"

Chapter Fifty-Two
02 April 1943

"*Atta boy*, Colonel!" A smiling Petty Officer Smith stood next to the treadmill as Rod Hurley reached the end of his workout. "That was a six-minute mile—not bad for somebody your age."

"'*Not bad?*' Are you kiddin' me?" Hurley tried to catch his breath as he stopped running and continued to walk as he cooled down. He grabbed the towel from the rail and wiped the sweat from his face. "I haven't run a six-minute mile since I was dating my wife back in high school. She snuck me into her bedroom one night and just as things were gettin' hot and heavy, we thought we heard her father comin' down the hallway. I shot out through the window like a bat outta hell. I didn't slow down 'til I'd made it all the way to my folks' place—clear on the other side of town."

Both men had a good laugh.

"You'd better get back up to your room, Colonel. You're gonna need to get cleaned up before the flight surgeon sees you this afternoon. The uniform you were wearin' when you got here was pretty fouled up. We managed to round you up a new one—everything except the flight jacket, that is."

Hurley stopped walking. He reached out and shook the Navy corpsman's hand. "I'll never be able to thank you enough, Smitty.

You worked my butt off these past few months. If it hadn't been for your willingness to stick with me through some tough times, I don't think I'd be takin' that flight physical today."

"It was no trouble, sir. I enjoy kickin' officers' butts. Try to make sure I don't see yours back in here."

"Thanks again, Smitty—*I mean it.*"

Chapter Fifty-Three
05 April 1943

Just after sunrise, the lone B-25 *Mitchell* rolled down the runway at Camp Springs Army Airfield in Eastern Maryland. The twin-engine medium bomber carried only 3,000 pounds of bombs—barely enough to take out the target.

The B-25 got airborne and climbed toward Chesapeake Bay, leveling off at 500 feet. The bomber accelerated to 230 miles per hour and turned southeast to avoid the German-held territory in the northern region of the Delmarva Peninsula.

Minutes later, a second *Mitchell* bomber lifted from the same runway.

When the first B-25 reached the Atlantic shoreline, it turned due east and headed out to sea. Seventy-five miles over the Atlantic, it turned northeast and paralleled the Delaware and New Jersey coastlines. From the point where it turned northeast, it took the lead B-25 one hour and eight minutes to cover the 250 miles to the eastern tip of Long Island.

Rounding the lighthouse at Montauk Point, the bomber descended and accelerated. The pilot leveled off at 100 feet and flew at 270 miles per hour toward the target at the western end of the sound. The small detachment of SS troops stationed on Hart Island never knew the *Mitchell* bomber was approaching until, twenty-two minutes after it had passed the lighthouse, all six of its 500-pound bombs hit their mark, laying waste to one of the island's two gas chambers.

The bomber banked hard left and headed due south, straight over Queens. Still hugging the deck, the pilot maneuvered the fleeing aircraft through the urban landscape at full throttle. He continually passed within feet of the buildings to either side of his route, making the aircraft virtually invisible to anyone who was not directly under or above its path.

Within minutes, the B-25 was skimming across Jamaica Bay. The Luftwaffe pilots at Floyd Bennett Field were only now beginning to start their engines. By the time the Bf 109s got airborne, the Allied raider had passed Rockaway Beach and was long gone over the Atlantic.

Back at Hart Island, the trailing B-25 released its bombs just wide of the second gas chamber. The errant drop caused only minor damage. Unlike the lead bomber, it turned southwest and cut straight across the Throgs Neck Peninsula, emerging over the East River. The low-flying bomber rattled the barracks at Rikers Island as it turned twenty degrees south and headed straight for Brooklyn. As it buzzed the airfield adjacent to the concentration camp at max speed, it passed directly over the building that housed the Luftwaffe Fighter Command Headquarters.

For the second time during the raid, Luftwaffe fighters were slow to respond. The pilots at the former New York Municipal Airport were still strapping into their cockpits as the fast-moving bomber passed 200 feet above their runways.

The anti-aircraft batteries that lined Manhattan's eastern shoreline began pumping 88-millimeter rounds at the low-flying B-25 from across the East River. As the bomber zigzagged through the ragged skyline, many of the rounds fell into neighborhoods in Queens and Brooklyn, killing and wounding a number of residents.

The fast-moving bomber passed a half mile east of Ebbets Field and continued south-southwest. The crew could see Coney Island, their final checkpoint, in the distance.

The Bf 109s that had earlier scrambled to intercept the first B-25 over Jamaica Bay were now at 2,000 feet, returning to Floyd Bennett Field. When the German pilots spotted the second bomber passing beneath them, they dove on it, attacking en masse. The B-25's gunners were quickly overmatched as the 109s intercepted the escaping bomber over Brighton Beach.

The initial pass from the lead German fighter disabled the starboard engine and killed the copilot as the stricken B-25 continued flying out to sea. During the ensuing passes from a half dozen 109s, so many rounds ripped into the Allied bomber that none of the Luftwaffe pilots was able to claim the kill as his own.

The B-25 lost a wing and cartwheeled into the Atlantic, slinging debris over a quarter mile.

The objective had been to halt the mass murders taking place on Hart Island; but the daring raid to neutralize the Nazi death mill had resulted in the destruction of only one of the camp's two gas chambers. It would take only two months for the SS to rebuild it. The raid had done little to interrupt the flow of Rikers Island inmates into the deadly chambers.

The mission was not a complete failure, however. The Allies came away from the raid having learned a valuable lesson. Although the German air defenses made it nearly impossible for massive bomber formations to hit targets in and around New York, the raid on Hart Island had demonstrated that a single, unescorted aircraft could take the Luftwaffe by surprise. A lone bomber stood a reasonable chance of getting through to New York City and taking out a target.

Chapter Fifty-Four
02 June 1943

No human on God's green earth is more irascible than a combat pilot chained to a desk. It had been two months since Rod Hurley's return to flight status. The flight surgeon in Bethesda had pronounced him fit for duty in all respects. Still, here he was—in Atlanta, shuffling papers in Hap Arnold's outer office.

Several times he had asked the general when he was going to receive his next assignment. Each time he had been told there were no command billets currently open. Anxious to get back into a cockpit, Hurley had even requested to be placed with a squadron in a subordinate billet. Unmoved, General Arnold had told him to be patient.

Hurley had made up his mind. Today was the day he was going to march into Arnold's office and demand that the commanding general of the Allied Army Air Forces accede to his demands and return him to a combat squadron. He was silently rehearsing his speech when General Arnold suddenly emerged from his office.

"Hurley—come with me," the general barked as he continued walking out the door into the hallway.

Hurley jumped to his feet and hurried to catch up. He was half-convinced that Arnold was somehow clairvoyant and that the general was taking him somewhere to bawl him out for what he was planning to say in his speech.

Arnold led him down several winding War Department passageways, to a secure room Hurley didn't even know existed. Two Marine sentries stood at parade rest, guarding the entrance. The armed Marines snapped to attention as the five-star general led Hurley through the door and into a conference room.

Convinced that the general would not have gone to this much trouble just to dress him down, Hurley now had no idea why he had been summoned to accompany Arnold to a room where a Navy admiral was sitting alone at the end of a long conference table. The admiral stood and walked toward Hurley and Arnold. General Arnold pointed to Hurley. "Admiral Fuller, this is Colonel Hurley."

Chauncey Fuller extended his hand. "I've been looking forward to meeting you, Colonel. General Arnold tells me you're about to go stir-crazy working in his office."

Hurley shook Fuller's hand. "The general's correct, sir. I guess I've been a bit of a nuisance lately."

"I'll vouch for that," General Arnold chimed in.

Admiral Fuller motioned to the conference table. "Take a seat, Hurley."

"Thank you, sir."

The three men sat. Admiral Fuller took a glass and a pitcher of water from a tray on the table. He filled the glass and offered it to Hurley.

"None for me—thank you, Admiral."

Admiral Fuller slid the glass in front of General Arnold and poured another one for himself. "General Arnold tells me you're the most experienced bomber pilot we have. More importantly, he says you're the *best* bomber pilot we have. Are you?"

"General Arnold is too kind, sir." Hurley thought back to the negative reaction he had received the last time he feigned modesty to a senior officer—sitting across from Colonel Morrow back at

Randolph Field. "But he's also *correct*," Hurley quickly added. "I *am* the best bomber pilot you have."

Admiral Fuller laughed. "I would've been disappointed in you if you hadn't said so. The general tells me you're also a natural leader and a good organizer. I won't put you on the spot again by asking you to affirm those two assessments."

Hurley smiled.

"You're probably wondering why you're here," Fuller continued. "General Arnold and I both think you're just the man we need for an important job. So, if you're—"

"*I'm in*," Hurley interrupted.

"You don't even care to know what the job entails before you agree to it?"

"I'm fairly certain it's a flying billet, or you wouldn't be concerned with my piloting skills. I'll take it."

Admiral Fuller chuckled. "Well, I certainly admire your enthusiasm, Hurley. Perhaps it's just as well you don't have a lot of questions. To be quite honest, I can't tell you much about your assignment—only that it's top secret. You'll be commanding a special operations squadron. I *can* tell you you're free to put your squadron together with whomever you choose. You'll be getting B-24Ds from the Consolidated plant in Fort Worth. They'll be modified to suit your needs. You'll use the B-24s to begin training your aircrews, but you won't be flying them operationally. You'll transition into brand new B-29s at the beginning of next year, as soon as Boeing has them ready to go. You and your crews will have to familiarize yourselves with the new bombers prior to your mission. You might not have much time to get that done."

Hurley leaned toward Admiral Fuller. "Sir—with all due respect, if you're trying to discourage me, you're not doing a very good job of it. You say I can have anyone I choose to stand up this new squadron? Isn't that going to tick off the other squadron commanders when I strip them of their best aircrews?"

General Arnold stepped in to answer the question. "You get anyone you want, Hurley. In fact, you get any *equipment* you want as well—anything. This project is code-named *Downrush*. You include that code word in the subject line of any requisition to any office in the War Department, and your request will be expedited—no questions asked."

Rod Hurley leaned back and shook his head in blissful disbelief. "This sounds like a license to steal," he said.

"That's *exactly* what it is," Admiral Fuller said. "There's no way I can impress upon you how critical this project is. When the time is right, you'll be briefed on all the details. In the interim, you and your aircrews will perfect a technique to deliver one bomb onto one target, from a high altitude, with absolute certainty."

"All this to deliver one bomb onto one target?" Hurley asked, slightly incredulous.

"*One* bomb—*one* target," Fuller repeated.

Chapter Fifty-Five
03 October 1943

Almost a year had passed since Marc Krbec and thirteen other Resistance fighters had brazenly hijacked two SS barges and rescued nearly six hundred prisoners from the Nazi gas chambers. In the eleven ensuing months, the Hart Island death camp had become an even more efficient operation. Despite the surprise Allied bombing raid that temporarily slowed the mass exterminations, the Nazis had gassed more than forty-seven thousand Rikers Island prisoners in the first nine months of 1943.

Now, thanks to intelligence provided by James Winston, the American Resistance was poised to eliminate the two men chiefly responsible for the systematic murder of a quarter million Jews in America.

Heinrich Himmler had secretly traveled to New York for an inspection tour of the North American concentration camps. The SS commandant, escorted by Ernst Kruger, was scheduled to arrive on Rikers Island at 1330 the following afternoon. The motorcade would be well guarded. To successfully attack it in broad daylight would be difficult and dangerous. But the target was too inviting. It was a risk the Resistance was willing to take.

Though Marc Krbec and his fellow Resistance fighters were not privy to the motorcade's route, there was only one way onto Rikers Island—the bridge across Bowery Bay. It was the perfect spot for an ambush. The wooded areas on both sides of the bridgehead would provide cover for the attackers. They would preposition themselves that evening and spend the night in the woods. A dozen men on either side of the road, armed with M1 carbines and grenades, would wait for their chance to take out the staff car in which Himmler and Kruger would be riding.

The biggest challenge would be escaping the scene afterward. After exiting the woods, they would have to make their way, under fire in all likelihood, across a seventy-five-yard clearing to a nearby wastewater treatment plant. They would then have to move along a narrow walkway next to the perimeter wall as they made their way across the East River shoreline, to the rear of the plant. Once the Resistance fighters made it to the pier on the back side of the plant, two nearby speedboats would be waiting to swoop in and extricate them from the fight. The operation was going to require perfect execution and precise timing.

That evening, several hours after darkness had overtaken the city, the two boats each offloaded a dozen men onto the deserted pier. Once the team was ashore, the boats retreated into the night.

Half a mile away, on the opposite side of Bowery Bay, a Luftwaffe sentry was patrolling the western boundary of the nearby airfield. As he happened to glance out across the bay, he noticed a group of men darting around the lighted perimeter of the wastewater treatment plant.

On the 59th floor of the Third Reich Expeditionary Headquarters, James Winston was working late into the night. He and several other maintenance workers were cleaning the conference hall in advance of the morning briefing for Heinrich Himmler.

Ernst Kruger was laying out the red carpet for the SS leader's visit to Rikers Island. James Winston hoped his fellow American Resistance fighters would provide Kruger's boss with an appropriate welcome.

Chapter Fifty-Six

04 October 1943

It was still several hours until daybreak. The two dozen Resistance fighters had long since settled in for the night. Two lookouts were posted at the edge of the woods on either side of the road. While everyone else was sleeping, the lookouts spotted headlights from a line of trucks approaching the bridge.

It was not unusual for the SS to transport new prisoners to the camp in the middle of the night. Both lookouts, hoping the vehicles would pass them by, moved into the woods. They hunkered down, making certain they were out of sight. As the headlights drew closer, the lookouts realized the convoy was much larger than the ones that routinely brought in new prisoners. There were at least a dozen trucks. The lookouts quickly woke the rest of the men on both sides of the road.

Marc Krbec, in charge of the group closest to the planned escape route, watched as the headlights from the long procession of trucks began to bathe the surrounding trees in light. At first, he thought they might continue past them and cross the bridge to Rikers Island. Instead, the trucks came to a stop immediately in front of the bridgehead. At least a hundred German soldiers began unloading from the trucks.

Two of the trucks carried large searchlights. When the lights were switched on and pointed toward either side of the road, the woods above Krbec's head were flooded with intense light. He weighed whether to try and take out the light or stay down on the ground and hope the Germans didn't see him and his men. Before he could make his decision, one of the Resistance fighters on the other side of the road lobbed a grenade at the light aimed in that direction. It exploded with a flash, shattering the light and killing the German soldier who was operating it.

All hell broke loose.

The Germans began fanning out into the woods on both sides of the road. Krbec immediately stood and lobbed another grenade, taking out the second searchlight. The eruption of muzzle flashes turned the darkened woods into a chaotic shooting gallery. Krbec frantically radioed for the speedboats.

The Resistance fighters on the far side of the road had no way to retreat. With their backs to Bowery Bay, it would only be a matter of time before they were wiped out.

Several of Krbec's men were already dead. He yelled for the rest to head for the wastewater plant. Firing on the run, Krbec and two others made it out of the woods and across the clearing. When they reached the concrete walkway that ran along the outside of the perimeter wall, they ceased firing and began sprinting single file along the narrow walkway, out over the river.

The Germans emerged from the woods and spotted the men moving in front of the illuminated wall. They stood at the edge of the clearing and opened up on the exposed Resistance fighters. The men fled toward the back side of the plant as rounds from the German rifles struck the ten-foot wall all around them. They ducked their heads and continued running as the bullets sent dust and stone fragments flying from the wall onto the walkway. The three men somehow made it to the corner of the walkway and disappeared behind the treatment plant. The German soldiers stopped firing and resumed their pursuit.

Krbec and the other two Resistance fighters, still on the walkway behind the plant, made a desperate dash. As they reached the pier, they could hear the boats speeding toward them in the darkness.

From seven hundred yards away, the helmsman of the lead boat could see the German soldiers running beside the lighted perimeter wall toward the men at the rear of the plant.

As they crossed the shoreline, the Germans were forced to move along the narrow walkway in a column. When the head of the column turned the corner, the three men on the pier began firing. The first two soldiers were cut down as soon as they appeared from behind the wall. The helmsman saw the muzzle flashes and heard the shots as the two Germans splashed into the dark water below the walkway.

But the soldiers continued coming—one behind the other.

Firing from the end of the pier, Krbec and the other two Resistance fighters emptied their carbines into the never-ending stream of German soldiers, sending a half dozen more into the East River. Marc Krbec was the only defender who still had a full magazine with which to reload—it wasn't enough.

More and more soldiers poured around the corner to join the fight. Many of them fell as they charged toward the pier, but for every one that was taken down, two more appeared from behind the wall. Within seconds, the Germans were on the back side of the plant in sufficient numbers to overwhelm the cornered Resistance fighters.

The helmsman watched as the silhouettes of the men at the end of the pier—first one, then all three—collapsed onto the concrete.

He quickly turned his empty boat around.

Chapter Fifty-Seven

11 November 1943 (Armistice Day)

Goodfellow Army Airfield, in San Angelo, Texas, was named for First Lieutenant John J. Goodfellow, Jr.

A native of San Angelo, Goodfellow had volunteered to fly with the United States Army during the First World War and had been assigned to the 24th Aero Squadron of the American Expeditionary Forces in France. He lost his life while flying a reconnaissance mission and was buried at the American military cemetery in Saint-Mihiel, France.

Now, as the world commemorated the armistice that had ended World War I, Goodfellow Army Airfield was home to a squadron of elite World War II aviators, all of them handpicked from the air forces of both the United and Confederate States of America—all of them training for Project Downrush.

It was a shiny new B-24D *Liberator*. It was the heaviest bomber in the Allied inventory; but despite being able to carry 8,000 pounds of bombs, the B-24 was still incapable of delivering the massive *Downrush* bomb. In addition to weighing 13,000 pounds, the bomb—if and when it was ready to be deployed—would be too large to fit inside the *Liberator's* bomb bay.

This particular B-24 sat inside a large hangar. It was one of seven bombers that had been modified specifically for Colonel Rod Hurley's 325th Special Operations Squadron. There were no turrets, no guns, and no life rafts or survival kits. The plane was unpainted, a weight savings of 400 pounds, and it had no drag-inducing gunners' windows in the sides of the fuselage. With the defensive armament and nonessential equipment stripped from the airframe, the modified bomber weighed only 31,000 pounds, nearly 7,000 pounds lighter than the empty weight of a standard *Liberator*.

The plane's pilot was the 325th SOS executive officer, Lieutenant Colonel Thomas Damron. Standing next to his plane, Damron was supervising his radio operator, who was painting large red letters on the nose section of their bare-metal silver bomber.

Rod Hurley walked up from behind Damron and stood beside him. Hurley watched as the radio operator, perched atop a stepladder, put the finishing touches on an elegant cursive "*M.*"

Without turning to look at his XO, Hurley spoke. "What's this, Tom?"

"We're naming her," Damron replied, looking straight ahead at his plane.

"You *do* remember we're getting brand new B-29s in just a few months. It's not as if you're actually going to fly combat missions in this bird."

"I know," Damron said as both men continued to watch the radio operator, who was now scripting a small "*e.*"

Over the next several minutes, the four other former *Yellow Rose* crew members attached to the 325th began trickling toward the corner of the hangar where Damron and Hurley were watching the young radio operator ply his painting skills.

Dave Murray was the next to join the two men. Shortly thereafter, Garry "Gabby" Crain moseyed up and stood next to

Murray. They scrutinized the new nose art as Damron's radio operator finished styling the next letter—a lowercase "*l*."

Lastly, Mark Lorance and John Spence strolled up to see what it was the others were watching. They stopped next to Crain and observed the beginnings of an "*a*."

After several seconds, Spence spoke up. "What the hell is this, Gabby? When did we start painting names on trainers?" The brash young navigator then bellowed down to the other end of the line of spectators. "Hey, XO—I thought we were gonna be gettin' brand-new birds for this operation! *What gives?*"

"Will you chowderheads please give a guy a break," Damron replied. "You're only mocking this because you don't understand it."

"We're listening," Hurley said with a wry smile. "Make us understand."

"Well…it's like this. I really love this bird, but I'm only gonna be able to fly her for a short time. It's kind of like…*well*…it's like I'm having a fling with her," Damron said, grinning.

"So, what are you naming her?" Hurley asked.

"*Melanie Anne*," Damron said proudly.

"Where'd you come up with *that* name?"

"She was my gal in London."

"You never had a gal in London," Hurley said derisively.

"I *did* so," Damron retorted. "It was after you guys left to come home. She was a gorgeous piece of work, *too*. She had dark hair…curves in all the right places…and legs that went on forever. The stories I could tell you guys…"

"I'll bet," Hurley said, nodding his head. "It's too bad I never got a chance to meet this dream girl."

"You *did* meet her," Damron said, smiling. "You *all* did."

"She must've made one hell of an impression on us," Spence chimed in sarcastically, "seeing as how not one of us remembers seeing her. Tell us, XO. When exactly did we meet this bombshell?"

"That day you guys brought the Johnnie Walker bottles up to my hospital room. She was the head nurse on my floor."

"*Wait one minute*," Hurley said incredulously. "Are you talking about the nurse who tried to throw us out of the hospital? You're telling me you and she—?"

"*Yep.*"

"You're *kidding.*"

"Nope."

Hurley shook his head in disbelief. "So, she tries to throw the rest of us out on our asses—but then she turns around and has a tryst with *you?*"

Damron grinned. "I'd say that proves she was an excellent judge of character."

Hurley shook his head again, this time laughing. "Okay, Romeo—when your winged mistress finishes putting her lipstick on, you think you and she can take my new copilot out and introduce him to the mission profile?"

Damron looked sideways at Hurley. "He's *your* copilot. Why aren't *you* training him?"

"Can't do it, partner. I have to fly to Atlanta." Hurley pointed to the open doors on the underside of the B-24's fuselage. "General Arnold and Admiral Fuller are finally gonna brief me on exactly what it is we're gonna be releasing out of that bomb bay."

Later that afternoon, Macaulay "Mac" Litchfield was sitting in the *Melanie Anne's* copilot seat, across the cockpit from Thomas Damron.

Damron flew the big bomber fast and low over the barren West Texas terrain. When they reached the initial point on the bomb run, Damron abruptly pulled the B-24's nose skyward and transitioned the stripped-down bomber into a steep climb. Mac Litchfield felt his two hundred pounds sink into the padded seat pan. Initially climbing at more than 1600 feet per minute, their climb rate began to slow as the bomber rose higher and higher.

The ascent lasted for almost half an hour. When the bomber had risen to 26,000 feet, Damron leveled off. His bombardier took control from the nose bay. The navigator had calculated their ascent from the IP perfectly. The *Melanie Anne* was on the final segment of the bomb run for only seven minutes before her bombardier released the dummy payload.

Damron banked hard and began a steep, descending turn away from the target. He called for max power. The flight engineer shoved all four throttles forward, causing the plane to accelerate as it descended.

Litchfield felt the airframe shudder as the B-24 approached its *never-exceed* airspeed. Any faster, and the bomber's wings could shear away from the fuselage. The flight engineer eased the throttles aft, just enough to avoid exceeding the maximum structural airspeed.

The *Melanie Anne* was already miles from the target when— from an elevated bunker in the wall of a nearby escarpment—the spotter watched the dummy payload land inside the 500-yard-diameter circle painted on the desert floor.

Chapter Fifty-Eight
26 April 1944

During his lifetime, the late William Johnson McDonald had amassed a small fortune as an East Texas banker. He had served in the 32nd Texas Cavalry during the war that divided the American nations. Upon his death in 1926, his estate endowed the sum of $850,000 to the University of Texas to construct an observatory in the Davis Mountains of West Texas.

Rising above the Chihuahuan Desert, the Davis Mountains were originally known as the Limpia Mountains. After the American Civil War, the range was renamed for Jefferson Davis, the first president of the Confederacy.

Inside the McDonald Observatory compound, the brightest physicists from both the Confederate and United States of America were on the verge of changing the course of history. Under the leadership of Robert Oppenheimer—at a cost of nearly two billion dollars—dozens of scientists were making final preparations to detonate the world's first atomic bomb.

Fifteen miles southeast of the McDonald Observatory, most of the residents of Fort Davis were unaware of the convoy that rumbled through their town just before 3 a.m. on that Sunday morning. The few who did get out of bed to investigate the unusual spectacle were witnesses to a long procession of military trucks, some filled with armed troops, some filled with equipment. The trucks were followed by an equally long procession of automobiles. Riding in one of the last automobiles was Toby Pozniak.

Pozniak was deeply conflicted. Having received news from Admiral Fuller that his lifelong friend had been killed while fighting with the Resistance in New York, he regretted that he and Marc Krbec had not parted on better terms the night he was smuggled out of Brooklyn by Lieutenant Commander Crofford.

As the convoy headed for the desert-floor detonation site, some fifty miles south of Fort Davis, Marc Krbec's death was not Pozniak's only compunction. For the past three years, the *Downrush* scientists had been concurrently developing two different atomic bomb prototypes. Robert Oppenheimer had appointed Pozniak to head up the team of physicists tasked with designing the uranium-fueled "gun-type" device. Although uranium was more plentiful than plutonium (the other radioactive element being considered for use), it was much more difficult than plutonium to enrich. The scientists in charge of producing fissile material were struggling to produce bomb-grade uranium in sufficient quantities. During the final stages of development, Pozniak's cylindrical weapon, even though it was smaller and would have been easier to deliver, had been cast aside in favor of the other design prototype—a spherical implosion device containing a plutonium core at its center.

Though it was significantly heavier and more massive than Pozniak's design, the implosion bomb was still small enough to be carried in the voluminous bomb bay of Boeing's new B-29 *Superfortress*. With a 20,000-pound max payload, the cutting-edge bomber, almost ready for production, was being specifically developed to deliver the larger bomb.

Even though he was disappointed that his was not the design that had ultimately been chosen, Toby Pozniak was nevertheless exhilarated at the prospect of witnessing the world's first nuclear detonation.

A little more than twenty-four hours after the *Downrush* scientists had reached their test site, in the predawn darkness near Marfa, Texas, a lone cattle rancher was getting ready to head out for the spring roundup.

Using the momentum he generated from a powerful pirouette, the old cowboy slung a saddle onto his horse's back. He lifted the left stirrup and placed it atop the saddle while he leaned down and attached the lower cinch strap. Leaning back for leverage, he gave the strap a hard tug, pulling it tight. He removed the stirrup from its temporary resting place and let it fall to the horse's side. The rancher picked up his rope and hung it around the saddle horn. Firmly grasping the top of the horn in his left palm, he raised his left boot into the stirrup and swung his right leg over the saddle. His horse seemed unusually nervous that morning.

The tough old rancher was an excellent horseman. He calmed his ride with a few gentle pats on the neck before giving him a nudge with the heels of his boots. The horse responded to the cowboy's command. After exiting the gate on the far side of the corral, the rancher rode into the night.

For years, many of the residents around Marfa had told stories of strange lights in the sky south of town. Those who claimed to have seen the illuminations described them as mysterious balls of light dancing over the desert. The old rancher had always been skeptical of the sightings, passing them off as local folklore. On this chilly spring morning, as he rode south to meet up with several of his fellow ranchers at a remote line shack, the night had only partially given way to the twilight in the eastern sky.

At first just slowing, his horse suddenly stopped in its tracks. The frustrated cowboy gave his mount several sprightly kicks to get him moving again. The frightened animal reared and tossed its head. In the next instant, the rancher and his horse were temporarily blinded by an enormous eruption of light on the southern horizon.

Chapter Fifty-Nine
12 July 1944

The Allies had their bomb. What they desperately needed now was a plane capable of delivering it.

Developing a superbomber was a complex task. When compared to other bombers of the period, Boeing's B-29 was a quantum leap in technology. It was to be the first bomber with pressurized crew stations. It was also going to be the first combat aircraft with a central fire control system for aiming remote-controlled gun turrets. But the biggest advancement was its tremendous range and payload capabilities.

Compared to the B-24, the B-29 could fly nearly twice as far and carry more than twice the bombload. Fully loaded, it weighed 120,000 pounds, 65,000 pounds more than a loaded B-24. The engines needed to power such a massive bomber didn't exist when the project began. They had to be designed and developed.

The early B-29 prototypes had been plagued by numerous setbacks, including several catastrophic engine fires. But the Boeing engineers had persevered. They had overcome the many challenges and had finally developed and built three successful prototypes.

At last, after months of delays, the first production B-29 was scheduled to roll off the Boeing assembly line by the end of the month.

At a time when the Nazis were beginning to advance south of Pennsylvania, the new bomber would soon provide the final piece to the Downrush puzzle.

The B-29 design team had been just as critical to the top-secret project as the physicists inside the McDonald Observatory. Everything about their state-of-the-art bomber represented new technology. It was proprietary technology—technology that only the Boeing engineers possessed.

It was a typical July morning along Puget Sound. The overnight fog had lifted several hours earlier. The clouds now hung several hundred feet above the water and surrounding shoreline. The prevailing visibility had improved to almost five miles—more than enough for the pilots from the Japanese carriers to navigate to their various targets.

As the twelve squadrons of attacking fighters and dive bombers, flying at an altitude of only 200 feet, made their way south from the main entrance into the sound, three squadrons peeled off to raid the naval air station on Whidbey Island. The fourth, fifth and sixth squadrons made for the naval shipyard at Bremerton, where the last few ships that still remained from the relocated U.S. Pacific Fleet were sunk in short order.

The remaining six squadrons flew directly over downtown Seattle and over Lake Washington, where three of them turned north, toward the naval air station at Sand Point. The final three squadrons headed south, toward Renton, where the Wednesday morning shift at the Boeing Aircraft Plant—including the B-29 design team—was three hours into the workday. The first bomb fell on the large conference room where the designers and engineers had gathered for a status briefing on the *Superfortress* project. It penetrated the roof before exploding. In an instant, the entire B-29 brain trust was wiped out.

As the bombs continued to fall, a Boeing test pilot and one of the B-29 flight engineers scrambled from inside a hangar onto the tarmac. The pair ran toward one of the three *Superfortress* prototypes in a desperate attempt to fly it away from the attack. As they climbed inside, the hangar behind them—the hangar housing the other two prototypes—erupted into an explosion of flames and debris.

In a frenzy, the two airmen simultaneously strapped into their seats and began their startup checks. They skipped all but the most essential steps as swarms of Mitsubishi *Zero* fighters strafed the bomber mercilessly. One by one, the four huge engines sputtered to life amid black clouds of exhaust. Even before the last of the engines began to turn over, the pilot released the brakes. The flight engineer pushed the first three throttles forward to begin taxiing toward the runway. As the number four engine began to catch, it was riddled by a hailstorm of bullets. Misfiring badly, the damaged engine began misting oil across the starboard wing.

The B-29 rolled onto the runway at a right angle to the centerline. The flight engineer, still struggling to get power from the starboard outboard engine, was unable to apply asymmetrical thrust to assist the hard-left turn. Standing on the left rudder pedal with all his might, the pilot simultaneously used the toe of his boot to apply the left brake. Straining to turn the colossal bomber ninety degrees with just his legs, he managed to align the aircraft on the long runway.

The desperate pilot yelled for takeoff power. The flight engineer pushed the three throttles on the operating engines to full power. He feathered the propeller on the disabled engine to reduce as much drag as possible. The pilot struggled to maintain the centerline as the fifty-ton behemoth slowly accelerated down the runway. All the while, the bomber continued to take hits as a relentless succession of *Zeros*, flying at low level and high speed, made pass after pass from above and behind. Through it all, the B-29 kept gaining momentum.

Just when it looked as if the lumbering *Superfortress* might achieve enough airspeed to become airborne on only three engines, a single *Val* dive bomber, trailing behind the strafing fighters, took dead aim at the escaping bomber. As the Japanese pilot released his ordnance, he pulled up, banked left, and looked back over his shoulder. He watched as the 550-pound bomb landed in front of the B-29, skipped once, then detonated. The disappointed pilot leveled his wings and climbed out straight ahead. Seconds later, the crater from his errant bomb ripped the portside landing gear strut from beneath the giant bomber's wing.

The last remaining B-29 prototype—the only aircraft capable of carrying the North American Allies' massive atomic bomb—spun off the runway, broke apart, and burst into flames.

In San Angelo, Texas, Colonel Rod Hurley and Lieutenant Colonel Thomas Damron were eating lunch at a local diner. Seated at the counter, they could hear the radio playing in the kitchen.

When the music was interrupted for a news bulletin, Rod Hurley strained to hear the report. He yelled through the serving window at the cook. *"Can you turn that up, please?"*

Once the cook turned up the volume, it didn't take long for Hurley and Damron to figure out what had happened. Each man tossed a couple of bucks onto the counter as they rushed out of the diner. They jumped into their car and sped toward the base. As Hurley drove, Damron spun the dial on the dashboard radio, frantically searching for a station with a clear signal.

Upon learning of the devasting attack on Puget Sound, Presidents Roosevelt and Truman concurrently and unceremoniously relieved U.S. Admiral Harold Stark as Allied chief of naval operations. They subsequently replaced him with Confederate Fleet Admiral Chester Nimitz.

The Japanese attack that Nimitz had warned was possible had come to fruition—and at the worst possible place and time. Without the B-29 to deliver it, the Allies' rotund implosion bomb was useless.

Robert Oppenheimer and Admiral Chauncey Fuller were in Atlanta for meetings. When Fuller informed Oppenheimer that the B-29 *Superfortress* program had been totally destroyed, the panicked physicist immediately picked up the phone. He asked the operator at the War Department switchboard to place an emergency, secure-line phone call.

Oppenheimer waited as the operator made the connection. He needed to pass the news to the only man who could now salvage the *Downrush* Project. After several rings, the McDonald Observatory operator came on the line. "How may I direct your call?"

"Put me through to Toby Pozniak," Oppenheimer said curtly.

Chapter Sixty

14 July 1944

Two years earlier, Admiral Nimitz's admonitions against moving the Pacific Fleet had gone unheeded. Four decades earlier, U.S. President Theodore Roosevelt had been unable to convince a reluctant Congress to complete the Panama Canal. As a result, the U.S. fleet was now trapped on the far side of the North and South American continents.

The large Japanese task force continued southward and, unchecked, delivered another devastating blow to the military installations in the San Francisco Bay area.

For now, Prime Minister Hideki Tojo's objective was unclear. General Dwight Eisenhower was convinced a Japanese land invasion was imminent but was unsure when or where it would come. Based strictly on a hunch, Eisenhower ordered General Douglas MacArthur, the commanding general of the Western Allied Forces, to prepare his defenses along the Southern California coastline.

For his part, General MacArthur doubted the Japanese would come ashore in a heavily populated area such as Los Angeles. He was convinced the invasion would come on the beaches north of San Diego. He began concentrating his defenses there, leaving Los Angeles virtually undefended.

In the meantime, the Allied leadership was meeting in Atlanta to brainstorm a solution to the Project Downrush setback. With the Germans steadily advancing down the East Coast, the prospect of a two-front war now made the atomic bomb even more critical to the Allies' survival.

...A wheelchair-bound man partially emerges from the darkness, his face still in the shadows. The faceless man points at Hitler and yells, "Do it, Pozniak! Pull the trigger!" Pozniak is still frozen. He doesn't know what to do. The two men continue shouting at him—

There were three quick rings from the bedside telephone. Trying to shake off the anxiety from the recurring nightmare, Toby Pozniak picked up the receiver.

"Good morning, Mr. Pozniak. This is your six-o'clock wake-up call."

It was Toby Pozniak's first time in Atlanta. Sitting inside the restaurant at the Georgian Terrace Hotel, he was sipping his morning coffee while he waited for Robert Oppenheimer. He gently replaced his cup onto the saucer made of fine china. As he tapped his cigarette ashes into a gold-lined porcelain ashtray, Glenn Miller's "Moonlight Serenade" played softly in the background. It was easy to get lost in the hotel's opulence. It was almost as if there wasn't a war going on.

But there *was* a war going on—a desperate war of survival.

Pozniak extinguished his cigarette as he rose to greet Oppenheimer. "Good morning, Robert."

Oppenheimer nodded his head. "*Pozniak,*" he said tersely. The aloof physicist sat down and unfolded the silk napkin at his place setting. He turned to one side in his chair as he crossed his legs at the knees and placed the napkin on his thigh. "How was your flight?"

"A little nerve-racking," Pozniak responded. "I'm not really used to riding in a military transport. I'm certainly not accustomed to looking out the window at a fighter escort."

As a waitress appeared at the table, Oppenheimer struck a match to light his pipe. The waitress unfolded breakfast menus and placed them in front of the two men. "Good morning," she said. "I'll be back shortly to take your orders." Oppenheimer seemed to ignore her as he lit his pipe and shook the match.

Pozniak looked up at the waitress. "Thank you," he said, smiling and nodding.

As the waitress turned and walked away, Oppenheimer took the pipe from his mouth. He leaned his elbow on the chair's upholstered armrest, holding the pipe high in the air. "So…are you ready for this meeting?" he asked.

Pozniak was unsure how to answer. "Should we even be discussing this in a public place?"

"It's fine," Oppenheimer answered condescendingly. "None of these people know what we're discussing. Even if they did, they don't possess the mental capacity to comprehend it. Are you ready for the meeting, or *aren't* you?"

"I suppose so," Pozniak answered. "Who's going to be there?"

"Roosevelt, Truman and several—"

"*Roosevelt and Truman?* I had no idea *they* were going to be there." Pozniak was taken aback that his boss had neglected to inform him he would be meeting with the two presidents. "Who *else* is coming?"

"General Arnold and Admiral Fuller, obviously. The commanding officer of the project bomber squadron will also be there, along with the design engineer from Consolidated. That reminds me—you and he need to get together following the meeting so you can pass him all the specifications he needs. Based on the preliminary information we've given him, he thinks he can design a modification to the B-24 bomb bay that will accommodate your device."

Pozniak was astonished. That was the first time he had ever heard Oppenheimer refer to the *Downrush* bomb as belonging to anyone other than himself.

"Just remember one thing," Oppenheimer continued. "Don't offer any opinions unless someone addresses a question specifically to you. I'll do most of the talking in there."

Toby Pozniak laughed to himself. That was much more like the Robert Oppenheimer he knew.

Later that morning, at the relocated War Department in Atlanta, Toby Pozniak sat with the Allied brain trust, waiting for the meeting to begin. While the others chatted, he surveyed his surroundings. He thought it was a large room in which to hold a meeting for such a small number of men.

There was a rap on the thick door. A Marine staff sergeant entered and took two steps into the room. He turned and snapped to attention as he held the door open. Everyone stood. President Truman was the first to enter, followed by President Roosevelt. As Roosevelt's personal aide rolled him into the room, Toby Pozniak was stunned. Just like most Americans, he had been unaware his president was confined to a wheelchair.

Chapter Sixty-One
19 July 1944

It had been nine days since the Japanese air strike at Puget Sound— seven days since the subsequent attack on San Francisco. Following more raids on military targets in and around San Diego, where General MacArthur was expecting the Japanese to come ashore, an invasion force finally landed that morning—at Los Angeles.

Against only light resistance, the Special Naval Landing Forces of the Imperial Japanese Navy came ashore on Alamitos Beach. The Japanese spearhead quickly moved west, across two temporary pontoon bridges, to Terminal Island, between San Pedro and Long Beach. After securing the virtually intact naval facilities at the massive Terminal Island complex, the offshore Japanese task force made quick and effective use of their new prize, sending in transport after transport to offload troops and supplies onto the U.S. Mainland.

From his headquarters in Atlanta, General Eisenhower issued an order calling for the tactical withdrawal of all Allied military units along the Southern California coastline. Few in number and ill-equipped, these "shell" units had only been left on the West Coast in the hope they would discourage the Japanese from attacking.

Eisenhower had known all along that these forces would be insufficient to repel an attack if one actually came. His plan now was to temporarily cede the West Coast to the Japanese to buy the Allies the time they desperately needed to resurrect the *Downrush* Project.

The Allied commander now hoped and prayed that a smaller, viable bomb could be completed while his army held the Germans at bay along the East Coast—a task that was becoming more difficult with each passing day.

At the Reich Chancellery in Berlin, Adolf Hitler was elated. This was the second front that Hideki Tojo, for the past year, had been promising would come. Hitler knew the Allies didn't possess the resources to fight a two-front war. It would only be a matter of time before Friedrich von Essen's forces would be able to overrun the Allies in the East.

Three years earlier, when he had set about diverting his Operation *Barbarossa* assets to North America, Hitler's only goal had been to occupy the United States and cut off the flow of arms to England. That goal was made more difficult when the Confederates unexpectedly intervened.

At first, the Confederates' war declaration had incensed Hitler; but now, with the Japanese invasion of California, it seemed as though, in addition to the United States, Hitler would soon be able to add the Confederate States of America to his list of conquered nations. He would, of course, be obligated to share some of the spoils of war with the Japanese Prime Minister; but Hitler was confident he would be able to exert his superior intellect over his Asian counterpart and come away with the lion's share of the conquests.

Unbeknownst to Hitler, however, Tojo had no intention of advancing inland. His only strategic interests lay in the Kern River Oil Field, north of Los Angeles. Tojo needed that oil to fuel his war effort against the Chinese, British and Australians in the Pacific. The Japanese military had no aspirations beyond Southern California. It was still the Nazi invaders to the east—not the Japanese—who posed an existential threat to the United and Confederate States of America.

Chapter Sixty-Two
28 October 1944

Washington, D.C., was in ruins. The German siege had lasted almost nine months. The U.S. and Confederate defenders had suffered more than fourteen thousand casualties. As the last Allied infantry units retreated across the Potomac into Virginia, they destroyed the only remaining bridge behind them. The evacuated capital—what remained of it—was relinquished to the victorious Nazi invaders.

As the German troops began rolling into the city, the only impediment to their progress was the debris from the bombed-out buildings. Every federal memorial, save for the Washington Monument, had been destroyed during the siege. At 1600 Pennsylvania Avenue, the White House was nothing more than a charred pile of rubble. But at the eastern end of the National Mall, one building remained intact—the U.S. Capitol.

Adolf Hitler understood the power of propaganda. When Paris had fallen at the beginning of the war, he had traveled there from Berlin to be photographed and filmed against the backdrop of the city's iconic landmarks. The Führer was on the other side of the Atlantic from Washington, D.C., but that was not going to stop him from seizing another opportunity to humiliate a conquered foe.

Throughout the siege, the Germans had purposely avoided targeting the U.S. Capitol. It was not hard for the Allies to envision why they had done so.

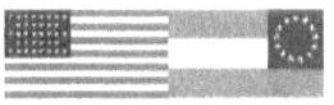

Lieutenant Junior Grade Wyatt Davis stood on the fo'c'sle of his motor torpedo boat. Resting his arm on the barrel of the PT-112's 37-millimeter deck gun, he surveyed the unbelievable destruction that surrounded him and the ten men under his command. After having navigated their way into the ruins of the Washington Navy Yard, they had tied their boat to the last small section of serviceable dock. Two miles to the north, they could see the dome atop the United States Capitol rising above the obliterated city landscape.

Lieutenant Davis's orders were to wait in the harbor for six passengers. He had no idea who they were or why they hadn't already fled the city ahead of the advancing Germans. Davis's superiors had made one thing clear, though: If his passengers did not arrive at the docks before the Germans did, he was not to wait for them. He was to extricate his boat and his crew without delay.

First Lieutenant Jason Wade represented everything Adolf Hitler and the Nazis despised about America's amalgamated society. His Catholic mother was the daughter of Salvadoran and Colombian immigrants. His Protestant father was the grandson of Irish and Welsh immigrants. The young combat engineer was the quintessential "melting-pot" American.

Hours earlier, as the last Allied troops were evacuating Washington, D.C., Lieutenant Wade and five of his men had volunteered to remain behind to complete one final task. On its face, their assignment seemed counterintuitive. They were to destroy the U.S. Capitol building.

The Allied high command knew that Hitler would make a grand show of occupying the Capitol and raising the Nazi flag. They were hoping the Führer would send his most senior representative, Field Marshal Friedrich von Essen, to be photographed climbing the steps to the front of the building. At the very least, the Allies understood that destroying the Capitol would deny the Nazis a propaganda victory. If they were fortunate enough to take out a senior leader in the process, so much the better.

Lieutenant Wade's men had worked feverishly for most of the morning, rigging the nearly two thousand pounds of explosives that would be required to bring down the building. The half dozen engineers had placed dynamite and blasting caps at critical points on the bottom two floors. The charges had been positioned to bring down the center portion of the edifice, including the two-hundred-and-eighty-eight-foot dome.

From the southeast corner of the building, Wade's engineers had laid two hundred yards of detonation cable, concealing it as best they could. They had run the cable to their observation post, which was hidden in the large mound of rubble where the Library of Congress once stood. Lastly, they had prepositioned two jeeps, in which to make their getaway, a block south of their position.

As they sat waiting for the Germans to arrive, Lieutenant Wade decided to send four of his men ahead to the waiting PT boat. The men were reluctant to leave, insisting they should stay in case the team was forced to fight its way to the Navy Yard; but after voicing their objections, they complied with their lieutenant's orders and departed for the docks in one of the two jeeps. As he and his sergeant waited in the shadow of the Capitol, Wade knew the Germans were already in the city, but he could only guess how much longer it would be before they arrived to claim their prize.

It wasn't long.

The two Americans hunkered down as they heard the panzers rumbling toward them. Lieutenant Wade extended the plunger on top of the box-shaped detonator. He connected the wires from the detonation cable to the terminals on the box. It seemed almost an eternity from the time they first heard and felt the seventy-ton *Tiger* tanks until they came into view. The column appeared from behind the northern end of the Capitol, rolling east on Constitution Avenue. The lead tank stopped and pivoted south onto First Street, eventually coming to a halt directly in front of the Capitol grounds. The column filled an entire block.

As the *Tigers* shut down their engines, the two men spotted a convoy of armored personnel carriers rolling south on Second Street. The vehicles turned west onto Capitol Street and drove straight to the steps of the building. Several dozen German soldiers leapt from the parked convoy and began patrolling the perimeter around the Capitol. Almost at once, a German staff car pulled to the front of the column and parked. The driver stepped from the car and opened the door for the rear-seat passenger.

Lieutenant Wade took off his helmet and removed the photo from the liner. Peering through his binoculars, he could see right away that the man was not Friedrich von Essen. He was not even a field marshal. He was only a general. Wade had his hands on the plunger, just waiting for the unidentified German general to get close enough to the building; but instead of moving toward the steps, the general walked farther away, surveying the Capitol in its entirety.

Just then, Wade saw that one of the patrolling German soldiers had discovered the detonation cable. Not knowing what it was, the curious soldier began tracing the cable toward the rubble where Wade and his sergeant were hiding. He was no more than twenty yards from the two men. For an instant, the young lieutenant contemplated destroying the Capitol without waiting for the general to approach it. Instead, he took out his combat knife and turned to his sergeant. "If this doesn't turn out well, blow the building and get the hell out of here."

Without waiting for his sergeant to acknowledge his order, he bolted from their concealed position into the open. At that same instant, a truck carrying the film crew and photographers arrived at the steps of the Capitol, diverting everyone's attention. Lieutenant Wade had never engaged in hand-to-hand combat. He and his engineers had only been given the most basic combat training before being sent to the front. Several seconds later, he was dragging the German soldier's lifeless body back into the rubble where he and the sergeant were hiding.

The sergeant was wide-eyed, shaking his head back and forth. "Son of a bitch, sir! Where'd you learn to do *that?*"

"I grew up in a rough neighborhood," Wade answered, out of breath.

The sergeant wasn't sure whether his lieutenant was joking or not. "Son of a *bitch*," he said again.

Finally, the general began walking toward the building. He informed his aide he was going to take a quick stroll inside while the film crew and photographers were setting up their cameras. He marched up the steps, past the huge marble columns that guarded the entrance. The jubilant general was still several strides from the door when Lieutenant Wade shoved the plunger into the detonator.

It took less than a second for the current from the spinning dynamo inside the box to reach the blasting cap inside the first dynamite charge. Those standing near the southeast side of the building were blown off their feet by the explosion. A split second after the last charge had detonated, the mammoth cast-iron dome cratered into the main section of the structure. The force from the collapsing dome toppled the walls outward, burying the camera crew and dozens of soldiers.

Lieutenant Wade and his sergeant didn't stick around for the dust to settle. As they sprinted toward their hidden jeep, one of the German soldiers lying on the ground spotted them and shouted at the others.

Several of the soldiers began firing at the fleeing Americans. A dozen others began piling into the only two armored personnel carriers not buried by debris. By the time the sergeant started the jeep and began racing toward the Navy Yard, the two German vehicles were less than a hundred yards behind them.

The Germans opened up on the jeep with the MG 42 machine guns mounted atop the personnel carriers. The young sergeant weaved the jeep through the piles of rubble that littered the street while Lieutenant Wade returned fire with his M1A1. The swifter, more-agile jeep began to pull away from the German pursuers as their heavier armored vehicles struggled to maneuver around the obstacles that blocked the roadway.

The four engineers waiting aboard the PT boat could hear the gun battle coming toward them. They scrambled back into their jeep to join the fight; but as soon as they had begun heading north, toward the Capitol, Lieutenant Wade and his sergeant appeared several hundred yards in front of them. The four men dismounted, taking cover behind their jeep. They cocked their weapons, waiting to lay down covering fire for their fleeing comrades.

As the Germans continued their pursuit, the gunners on the deck of the PT-112 began firing at the personnel carriers with the boat's four .50 caliber machine guns. Most of the remaining sailors were firing M1 rifles. Lieutenant Junior Grade Davis gave the order to start the 112's engines. He had been briefed on what to do if the Germans showed up before his passengers; but no one had instructed him on how to proceed if the Germans and the passengers arrived simultaneously.

Less than a hundred yards from the dock, as the sergeant driving Lieutenant Wade's jeep continued weaving through piles of debris, he was raked by fire from one of the German machine guns. The mortally wounded sergeant lost control of the speeding jeep. It ran up the side of a debris pile and became airborne, flipping upside down. Wade was thrown from the vehicle and landed hard on the pavement, breaking both his legs.

Under heavy fire from the 112's machine guns, the two armored personnel carriers stopped short and took up defensive positions within view of the dock. A dozen German foot soldiers poured out of the vehicles and joined the fight from behind a large mound of rubble.

Lieutenant Wade, under fire, began crawling toward the waiting boat. His four remaining engineers were pinned down behind their jeep.

Lieutenant Junior Grade Davis passed the helm of the 112 to his executive officer. He leapt from his boat to the dock and began sprinting toward Wade. Just as the Germans were about to open up on Davis from behind the pile of rubble, the pile exploded, sending rocks and German soldiers into the air. When the flying debris settled, several of the Germans lay dead, victims of the 112's powerful deck gun.

As the remaining Germans fired at him, Davis reached Wade's side. He knelt and lifted the wounded Lieutenant onto his back. The young skipper stood and, with Wade draped across his neck and shoulders, began lumbering toward his waiting boat, weaving his way through piles of debris. Just before Davis reached the dock, a German round ripped through his calf. He fell, dropping Wade onto the ground in front of him.

As the 112's deck gun took out several more of the German soldiers, Lieutenant Wade's engineers abandoned their cover behind the jeep and dashed toward the boat. Two of them grabbed Davis. The other two grabbed their fallen lieutenant. One of Davis's sailors cast off the last dock line just as the men were scrambling aboard.

The 112's executive officer quickly maneuvered the boat away from the dock and shoved the throttles all the way forward. Below deck, the 112's machinist's mate responded to the engine order telegraph and applied full power to her three 1200-horsepower engines.

Within seconds, the PT-112 was clear of the harbor and speeding down the Anacostia River at 40 knots—well out of range.

<u>*Chapter Sixty-Three*</u>

23 November 1944

Washington and Richmond had fallen. Both permanent capitals had been overrun and smashed by the advancing Germans. General Eisenhower's forces had managed to fall back into Southern Virginia and establish another defensive line along the Roanoke River; but Eisenhower did not expect the new line to hold for much longer.

Admiral Nimitz had managed to move his ships out of Norfolk ahead of the Nazi advance. The Allied fleet had relocated to Charleston, South Carolina, where it remained a deterrent to German attacks along the Southern Coast.

The design team at Consolidated had managed to modify the 325th's B-24s so they would be capable of carrying Toby Pozniak's downscaled bomb; but Pozniak's team had, as of yet, been unable to construct one. One of the major obstacles Pozniak and his colleagues faced was a lack of fissile material.

The implosion bomb had been a plutonium-fueled device. At the beginning of the Downrush Project, bomb-grade plutonium had been easier to obtain than uranium. The larger bomb's plutonium core was the reason Oppenheimer had chosen it over Pozniak's uranium-fueled device. In the months following Oppenheimer's decision, the Allies had dedicated all their enrichment resources toward producing plutonium. Now, they desperately needed uranium. Racing the clock, the Downrush scientists were struggling to enrich enough of it for Pozniak's team to build their bomb.

The Allies were on the brink. The Nazis were less than five hundred miles from Atlanta. As winter approached, Eisenhower hoped von Essen would delay his next offensive until spring.

One of James Winston's daily duties at the Third Reich Expeditionary Headquarters was to clean the office belonging to SS General Ernst Kruger. The arrogant Nazi detested being in the same room with the man he called the *"großer affe"* [big ape], so he insisted Winston complete the task of cleaning his office prior to his arrival each day.

The repugnant nature of the demand aside, Winston didn't exactly look upon this as a hardship. Kruger routinely stayed out late, drinking and carousing. As a result, the debauched general rarely came in before midmorning. Kruger's refusal to be in the room with Winston gave the Resistance operative free rein to read through Kruger's correspondence, allowing him to mine large amounts of valuable intelligence for the Allies.

On one occasion, Kruger's aide unexpectedly entered the office and found Winston shuffling through papers on the general's desk. The aide simply assumed he was tidying them as part of his janitorial duties. Because of his Nazi-ingrained racism, it never occurred to Kruger's minion that this "großer affe" was more literate in German than he himself was.

It was Thursday morning. Thursday was the day Kruger held his weekly staff meetings to discuss the status of the occupation and to lay out his plans for moving the Nazi cause forward, not only in New York—but in the other occupied regions as well. Kruger always made agenda notes for the meetings on Wednesday afternoon and left them on his desk overnight. Often, the information Winston extracted from Kruger's preparatory notes was political in nature and of little strategic value.

That was not the case today. Today, James Winston learned that Wilhelm Keitel, Field Marshal of the German Army and Hitler's top military adviser, would be arriving in New York on December 16th, nine days ahead of a Christmas Day conference with Field Marshal Friedrich von Essen.

Buoyed by the Japanese attack on the West Coast, Hitler was sending Keitel to outline the Führer's plan for the final offensive—a monumental push to break the stalemate and end the war in North America. It was to be a blitzkrieg of epic proportions—beginning in the spring of 1945.

Chapter Sixty-Four

25 December 1944

It was 4:30 a.m. on Christmas morning. James Winston, inside the Empire State Building, had spent the last six hours stripping, waxing and buffing the marble-tile floor inside the 59th-floor conference room. In just a few hours, Field Marshal Keitel, Field Marshal von Essen and SS General Kruger were scheduled to meet here.

They would be discussing Hitler's plans for the final push against the North American Allies. The three men and their various aides would occupy fewer than a dozen of the forty chairs that surrounded the large sectional table.

As he moved the last section of the table back into place, the one closest to where the Nazi war planners would be seated, Winston knelt and peered underneath it. He opened his toolbox and removed the special "tape measure" that had been given to him by Lieutenant Commander Mike Crofford. Utilizing a bracket he himself had fabricated to hold the battery-powered device in place, Winston screwed it to the underside of the table and extended the "ruler" that would function as an antenna.

As James Winston was activating the listening device inside the Empire State Building, Natalie Rosenbaum was lying awake in her barracks at Rikers Island.

Natalie examined the numbers that were tattooed on her forearm. She knew that even if she somehow survived her living nightmare, she would never be the same person she used to be. As she contemplated her fate, Natalie knew she would never again see her parents. She had lost all hope that she would ever be reunited with Toby Pozniak.

She wondered why God had abandoned her. Once a vibrant, joyful young woman, Natalie Rosenbaum had been reduced to hopelessness and anguish. She began to contemplate ways to end her life—to end her misery.

As she closed her eyes and slipped into a restless slumber, she decided it would be easier to let death run its natural course.

Chapter Sixty-Five
26 December 1944

On the Tuesday morning following Christmas, the 34th Street-Penn Station subway exit was packed with people making their way to work, many of them as forced laborers for the Nazi regime. As James Winston approached the top steps of the exit, Mike Crofford began making his way down, against the flow. As Crofford bumped ever so slightly into Winston, the intelligence officer took the small notebook that his operative placed in his hand and slipped it inside his coat pocket.

The notebook contained Winston's report from the Christmas morning meeting between Keitel, von Essen and Kruger. Winston had taken detailed notes—all in the original German—as he sat on a bench in Greeley Square, a block away from the Empire State Building. He had spent the rest of that day translating and organizing the conversations into a comprehensive intelligence report.

Now in Crofford's possession, it wouldn't be long before the report reached the Allied high command. The urgency surrounding the *Downrush* Project would soon be further heightened.

Chapter Sixty-Six
12 February 1945

Barely seven months after resurrecting their previously cast-aside design, Toby Pozniak's team was ready to test the weapon they hoped would save America.

The speed with which they had completed their project and the methods by which they had fabricated the prototype had been nothing short of miraculous. The fact that they had been able to produce their complex bomb and also comply with their mandated size restrictions represented a feat of genius. Even Robert Oppenheimer, not one to lavish praise upon others, was impressed, which made it even harder for the lead *Downrush* scientist to give Pozniak and his team the news he now had to deliver—there would be no test.

The enrichment facility had only been able to produce enough uranium for two bombs. Oppenheimer informed Pozniak that they couldn't afford to waste one of the bombs on another test detonation. When Pozniak asked why two bombs were necessary, Oppenheimer refused to answer.

Chapter Sixty-Seven

17 February 1945

At the War Department in Atlanta, the Allied war planners were anxious. Presidents Roosevelt and Truman, along with General Eisenhower and Admiral Nimitz, as well as their top staffers and aides, had gathered to receive a briefing from Robert Oppenheimer and Admiral Fuller.

As Admiral Fuller laid out the status of the *Downrush* Project, the decision makers were relieved to learn that the new bomb was ready to be deployed. Their elation was only slightly dampened when they learned that there was only enough enriched uranium for the two bombs the *Downrush* team had already assembled. Nearly all of them believed two bombs would be one more than they needed.

However, when Fuller informed them that this new bomb, which employed a much more sophisticated detonation mechanism than the earlier bomb, had not been tested, some in attendance voiced concern.

"Can we really decide how best to utilize this new weapon if we're uncertain it's going to work?" President Roosevelt asked.

"The device will work," Fuller stated flatly. "I'm confident of that."

"Then we'll hit Berlin with both bombs," Roosevelt posited, receiving nods of concurrence from most in the room.

"What about the Japanese?" President Truman asked. "Need I remind everyone there are *two* invading armies on our shores?"

General Eisenhower quickly stepped up to answer his president. "It's a fair point, sir. While it's true the Japanese hold Southern California, Emperor Hirohito is only interested in our natural resources. The Nazis, on the other hand, are here to end our way of life—to subjugate us. Their goal is to vanquish our culture and invalidate everything we stand for."

"So, you're saying Japan will capitulate once we destroy Berlin?" Truman shook his head. "I don't think so, General. They're fanatical fighters—you know that."

"Mr. President, the Japanese only have enough military assets on our shores to defend the California oil fields against an enemy fighting a two-front war. Once we've defeated Hitler, driving the Japanese from the West Coast will be straightforward. Even if that weren't the case—as a practical matter, we have no means with which to deliver a bomb all the way to Tokyo. Even the B-29 wouldn't have given us that kind of range."

Truman seemed satisfied with Eisenhower's answer.

Roosevelt turned to Admiral Nimitz. "Chester, do we have the naval assets to deliver the bombs, planes and aircrews to England?"

"We do, Mr. President, but it won't be without risk. We can deliver the aircrews and bombs using submarines; but I think we should consider flying the B-24s across. I think it would be a much safer bet than transporting them aboard surface vessels."

Roosevelt looked at Eisenhower. "How about that, Ike? Do the bombers have the range to make that flight?"

Eisenhower quickly turned to General Arnold for confirmation. Arnold gestured in the affirmative.

As Robert Oppenheimer continued to sit in silence, President Truman looked past Eisenhower, directly at General Arnold. "Hap, if we fly the bombers across, how many will we need to send to ensure at least two of them safely reach England?"

"If you're worried about the Germans shooting them down, Mr. President, the biggest threat is here at home. Once we get them clear of our own coastline, and if we keep them far enough north of the German patrols out of the Azores, they should be able to reach England unmolested. Getting two of them safely to Berlin will be the bigger challenge, by far."

General Arnold looked around. He sensed that everyone in the room was waiting for him to elaborate on his previous statement. "As you probably know, the B-24s have been stripped of all their defensive armament in order to fly the delivery profile the *Downrush* pilots have been perfecting. As we learned from the Hart Island raid, separating them and sending each of them in alone will give us our best chance of success. The one thing we have going for us is that the Germans have geared their air defenses around Berlin to counter large groups of RAF bombers at high altitude, almost always at night. They won't be expecting a single, low-level bomber in broad daylight. In addition—"

The senior aviator realized he was veering off course. "I'm sorry, sir. To answer your question, I would dispatch all seven of the 325th's B-24s to England. Even if only three survive the ferry mission, we'll still have one available as a backup."

"If that's the case," Truman responded, "it will require all of the 325th's aircrews to ferry them across. What if the loss rate is higher than you anticipate? Can we afford to lose most or all of the men we've trained for this mission?"

"The way I see it, Mr. President, we have seven modified airplanes, seven crews, and two bombs—and no time to increase those numbers before Hitler's spring offensive. At this point, sir, a crew without a plane is just as useless to us as a plane without a crew. I see no reason why all the aircrews shouldn't fly to England."

The look on Truman's face let Arnold know he had succeeded in making his point, harsh as it was.

"Well…that makes *my* job easy," said Nimitz. "We'll load the bombs aboard two separate subs and transport them across the Atlantic. Nothing can ever be certain, but I believe we'll be able to deliver them both to England intact."

"Then it's settled?" Truman asked, directing the question to no one in particular.

President Roosevelt pushed his wheelchair away from the conference table. "Gentlemen, I believe we have a consensus. We'll leave it to Ike and Chester to work out the details and report back to us when the plan is finalized. Any other questions?"

Robert Oppenheimer, who had sat quietly in the background to this point, abruptly broke his silence. "Perhaps we should be asking ourselves if sending both bombs to England is the best option, gentlemen."

Everyone in the room was now focused on the eccentric physicist—about whom most of them knew very little—and with whom most of them had little in common. Roosevelt rolled his wheelchair back to the table. "Go ahead, Doctor Oppenheimer. You have something to say?"

Oppenheimer had always been equal parts scientist and philosopher. He struck a match and lit his pipe. For a few annoying seconds, he puffed long and hard while gazing at the ceiling. Finally, he set the pipe aside and rose to address the room. After several more exasperating seconds, he began. "When we deny the evil within us, we dehumanize ourselves. We deprive ourselves not only of our own destiny—but of any possibility of dealing with the evil in others."

Everyone in the room sat silently. No one was quite sure what the erudite physicist had just said. They certainly didn't know how to respond to it.

Oppenheimer continued. "My childhood didn't prepare me for the fact that the world is full of cruel and bitter things. That fact notwithstanding, it's perfectly obvious that the whole world is going to hell as we speak. The only possible chance that it might *not*…is that we not fail."

President Truman, losing patience with Oppenheimer's rambling, implored him to make his point.

Oppenheimer ignored him. "We find ourselves in the death grip of a terrible beast. If we can't be sure that we're capable of severing the head of the beast, we should be prepared to cut off his hands as a last alternative—even if we cut ourselves in the process."

Truman exploded. "*Dammit, man!* We don't have time for this crock of—"

Roosevelt calmly held up his hand and interrupted his Confederate counterpart. "Mr. Oppenheimer, are you offering us an alternative plan? If so, please get to the point."

Oppenheimer turned to Chester Nimitz. "Admiral, can you guarantee both bombs will make it across the Atlantic? For that matter, can you guarantee at least *one* of them will make it?"

"No—I can't *guarantee* it," Nimitz answered. "But I can—"

Oppenheimer cut him off, directing his next question at General Eisenhower. "General, can we afford to fail at delivering at least one of these bombs against the Nazis?"

Eisenhower, though he did not voice a response, knew the answer to the question, as did everyone else in the room.

Oppenheimer waited momentarily, then laid his cards on the table. "Tell me, then—how much more difficult will it be to deliver both bombs to Berlin than it would be to deliver one of them to New York City?"

"*In God's name!*" One of the aides shouted from the back of the room.

General Eisenhower and Admiral Nimitz were quietly stunned. President Truman shook his head in disgust. Most of the military officers in the room were incredulous that this egghead physicist was daring to postulate military strategy, never mind the insane nature of his suggestion.

There was one person in the room, however, who was not totally dismissing the validity of Oppenheimer's question—Franklin Delano Roosevelt.

Chapter Sixty-Eight

19 February 1945

In San Angelo, Texas, Rod Hurley was sitting in his office with his XO, Thomas Damron. As they were discussing the recent modifications to their B-24s' bomb bays, Major Harold Stovall, the 325th's adjutant, appeared in the doorway.

Hurley looked over and saw Stovall holding a sheet of teletype paper. "Whatta ya got, Harry?"

"This just came off the C-RATT, sir." The C-RATT (coded radioteletype) was the Allies' secure messaging machine.

"What is it?"

"It's a message from Eisenhower." Stovall walked in and handed Hurley the following message:

FM SUPREME COMMANDER ALLIED FORCES
TO COMMANDER 325TH SPECIAL OPERATIONS SQUADRON
TOP SECRET//
SUBJ//DOWNRUSH

YOU ARE HEREBY DIRECTED TO PROCEED WITH ALL DOWNRUSH
ASSETS TO CNAS JACKSONVILLE, FL, ON OR ABOUT 28 FEB.
UPON ARRIVING CNAS JACKSONVILLE, YOU WILL DETACH TWO
AIRFRAMES AND TWO AIRCREWS TO YOUR EXECUTIVE OFFICER, AT

WHICH TIME HE WILL BEGIN REPORTING SEPARATELY TO COMMANDER ALLIED ARMY AIR FORCES.
YOU WILL SUBSEQUENTLY PROCEED FROM CNAS JACKSONVILLE TO RAF KIRMINGTON, LINCOLNSHIRE, ENGLAND—ARRIVING NO LATER THAN 07 MAR—AND AWAIT FURTHER ORDERS. YOU WILL CONTINUE REPORTING DIRECTLY TO THIS COMMAND.
YOU ARE FURTHER DIRECTED TO DISPATCH YOUR ASSETS FROM CNAS JACKSONVILLE TO RAF KIRMINGTON IN SINGLE-SHIP FLIGHTS, ALLOWING AT LEAST THREE HOURS BETWEEN DISPATCHES.
GODSPEED.

BREAK TRANSMISSON

Chapter Sixty-Nine
09 March 1945

The Friday morning commute was heavy in Midtown Manhattan. Lieutenant Commander Mike Crofford waited nervously at the top of the 34th Street-Penn Station subway exit. He tried not to be conspicuous as he continually leaned over the concrete wall, looking down into the stairwell.

The No. 3 Train from Harlem was running late.

Finally—Crofford spotted James Winston coming up the steps. Crofford nonchalantly entered the stairwell. The report Winston handed off to Crofford held the crucial intelligence the Allied high command had been waiting to receive.

Chapter Seventy
10 March 1945

Inside his office at Allied Headquarters in Atlanta, General Eisenhower was sitting behind his desk, carefully studying situation reports from the fight along the Virginia Front. Most of the reports were discouraging. Eisenhower knew that the circumstances there were becoming dire. He also knew that if the _Downrush_ Project failed to bring about a German surrender prior to the nearing spring offensive, the war would be lost. The United and Confederate States of America would cease to exist. After that, the tiny island nation of England would be the last line of defense against Hitler's goal of world domination.

As the Allied commander paused in a moment of reflection, Eisenhower rued the day, some eighty years earlier, when President Abraham Lincoln had been forced to surrender the Union cause. He was virtually certain that, had his Confederate predecessors not prevailed in their war of secession, the enemy would not now be at his gates. If the United States had been allowed to achieve its pre-Civil War destiny—if America had not been divided—Eisenhower was convinced the Germans would be the ones desperately defending their homeland. _They_ would now be the ones on the verge of defeat.

Casting his momentary ruminations aside, Eisenhower returned to the task at hand. As he reached across the desk for the next report, his aide knocked on his open door. The aide, holding a dossier in his hand, had an anxious expression on his face. "It's here, General—the intelligence report from Lieutenant Commander Crofford. I'm afraid it's even bigger than we thought."

Eisenhower spent the next several hours poring over the details in James Winston's report. The spring offensive was going to be cataclysmic. Hitler knew the British weren't prepared to invade the European Mainland. He was banking on the fact that he could redeploy half his infantry and panzer divisions from the occupied nations in Western Europe long enough to deliver a death blow to the North American Allies. Once his enemies in America were defeated, he could remove the redeployed troops and tanks from America and return them to Europe before the British would be able to mount a cross-channel invasion. The Germans were rapidly moving forces across the Atlantic. Tons of equipment was already stacking up on the piers along Manhattan's West Side.

Several hours later, the following message was handed to General Hap Arnold:

FM SUPREME COMMANDER ALLIED FORCES
TO COMMANDER ALLIED ARMY AIR FORCES
TOP SECRET//
SUBJ//DOWNRUSH

TIMING AND DECISIVE SCOPE OF SPRING OFFENSIVE NOW KNOWN. NYC MEETING BETWEEN KEITEL, VON ESSEN, AND ALL GERMAN DIVISION AND BRIGADE COMMANDERS TO OCCUR AT THIRD REICH HQ ON 08 APR AT 1800 GMT.
SPRING OFFENSIVE TO BEGIN 07 MAY.
BERLIN SOURCE REPORTS HITLER CURRENTLY MEETING WITH ROMMEL IN OCCUPIED FRANCE—SPECIFIC WHEREABOUTS UNKNOWN.
SOURCE REPORTS HITLER SCHEDULED TO DELIVER SPEECH AT REICHSTAG BEGINNING 1900 GMT ON 04 APR. NO FURTHER TRAVEL EXPECTED UNTIL MID-APRIL.

BERLIN DOWNRUSH MUST OCCUR NET 1900 GMT ON 04 APR AND NLT 1300 GMT ON 08 APR.
IF CONFIRMATION OF BERLIN DOWNRUSH NOT RECEIVED AT THIS COMMAND BEFORE 13OO GMT ON 08 APR, THIS COMMAND ONLY—REPEAT, THIS COMMAND ONLY—WILL ISSUE ORDER TO BEGIN ALTERNATE DOWNRUSH MISSION.

BREAK TRANSMISSON

Chapter Seventy-One
19 March 1945

In the dead of night, a nondescript tractor-trailer pulled away from the submarine docks at Her Majesty's Naval Base, Clyde, in Scotland. In the rear of the truck, in addition to its carefully crated cargo, were a half dozen Royal Marines and one nuclear physicist.

The physicist, a young Confederate from Tennessee, was carrying with him three benign-looking plugs, each about the size and shape of an automobile cigarette lighter. Each of the metal plugs had a bright red plastic cap on one end. Carter King settled in for the long drive across the English countryside. His destination lay three hundred miles to the southeast—RAF Kirmington.

Twelve hours later and three thousand miles away, another nuclear physicist climbed inside the belly of Lieutenant Colonel Thomas Damron's B-24 at the Confederate Naval Air Station in Jacksonville, Florida. Inside Damron's B-24 was a mock-up of the atomic bomb the physicist and his team had designed. Toby Pozniak was demonstrating how he planned to climb into the _Melanie Anne's_ bomb bay to arm the bomb while the aircraft was in flight.

Damron was crouched in a cavity just aft of the bay—the cavity from which the B-24's belly gunner would have entered the retractable lower ball turret. The ball turret was no longer there. It had been stripped from the airframe as part of the Project *Downrush* weight-saving modifications. Damron watched as Pozniak, at the rear of the bomb, disconnected the primer wires, removed the breech plug, and inserted four bags of cordite powder into the rifle mechanism.

"When the primer wires ignite the cordite," Pozniak explained, pointing to the breech, "the explosion will propel the stack of uranium *projectile* rings forward through the gun tube inside the bomb." He swept his finger toward the front of the bomb. "The rings will be melded around the smaller uranium *target* rings at the other end of the bomb. It's sort of like slipping a large donut onto a smaller one, except it's such a tight fit, you have to compress the inner donut in the process. This will result in a critical mass of uranium, which will produce an atomic explosion."

Pozniak replaced the breech plug and reconnected the primer wires. He made his way around to the left side of the bomb, being careful to step only on the box-beam catwalk and not on the lightweight bomb bay doors. The catwalk, originally located between two conventional bomb racks, had been moved from the center of the bay all the way to the port side. It had been moved to accommodate the single, massive atomic bomb, which weighed nearly 10,000 pounds—twice the B-24's normal long-range bombload.

Damron leaned to his left and watched as Pozniak, standing beside the bomb, unscrewed three small green-capped plugs from near the top of the bomb's outer casing. He replaced them one at a time with three red-capped plugs. "These are the arming plugs," Pozniak explained. "Once I've inserted them, the bomb is armed and ready to drop. At this point, the only way to disarm it is by removing the red-capped plugs and reinserting the green safety plugs."

"Can't you disarm it just by unscrewing the arming plugs?" Damron asked.

"That won't do it," Pozniak answered. "There are cams on the arming plugs that rotate relays inside the bomb casing. The closed relays complete the circuitry. Simply removing the red-capped plugs won't reopen the relays. The bomb is still armed until I reinsert the safety plugs, which have cams that turn the relays in the opposite direction." He held up one of the green-capped plugs and showed the cam to Damron.

Pozniak slipped the plugs into his pocket and made his way aft along the catwalk, toward Damron. He squatted as he negotiated the ninety-degree turn that took him back to the centerline of the bay. Duckwalking along the catwalk, he slipped beneath the box-shaped stabilizing fin at the tail of the bomb.

Stepping aft of the bomb bay, the smiling physicist stood upright and faced Damron. "That's all there is to it, Colonel. I'll arm the device after you've climbed above ten thousand feet on the bomb run. Once it's armed, the barometric altimeter will become active. When the bomb falls through five thousand feet, it'll activate the radar altimeter, which will detonate the bomb at an altitude of nineteen hundred feet above the target—the height that yields the maximum blast radius."

The pilot and physicist had quickly struck a chord with one another. Both Damron and Pozniak were native New Yorkers, Damron from the Bronx and Pozniak from Brooklyn. Neither of them realized this was the primary reason they had been assigned, at the personal behest of President Roosevelt, to the backup *Downrush* bomber.

Not knowing if or when they would be called upon to deliver their bomb, neither man was aware of their intended target.

Chapter Seventy-Two

04 April 1945 (Operation Downrush—the first day)

(13 hours, 54 minutes GMT—04 hours, 06 minutes to Hitler's Reichstag speech) It was a rainy, unseasonably cold afternoon at RAF Kirmington. A single B-24D bomber taxied away from a remote hangar, toward a specially constructed concrete pit on the heavily guarded tarmac.

The taxi director, aligning the B-24's low-slung fuselage with the elongated pit, signaled for the bomber to turn ninety degrees to the right. As the aircraft turned, several dozen curious onlookers, watching from the 325th's open hangar bay, were able to make out the artwork on the bomber's starboard nose section. It was a freshly painted image of an especially curvy blonde with a come-hither look in her eyes. Leaning back in a provocative pose, she was wearing a cowboy hat, boots—and little else. Beneath her derrière, painted in elegant script letters, were the words "*Yellow Rose.*"

Once the B-24's open bomb bay was positioned over the pit, the taxi director crossed his arms, signaling for the pilot to apply the brakes. Three men inside the pit, led by Carter King, set about loading the *Downrush* bomb into the *Yellow Rose's* underbelly.

King, carrying a heavy chain, climbed a ladder into the bomb bay. The young physicist threaded the chain through a pulley that was mounted on the main spar at the top of the bay. Then, he lowered the loose end of the chain back down to one of the men still in the pit. The man attached it to a large hook at the bomb's center of gravity. King signaled the other man to activate the winch inside the pit. Slowly—carefully—all three men guided the 10,000-pound bomb as the winch lifted it into the B-24.

Once the bomb was at the proper height, King stood on the catwalk inside the bomb bay. He stretched his torso and arms across the top of the bomb's outer casing and swung the forward bomb-release hook down from the main spar. He attached it to an eyebolt on top of the bomb, just forward of the hook where the chain was attached. He locked it in place.

Repositioning himself to the rear of the bay, King swung the aft bomb-release hook down and signaled the winch operator to raise the bomb slowly. As the back of the bomb rose ever so slightly, King aligned the aft release hook with another eyebolt. He signaled the winch operator to stop as he locked the second bomb-release hook into place.

King detached the chain from the top of the bomb and extracted the loose end from the pulley. He held onto it as he descended the ladder, links of chain collecting on the concrete beneath him. Once down, he dropped the rest of the chain, shook hands with the other three men in the pit, and scurried back up the ladder. As one of the other men lowered the ladder onto the floor of the pit, Carter King grabbed an interphone headset from a hook inside the bay. He informed Rod Hurley that the bomb was properly secured aboard the aircraft and cleared the bombardier to close the bomb bay.

When the bomb bay doors began to scroll shut, the young physicist waved goodbye to his two colleagues. Each man acknowledged King's wave with a thumbs-up as they both disappeared beneath the closing doors.

(15 hours, 47 minutes GMT—02 hours, 13 minutes to Hitler's Reichstag speech) Twelve miles southwest of Berlin, near the town of Stahnsdorf, Stefan Rosinger sat on the second-story balcony of his farmhouse. A fervent anti-Nazi, the dissident farmer had been spying for the Allies for most of the war.

Rosinger's family had immigrated to Germany from Austria in 1921. Even though he was a loyal German citizen, he believed the destruction of Hitler's Third Reich was the only way to save his country. In addition to working for the Allies, he and his wife Elza prayed daily that the Nazi war criminals would soon receive the hard reversal they deserved.

Elza had grown up in the western regions of Czechoslovakia. The only child of wealthy Jewish parents, she had come to Berlin in 1929 to study music at the Berlin University of the Arts. It was in Berlin where she had met the young Austrian farmer who later became her husband.

Stefan and Elza Rosinger had purchased their farm near Stahnsdorf two years before Hitler's rise to power. From the time the Nazis took control of the Reichstag, the couple had been careful to conceal Elza's ethnicity. Stefan and Elza had thus far managed to keep her Jewish lineage a secret, but the couple lived in constant fear.

When the Nazis occupied Western Czechoslovakia in 1939, Elza's parents had been forcibly relocated to the Terezin ghetto in the northern part of the country. Eventually, they had been shipped to Auschwitz, the Nazi death camp in Poland. Shortly thereafter, Stefan and Elza had met a fellow dissident, who put Stefan in touch with his Allied handler in London.

Today, Rosinger had been told to keep his eyes trained on the horizon, toward downtown Berlin. His handler had instructed him to remain at his post for the next four hours. Because of the rain and low clouds, he could barely see beyond the fence at the edge of his farm. He had no idea what it was he was waiting to see; but if and when he saw it, he had been directed to dispense with his code book and broadcast an immediate, in-the-clear report to the Allies.

Pressing his handler in London for more information, Rosinger had asked him how he would know when he had observed whatever it was he was supposed to report.

"You'll know," his handler had responded.

(16 hours, 07 minutes GMT—01 hour, 53 minutes to Hitler's Reichstag speech) Practically nothing was going as planned aboard the *Yellow Rose*. An hour into their three-hour flight to Berlin, Rod Hurley and Mac Litchfield were still flying in the clouds at 9,000 feet. They were supposed to be flying below 200 feet to avoid detection. Even so, they dared not descend with no visibility. They could climb and hope to break out on top of the clouds, but that would do them no good if their target was still obscured when they arrived over Berlin.

Making matters worse, all but one of the B-24's oxygen canisters had been removed to conserve weight. The crew was only supposed to go on supplemental oxygen during the high-altitude segment of the bomb run. If they climbed now, they would exhaust their oxygen supply well before they started their bomb run.

John Spence, the *Yellow Rose* navigator, was using radio beacons out of England to keep the bomber headed toward Berlin; but with no ground reference, he would be unable to locate the IP and successfully navigate the bomb run to the Reichstag. After another twenty minutes of frustration, Rod Hurley reluctantly decided to abort the mission and return to RAF Kirmington.

(19 hours, 12 minutes GMT) At twenty-two minutes before sunset, as Hitler was delivering his speech at the Reichstag in Berlin, the *Yellow Rose* broke out of the clouds 600 feet above RAF Kirmington. Mac Litchfield circled to land on the rain-soaked runway. As Litchfield taxied toward the concrete pit to offload one of only two *Downrush* weapons in the Allied arsenal, Rod Hurley knew he had expended one of the days in his five-day window to deliver the bomb to Berlin.

Hurley had no idea why he had been saddled with this narrow window in which to complete his mission. He only knew that he had four opportunities remaining.

Chapter Seventy-Three

07 April 1945 (Operation Downrush—the fourth day)

(1900 hours GMT—18 hours to the deadline for launching the second bomber) At RAF Kirmington, Rod Hurley and the crew of the *Yellow Rose* were becoming increasingly frustrated. Three more times they had launched into the dismal weather over England and Western Europe. Three more times they had been forced to abort and return to Kirmington.

They would have one final day in which to accomplish the task they had been working toward for more than a year—one more opportunity to defeat the Germans on their own soil. Rod Hurley and his crew were growing desperate to complete their mission. Had they understood the consequences that loomed if they failed to deliver their bomb by General Eisenhower's deadline, they would have been even more desperate.

In Jacksonville, Florida, Thomas Damron and his backup crew had been placed on twenty-four-hour alert by General Arnold. Damron couldn't understand why the *Melanie Anne* hadn't been deployed to

330

England with the rest of the 325th SOS. He and his crew were becoming impatient for an answer.

The *Melanie Anne's* skipper had placed several secure-line phone calls to General Arnold in Atlanta; but Arnold had yet to answer any of them. Damron was considering going over Arnold's head, directly to General Eisenhower.

Chapter Seventy-Four

08 April 1945 (Operation Downrush—the final day)

(0515 GMT—07 hours, 45 minutes to the deadline) General Dwight Eisenhower knew what was at stake. If he didn't receive confirmation of a successful detonation over Berlin by 1300 GMT, the backup mission would have to launch from Jacksonville and begin the five-hour flight toward New York City.

Five hours after the deadline, at 1800 GMT, hundreds of the most important Nazi military commanders in North America were slated to meet at the Third Reich's headquarters in New York. But the thought of using an atomic bomb on a U.S. city—even as a last, desperate attempt at survival—was more than the general could process on his own. He needed to speak with the U.S. President. Eisenhower requested a late-night meeting at FDR's private residence to discuss the grave decision one final time.

In Atlanta, it was fifteen minutes past midnight on Sunday morning—a quarter hour into what would be the most consequential day in modern history.

General Eisenhower, waiting in President Roosevelt's study, rose to greet him. "Good evening, Mr. President."

The president's personal aide rolled him into the room and positioned his chair at the corner of the large oak desk. "Hello, Ike. I think 'good *morning*' would be more appropriate." The aide placed a blanket across his lap. The president looked even more frail than usual. It was obvious his health was deteriorating.

Eisenhower sat back down in the chair, directly in front of Roosevelt. The president took a silver cigarette case from his desk and opened it, offering one to Eisenhower. The general took a cigarette, nodding his head in appreciation as he removed his lighter from his jacket. He flicked the lighter open and waited for the president to remove another cigarette for himself. He leaned forward to light the president's cigarette before lighting his own.

Roosevelt replaced the case and moved an ashtray across the desktop, positioning it so he and the general could both reach it. He looked at Eisenhower and mustered a faint smile. "I believe Scotch is your drink, isn't it?"

"Scotch will be fine, sir."

The aide went to the liquor cabinet in the corner of the study. After pouring a Scotch for General Eisenhower, he mixed a dry martini, the president's preferred drink. He handed the drinks to the two men and asked the president if he needed anything else.

"No—that's all, thank you. Please give us the room now."

"I'll be outside the door if you need me, sir." The aide walked from the study, turning to pull the large double doors closed as he left.

Roosevelt looked at Eisenhower. "So…what's on your mind, Ike? Having misgivings about our secondary target?"

The look on Eisenhower's face confirmed the president's intuition. The general shook his head. "The forecast over Western Europe doesn't look good, sir."

Roosevelt laid his cigarette on the ashtray. He looked down at his drink for several seconds before setting it on the corner of the desk. His hands were clasped as he rested them on the blanket across his lap. "*Well,*" the president said thoughtfully, "I think we knew it might come to this. Let's not give up hope, though. If anyone can get through to Berlin, I think it's this Hurley fellow. Hap says he's the best aviator he's ever seen." Roosevelt leaned forward in his wheelchair. "Ike—do you think we should go ahead and tell Hurley what's at stake here? Should we tell him what the secondary target is?"

"I honestly don't think it would make a difference, sir. And that's not why I'm here."

Roosevelt took his cigarette from the ashtray. "Say what's on your mind."

"I talked to Hap several hours ago. He says we can still throw together another massive strike in time to hit New York during the meeting. The plans have been on the table for a long time. Yes, there will still be civilian casualties; but, if we use conventional bombs, at least we won't destroy the entire city."

"*Ike*…haven't we already hashed this out?" The president leaned back. "Tell me—what happened the last time we hit New York with a massive air strike? Did we take out our intended target?"

Eisenhower knew it was a rhetorical question.

"Let me ask you straight up," the president continued. "If we throw everything we've got at 'em tomorrow…even if we put every available bomber in the air…what are the odds we'll take out the people in that meeting? Even if we get lucky and score a direct hit, won't they already be in the shelters? It's not as if we can take their air defenses by surprise if we send a thousand bombers over the city."

Roosevelt leaned forward. His expression was more somber than Eisenhower had ever seen it. "Ike—listen to me. They have tons of equipment stacked along the Hudson. A third of their fleet is in New York Harbor *right now—as we speak.* At one o'clock tomorrow afternoon, every German commander above field grade will be inside the Empire State Building. Hitler is gearing up for the largest military campaign in history, and it's coming at us in four weeks. We simply *can't* fail here. This will be our final opportunity to survive this war."

General Eisenhower knew the U.S. president's assessment was accurate. He just needed to hear it one last time. He tamped out his cigarette in the ashtray and stood to leave. "Very well, Mr. President. Let's hope Colonel Hurley comes through in the morning. One more thing, sir—I'll be flying down to Jacksonville in a few hours. If it *does* come to pass that I'm to order Colonel Damron and his men to do the unthinkable, I think I should do it face to face."

"You're absolutely right," the president said, nodding his head. "It *should* be done face to face. In fact, I'm going with you."

"That's not necessary, sir. The responsibility is mine."

Roosevelt shook his head. "No…that's where you're wrong, General Eisenhower. Please—sit back down for a minute."

Eisenhower sat back down in the chair.

"Ike—if you don't remember another word that was said here tonight, I want you to remember what I'm about to tell you."

Eisenhower leaned in close, obliging the president with his undivided attention.

Roosevelt leaned in as well. "The accountability for this terrible situation rests solely with me—no one else. Not President Truman—not you. No one but me. *I'm* to blame for not preparing—for not recognizing the war was coming to our shores. If we should fail tomorrow, history will show that the fault was mine—and mine alone."

General Eisenhower stood. He reached over and took the glass of Scotch from the desk. He held it in his hand, reflecting on what he was about to say. After several seconds, the Confederate general downed the last of the Scotch and set the glass on the desk. "Abraham Lincoln once admonished us that a house divided cannot stand. With all due respect, Mr. President, I disagree with what you said just now. If we lose this war, I believe history will show that it wasn't lost because of anything that happened four years ago…or anything that might happen tomorrow. Sir…if we lose this war, it will be because we lost it generations ago…on a bloody battlefield beside Antietam Creek."

(0604 GMT—06 hours, 56 minutes to the deadline) Unable to sleep, Thomas Damron was lying awake in his room at the Bachelor Officer Quarters. It was just after 1 a.m. in Jacksonville. Damron was tossing and turning, trying to decide if he should jump his chain of command and contact General Eisenhower. He and his men deserved to know why they hadn't been sent to join the rest of the 325th SOS in England.

Why were they on alert here in Florida? It didn't make any sense. He had tried talking directly to General Arnold, his immediate superior, on three separate occasions. Each time the general had refused to accept his call.

Finally, Damron made his decision. He would try to contact General Arnold one more time, first thing in the morning. If he was unsuccessful, he would try calling General Eisenhower directly.

(0712 GMT—05 hours, 48 minutes to the deadline) For the fifth day in a row, the *Yellow Rose* rumbled into the rainy, cloud-laden skies over RAF Kirmington. It didn't look promising. The ceiling was lower today than on any of the previous four days.

At least it was a smoother ride. This was the first time they had launched in the early morning air. Carter King, as he sat strapped into his side-facing seat aft of the bomb bay, hoped this would be the day he didn't get airsick from bouncing around inside the belly of the poorly ventilated bomber.

Rod Hurley, as he concentrated all his attention on his flight instruments, continued to climb through 6,000 feet on an easterly heading, out over the English Channel. Three minutes later, passing 8,000 feet, his B-24 was still in the clouds. Then, as he began to level off at 9,000 feet, the cockpit grew noticeably brighter. Hurley started to become cautiously optimistic that this would be the day—the day he and his crew would finally deliver their history-altering payload to the heart of Hitler's Third Reich.

Stefan Rosinger, for the fifth straight day, sat down on his balcony. Elza brought him his morning cup of coffee and gave him a kiss.

His instructions on this day were different than on the previous four days. His handler had told him that if he didn't see anything by 2 p.m. in Berlin (1300 GMT), he was to contact London and report that nothing had happened.

He looked toward Germany's capital and waited.

(0743 GMT—05 hours, 17 minutes to the deadline) Cruising at 9,000 feet, still over the English Channel, the *Yellow Rose* broke into the clear for the first time in the past five days. Everyone in the crew breathed a sigh of relief. Rod Hurley passed the controls to Mac Litchfield and pressed his throat mic. "How about it, John? Can you fix our position?"

"Stand by, Skipper." John Spence got up from his navigator's station. He stood behind Mark Lorance, who was seated closest to the B-24's forward plexiglass. Spence peered anxiously over the bombardier's shoulder, scanning the coastline beyond the channel. He searched for a recognizable landmark. He made out a series of barrier islands at eleven o'clock, stretching northward and bending toward the coast. He went back to his chart. "Got it, Skipper! We're headed straight for Amsterdam. Come left to zero niner two."

Hurley looked at his copilot and smiled. "You heard him, Mac—zero niner two." He pointed and made a downward motion with his finger. "Take her down to two hundred feet and put the spurs to her."

Litchfield was from New England. He had never even seen a set of spurs. Still, he knew exactly what his skipper wanted him to do. He began a gradual descent, leaving the throttles forward. As the heavy bomber picked up speed, the men inside her felt a rush. The feeling of relief they had experienced breaking into the clear minutes earlier now turned to nervous anticipation.

They were going to Berlin.

(0758 GMT—05 hours, 02 minutes to the deadline) It was clear and sunny. Crossing the Dutch coastline at 200 feet and 248 miles per hour, the *Yellow Rose* began to bounce in the thermals that were rising from the plowed fields below.

Seated in the bowels of the fuselage, Carter King was vomiting violently into a paper bag. The windows that once would have accommodated two waist gunners, had been eliminated from either side of the fuselage. King had no way to look outside the aircraft. He was beginning to worry that, if his condition didn't improve, he wouldn't be able to arm the bomb after the *Yellow Rose* reached the IP and started her steep climb.

From his station immediately aft of the copilot's seat, Garry Crain attempted to pass a coded position report over the long-range HF radio, but something was wrong. It wasn't transmitting. Using the VHF radio, he transmitted the position report "in the blind," hoping they might still hear it back at RAF Kirmington. With the bomber no longer in line-of-sight range from England, Crain knew it was unlikely that the 325th's operations officer would receive the report.

(0804 GMT—04 hours, 56 minutes to the deadline) In Atlanta, several hours before dawn, a specially modified Consolidated C-87

Liberator Express (a variant of the B-24) began rolling down the runway at Candler Army Airfield. With barely a third of the 5000-foot runway behind it, the VIP transport rotated, lifted into the cool Georgia night, and headed south-southeast.

It was a ninety-minute flight to the Confederate Naval Air Station in Jacksonville, Florida.

(0913 GMT—03 hours, 47 minutes to the deadline) Just over two hours into the flight, *Yellow Rose* navigator John Spence announced the IP—a distinctive bend in the Elbe River.

Hugging the terrain at fast cruise airspeed, the lone B-24 bomber and her crew were now sixty-three miles west of the Reich Chancellery. They had met no resistance. Those on board could only assume that the Luftwaffe was unaware of their presence. Seeing as how the *Yellow Rose* was carrying no defensive armament, her crew was relieved that their stealthy flight profile had gotten them this far into Germany undetected.

Unfortunately, they now had to begin a lengthy climb that would make them vulnerable to radar detection. If they encountered any German fighters during the long, slow-airspeed climb, they would be sitting ducks. Rod Hurley took the controls from Mac Litchfield and called for max climb power.

Dave Murray, from his flight engineer station, leaned forward into the cockpit and toggled four switches to open the electric cowl flaps. The flaps would remain open for the duration of the climb, allowing more cooling air to flow around the engines. Then, he pushed the four prop levers forward, increasing the speed on each of the propellers by 200 RPM. Lastly, he advanced all four throttles to maximum climb power.

Hurley pulled back on the yoke to initiate the uphill bomb run. Because of the fuel she had burned, the *Yellow Rose* was almost 7,000 pounds lighter than when she had lifted off at RAF Kirmington. Each of her four Pratt & Whitney engines was churning out more than 1,100 horsepower as the *Yellow Rose* began to climb at 1,540 feet per minute and 135 miles per hour—straight toward Berlin.

Twelve minutes into her bomb run, the *Yellow Rose* passed 13,000 feet, the halfway point of her ascent. From the crystal-clear skies over Germany, her crew would soon be able to see Berlin.

The much smoother air at the higher altitude made it easier for Carter King to arm the bomb. He successfully pulled the safety plugs and replaced them with the red-capped arming plugs. No longer airsick, he felt a combined sense of satisfaction and anticipation as he returned to his station aft of the bomb bay and strapped into his seat.

The bomber's rate of climb continued to decrease in the thinning air. Dave Murray reached forward to advance the "boost" levers that controlled the *Yellow Rose's* four superchargers. As he increased the RPMs, the superchargers forced more of the thin air into the engines' carburetors. As the bomber continued to climb, the meticulous flight engineer noticed the number three propeller had lost some RPM. He tried to sync it with the others. As he applied forward pressure to the prop lever, it wouldn't budge. He tried retarding the lever to free it up.

Suddenly, there was no resistance on the lever. The number three propeller began to rotate faster and faster. It was spinning out of control. *"Overspeed on number three!"* Murray shouted as he grabbed the number three throttle and retarded it to the *idle* position. He simultaneously pulled the number three mixture lever to the *fuel cutoff* position, shutting down the number three engine as the propeller continued to spin dangerously out of control.

Rod Hurley stood on the left rudder pedal to counter the abrupt right yaw from the loss of thrust on that side of the aircraft. He immediately dropped the nose to gain airspeed. The increased airflow over the *Yellow Rose's* twin rudders made it easier to correct for the spontaneous yaw. The airframe started to vibrate violently as the overspeeding propeller pegged the number three RPM gauge.

Descending at 2,300 feet per minute, Hurley had the presence of mind to call for Carter King to disarm the bomb. He desperately needed to get his aircraft down on the ground before the out-of-control propeller separated from the engine and caused a catastrophic structural failure.

For a fleeting moment, Hurley considered jettisoning the bomb instead of disarming it. He quickly thought better of it. If he jettisoned the bomb from this altitude, the blast above the German countryside would take the B-24 out anyway.

A startled King checked to make sure he still had the three green-capped safety plugs in his flight suit. He had no idea how high the bomber was, but he knew if they descended through 5,000 feet, the radar altimeter would activate while the bomb was still inside the bomb bay. The bomb would detonate. He quickly unstrapped and called for an altitude check.

"Ten thousand, eight hundred!" Mac Litchfield called out from the copilot station.

"Keep giving me hacks!" King shouted back, still fumbling for the safety plugs inside his lower, right-leg pocket.

"Ten thousand, five hundred!"

King pulled the plugs from his pocket. In his haste to scramble from his station into the bomb bay, he forgot that his interphone cord was still plugged into the jack above his seat. As he was scrambling into the bomb bay, safety plugs in hand, the cord jerked his head back abruptly, causing him to stumble and fall. He dropped the plugs. All three hit the catwalk and bounced into the bay, rolling beneath the bomb. Because of the bomber's nose-down attitude, the plugs bounded all the way to the forward bulkhead, at the far end of the bay.

"Ten thousand!" came the next hack from Litchfield.

King didn't hear it. He had disconnected his interphone cord and was racing forward on the catwalk. Reaching the forward end of the bay, he quickly threw himself prostrate onto the catwalk and stretched his arm beneath the bomb, reaching for the plugs.

As the aircraft continued to vibrate, the plugs bounced wildly on top of the thin bomb bay doors. King frantically tried to retrieve the plugs. Holding onto the catwalk with his left hand, he somehow managed to gather two of the three plugs in his free hand. He desperately tried to corral the third plug without dropping the first two; but as King opened his fingers slightly to grab the last plug, the first two slipped from his grasp.

It was taking too long.

As the plane continued to buffet, he tried again. Just as before, he quickly managed to pick up two of the plugs. This time, as King pinned the third plug against the bomb bay door with his closed fist, he used only his index finger to pick it up. He held onto the plugs for all he was worth as he extricated himself from the underside of the bomb.

King sprang to his feet and sprinted aft, balancing himself on the narrow catwalk. As he plugged his interphone cord into the jack, he heard Litchfield yelling *"six thousand, five hundred!"* In less than a minute, the radar altimeter would activate. The bomb would vaporize the *Yellow Rose.*

"Open the bomb bay doors!" King shouted.

Mac Litchfield started to question King, but Mark Lorance cut him off from the bombardier station. "Opening bomb bay doors!" Lorance yelled as he toggled the switch that opened the doors. He understood that King was trying to stop the radar altimeter's signal from bouncing off the closed metal doors, buying the young physicist more time to disarm the bomb.

As the doors opened, the violent rush of wind through the open bomb bay forced King to steady himself on the catwalk. The narrow steel-mesh walkway was now the only thing preventing the young physicist from falling out of the bomber.

"*Five thousand!*" came the next hack from Litchfield.

The radar altimeter was now activated. Unless King could disarm the bomb in time, it would detonate when they reached 1,900 feet above the ground. He carefully placed the three safety plugs in his pocket. If he dropped even one of the plugs out of the open bomb bay, there would be no way to disarm the bomb.

"*Four thousand, five hundred!*"

Carter King, while balancing himself on the shaking catwalk, leaned against the bomb and removed the first of three arming plugs from the bomb's outer casing. His first inclination was to let it fall through the open doors to free both hands before handling the safety plugs. Not knowing why, he decided to place it in a separate pocket before reaching for the first of the three green-capped plugs.

"*Four thousand!*"

King carefully grabbed one of the safety plugs from his other pocket and threaded it into the bomb casing. He moved to the next plug.

"*Three thousand, five hundred!*"

He repeated the tedious process a second time. Two of the safety plugs were in.

"*Three thousand!*"

King removed the third arming plug from the bomb and slipped it into his pocket beside the other two. Still balancing himself on the vibrating catwalk, he reached into the other pocket for the remaining safety plug.

Just as he pulled the last plug from his pocket, the aircraft hit a powerful thermal that jolted King so hard he slammed his elbow against the bomb. He lost his grip on the plug. It momentarily levitated inches above his hand. He instinctively raised his hand and slapped the plug higher into the air.

"*Two thousand, five hundred!*"

As it fell, the plug ricocheted off the side of the bomb. King made a desperate attempt to snag it before it fell from the open bomb bay.

(0936 GMT—03 hours, 24 minutes to the deadline) At the Haselhorst air defense complex, west of Berlin, an alert Luftwaffe radar operator saw an unidentified contact momentarily appear on his scope, then disappear.

The young lance corporal reported his observation to his staff sergeant, who dutifully reported it to the lieutenant in charge of the Sunday duty section. The lieutenant, knowing that the RAF rarely attacked on Sundays, that they never attacked in daylight, and that they always attacked in large formations, obligingly thanked the sergeant for his report and dismissed it.

(0938 GMT—03 hours, 22 minutes to the deadline) His heart pounding, Carter King scrambled back to his seat aft of the bomb bay and strapped himself in. The young physicist had managed to disarm the bomb with only seconds to spare.

Mark Lorance closed the bomb bay doors while Rod Hurley and Mac Litchfield desperately searched the German countryside for a place to set the disabled bomber down. The runaway prop was shaking the plane even more violently. The crew expected the airframe to come apart at any second.

In a moment of clarity, Hurley turned to Litchfield. "Mac, we can't gift this bomb to Hitler." He banked the *Yellow Rose* south, toward a series of lakes in the distance.

"You're going to ditch her—aren't you, Skipper?"

Hurley announced his intention to the rest of the crew. He took a quick look back at his radio operator. "Gabby, the kid won't know what to do back there. Go help him."

Garry Crain unstrapped and began making his way aft and down, through the bomb bay, to help Carter King prepare to ditch. After watching the original *Yellow Rose* sink into the English Channel four years earlier, Crain had hoped he would never have to do this again.

As Rod Hurley was setting up for his final approach to the large lake near Brandenburg, Germany, the rest of the crew was making final preparations to ditch. There were no survival rafts aboard the stripped-down bomber, so once they hit the water, each man would be on his own, with nothing but his Mae West to keep him afloat in the lake.

Hurley briefed them to swim for the southern shoreline, where they would try to join up. He hoped the *Yellow Rose* would settle to the bottom of the lake, taking her top-secret payload with her. As he began a steep left turn onto final, Hurley banked the B-24 almost sixty degrees to get her lined up into the wind. Halfway through the two-*g* turn, the vibrations from the number three prop suddenly ceased. The number three RPM gauge began winding down toward zero.

The *Yellow Rose* was flying smooth as silk.

Looking out the window on his side of the cockpit, Mac Litchfield confirmed what Rod Hurley and Dave Murray had already surmised. "*Number three's feathered!*" Litchfield announced.

"*Max power!*" Hurley barked as he leveled the wings and rolled out straight ahead. Murray immediately shoved the throttles on the three operating engines to the firewall. Hurley tugged back on the yoke to arrest the bomber's descent and level off. Relieved that the runaway prop was no longer shaking his bomber apart, Hurley's mind began to race, trying to figure out his next move. "*Talk* to me, Dave—what's goin' on with the prop?"

"It's gotta be the governor pulley, Skipper. The cable must've snapped, and the pulley somehow jammed hardover—all the way past the *full-increase* position. That's what caused the overspeed."

"So why is it feathered *now?*"

"The hard-g turn must've freed the pulley. Once it was free, it's designed to fail-safe to the feathered position. I think we're okay now."

"Can we make the bomb run on three engines?"

"Not a chance," Murray said, shaking his head emphatically. "She'll never be able to climb to twenty-six thousand. We could try to go in lower, but according to the whiz kid back there, we'll never outrun the blast unless we're above twenty-three thousand. We'll be lucky if we can climb to twenty."

There were several unsettling seconds of silence over the interphone—none of the men in the *Yellow Rose* wanted to be the first to break it. Everyone knew Hurley was considering sacrificing the bomber and her crew to deliver the bomb. Finally, Hurley pressed his mic. "All right, Dave—let me ask you this: If I can find a place to set it down, you think you can fix the governor?"

"You get 'er down, Skipper, and I'll make it work even if I have to walk to Fort Worth for parts."

Rod Hurley thought back to a conversation he had once had with his RAF tail gunner, Aleksander Nowak. It was a conversation about an isolated airstrip along the Baltic coastline—in Poland. It was an airstrip controlled by the Polish Resistance. He began a slow turn to the north, toward the Baltic Sea.

Rod Hurley had not been briefed on the alternate *Downrush* mission. He had no way to know that, back in Florida, his decision not to sacrifice his crew was about to set a calamitous chain of events into motion.

(1103 GMT—01 hour, 57 minutes to the deadline) It was three minutes past 6 o'clock in the morning on the East Coast. Thomas Damron had been on hold for the past half hour. The War Department switchboard operator finally came back on the line and told him it would only be a few more minutes. Damron continued to hold, waiting for his chance to finally speak with General Arnold.

Seated with his feet propped on the windowsill, Damron gazed out of the operations shack that was perched atop the corner of his detachment's hangar. He spotted something unusual out across the tarmac. There were several jeeps approaching. Behind the jeeps was an Army staff car with a five-star flag fluttering above each of the front fenders.

Following immediately behind the staff car was an even more impressive vehicle—a limousine. It was a navy-blue convertible, carrying a lone rear-seat passenger. The shimmering 1939 Packard Super 8 Phaeton, replete with U.S. flags on the chrome bumper and armed guards riding upright on both running boards, was a spectacular sight in the early-morning sunshine.

The motorcade headed straight toward Damron. He got up from his chair and stood on his toes as he watched the vehicles drive beneath the elevated operations shack.

Having lost sight of the unusual procession, Damron grabbed the phone base from the desktop. Contorting his shoulder to hold the handset against his ear, he used his free hand to pick up the long cord that connected the base to the wall-mounted jack. He took several quick steps to the hangar side of the shack, awkwardly paying out the excess cord as he crossed to the window on the opposite side.

As the switchboard operator came back on the line, Damron quickly dropped the cord on the floor and returned the handset to his free hand. Still holding the phone to his ear, he extended his head through the open window and strained to look down at the vehicles that were parking inside the hangar.

The operator informed Damron that General Arnold would speak to him now.

Damron told the operator to stand by. He watched as an aide jumped from the front of the staff car and opened the aft-swinging rear door. General Dwight D. Eisenhower emerged. He stood erect and tugged down on the bottom of his waist-length uniform jacket. With a stoic expression on his face, Eisenhower turned and walked toward the man still seated in the back of the limousine—President Franklin Delano Roosevelt.

For the next few seconds, Damron didn't know what to do.

The operator spoke. "Are you there, Colonel? General Arnold will speak to you now...*Colonel?*"

Damron finally answered. "Please pass along my gratitude to the general for taking time out of his busy morning. I won't be needing him now."

(1300 GMT—the deadline for launching the second bomber) In Berlin, the 2 p.m. deadline came and went. Stefan Rosinger made his way to his barn and climbed a ladder to the loft. Removing a hidden crate from a haystack, he set up a long-range HF transceiver assembly and extended the antenna lead. He attached the lead to an inconspicuous wire that ran to the outside of the barn and across the barn's west-facing, ivy-covered roof.

In London, Rosinger's handler decoded the following seven-word message: *"Am Himmel über Berlin ist alles normal."* [Everything normal in the skies above Berlin.]

(1317 GMT—17 minutes past the deadline) At 8:07 Eastern Standard Time, Thomas Damron and his crew, carrying the second *Downrush* bomb, lifted off in the B-24 *Melanie Anne*. Shortly after departing CNAS Jacksonville, they were joined by an escort of twenty-six P-51 *Mustangs*.

The flight plan called for the formation to fly northeast, at an altitude of only 500 feet. They were to continue on that heading until they were 400 miles over the Atlantic, at which point they would turn due north, toward New York City. The fighters would escort them for another 200 miles.

After that, the *Melanie Anne* would be on her own.

(1323 GMT—05 hours, 25 minutes to the *Melanie Anne's* estimated bomb drop) John Spence had pulled off a minor miracle. With only a secondhand description from Rod Hurley and some outdated charts, the *Yellow Rose's* navigator had managed to locate the Polish Resistance airfield on the Baltic coastline.

Dave Murray stood atop a ladder that had been provided by the Polish Resistance fighters at the airstrip in Debki, Poland. His repair complete, he began tightening the fasteners around the *Yellow Rose's* number three engine cowling. Unable to successfully splice the pulley cable, he had permanently fixed the prop governor to a position he hoped would yield a suitable RPM when the number three engine was at cruise power. It was a crapshoot. Once they were airborne, the crew would have no way to adjust it from the cockpit.

As Murray was finishing his makeshift repair job, Rod Hurley chatted with Aleksander Nowak and the other Polish Resistance fighters. His old tail gunner had been understandably surprised to see an Allied B-24 landing in Poland. Upon seeing the familiar blonde painted on the nose of the bomber, he had been even more surprised. Nowak had recognized her right away.

Even though the *Yellow Rose's* mission was top-secret, Hurley decided secrecy didn't much matter at this point. They were either going to succeed or fail in the next few hours anyway. He explained to Nowak and his comrades that the weapon they were carrying could end the war.

The Resistance fighters shared what little aviation gasoline they had, dispensing dozens of five-gallon cans into the *Yellow Rose's* wing tanks by hand. Rod Hurley doubted it would be enough to get them back to England, but that wasn't important anymore. Right now, the only thing that mattered was delivering the B-24's payload to Berlin.

Dave Murray climbed down the ladder. He walked to where Hurley and Nowak were chatting. "I think we're ready, Skipper."

Rod Hurley turned to Aleksander Nowak. The two men embraced. One by one, Nowak hugged his former *Yellow Rose* crewmates, slapping them on the back and wishing them "*życzenia powodzenia*" [good luck].

(1634 GMT—02 hours, 14 minutes to the *Melanie Anne's* estimated bomb drop) It was 11:34 a.m. in New York. James Winston was testing his short-range listening device in preparation to eavesdrop on the high-level meeting scheduled to begin in less than ninety minutes. Contrary to the way it had been on Christmas Day, Greeley Square would be teeming with people this Sunday afternoon.

Over the next few hours, Winston would listen in on the Nazis' top-secret briefing—a briefing that would include hundreds of the most senior German military officers in North America. Winston knew the Allies were likely to attack the strategic summit with everything they had. The Resistance operative was well aware that he and those around him might become collateral damage.

Still, James Winston remained at his post. He was a block away from the Empire State Building.

(1642 GMT—02 hours, 06 minutes to the *Melanie Anne's* estimated bomb drop) The *Yellow Rose* began her takeoff run on the short asphalt runway in Debki, Poland.

The refueled bomber was slow to accelerate. With her nose raised, the B-24 was barely light on her wheels as the pavement beneath her two main landing gear came to an abrupt end, giving way to weeds and rocks.

Rod Hurley quickly called for "gear up." The crew could feel the *Yellow Rose* shuddering—barely flying above her stall speed. As the nose wheel disappeared into the fuselage and the main landing gear folded into the wings, the bomber gained some flying speed. Hurley pulled back on the yoke just enough to nurse the unsteady bomber over the trees near the end of the airstrip.

In the nose bay, John Spence and Mark Lorance felt the tops of the trees slap the underside of the bomber's fuselage. The impact cracked the bottom pane of plexiglass, just forward of Lorance's feet. As they cleared the tree line, Spence reached out and jabbed Lorance on the shoulder. "I keep tellin' you this is a horseshitty job," he said glibly.

The *Yellow Rose* was airborne—one hour and three minutes from Berlin.

...The faceless man points at Hitler and yells, "Do it, Pozniak! Pull the trigger!"

The *Melanie Anne* was two hours from New York City.

Toby Pozniak and the other six men sat silently at their crew stations, each man reflecting on the gravity of their mission. Pozniak listened to the steady drone from the engines. In an almost-hypnotic state, he replayed his recurring nightmare. He knew now that the faceless man in the wheelchair was the man who, hours earlier, had ordered him to drop his apocalyptic bomb on New York City—Franklin Delano Roosevelt.

He also knew that Natalie might still be alive. Rikers Island was seven miles from the Empire State Building. There had been no test—no way for Pozniak to predict the effective blast radius from his bomb. His nightmare was coming to fruition. This was it—this was his moment of truth.

Toby Pozniak studied the three red-capped plugs in his hand.

(1737 GMT—01 hour, 11 minutes to the *Melanie Anne's* estimated bomb drop) In Midtown Manhattan, more than two hundred members of the Nazi command structure began congregating on the 59th floor of the Empire State Building.

In Germany, the sun was beginning to set west of Berlin.

Adolf Hitler was celebrating the end to a glorious day in the Reich, dining with Field Marshal Hermann Göring and Grand Admiral Karl Dönitz in the Reich Chancellery. Hitler was discussing the conference that was about to take place in New York.

Göring and Dönitz, two of Hitler's three senior-most officers, listened as Hitler regaled them with details of the plans being disseminated by his other senior-most officer, Field Marshal Wilhelm Keitel.

Hitler had entrusted Keitel to disseminate details of the spring offensive to his commanders in North America. In less than half an hour—at the afternoon meeting inside the Third Reich's New York City headquarters—Keitel would begin laying out the final plans for America's defeat.

Adolf Hitler could barely contain his rapture.

Approximately sixty miles east of Berlin, the *Yellow Rose* crossed the Oder River, the border between Poland and Germany. She began climbing on her bomb run. The number three propeller, only slightly out of sync, was performing just as Dave Murray had hoped it would.

Just outside New York Harbor, the USS *Billfish* took up a position within visual range of the Manhattan skyline. At 1800 hours GMT, she would come to periscope depth and float a tethered antenna buoy.

(1751 GMT—57 minutes to the *Melanie Anne's* scheduled bomb drop) The young Luftwaffe corporal was manning one of the mobile radar stations on the eastern outskirts of Berlin. His scope began to paint a single contact some thirty miles away. The contact was obviously not a formation of bombers, but it was flying too slow to be a fighter.

Must be a trainer, the corporal told himself.

(1801 GMT—47 minutes to the *Melanie Anne's* estimated bomb drop) Inside the Empire State Building, SS General Ernst Kruger welcomed Field Marshal Wilhelm Keitel and Field Marshal Friedrich von Essen to the Third Reich Expeditionary Headquarters. As he yielded the floor to Wilhelm Keitel, Kruger took a seat at the back of the huge conference room and surveyed the scene. He was pleased with himself for the way he had hosted this critical summit.

Ernst Kruger was certain his Führer would be pleased with him.

One block away from the Empire State Building, James Winston—as discreetly as he could—listened to the dialog in his ear and began transcribing.

Just outside of Stahnsdorf, Germany, Stefan Rosinger had just finished helping Elza clear their dinner table. Rosinger settled into his favorite chair. He lit his pipe and began reading from a book of poems by Arno Holz.

(1802 GMT—46 minutes to the *Melanie Anne's* estimated bomb drop) Rod Hurley leveled the *Yellow Rose* at 26,000 feet. As soon as the B-24 was steady and on course, Mark Lorance began twisting two knobs to level the vertical gyro in his Norden bombsight.

John Spence tapped Lorance on the shoulder and pointed toward an unmistakable landmark—the Moltke Bridge. The nineteenth-century bridge spanned a distinctive bell-shaped curve in the Spree River, making it easy to identify from the air. Only six hundred yards from the Reich Chancellery, the bridge was the perfect guidepost from which to pinpoint their target.

Even from five miles above the city, the *Yellow Rose*'s bombardier could make out the reflection of the setting sun's rays as they illuminated the glass dome atop the Reichstag. Directly across the street from the Reichstag was the building Mark Lorance would line up in his crosshairs. It was the Reich Chancellery—Adolf Hitler's residence.

"Target in sight, Skipper!"

Rod Hurley responded in a calm, settling voice. "It's your aircraft, Mark." Hurley removed his hands from the yoke as he engaged the autopilot and transferred control to his bombardier.

Lorance opened the bomb bay doors and peered through the bombsight's optical lens. Using his right hand to manipulate a pair of large knurled knobs, he aligned the crosshairs over the bridge, then moved them south to the Chancellery.

Still looking through the lens, he used his left hand to arm the automatic release on the bombsight. "Here we go, boys." The nervous excitement in Lorance's voice steadily increased. "Steady...*stand by...that's it! Bombs away!*"

Seated at his station just aft of the bomb bay, Carter King watched the massive 10,000-pound bomb depart the aircraft. He clicked the *start* button on his stopwatch.

Lorance closed the bomb bay. *"She's all yours, Skipper!"*

Rod Hurley disengaged the autopilot and banked hard left, heading downwind. He lowered the B-24's nose, trading altitude for precious airspeed. With the airspeed indicator reading 325 miles per hour (her maximum structural airspeed), the *Yellow Rose's* true airspeed in the thin air was more than 450 miles per hour. Riding a strong tailwind as she descended through 25,000 feet, the bomber was racing over the ground at eight miles per minute.

The number three propeller was now badly out of sync. The crew of the *Yellow Rose* waited to see if their skipper could outrun the blast from the bomb.

As Carter King's stopwatch hit 46 seconds, at an altitude of 1,900 feet above the Reich Chancellery, the cordite bags inside the breech of Toby Pozniak's trigger mechanism ignited. The uranium inside the *Downrush* bomb instantly went to critical mass.

The world entered the age of nuclear warfare.

Shortly after dusk had overtaken his farm, Stefan Rosinger was dazed by a brilliant flash outside his windows. Seconds later, the windowpanes on the north side of his house imploded. Shards of glass flew just past his head and into the interior of his suddenly darkened home.

Stefan shouted to his wife in the next room, but she was unable to hear him. Elza Rosinger's ears were still ringing from the blast that had originated more than twelve miles away.

The men aboard the *Yellow Rose* braced themselves as their aircraft was tossed about so violently that it felt as if it would be ripped apart. As the turbulence subsided, Rod Hurley pressed his throat mic and called for everyone to check in. To his amazement and relief, everyone in his crew was okay. The bomber was still intact.

As he banked to the left and put the *Yellow Rose* on a course for the English Channel, Hurley and his crew could see the enormous, mushroom-shaped cloud boiling into the twilight sky above Berlin. Carter King scrambled through the bomb bay and up to the flight engineer's station to catch a glimpse through the side of the cockpit.

John Spence was the only *Yellow Rose* crew member not at a loss for words. He turned to the silent bombardier sitting next to him. "I think we just opened the gates to hell," he said in a reverent tone that Mark Lorance had never heard him use.

(1816 GMT—32 minutes to the *Melanie Anne's* estimated bomb drop) Thomas Damron and his crew were sixty-eight miles south of New York City. Now flying at only 200 feet above the Atlantic Ocean, they were covering more than four miles a minute. The *Melanie Anne* was seconds from the start of her bomb run.

Having gathered his wits, Stefan Rosinger held a coal oil lantern as he climbed the ladder to his loft. He knew he had to get his message through to the Allies. He quickly set up his HF radio and switched the power on—nothing.

The Project *Downrush* physicists had failed to account for the electromagnetic pulse that would be generated by their bomb. No one in the Allied chain of command was aware that Berlin had been destroyed.

(1848 GMT) Natalie Rosenbaum wandered into the bright sunshine at Rikers Island.

Looking into the southern sky, Natalie experienced a premonition—her deliverance was close at hand. Shielding her eyes from the afternoon sun, she saw four narrow white streaks against the deep-blue sky. As the streaks extended northward, the trailing ends billowed, merging into one long trail across the heavens. For the first time since her parents had been taken away, she felt she was not alone in the world.

Natalie watched as the path of the silent streaks began to curve. She felt a nearness to God.

In Greeley Square, James Winston continued to monitor the meeting being held a block from where he was sitting. He was unaware of the lone B-24 above the city.

Scribbling on his notepad, he was momentarily distracted by a group of children frolicking on the other side of the park.

High above Natalie Rosenbaum and James Winston, the second *Downrush* bomb was arcing toward New York City.

(2114 GMT) At CNAS Jacksonville in Florida, President Roosevelt and General Eisenhower anxiously awaited the phone call from the Naval Intelligence Office in Atlanta—the phone call to relay confirmation from USS *Billfish* that the New York bomb had detonated. It was more than two hours past due.

At RAF Kirmington in England, the 325th SOS duty officer sat inside the squadron's dimly lit operations shack. His feet were propped on the desk where the VHF radio sat silent. Dozing off in his chair, he suddenly sat upright as the radio came alive with static.

Seconds later, the startled duty officer recognized a voice he had last heard more than fourteen hours earlier—the voice of a man he had given up for dead. It was the voice of his commanding officer, Colonel Rod Hurley.

(2138 GMT) In Jacksonville, Florida, the phone inside the VIP lounge at the 325th's hangar finally rang. It was the much-anticipated call from Naval Intelligence. But it wasn't the message President Roosevelt and General Eisenhower were expecting to receive.

When the aide handed the phone to Eisenhower, the caller informed the general that the Berlin bomb had successfully detonated. Initial reports indicated that everything within a three-mile radius of the Reich Chancellery had been completely destroyed. Adolf Hitler, along with a staggering number of his top officers and administrators, were thought to be dead. The Nazi regime in Berlin was effectively wiped out.

Eisenhower relayed the message to Roosevelt. Both men were stunned—*but what about New York? Was it too late to recall the second B-24?*

"Any word from *Billfish?*" Eisenhower asked.

President Roosevelt rolled his wheelchair closer to the phone, scrutinizing Eisenhower's expression.

"No word yet, General."

Eisenhower looked at Roosevelt and shook his head as he shouted into the phone. "Listen to me! We've got to contact Colonel Damron! *Tell him to abort!*"

The caller hesitated. "We're trying to raise Damron now, but the stripped-down bomber is only equipped with VHF. We were supposed to relay our communications through *Billfish* over their HF. Damron is out of our VHF range."

"Then get the sub on HF and have them pass the abort order to the bomber—*now!*"

"That's just it, General—we can't raise the sub either."

Two hundred feet beneath the waters southeast of New York Harbor, the USS *Billfish* lay at the bottom of the Atlantic—her crew victims of depth charges from a German destroyer.

(2251 GMT) President Roosevelt and General Eisenhower were beside themselves. Fearing the worst, they agonized as they waited. What should have been a time of celebration in the wake of the successful detonation over Berlin was instead a time of dread. Roosevelt was especially distraught, fearing he might have needlessly ordered the destruction of New York City and killed millions of his own citizens.

Not long after sunset, the phone inside the VIP lounge rang again. As he answered the phone, the aide's expression indicated the call was not from Naval Intelligence. After several seconds, he hung up the phone. "That was Base Operations," he announced. "Lieutenant Colonel Damron and his crew are twenty minutes out."

(2317 GMT) As the last of her four propellers clacked to a stop, the *Melanie Anne* was besieged by those waiting for her on the tarmac.

The exhausted crew members began to exit, one by one, from the open bomb bay doors beneath the fuselage. Even though his station was closest to the exit, Toby Pozniak was the last to emerge from the darkened B-24's interior. As he stepped away from the bomb bay, he could see President Roosevelt and General Eisenhower waiting.

Without speaking, Eisenhower rushed past the crew, toward the B-24. He knelt next to the open bomb bay and peered inside—it was empty. The frantic general turned to Pozniak. "Did it *detonate?*"

Pozniak didn't answer.

"Dammit, man! The bomb! *Did it detonate?*"

Everyone on the tarmac watched as the young physicist approached the general and extended his closed hand. Eisenhower instinctively placed his hand directly beneath Pozniak's. The physicist opened his fist and dropped the three red-capped arming plugs into Eisenhower's palm.

Eisenhower was confused.

"I didn't arm it, General."

"You mean, *it didn't detonate?*"

Pozniak shook his head. "No—it didn't detonate."

Seated in his wheelchair, President Roosevelt slapped his hand down hard on the armrest and shouted at Pozniak. "*Come here!*"

Startled, Pozniak cautiously approached the president.

Visibly trembling, Roosevelt began lifting himself from the shaking, rattling chair. Two of his secret service agents, recognizing that the president was trying to stand, rushed to his side and lifted him upright. When Pozniak was within reach, Roosevelt threw his arms around him. He hugged the dumbfounded physicist with a vigor that belied his deteriorating health. As tears welled up behind his wire-rimmed spectacles, Roosevelt patted Pozniak on the back. "God bless you for what you've done, my boy—*God bless you.*"

Pozniak was baffled, as were all the *Melanie Anne* crew members. "I don't understand, Mr. President. We failed—*I failed.*"

Roosevelt laughed and shook his head. He turned and shouted loudly enough for the rest of the crew members to hear his words. "You boys don't know—do you? Colonel Hurley and his crew got through!"

Roosevelt removed his hat and waved it in a heralding motion. He projected his voice even louder. "Berlin has been destroyed, gentlemen! We *did* it—*you* did it!" He turned back toward Pozniak. "Son—*you* didn't fail. You kept *us* from failing. You saved us from the greatest calamity in the history of our nation."

(2357 GMT) It was 8:57 p.m. in Jacksonville. All seven of the *Melanie Anne's* crew members were escorted into the hangar by naval intelligence officers. Each man was placed in a private space to conduct his debrief apart from the others. The questions and answers flew back and forth well into the night.

Even as the men were providing details of the failed detonation over New York, news of the successful detonation over Berlin was beginning to spread across the globe.

The following afternoon, Thomas Damron and his crew would be debriefed again—this time as a group.

At the conclusion of the three-hour, closed-door debrief, the remaining members of the 325th's Jacksonville detachment would also be brought into the meeting. Everyone in the room would be ordered never to speak of the failed mission.

With the *Melanie Anne's* fateful bomb run permanently shrouded in secrecy, the world would never know that Toby Pozniak had personally saved millions of his fellow Americans from a nuclear holocaust. For Toby Pozniak—the great nephew of Stanislaw Pozniak—that didn't matter. He had lived his defining moment.

His recurring nightmare was over.

<u>*Chapter Seventy-Five*</u>
09 April 1945

During the initial hours following the Reich's decapitation in Berlin, Field Marshal Wilhelm Keitel rushed to return to Germany. He was desperate to salvage the Nazi war effort. Well before dawn, Keitel and his staff arrived pierside along the Hudson. The last surviving member of Hitler's inner circle boarded the light cruiser KMS *Nürnberg*.

In the early morning darkness, the German cruiser got under way—alone—to begin the long Atlantic crossing.

Keitel and his staff had improvised their emergency plan to resurrect the Reich in the conference room where, only hours earlier, they had presented Hitler's grand scheme for America's final defeat—the same conference room where James Winston had placed his listening device.

As the *Nürnberg* slipped through the Verrazano Narrows, two Allied submarines, not far from where their fellow submariners had been entombed aboard the USS *Billfish*, were lying in wait outside the harbor. The commanders of the two subs quickly calculated their firing solutions. The first torpedo struck the *Nürnberg's* stern on the starboard side. It destroyed one screw and disabled the other. The proud warship was dead in the water.

The second and third torpedoes simultaneously struck the paralyzed cruiser amidships, one from each side. The blasts severed her keel, splitting her apart. As she broke into two sections, a fourth torpedo penetrated her bow and ignited her forward magazine, destroying the superstructure and setting off a rapid succession of secondary explosions. The forward half of her hull ceased to exist.

As the *Nürnberg's* rudder and remaining screw rose from the water, her severed stern section slipped beneath the dark, cold waters of the Atlantic. More than five hundred of her six hundred and seventy-three crew members were lost.

Field Marshal Wilhelm Keitel and his staff were not among the survivors.

Chapter Seventy-Six
10 April 1945

At a château in Southern France, Field Marshal Erwin Rommel was now the senior-ranking officer in a decimated German command structure.

Whether or not Erwin Rommel was a committed Nazi was debatable. One thing was certain, however. The man known as the "Desert Fox" possessed a brilliant military intellect. Above all else, Rommel was a pragmatist. He understood that if the war continued, there would be more bombs like the one that had destroyed Berlin. He knew Germany would be annihilated.

Rommel understood what all but the most ardent of Nazis understood—the war was lost. From his headquarters in occupied France, Erwin Rommel directed Field Marshal Friedrich von Essen to begin the process of capitulation to the North American Allies.

Von Essen, himself a military pragmatist, dutifully complied with Rommel's directive.

As the Nazi leadership began to evacuate their headquarters inside the Empire State Building, the situation quickly became chaotic.

Many of the highest-ranking officials were attempting to flee North America aboard several of the remaining Kriegsmarine warships in New York Harbor.

SS General Ernst Kruger was clearing his office as his aides were packing his possessions into boxes and loading them onto dollies. When they had finished packing and loading the boxes, Kruger's aides wheeled the dollies out of the office, to the large freight elevator at the other end of the hall. The general followed them, stopping at the doorway. He watched them load the dollies onto the elevator and disappear behind the closing doors.

Kruger turned and walked back into his office to retrieve his briefcase from his desktop. Before leaving, he walked to the window and paused to look out across the city he and his fellow Nazis had terrorized for the past four years. From his office on the west side of the building, Kruger could see the piers along the Hudson. He saw black smoke rising from the stacks of the waiting destroyer. He could see the large white "43" painted on the *Hermann Künne's* dark gray bow. His escape vessel was firing her boilers, preparing for the voyage to South America.

As Kruger turned to leave his office, he was startled by an unexpected sight. James Winston was standing in the doorway, blocking his exit. Kruger wished he had been wearing his sidearm. He would have used it to murder the *großer affe* as a parting act of insolence toward the Americans and their mongrel society. "Stand aside!" he shouted at Winston.

The general was stunned beyond belief when Winston spoke back to him. *"Du gehst nirgendwohin, du bösartiger kleiner Bastard."* [You're not going anywhere, you malignant little bastard.]

"You!" Kruger shouted at Winston. The SS general was incredulous. This insignificant janitor spoke perfect German. "You understood everything! Everything we said—everything we wrote! You knew all along what we were doing—*Mein Gott!"*

Winston moved toward Kruger.

The general began shouting for his aides, but his cries went unheard. Kruger and Winston were all alone on the 82nd floor.

Kruger swung his briefcase at Winston. The Resistance operative grabbed it and jerked it from Kruger's grasp. Kruger produced a dagger and lunged at Winston. The dagger lodged in the briefcase as Winston used it to shield himself. He slung the case and dagger aside as he subdued Kruger and placed him in a stranglehold under his arm. With his free hand, Winston pulled one of the photos of the Hart Island gas chambers from his pocket and shoved it in the arrogant Nazi's face.

Kruger began shouting and cursing, thrashing his fists against Winston's solid frame. While tightening his arm around the flailing general's neck, Winston reached over and unlocked the hinged window. He swung it open. When Kruger felt the brisk air through the open window, he became frantic. He tried with all his strength to break free—it was futile.

Winston hoisted the horrified Nazi up and through the open window. He held him by his ankles. Winston ignored Kruger's bloodcurdling screams as he waited until the street and sidewalks were clear of cars and pedestrians. Ernst Kruger desperately pleaded for his life, but his pathetic pleas went unheeded. James Winston, perhaps more so than anyone else, had borne witness to the unspeakable evil that resided deep within Kruger's irredeemable soul.

The eight-hundred-foot fall took seven seconds.

Chapter Seventy-Seven
11 April 1945

Fifty-four hours after the *Yellow Rose* had dealt a deathblow to the Third Reich, the Allied planes began landing at the New York Municipal Airport. They came in waves. So many landed in the first few hours that rows of Luftwaffe airplanes had to be bulldozed into the East River to make room on the tarmac.

The winds that day were from the southeast. As each arriving Allied plane made its turn onto the final approach, it passed directly over Rikers Island. The hundreds of SS guards and camp administrators had already fled the camp. Dressed in civilian clothes, they had disappeared into the city, securing the gates and destroying the bridge behind them.

Natalie Rosenbaum knew exactly what to do. She began gathering her ledgers—the ledgers that could be used to prosecute the Nazi war criminals who were responsible for the depravity that had been perpetrated in this godforsaken place. She clutched the ledgers against her body and sat down inside the tiny shack where she had done her accounting for the past three years.

She sat—waiting.

"...Saul Rosenbaum reached out subliminally to communicate his dying message to the slowly fading vision of his daughter—It's going to be okay, Ketzel. He'll send for you soon."

All he had was a faded photograph.

Lieutenant Commander Mike Crofford and his fellow Resistance fighters led the Allied flotilla of small vessels across the narrow channel that separated Rikers Island from the airport. Crofford was aboard the first boat to land on the rocky shoreline next to the concentration camp.

Most of the Resistance fighters had known what to expect. It was the newly arrived Airborne Rangers who were most horrified by what they saw as they looked through the barbed wire fence that surrounded the compound. One of the Rangers cut the chain on the gate with a pair of long bolt cutters.

As the Allied soldiers swung the gate open, Crofford led the way into the camp. He and the others were quickly surrounded by a throng of ghostlike figures—all with sunken cheeks and dark, pain-weary eyes. The emaciated prisoners, many with open sores and missing teeth, all wanted to touch the men and kiss their hands. A number of the prisoners, as well as many of the soldiers, were overcome with emotion.

Crofford questioned everyone he passed, but no one recognized the time-worn image of the young woman in the photograph. He held the photograph high in the air. *"Natalie Rosenbaum?"* he shouted.

One of the prisoners in the middle of the throng pointed toward the shack near the gate.

As everyone continued to mingle in the center of the compound, the apprehensive intelligence officer walked toward the small wooden building at the edge of the camp. He wasn't sure what he would find inside.

Crofford opened the creaking door to the shack. He saw the anxious woman seated on the crate, alone in the darkness. She was holding several ledgers against her frail body as she rocked back and forth. She stared straight ahead, through the cracked lens in her eyeglasses, as if she were catatonic. "Are you Natalie Rosenbaum?" he asked softly.

"Yes, I am," she answered, turning to look at the man who had asked the question. She stopped rocking and stared back at him. "Who are you?"

"No one's going to hurt you anymore, Natalie. My name is Mike Crofford. Toby Pozniak sent me to take you away from this place."

Chapter Seventy-Eight
08 May 1945

Field Marshal Erwin Rommel, acting on behalf of the Third Reich, boarded the British battleship HMS *Valiant* at the Belgian port of Antwerp. Among those representing the Allied military as Rommel signed the unconditional surrender on the *Valliant's* quarterdeck was Brigadier General Roderick Hurley.

Across the Atlantic, spontaneous celebrations had already broken out throughout America. Missing from those who celebrated the historic ceremony was Franklin Delano Roosevelt. Three weeks earlier, on April 12th, the 32nd president of the United States had died from a cerebral hemorrhage at his residence in Georgia.

Two grateful nations mourned his passing.

Chapter Seventy-Nine
14 August 1945

The several thousand Japanese soldiers who had not been killed were in disarray. They had retreated from the Kern River Oil Field into the San Gabriel Mountains, north of Los Angeles. Surrounded by General MacArthur's army and cut off by Admiral Nimitz's Pacific Fleet, those who chose not to commit suicide finally surrendered at Newhall Pass, near Santa Clarita, California.

America's war had ended.

<u>*Chapter Eighty*</u>

26 September 1945

It had taken six months.

After a massive citywide search, during which all but a few of the searchers weren't even sure what it was they were trying to locate, the large metal object was found. The search had covered two thirds of Manhattan and parts of Brooklyn and Queens. Using sonar, its position had finally been pinpointed seven blocks away from the Empire State Building, at the bottom of the East River.

In the dead of night, a Navy salvage vessel recovered the mysterious object. Even the crew of the salvage vessel was unaware of the hundred and forty-one pounds of uranium-235 still inside the casing.

Chapter Eighty-One
13 December 1946

In Atlanta, Georgia, it was one of the final concurrent acts of the relocated Allied governments.

As rebuilding efforts neared completion at the U.S. Capitol in Washington, D.C., President Harry S. Truman and First Lady Eleanor Roosevelt presided over the ceremony. The pair concurrently awarded Distinguished Service Crosses to the six military crew members of the *Yellow Rose*.

Mike Crofford, now a full commander, received the Navy Distinguished Service Medal for organizing and leading the American Resistance in New York City.

Commander Crofford's former boss, Rear Admiral Chauncey Fuller, was awarded the Legion of Merit for his leadership on the *Downrush* Project.

For *his* part on the project, Toby Pozniak became the first recipient of a new award—the Medal of Freedom. Even though the citation was officially for his work in developing the bomb that had defeated the Germans, there was more to it. President Truman privately confided to Pozniak that he and President Roosevelt had decided to accord him the honor for his unheralded action aboard the

Melanie Anne over New York City. The decision to create the award had been made only hours before the late president's death.

For their selfless efforts as non-military combatants against a foreign enemy, Carter King and James Winston were each awarded Congressional Gold Medals. Three dozen members of the American Resistance received the same award. Many of them, including Marc Krbec, were awarded the medal posthumously.

Observing the ceremony from off to one side of the room, Margaret and Samuel Hurley stood with the other family members of those being honored. Also standing among the family members—nineteen months removed from the Rikers Island concentration camp—was Natalie Rosenbaum Pozniak.

Chapter Eighty-Two
20 February 1947

More than a year and a half after World War II had ended, many of those who had participated in Adolf Hitler's Final Solution were finally brought to justice.

In Europe, months earlier, the Nazi war crimes trials had been held in Nuremberg, Germany. Many of the defendants at Nuremburg had died when the atomic bomb was dropped on Berlin. Even so, they had been tried and convicted in absentia lest the world forget their atrocities.

In America, the trials were held in New York City. One hundred and seven defendants were charged with crimes against humanity. Of those, three were acquitted, eleven were found guilty of lesser crimes, and sixty-four were sentenced to life imprisonment. Twenty-nine of the defendants, including SS Colonel Helmut Kraus—commandant of the Rikers Island concentration camp—were sentenced to death by hanging.

The Allied prosecutors had been extremely thorough in the cases they presented before the international justices. The half dozen military lawyers had submitted tons of physical evidence, including the photographs obtained by James Winston of the Hart Island death camp.

In the end, however, it was the written evidence that had proven to be the most damning in placing blame for the horrible crimes depicted in the photos. When the trial finally concluded, it was the evidence that had been gleaned from Natalie Rosenbaum's ledgers that sent Helmut Kraus and his ilk to the gallows.

Chapter Eighty-Three
20 January 1953

It was not particularly cold for a late January morning in Brooklyn. Having warmed up the car, Toby Pozniak tossed three lightweight winter coats into the trunk. He was anxious to get started on the seven-hour drive to Washington, D.C.

Frustrated, he tried to hurry Natalie along as she tended to Marc, their five-year-old son, on the front porch of their Prospect Heights brownstone. Natalie insisted Marc needed a heavier coat for the outdoor event.

"*Fine*. I'll go back in and get it," Pozniak told his wife. "You two go ahead and get in the car. We're already cutting it close."

"We have plenty of time," Natalie said calmly as her husband headed back toward the front door. "It doesn't start until three o'clock. It's not even six-thirty yet."

Pozniak looked straight ahead as he passed his wife and son on the porch. "*Traffic*, Natalie—*traffic*."

As the family finally settled into the car, Natalie leaned over and gave her husband a kiss. He looked at her apologetically and smiled. Then he turned toward the back seat. "All set, buddy?"

Marc smiled at this father. "All set, Pops."

After crossing the Manhattan Bridge and battling their way across the city in rush-hour traffic, the Pozniaks made it through the Holland

Tunnel, to the other side of the Hudson. They headed south out of Jersey City and crossed the Bayonne Bridge to Staten Island. Then, they followed State Highway 440 across another bridge—back into New Jersey.

Natalie looked over at her husband. "Are you *sure* this is the shortest way, sweetheart?"

He looked at her and laughed. "I'm a nuclear physicist, honey. You think I don't know how to drive? Trust me—this is the quickest route."

Natalie looked back at Marc. "I sure hope you grow up to be as smart as your father," she said with a sly grin.

Pozniak looked at her and winked.

The middle portion of their trip took them along U.S. Highway 40, across the Delaware River to Wilmington. From there, they crossed into Maryland and south to the Susquehanna River— where they drove onto the Eddie Ramirez Memorial Bridge.

After crossing the river to the south side of the bridge, Toby Pozniak pulled to the side of the road. He held Marc's and Natalie's hands as they walked through the memorial plaza that honored Eddie Ramirez's valiant sacrifice.

There was a Sherman Tank sitting atop a large stone pedestal at the spot where the young private had fired the shots that toppled the original bridge. On the pedestal was a plaque describing how—in 1941, during the initial days of the Nazi invasion—his actions had single-handedly stalled a column of advancing panzers headed for Washington, D.C. Even though he had received the award posthumously, the plaque contained an engraved image of Eddie Ramirez wearing the Medal of Honor.

Toby Pozniak knew his son was too young to understand the significance of the site where they now stood. He knew that, someday, he and Natalie would have to explain the grotesque numbers on her forearm. He hoped that when his son grew older, he would appreciate the magnitude of the historic event he was about to witness.

He hoped Marc would remember this day.

Several hours later, Toby and Natalie Pozniak stood with their son in a crowd that numbered in the hundreds of thousands. As the newly elected president stepped to the podium at the east portico of the rebuilt U.S. Capitol Building, Toby Pozniak hoisted Marc onto his shoulders so he could watch him take the oath of office.

They looked on as the president-elect placed his hand on the Bible and recited the oath. Then, they bowed their heads as the 34th president of the United States offered up the following prayer:

> Give us, we pray, the power to discern clearly right from wrong. Allow all our words and actions to be governed thereby—and by the laws of this land.
>
> Especially, we pray that our concern shall be for all the people—regardless of station, race or calling. May cooperation be the mutual aim of those who, under the concepts of our Constitution, hold to differing political faiths—so that all may work for the good of our beloved country and Thy glory.
>
> May our nation never again be divided.
>
> Amen.

It had taken several years of diplomacy to finally become a reality; but with those few words, history was made. Dwight David Eisenhower—born and raised in the former Confederate States of America—became the first president of all forty-eight United States.

Also from Braveship Books...

www.ingramcontent.com/pod-product-compliance
Lightning Source LLC
Chambersburg PA
CBHW051557100726

47898CB00001B/129